She'd turned in her badge. But she hadn't lost her instincts . . .

The shrill wail of a siren came closer. The sound always made her heart pound. It was the Friday-night horrors, starting a little earlier than usual.

A paramedic truck sped past her and made a U-turn. It pulled up to the railroad tracks crossing Las Almas Boulevard.

Hannah watched it double back. Then she saw the Range Rover.

Bradley's car sat on a side street near the crossing gate. Under the orange streetlight, the bottle-green finish was a sickly black, like something rotting in water. She felt herself go shivering cold, down to the bone. She knew what that intuition meant . . .

MORE MYSTERIES FROM THE
BERKLEY PUBLISHING GROUP . . .

JENNY McKAY MYSTERIES: This TV reporter finds out where, when, why . . . *and* whodunit. "A more streetwise version of television's Murphy Brown." —*Booklist*

by Dick Belsky
BROADCAST CLUES
THE MOURNING SHOW

LIVE FROM NEW YORK
SUMMERTIME NEWS

CAT CALIBAN MYSTERIES: She was married for thirty-eight years. Raised three kids. Compared to that, tracking down killers is easy . . .

by D.B. Borton
ONE FOR THE MONEY
THREE IS A CROWD

TWO POINTS FOR MURDER
FOUR ELEMENTS OF MURDER

KATE JASPER MYSTERIES: Even in sunny California, there are cold-blooded killers . . . "This series is a treasure!" —*Carolyn G. Hart*

by Jaqueline Girdner
ADJUSTED TO DEATH
THE LAST RESORT
TEA-TOTALLY DEAD

MURDER MOST MELLOW
FAT-FREE AND FATAL
A STIFF CRITIQUE

FREDDIE O'NEAL, P.I., MYSTERIES: You can bet that this appealing Reno private investigator will get her man . . . "A winner." —*Linda Grant*

by Catherine Dain
LAY IT ON THE LINE
WALK A CROOKED MILE
BET AGAINST THE HOUSE

SING A SONG OF DEATH
LAMENT FOR A DEAD COWBOY

CALEY BURKE, P.I., MYSTERIES: This California private investigator has a brand-new license, a gun in her purse, and a knack for solving even the trickiest cases!

by Bridget McKenna
MURDER BEACH
CAUGHT DEAD

DEAD AHEAD

CHINA BAYLES MYSTERIES: She left the big city to run an herb shop in Pecan Springs, Texas. But murder can happen anywhere . . . "A wonderful character!"
—*Mostly Murder*

by Susan Wittig Albert
THYME OF DEATH

WITCHES' BANE

LIZ WAREHAM MYSTERIES: In the world of public relations, crime can be a real career-killer . . . "Readers will enjoy feisty Liz!" —*Publishers Weekly*

by Carol Brennan
HEADHUNT

FULL COMMISSION

BONNIE INDERMILL MYSTERIES: Temp work can be murder, but solving crime is a full-time job . . . "One of detective fiction's most appealing protagonists!"
—*Publishers Weekly*

by Carole Berry
THE DEATH OF A DIFFICULT WOMAN

GOOD NIGHT, SWEET PRINCE

MURDER
IN
BRIEF

—⅏—

CARROLL
LACHNIT

BERKLEY PRIME CRIME, NEW YORK

MURDER IN BRIEF

A Berkley Prime Crime Book / published by arrangement with the author

PRINTING HISTORY
Berkley Prime Crime edition / June 1995

ISBN: 0-425-14790-8

Berkley Prime Crime Books are published by The Berkley Publishing Group, 200 Madison Avenue, New York, NY 10016.
The name BERKLEY PRIME CRIME and the BERKLEY PRIME CRIME design are trademarks belonging to Berkley Publishing Corporation.

PRINTED IN THE UNITED STATES OF AMERICA

10 9 8 7 6 5 4 3 2 1

For Alec

1

Hannah Barlow knew she was in trouble. But she didn't know what she'd done. Not yet.

She routinely parked in the faculty lot, but she'd never been caught—she thought. She'd kept *McCormick on Evidence* longer than the five days the library allowed, but she paid the fine. She posted her bike's for-sale notice on the Student Activity Council's bulletin board without its permission. Mea culpa. Perhaps she could plead that the constitutional-law professor's lecture on the First Amendment drove her to a free-speech frenzy.

None of those things should have brought her here, to the law-school dean's chilly waiting room.

Lois Popich, the dean's secretary, had opened the door during corporations class that morning and passed the professor a note. He called Hannah's name and handed it to her. It said: *Be at Dean Weiss's office at noon.*

A chilling summons. She stopped in the bathroom before she went upstairs. She assessed the state of her hair, which seemed to have moods of its own, from demure to demonic. It was red, dark as paprika, and it curled down to her shoulders. On some days, like today, it twisted, turned wild. A bad omen, she thought as she pulled a brush through the thicket. The bristles bit into her scalp and tugged the hair until her eyes stung. She pulled the strands back and tamed them with a hair tie.

Her eyes were green, shot with blue. But she had been studying late, and sleeplessness had dulled their color. The irises were gray. The circles under her eyes were deeper, too. She dabbed on some concealer and took a deep breath.

The last time she'd been called to an academic boss's office, she'd been running for sophomore-class president at Maria Goretti High School. And that time, she'd been suspended.

She had been arguing minor-league theology with her pious, seminary-bound brother that semester. One of her New Testament arguments had made him so eye-poppingly mad that she decided she could use it to great advantage in her campaign speech.

She mentioned that a new Bible translation clearly said that Mary and Joseph did not have relations, as the translation delicately put it, until after the baby Jesus was born. So despite everything the nuns have ever told you, she had said, they obviously did have a sexual relationship once the infant made an appearance. The point: Reexamine what you've always taken as Gospel truth. Gospels change.

Her classmates applauded, but not at the analogy. They loved anything that mentioned sex, a fairly taboo subject at Maria Goretti. The principal, Sister Mary Immaculata, acted without hesitation. Her namesake was ever-virgin and Hannah's speech was nothing less than heresy. The memory of sitting in the school office, watching the quaking, furious nun make the phone call to her parents still made her heart pound.

So here she was, twenty years later, a sophomore in trouble. Gospels might change. Some things didn't.

Lois Popich glanced over her computer screen at Hannah once, but then went back to work.

Hannah didn't like Lois much. Even though she was barely out of college herself, she had always been somewhat aloof from the Douglas students. But she had at least deigned to chat from time to time during Hannah's first year. Lois worked in the faculty support office's word-processing center then, typing outlines, tests, and the occasional treatise. Over the summer, she had been promoted to this job. Now that she worked for the dean, Lois was officious and sometimes downright hostile. A guard dog in a severe wool suit.

She glanced up again. Hannah caught her eye.

"Do you know what this is about?" Hannah said.

Lois primly shook her head and kept typing.

Hannah tried to relax. It could be nothing. It could be something good. She doubted it. She looked at the pictures of the dean on the waiting-room walls to pass the time.

Dean Frederick Weiss ran the William O. Douglas School of Law, named for a liberal hero, but the gallery showed precisely the opposite political affiliation.

Weiss shook hands with a conservative Republican governor. He took a check from a moderately liberal Republican senator and laughed uproariously with a congressman so reactionary that he bordered on the Cro-Magnon. But Weiss was only being shrewd. Douglas needed friends, patrons, funds. And too close an identification with a liberal icon would close so many doors. Especially in Orange County.

Hannah felt lucky to still be at Douglas. Fifteen percent of the first-years had washed out. She'd weathered it, although it had been harder than she could have imagined. She had been out of college for thirteen years, out of the habits of study. The law books were impenetrable at first. The reading requirements for eight classes staggered her.

But at least her eleven years as a cop weren't completely wasted, particularly in criminal law and evidence. She had more than heard of *Miranda* v. *Arizona*—she knew the advisement of rights by heart. *Nardone* v. *United States* was nothing new to her: she knew how an illegal search tainted evidence, making it, as Justice Frankfurter called it in *Nardone,* "a fruit of the poisonous tree," and thus inadmissible in court. One of Las Almas's own cases—whether the cops had indeed made a "plain view seizure" when they skimmed a half-used bindle of heroin out of a drug dealer's curbside trash can— had made it up to the Supremes. The city lost the case— poisoned fruit, the court ruled.

She had been rigorous with herself in first year, studying incessantly, ignoring anything that wasn't school and books and note taking. It was a life of cold logic, hard work, black-letter law. She had created an ice cave, a place to keep her heart and soul safe but inactive. Frozen, to be revived when she was ready. She had no way of telling when that would be.

She had quit the Las Almas Police Department as a last resort. A string of ugly cases had weakened her resilience. And the last case, Janie Meister's case, threatened to break her. She thought she could get past her guilt over Janie by disowning it, by being the order-following, case-clearing drone her superiors wanted. But the price had been too dear, finally. A life had been lost. Two, if you counted Hannah among the dead. And Hannah did, for a long time.

Now, in January, halfway through second year, Hannah felt a wave of warmth that hinted at resurrection. Law school was bringing her back to life. The work was hard, but not impossible. Briefing a case had taken her a day during first year. Now she could do it in an hour. She looked forward to some of the classes. She had made friends. People treated her as though she were competent, reasonable, and wholly human. So perhaps she was.

She heard someone laugh in the hallway. The door opened and Bradley Cogburn strolled in. He leaned over Lois Popich's screen and showed her a note.

"I didn't get a hall pass. Is that a problem?" he said, pouting like a little boy.

Popich didn't even look up. "Take a seat. The dean will be with you shortly," she said.

Cogburn saw Hannah then. He sauntered over, sat down in the chair next to hers, stretched his long legs, and ran his fingers through his hair. Honey blond, streaked with strands the color of wheat. Ten years ago, Hannah thought, I would have wanted this guy. Bad.

He usually wore wire-rim glasses, which put a studious frame around his violet-blue eyes and tempered his handsomeness. But, Hannah noticed, he slipped them off sometimes and traced the faint laugh lines around his mouth with one curling gold earpiece. The gesture hinted at thoughtfulness. But Hannah thought it was self-consciously seductive, probably even rehearsed.

He'd used it on her before, as he waited for her to solve whatever research problem had erupted in the moot-court brief they were writing together.

Douglas required every student to participate in the moot-court competition. Two-person teams were assigned a legal problem and a side to argue. The teams researched cases and wrote a brief, such as a lawyer would present to an appeals court. Then the teams went before one of two panels of judges—actually, law professors—and made oral arguments.

For nearly six weeks, she and Bradley had been meeting twice a week at Rattigan Library. As they called up cases on the LEXIS service and photocopied treatises, Bradley teased her that his wife, Alicia, was getting suspicious. Hannah rolled her eyes.

"You're ten years younger than I am," she said.

"What does that matter?" he said.

Hannah gave him a stern look, and that was the end of it. But he continued to touch his face with the gold glasses and tell her that—intellectually, of course—they were an unbeatable team.

Hannah wasn't so sure about that. As far as she could tell, he found law school a lot less challenging than she did. And they hadn't chosen to be a team, anyway. Cogburn merely followed Barlow on their section's roll sheet.

In Douglas's mock courtroom, the three-professor panel bombarded them with the flaws in their reasoning, the holes in their arguments, and the inconsistencies in their positions. Then the three congratulated the team on its work. It had been a nerve-racking experience, and Hannah half hoped they hadn't scored high enough to be selected for the interscholastic team.

Now, seeing Bradley here, Hannah could narrow down the reasons for Weiss's summons. Something about moot court. Maybe they had been good enough for the school team, after all. Weiss would have loved to beat Loyola and UCLA. Moot-court competition was the law-school equivalent of football, Hannah thought. Weiss wanted his team to be the killer LitaGators. The bruising Barristers.

"What's the deal here?" Bradley said.

Hannah shook her head. "Since it's both of us, I'd guess it's about moot court. I can't imagine what."

Bradley shrugged. "I'm sure it's no big thing. If we'd cited a depublished case, the Parson would have lectured us on it for an hour—right there in the courtroom."

Hannah smiled at the image of the sermonizing professor glowering at them from a pulpit and instantly felt calmer. This pastime of Bradley's, nicknaming and demythologizing the entire Douglas faculty, was part of his charm. The Parson was perfectly named: a dull, preachy man who droned contract classes to sleep. The Queen of the Night was Emilia Dove, a criminal-law professor who screeched at slow-witted students in staccato bursts. The Ruminator was a bovine man who chewed his way through tort and evidence law with excruciating, numbing slowness.

Where Bradley found the energy for such pursuits, Hannah never knew. Douglas was, variously, a swamp and a jungle and a free fall for Hannah, and nearly every other student. But it was an amusement park for Cogburn. Bradley's Land o' Law.

It had been so from the start. Hannah and the rest of the class spent the first months puzzling out the syntax and structure of legal reasoning. It so twisted her brain that Hannah was sure reading *War and Peace* in Urdu would have been easier. But Cogburn immediately seemed to think like a lawyer. He knew the argot, volunteered answers, and still had time to be the class wit. Truth be told, Hannah told herself, you're jealous of him.

She knew why, specifically. He had made the staff of *Law Review,* and was rumored to be a contender for the editor's job in third year. He was not the shoo-in, however. Catherine Spinetti, an aspiring prosecutor with a white-hot GPA, was reportedly dead set on getting the position.

Hannah, meanwhile, hadn't even made it onto the staff and thus lost her best chance at a summer clerking job at a top-notch firm. Interviewers wanted to see law review on the résumé. The *Law Review* editor, a third-year copyright wiz named Harrison Onizaki, told Hannah the article she wrote as a tryout—her "write-on"—was solid, but there had been better ones. Bradley's was one of those. And it still rankled.

Hannah had managed to line up a summer job with Dare and Dare, a small, hardworking, low-paying firm that specialized in bankruptcies. The landslide in Orange County's economy was keeping the lawyers there busy and they seemed a friendly, professional bunch. But it wasn't the leap into the legal firmament she had hoped for.

With annoyance, she found she couldn't let go of the envy. The first day she and Bradley started working together, she asked him if she could read his write-on. He seemed flattered, and brought it to her the next day. It was the next-to-last version, he said, forgive the edits. She saw that he'd sandwiched in a handwritten footnote—7a—between 7 and 8.

"Writing is rewriting," he said.

From the first paragraph, she felt the prickle of jealousy. Her article had been well organized, thoroughly footnoted. Thoroughly dull, she thought, nothing like this. Bradley's writing was lucid, engaging. Memorable, for an academic paper on the finer points of lying in wait and premeditation. Every sentence was honed to a cogent point. Each paragraph built to an unarguable conclusion. The transitions flowed effortlessly. She flipped the pages faster, hoping to see some flaw, someplace where the mortar was a bit too thick, the structure out of alignment. But he'd trimmed here, straightened there, with a flick of black ink. There was nothing to criticize.

So it bothered her all the more when she realized that Bradley was slacking off on the moot-court brief. Several times he showed up with only vague notes on the issues he was supposed to have researched. When it came time to finish the brief, he told Hannah his two sections weren't quite ready. Hannah finally gave him the floppy disk of her draft and let him work his issues into it. She would have liked to give the piece a final collaborative gloss, but he told her there wasn't time and assured her it was fine.

She read the finished product, just before oral arguments. It was her best effort, but the seams that joined it with Bradley's work showed. And his writing needed a little more rewriting, she thought. The brief wasn't going to win any prizes. If he'd tried a little harder, it could have. It irked her that this time Bradley had decided to be less than perfect.

"We probably made the interscholastic team after all," Bradley said to her. "That's why we're here."

"I don't know if I'm interested," Hannah said. She wasn't sure she wanted to work with him again.

"It'll look good on your transcript," he said. "The big firms want to see perfect grades, law review, moot court. All that honors stuff. You're not going to settle for those drones at Dare and Dare after you graduate, are you?"

The gibe hurt. It was too close to how she really felt.

"It's a good boutique firm," she said. "I'll be perfectly happy there."

He snorted.

"Besides, who has time for moot court and law review? When would you study?" Hannah said.

"Piece of cake," Bradley said.

Hannah bit the inside of her lip. She hated feeling like this. Some people are just born to this law-school stuff, she thought.

It's in their blood. Sometimes she feared she wasn't one of them.

Twelve-fifteen. How long did Weiss mean to keep them waiting? Hannah's palms were damp. She felt like the shaky-kneed girl in Sister Mary's office again. Weiss probably wanted it that way.

The door from the hallway opened to a riot of noise as the students fled their classes for lunch. Celestina Pacheco came in first, followed by Fernando Ruiz. Although they were second-years, too, Hannah didn't know either one of them well.

She knew Celestina held some office in the Latino Law Students Association. Ruiz had been in Hannah's first-year criminal-law class. He had a fierce face and a silence that bordered on broodiness. And he seemed to know a lot about illegal vehicle stops and body searches.

This is definitely something about moot court, Hannah thought. Pacheco and Ruiz were partners. Hannah remembered seeing them sitting outside in the hall when she and Bradley finished their oral arguments.

Hannah nodded a hello at them. Celestina smiled tentatively. Ruiz ignored her. He perched on the edge of the plastic-upholstered sofa and glared across at Cogburn.

"Asshole," he hissed.

Bradley blinked mildly and glanced over his shoulder, as though someone might be standing behind him.

"Is there a problem?" he said.

"You're the problem," Ruiz said.

Lois Popich stopped typing, picked up the phone, and muttered into it. She stood up.

"Dean Weiss will see you now," she said.

Weiss, a thin, freckled man who combed wisps of reddish-brown hair across his scalp, stood at his desk, his hands clasped behind his back. Two documents sat on the polished desktop. Hannah saw that they were typed on pleading paper.

Weiss parted his hands above the documents, like a magician making a hocus-pocus pass.

"Do you recognize these?" he asked the students.

All four edged toward the desk. Hannah saw the Cogburn-Barlow moot-court brief. The other paper belonged to Celestina and Fernando.

Hannah tapped the brief. "Bradley and I wrote this for moot court," she said.

"We did this one," Fernando said, stabbing his finger at the other document.

Weiss nodded and sat down. The students stepped back from the desk, but Hannah knew Weiss expected them to stay on their feet. We are in trouble, she thought. And it's bad.

"You're familiar with the student honor code," Weiss said, and waited until they all had nodded. "Then you know that the most serious infraction of the code, the one that can draw an immediate expulsion and a report to the state bar, is plagiarism. And I assume you know what plagiarism is."

Hannah felt her mouth go dry. In all the notes she took, had she cribbed a phrase for a footnote without realizing it? She didn't think so.

"When the teams had finished their oral arguments, the two panels met and swapped the briefs you'd all submitted," Weiss said. "We like to have the judges who didn't hear the oral argument give the briefs a read. Just to make sure the writing stands on its own."

Hannah heard Ruiz catch a sharp breath. But his face was impassive.

"That's when the judges noticed it. Whole sections of these briefs are identical. Down to the last comma."

"Will you show us the sections you're talking about?" Hannah said. She tried to sound untroubled, but her voice seemed feeble, shaky.

"You'll be able to review the evidence in due time," Weiss said. He slid the briefs out of reach and held out four sheets of paper.

"These are the formal complaints. You'll have a week to obtain counsel, if you want it, prepare an answer, and file it with this office. We will then set dates for discovery and a hearing."

Hannah heard the growl first. Then Fernando lunged at Bradley, toppling him onto the desk. The briefs fluttered to the floor as Bradley skidded across the surface. His head hit Weiss in the gut. Weiss stumbled backward and broke his fall by grabbing the drapes.

Hannah didn't think. She just moved. She grabbed Fernando by the back of his shirt and yanked him off Bradley. Bradley staggered to his feet, found his balance, and slammed his palm against Fernando's chest. Hannah summoned up the ghost of cop-takes-charge.

"Back off, Bradley," she barked.

He wavered, fist clenched. Then he stepped back.

Weiss freed himself from the drapes and picked up the phone. It quivered in his hand and his voice shook as he summoned a security officer.

Fernando squirmed in Hannah's grip.

"Let go of me," he said.

"Are you going to do anything stupid?" Hannah said.

"No," he whispered.

She let go. Weiss hung up the phone and cleared his throat.

"Mr. Ruiz, you will be escorted to your car," he said. The authority filtered back into his voice. "You'll be barred from this campus until your hearing, unless you have business here related to your case. In that event, call in advance and you will be admitted to the school grounds."

Ruiz said nothing. He glowered at Hannah and Bradley. Celestina, who had been standing paralyzed during the ruckus, took his arm and walked him out of the office. She stopped at the door and looked over her shoulder at Bradley.

"You can't do this to him," she said.

Bradley barreled out the door behind them and down the stairs, two at a time. Hannah followed him, calling his name. He disappeared into the Memorial Grove.

Douglas's campus had once been Orange Flame, one of the citrus orchard and packing plants that gave the county its name. The land had been given to the school with the requirement that it always keep the mother trees. Neat white metal signs ordered students not to cut through the grove, but Bradley stormed down the rows, slapping at the branches as he passed and ignoring Hannah's calls for him to wait.

This morning all she had to worry about was understanding shareholders' lawsuits, she thought. Now it was plagiarism and a fistfight in the dean's office. What next?

She pushed back one last branch and emerged onto Founder's Walk. Bradley slouched on a bench and peeled off his glasses. The sun hadn't burned through the morning clouds yet, and the air seemed unusually chilly. Or maybe, Hannah thought, it's just me that's turned to ice. Fear did that to her.

"What's going on?" Hannah said, sitting next to him. "Parts of the briefs are nearly identical? How did that happen?"

He didn't answer at first. Then he put his glasses back on and shrugged.

"Relax, Hannah. It's all a big mistake." He reached over and patted her shoulder, giving her the slow, sly smile that must have churned the hormones of countless college girls. It had its charm, but now it only made her mad.

"This is serious," she said.

He snapped off the expression, easy as flicking a light switch.

"It is," he said. "Fernando plagiarized our brief."

"Fernando?" Hannah narrowed her eyes at Bradley. Something was out of kilter, she thought. "Then why did he assault you? Shouldn't it have been the other way around?"

"I ratted him out," Bradley said. "I didn't expect it to turn out this way. I'm sorry."

Bradley said he'd stopped by the Ruminator's office, just before the oral arguments began. He'd seen the Ruiz-Pacheco brief on his desk and started reading it.

"Jesus," Hannah said. "You're not supposed to do that."

"It didn't matter," he said. "I knew they weren't our opposition. They briefed the same side of the case that we did. Besides, we didn't even have the same judges."

Since the moot-court scenario dealt with a wrongful termination case with racial overtones, he said, he wanted to see how two Latinos handled it. As he skimmed the paper he realized whole chunks were identical to their brief.

Then, he said, he remembered seeing Fernando at the library one day, walking away from a carrel where Bradley had been working on the brief. Bradley said that when picked up the paper, it was warm to the touch. He thought it had been the sun, or the study lamp. But in the Ruminator's office, he realized what had happened. Fernando had just photocopied the brief.

"So I told him," he said. "I let him know Ruiz had cribbed our brief. I thought they'd just deal with him and Celestina."

Hannah didn't say anything for a moment. Things were moving so fast, it was hard to keep it all straight.

"But Weiss said the two panels realized the briefs were the same after they swapped them," Hannah said.

Bradley looked cautiously at her. "Maybe they want to preserve the myth that they actually read what we write."

"Level with me, Bradley. Are you telling me what really happened?" Hannah said.

Bradley looked offended. "Why would I lie to you? Why would I plagiarize something Fernando Ruiz wrote? He's barely hanging on by his fingernails here. If I was going to steal from somebody, I'd do better than that."

Hannah didn't answer him. Don't panic, she told herself. Bradley wouldn't cheat. He's glib and he can be a smart-aleck pain in the ass. But he's a good student. He's in line for editor of the *Law Review*. You, she reminded herself, didn't even make the staff.

"Look," Hannah said. "You have the sections I wrote, and you have your drafts. That shows a work-in-progress. We have our research notes. We can trace the development of the brief. We can prove we wrote it."

"Right," Bradley said. "That's what I mean. There's nothing to worry about."

"So you'll round that stuff up? We can meet tomorrow and go over it, start outlining the defense," she said. Now the lawyer in her took over. She felt calmer. "I think Bobby Terry would act as counsel, if we want him."

Bradley stared down at the pavement and tapped his lip with his fingertips.

"You've got my floppy disk, right?" Hannah said.

He didn't answer her, and Hannah felt a sick wave in her stomach.

"Bradley, that was the only copy. My hard disk crashed last week. I lost everything that was on it."

"I know I've got it. It's just a matter of finding it. If I can't, Alicia can. She cleans up after me."

But he was frowning.

"What is it?" she said. "Jesus, Bradley, you've got me really worried."

"Don't sweat it," he said, clicking on the smile. "Look, we're innocent. The innocent have nothing to fear, right? You told people that, all the time, when you were a cop, right?"

She nodded. But she had realized she had been stupid, offering assurances like that. She had learned the hard way: innocence was trampled, all the time.

2

It was nearly five on Friday afternoon. And in Hannah's experience, that was the least likely time to find a knot of students outside the library. People fled campus as early as possible on Friday, trying to escape from law overload, a condition marked by headache, jitters, and a marked tendency to yammer about parol evidence or corpora delicti.

But there were twenty-five or thirty people clustered on the steps of the Rattigan Library, still and rapt. Hannah saw one head above the rest. A woman, standing a step up from the crowd. With a jolt, she realized it was Celestina Pacheco, wearing the twisted face of a Fury.

She slammed her fist into her palm. She pointed at the administration building. She stretched her mouth as she spoke, as though it could not encompass her rage.

Hannah edged closer to the little crowd. And now she saw the posters propped up at Celestina's feet. They bore pictures, grainy blowups from the student directory. Bradley on one, her own face on the other. The third one showed a doleful Fernando Ruiz and the words printed in block letters: RICH KID AND ROGUE COP GET THE BREAKS—YOUR HERMANO GETS THE SHAFT.

Celestina shifted in and out of Spanish, but Hannah got the drift. The administration had made up its mind about who was guilty in the plagiarism incident. The scales of justice were unbalanced once again. We've seen it before: Rodney King, the L.A. Four. It's going to happen again, unless we stop it.

Hannah felt sick. Whatever they'd ferreted out about her

departure from the Las Almas police had been twisted. By whom, she didn't know. Rogue cop. Jesus.

The crowd was shifting, answering, catching Celestina's outrage. Hannah knew a few of them. Some were people she liked. People she'd studied with. She'd never made a secret of her first career. She'd been proud of the work she did. But she'd steered away from talking about the end. Now she realized she'd set up a mystery that could be exploited.

A guy at the fringe turned around and saw her. He glanced at the poster, back at Hannah. She cut across the lawn to the parking lot. She wasn't going to wait around for what would have come next.

At home, she spent two hours trying to find her rough-draft notes, but it was useless. Nothing generated paper like law school. Outlines, books, folders, binders, and notepads were tumbling off her desk and stacked in towers around the living room. She went through every leaf of it. Nothing.

Bradley called at eight.

"I've got everything," he said. "We're set."

"Thank God," Hannah said, dropping onto the sofa.

"I'm going to M'Naghten's in a while," he said. "Why don't you come by?"

Hannah warned him about the rally, but he shrugged it off.

She arrived downtown just after nine. She parked a couple blocks away from campus and walked down Grove Street, formerly the town's main drag. It usually brought back good memories.

Las Almas had always been home, a place she'd explored in expanding circles as she grew up. As a kid, she had ridden around its old neighborhoods on her bike. As a high-school junior, she learned to negotiate the traffic zipping around the Plaza (only blatant newcomers to town erred by calling it the Circle). As a cop, she'd walked the downtown beat for more than a year.

The city was one of the county's oldest. It had begun as a collection of adobes in the middle of a vast Spanish land grant, one of those that divided up the rolling stretches of coastal plain south of Los Angeles.

The history of the town's Spanish name was debated in

historical journals from time to time. Las Almas meant the souls, or the inhabitants. Or the spirits. It didn't literally mean ghosts. But there were ghosts here, for Hannah. Two spirits, two souls—Hannah's mother and the girl, Janie—haunted Hannah's dreams. She couldn't do anything about their appearance when she was asleep, but when she was awake, she tried to keep them at bay. So far, she had been spared seeing their apparitions strolling on Grove Street.

She headed for M'Naghten's, the bar across the street from school. It was one of the oldest buildings on the street, having been a print shop, a pharmacy, and then, for years, Lucy's, a depressing hangout for the town's hard-core drunks.

The current owner had flunked out of Douglas after his first year. He took over the bar and painted the legend on the plate-glass window, THE BAR YOU DON'T STUDY FOR, and changed the name to M'Naghten's. This delighted the law students to no end. Most of them had met M'Naghten, after a fashion.

In 1843, M'Naghten, an Englishman, had made legal history. He killed the prime minister's secretary, but pleaded insanity and was acquitted. His case established the first modern test of legal insanity: people were deemed insane if they could not distinguish right from wrong. If, in the words of the court, they did not know they were "violating the laws both of God and man."

According to the casebook, M'Naghten was obsessed with "certain morbid delusions." These were depicted in a mural on the bar's back wall, and with the owner's permission, any artistic student could further embellish the scene.

It didn't take long for M'Naghten's to become a campus annex, where students, faculty, and staff mingled, more or less without formality. Sometimes classes adjourned there for further discussion, which usually devolved into a gossip fest.

M'Naghten's was not universally loved, however. The fundamentalist Christian church down the street kept up a permanent protest on its marquee: THE BEST SIDE OF A BAR IS THE OUTSIDE.

Generally, Hannah thought so, too. It was a lesson she wished her mother had learned.

But M'Naghten's was an exception—it was less a bar than an emergency room for law-twisted psyches.

Even after mastering some of its turns, she still felt Douglas was like a rat maze. Nearly a thousand students spent the week scurrying through classes, reading and studying, bonking their heads on mens rea or rebuttable presumptions, all in search of the goodies around the corner. A ninety in an exam. A position on *Law Review*. A place in the top ten percent of the class. All of those were necessary to get a decent job after graduation. The law business had suffered in California's economic depression, and the competition for any job was keen.

It made the race even more exhilarating, exhausting, terrifying. Sometimes, the pressure built until Hannah felt she would explode. She could feel the tension, a thickness in the air that made her eardrums throb. Everyone felt it. Intellectual sparring matches erupted into vicious ad hominem bouts. Study partners broke up, belting recriminations like divorce-court combatants. And sometimes the misery slopped over into other partnerships. She knew that more than one marriage had failed during the first year.

At the end of every week, students crawled into M'Naghten's to anesthetize themselves and bemoan their choice of career. Hannah usually stopped in on Fridays, whined with the rest of the rats, and got a précis of the week's best dirt from one of the bartenders.

But no matter how much we all hate Douglas on Friday, we're back there on Monday, Hannah thought. The importance of law school is our morbid delusion. In that, we're just like M'Naghten, bless all our little addled heads.

She pushed through the crowd clustered around the hissing espresso machine next to the front door. She didn't think people whose nerves already were tighter than piano wire really needed to knock back two-ounce shots of concentrated caffeine. But sometimes it was a nice alternative to alcohol. She ordered a single latte and sat down at the bar, looking for Bradley.

If it had been up to her, they would have met somewhere else. She feared the crowd from the afternoon had adjourned here to plan its next move. But so far, she only saw the regulars.

Weaving their way to the back of the room were the Texas Twins. The party-hearty boys from Austin were headed for a flunk-out, according to the rumor mill. She also saw Guillermo Agustin, her copyright-and-trademark professor. There was someone she'd like to know better—after she graduated. Her last relationship had been a yearlong roller coaster with a slim, moody, dark-eyed patrol sergeant who sent her through peaks of joy and troughs of misery. And when the ride ended, they had to pass each other in the halls and pretend nothing had happened. That taught her to keep work and romance far apart.

Catherine Spinetti sat in a booth against the bricked back wall, casebook in front of her. She was not a regular. Much too serious for that. Some people negotiated every twist of the maze just right, usually because they avoided places like M'Naghten's. Catherine was one of them.

But if she was going to be named *Law Review* editor, she would have to do some politicking, and M'Naghten's was a good place to do that.

Students ran the *Review*, top to bottom. The editor had to be more than studious. He or she would have to be able to manage a sometimes querulous staff. He or she would have to be both a writer and a referee. And a glad-hander, to get the job in the first place. Bradley seemed like the obvious choice, but Spinetti could probably handle it if she would just melt a bit, Hannah thought.

Hannah watched as Spinetti tossed back a big swallow of wine, never taking her eyes off the casebook. She sat alone in the booth.

She was tall and big-boned, but slim. She had straight hair the color of mahogany and always wore it in a simple braid at the back of her neck. She wore her usual ensemble: voluminous black jacket, white blouse, black wool pants, and black, low-heeled, waxed-leather boots. Somehow, Hannah thought, she managed to look anything but bohemian in that outfit. The clothes, and the woman, had a daunting austerity. Hannah wondered if she'd once been in a convent, or a convent school. After twelve years of Catholic school and daily contact with the nuns, Hannah thought she could spot the signs. It seemed to her that the cloister's world of self-denial clung to Catherine like a veil.

Maybe early rising and self-abnegation were the secrets to Catherine's success. She never talked about her ranking, but Bobby Terry, the class handicapper and Hannah's study partner, figured she had to be number one.

Hannah sighed to herself. What would it take to be that

good? She couldn't imagine. When she wasn't seeing Douglas as a rat maze, she imagined herself as a frantic mouse in a wire wheel. She ran and ran and never seemed to get ahead. It was exhausting, just staying in place.

A flurry of noises erupted in the back of the bar: a yell, a thump of furniture, feet scuffling on the brick floor. She stood up and saw one of the twins—popularly known as Big Bubba—being heaved to his feet by the neck of his Alamo T-shirt. Despite his inferior position, he screamed twanging oaths in the face of his opponent, a burly first-year who sported a Che Guevara beret. Battling symbols, she thought, just what we don't need.

The bartender waded into the melee and yelled for them to break it up. As the crowd parted, Hannah saw Fernando and Celestina on its edges. Then, to her horror, she heard Big Bubba shouting her name back at them.

"You all have got to understand that Bradley and Hannah and the rest of the white race have rights, too," he bellowed.

Great, Hannah thought. Next, she'd be a Klan pinup girl. She had avoided the rally earlier, knowing she was no match for serious, studious, inflamed Latinos. But she knew Big Bubba was nothing but a tipsy loudmouth, and she could defuse him before he got them both in more trouble. She pushed through the onlookers and helped the bartender lead him away. She ordered a cup of coffee and slid it in front of him. His breath reeked of beer. She managed to pluck his real name out of memory.

"Look, Dave. You can pick your own fights all you want," she said, trying to hold his weaving eyes. "But don't drag me into it. This racist crap only makes it more difficult for Bradley and me. We've got enough problems as it is."

He scowled at her. "I was only trying to help," he said.

"This kind of help we can do without," she said.

She picked up her backpack and started to leave. She'd call Bradley later, but she wasn't going to wait around anymore. She felt like the fuse in a stick of dynamite.

She turned to see Bradley sitting with Catherine Spinetti. He seemed deaf to the ruckus in the bar, and apparently didn't know he was the cause of it.

Bradley and Catherine were staring at each other. He was smiling, his arms crossed lazily over his chest. She was tapping her pen on the open book, over and over, until she suddenly jabbed the point into the page. He leaned close and said something. She nodded and smiled at him. As though he'd won and she had grudgingly acknowledged it.

Bradley spotted Hannah. He grinned at her and gave her a thumbs-up.

He waded to the bar and suddenly, Hannah noticed, the room wasn't as noisy as it had been. It grew even quieter as they sat down. The silence, she noted, had begun at Celestina and Fernando's table. It was a fog, moving toward them.

"I'm buying," Bradley said. The bartender brought him a double scotch and he downed it. "We're home free."

"You've got everything?" Hannah asked. "Your notes, my disk, everything?"

He nodded and waved at Catherine Spinetti, who had gathered up her books and was gliding out the door.

"They're sunk," he said to Hannah. Then, seeing Fernando, he yelled, "Now who's the asshole?"

"Quiet down," she said. "Things have been a little tense here."

"Well, let's drink and split."

"Where are they?"

"Where are what?"

"The notes, the disk, what we've been talking about, for God's sake," Hannah said. "We need to talk, figure out how to write the answer. What else are we doing here?"

He rubbed his forehead, motioned for the bartender to hit him again.

"Christ Hannah, I didn't bring all that stuff."

"Goddamn it, Bradley!" she said, slamming down the coffee cup. "We've got less than a week. I want to see what we've got."

Bradley groaned. "It'll take me an hour, and I don't want to come back here. It'll be the Friday-night free-for-all in an hour."

"La Luna, then. It'll be quiet there," Hannah said.

"Okay, fine," he said, sighing. "La Luna. Ten-thirty."

Hannah watched him as he knocked back the second scotch and headed for the door. But near the entrance, Bradley stopped. He called the bartender and pointed to the glass-doored refrigerator. It held some wine and a bottle of Perrier-

Jouet champagne. The green glass was swirled with pastel Art Nouveau flowers.

"Let me have that," Cogburn said.

"It's decoration," the bartender replied. "The boss thinks it gives the place a little class."

"Give it to me," Bradley insisted.

"It's sixty dollars," the bartender said.

Fernando strode toward Bradley, his hands flexed at his sides. Hannah noticed, for the first time, the blue star tattooed between his thumb and forefinger.

Bradley pulled out his wallet. Hannah got up and stood next to him.

"What are you doing?" Hannah asked.

"It's a little ritual my father had," he said. "When he hit a snag in a project, he'd buy a good bottle of champagne and pop it open. He said it brought him luck. And the one time he didn't do it, everything turned to shit. I'm not making that mistake."

The notion made her uneasy.

"It's a damned jinx," she said.

Bradley shook his head and jutted his chin at Fernando.

"I want him to see this."

"Rubbing Fernando's nose in it is going to piss these people off," Hannah said.

"Screw 'em all," Bradley said, handing the bartender three twenties.

As Fernando passed he bumped Bradley with his shoulder. Hannah thought she would have to referee round two, but Bradley just smiled at him.

"You're excused," he said.

Fernando shoved open the door and was gone. Celestina stayed at the table in the back with the bereted first-year, staring at them.

"Okay, I'm gone," Bradley said, waggling the bottle at Celestina as though it was a trophy.

Hannah tried to convince him to wait a few minutes. Fernando was probably waiting outside, and although Bradley deserved a slug, the cop in her wanted to defuse a brawl, if possible. But Bradley wouldn't stay.

"I don't like the crowd here," he said, raising his voice. "Kind of . . . cheap and rowdy, you know? And it smells like a Tijuana cantina, where they don't even bother with bathrooms. They just piss on the walls."

"Cut it out," Hannah said. "It's not funny."

"See you in an hour," he said.

She watched him from the door. He walked down the block, past the closed stores. He disappeared for a moment in the darkness of the Plaza and its ring of Italian cypresses. Hannah saw someone moving behind the trees; Fernando, she thought. She nearly called to Bradley. But he emerged on the other side, next to his Range Rover. No one followed him.

He turned around, as though he knew she was watching him, and raised his arms in a V. He pretended to guzzle the champagne and flashed that smile at her. She refused even to nod at him. He shrugged, got into the car, and peeled out into the night.

$$3$$

She left M'Naghten's at ten-fifteen, rehearsing what she would say to Bradley. From the east, where the Santa Fe railroad cut through town, she heard the long, unbroken howl of a train's air horn. He's really leaning on it, Hannah thought, about to cover her ears. It could wake the dead. The horn stopped abruptly.

No more fooling around, she would tell Bradley. It's not a joke, and we don't need a politically incorrect sideshow or your cavalier attitude.

Maybe, she thought, his childishness ticks me off because I'm not twenty-five anymore. I've been around enough to know what's at stake here. I don't have time to go window-shopping for another career, another life. Bradley, fair-haired child that he is, can dust himself off and reinvent his future—sales, politics, modeling, personal-transformation infomercials—who knew what he was capable of doing? But for me, it's life and death.

She stopped at a light. Her Hyundai Excel sputtered and nearly died. It was four years old and she had missed a tune-up or two in the last eighteen months. Law school had made her a pauper. Hannah pumped the gas pedal and the car settled into a rough idle.

From the corner of her eye, she saw someone dart across a side street, full speed. The runner jumped a low wall and disappeared down an alley. Hannah reached across and locked the passenger door. God knows what that was. The aftermath of a gang bang. Or a prelude to one. The warehouse walls and splintering picket fences in this part of town were coated in layers of competing graffiti. She had worked patrol here, years ago, and it had been bad enough then. But gang warfare had made the neighborhood even worse.

The shrill wail of a siren came closer. The sound always made her heart pound. It was the Friday-night horrors, starting a little earlier than usual.

A paramedic truck sped past her and made a U-turn. It pulled up to the railroad tracks crossing Las Almas Boulevard.

Hannah watched it double back. Then she saw the Range Rover.

Bradley's car sat on a side street near the crossing gate. Under the orange streetlight, the bottle-green finish was a sickly black, like something rotting in water. She felt herself go shivering cold, down to the bone. She knew what that intuition meant. She swung the car around.

Paramedics piled out of the ambulance with a stretcher and raced along the track, turning to shadows as they ran into a tunnel of cold white light.

Hannah parked behind the fire truck. Police cars pulled in behind her. A Las Almas cop got out. He was a breath away from giving Hannah his move-along speech when he recognized her.

"Hannah Barlow. Literally ambulance chasing. Nice career move," he said.

"Hey, Bryant," she said. He'd gained a little weight since they rode together. She locked the car and followed the paramedics down the siding. The ballast crunched under her feet.

"Where do you think you're going?" Bryant asked, a pace behind.

"I saw a friend's car over there. It's a bad place to stop at night. I was afraid he might have been in trouble."

"Well, unless he decided to take a snooze on the tracks, I don't think this concerns him. Why don't you—hey!"

Hannah was sprinting away from him, her feet wobbling in the loose rocks. She could hear him running after her.

The pure light flooded the tracks, angling sharply down from the hulking diesel locomotive. Its engines thrummed low, more sensation than sound. The light washed over the paramedics and cops, outlining them in white. One officer helped a man dressed in a denim uniform climb down the ladder from the locomotive. The man's hands shook as he moved them slowly down the handrails. His foot dangled, unable for a moment to find the metal step. He nearly fell back into the cop's arms as he miscalculated the last, long drop to the ground.

The cop held him by the shoulder and the wrist. The man seemed dazed.

"It's okay. You did what you could," the cop said as Hannah passed them.

"It's takes a mile to stop," the man said, his voice getting faster and louder as he talked. "I couldn't big-hole it. The wheels would have locked up. Could have derailed. All those houses back up to the tracks. I couldn't stop. He just laid there."

And then he began to sob.

Hannah ran for a few more yards, until she saw the paramedics coming toward her, the stretcher empty. She hurried past them, block after block, a quarter mile, toward the crumpled mound on the tracks.

In the first glance, before she closed her eyes, Hannah saw a nightmare portrait of Bradley. Glasses splintered into shards. Red-streaked hair. His face was crushed into a bowl of blood and mangled skin.

She looked again. His left arm was gone. The legs of his black jeans were shredded, gory tatters below the knees.

She closed her eyes once more. The afterimage burned on, changed, slipped into the film in her head, the one that always played, never varying, never forgiving.

A hot day, too hot for June. White lambskin rug, brand-new, drenched with red. Her mother sinking into the slick. The gash in her forehead, deep as a nightmare. Her eyes open, staring, at Hannah. Dead, but they spoke to her. Your fault, your fault. Always your fault.

Hannah shook the picture away, opened her eyes again. A cop was checking Bradley's pockets.

"No wallet," he said.

Robbery, Hannah thought. Why did Bradley stop here? It could have been a car-jacking. The runner she saw. A car jacking, and something had gone wrong. A hand landed on her shoulder and whirled her around.

"Goddamn it, when I tell you to stop, stop," Bryant screamed at her.

"His name is Bradley Cogburn," she said. She was so cold, suddenly. She fought to stop her teeth from chattering. "He's a second-year law student at my school. He lives in Newport Beach. His wife's name is Alicia."

"What the hell was he doing lying on railroad tracks in the middle of the night?" Bryant said.

"I don't know." She felt dizzy, pummeled by the shock of seeing Bradley there. Her knees were weak, and she knew she would have to sit down soon or fall down.

"We were talking at M'Naghten's about forty-five minutes ago, and he was going home to get some research notes, but he couldn't have gotten there and back. There wasn't enough time. I was supposed to meet him at La Luna at ten-thirty."

He released her arm, and Hannah swayed. He steadied her. "Wait here for a minute."

Hannah sat on the curb and took slow breaths. Life and death, she thought. I elevated a goddamn school paper to life and death while Bradley was broken and bloodied and dying. She felt suddenly ashamed and shallow. Maybe she shouldn't have let him leave M'Naghten's alone. He was buzzed, vulnerable. She closed her eyes and saw his corpse again. She thought she might throw up and she pressed her icy-cold hands to her cheeks. The nausea passed.

Bryant came back with a Las Almas lieutenant and a detective from Santa Fe Railway Police. She repeated what she knew for them.

As she talked she watched the crowd gathering—incredible, how many people would come out to gawk so late. Even a kid, out past Las Almas's curfew.

He was eleven or so. His hair was strawberry, shades lighter than Hannah's. He wore thick glasses and his front teeth nibbled at his lower lip. He looked like an anxious rabbit.

He was staring down at the yellow tarp they had thrown over Bradley's body. Padded headphones covered the boy's ears. His eyes darted back and forth, went wide, and fixed again on the tarp. Then he pushed through the back of the crowd and ran.

After a while the police told her she could leave and she walked slowly back to the Hyundai. She searched the backpack for her key chain, her hand running over all the junk in the bottom. Where is it? She peered into the window and saw the chain dangling from the ignition.

Goddamn it, she thought. Not again. She'd been in such a hurry, she'd locked herself out.

The crowd of cops was thinning. The Santa Fe detective let her use his cellular phone to call the auto club and offered to wait with her until the locksmith came. She told him she'd be fine.

The locksmith's van was there in minutes. He'd opened her door and Hannah was ready to go when she saw the key duplicator in the van. As Hannah watched him grind a duplicate key for her, she found herself thinking about the draft of the brief. She pushed the notion away. Bradley was dead, and she was considering only herself and the disciplinary hearing. But the thought wouldn't leave: the cops would impound the car and it could take weeks to get anything out of it.

She tried out the new key on the Hyundai's trunk and dropped it in the backpack's zippered pocket. Bryant stood nearby, radioing a tow truck.

"A favor?" she said when he was finished.

"Shoot," Bryant said. "I owe you. You saved us about eight hours of investigative time tonight."

"I think Bradley has something of mine in the car."

"You can look," Bryant said. "But I can't let you take anything. You see something that's yours, follow up with the detectives in the morning."

She thanked him, got out her flashlight, and walked to the Range Rover. She played the beam inside it. The interior was empty, except for a jacket and sunglasses. No envelopes, no disks, no notebooks. So he never made it to Newport Beach. But something bothered her, nibbled at her all the way home.

4

Hannah shoved open the gate to the jungle backyard that lay behind it. The overgrown bougainvilleas, spilling bracts of sherbet orange and vermilion, had pulled down a wire fence. Oleanders ballooned around desiccated palm trees. A tide of ivy crept across the lawn. Hannah imagined that it bore a battalion or two of rats. Rats loved ivy.

Hannah hustled up the steps, rodents on her mind. Her apartment was on the second floor of the Victorian house.

The yellow mansion dwarfed the cottages around it, a clapboard Jungfrau jutting out of a stucco plain. It must have been beautiful once. But now its columns were gray and cracked. The white scrollwork had rotted in a dozen places. Decades of sun and rain had pummeled the second-story frieze so that the sculpted wood design of fat grape clusters and curling tendrils had shriveled to a low, almost indecipherable relief.

The house's owner, Emma Snow, pale, stooped, and stubborn, lived downstairs, where she was methodically filling her rooms with junk. She had packed most of them full, and spent her days and nights in the parlor.

Hannah knew Mrs. Snow had a packrat problem. She'd met people like this before. They started saving newspapers, and before they knew it, they couldn't part with anything. Not tinfoil, or cans, or even foul refuse. Mrs. Snow wasn't that far gone, not yet. Every few weekends Hannah convinced her to let the kids from Holy Family shovel out a room and take the findings to the recycling center. Nevertheless, it was getting harder to get Mrs. Snow to listen. She was beginning to take the haul-aways personally.

When it came to Hannah's apartment, though, she was the angel landlady. She let Hannah deduct the cost of whatever needed fixing. During a hot spell that pushed the temperatures into the nineties in December, Hannah made up a list of estimates for window air conditioners and gave it to her. Mrs. Snow agreed to review the list, but in the end, she told Hannah to do whatever she wanted and just send her the bill.

Mrs. Snow stayed up late most nights, walking around the parlor talking to herself, or sometimes to her husband, Walter, who had died in 1954. But the lights in the parlor were out now. Hannah looked at her watch. Midnight.

Hannah paused on the little landing outside her rooms. From it, she could look west to the old town and the law school. To the east, two blocks away, lay the city's barrio. Ranchera music on Friday nights. Holy Family Church and School. In the morning, she could hear the rattling parade of shopping carts as men pushed them, heaped with bagged oranges and peanuts, to the busy streets where they sold them to commuters.

Inside, she turned on the mica-shaded lamp. Its amber glow filled the center of the room, leaving the corners in deep shadow.

Hannah had found the apartment after she graduated from college. It had only one bedroom, a midget kitchen, a massive, flamingo-pink tiled bathroom with a claw-footed tub, and a living room. It must have been an upstairs library once. The ceilings were high, crossed with beams of fumed oak. The floors were oak, too. Hannah had found them under a layer of pea-green carpet and sanded and buffed them until they gleamed. The glass in the mullioned windows was artfully bubbled and cracked. Red stained-glass medallions anchored each corner.

She filled the apartment with the Mission furniture her grandmother had left behind when she went to the nursing home. Hannah had been in high school then. Other pieces she discovered at garage sales when she was in college. The dark oak furniture, serious and masculine, made her feel rooted. Secure.

Later she found out that collectors were paying thousands

for an L. and J. G. Stickley bookcase like hers, or the Limbert sideboard that held her mismatched garage-sale dinnerware. She sold a tiny Roycroft tabouret to pay for summer school. The huge Gustav Stickley library table, now covered with stacks of books, papers, and her computer, was due to go up for sale next, unless she got a scholarship for third year.

Hannah gathered up a heap of mail on the floor. She sat on the leather sofa and flicked through the bills and junk until she came to a creamy vellum envelope. The card within was embossed with a Celtic cross. It informed her that the Reverend Michael Barlow had been named vicar of religious education for the South Coast Diocese. So, Hannah thought, he's moving up the Catholic corporate ladder. A second paper fluttered out.

In his fine, fluid hand, in blue-black ink, Michael wrote that he was sorry she could not attend the celebratory Mass and reception, as the rest of the family had. He felt sure that even their mother had been there, watching from the ranks of the saints.

She read it again. Each word carefully chosen to inflict a jab of pain and guilt, but coated in pious sentiments. Their mother wasn't with them. Hadn't been for eighteen years. And Michael never missed an opportunity to remind her, obliquely, of whose fault that was. Hannah shredded the paper and threw it in the kitchen trash.

Hannah tried to sleep, but it was useless. She saw Bradley's mangled body every time she closed her eyes.

She got up and went to the bathroom. She fingered the fine lines around her eyes. They grew more pronounced every year. She was beginning to look like her mother, she thought. She had her mother's skin, shell pale and smooth. The freckles were her mother's, too. She hated the faint ginger dusting across her nose when she was little. Now she accepted it as a constant reminder of her mother. Hannah had loved her.

But she didn't know the woman who, drunk and seething with manic rage, lashed out at her on that last day. The argument had escalated. She slapped Hannah, and Hannah shoved her. Had Hannah hit her, too? She couldn't remember. But her mother slammed against a wall. And although Hannah had been told a hundred times it wasn't her fault, she didn't believe it. She didn't know her mother had cracked her head as she fell, but that wasn't the issue, Hannah thought. She had run. And her mother had died there, alone.

She turned away from the mirror and went back to the living room. Someone to talk to, she thought. She called Bobby. It was late, but he didn't usually mind. Law school bred insane competition, but it also fostered friendships. Bobby and Hannah had been studying together since the first week of school.

In those days, students were leaping into study groups like passengers ditching the *Titanic* for the lifeboats. The others in their group had drifted off, dropped out, or flunked out. She and Bobby kept at it. They outlined their class notes, photocopied them, and argued over what they really meant. He'd saved her butt in property, she saved his in torts. Hannah knew she was lucky to have a study partner as solid as Bobby.

Best of all, they hadn't slept together, though Bobby had suggested it once, after one too many glasses of good Sonoma cabernet. After that, they agreed that late-night studying shouldn't involve wine.

On the fifth ring, Bobby's answering machine clicked on. Hannah remembered: he was visiting his parents in Oakland and picking up a weekend cooking class in Berkeley. One thing she could say for Bobby. He hadn't gotten to 270 pounds by eating bad food.

She made a cup of camomile tea and sipped it while she watched a bad movie on the sci-fi channel. She dozed off as a giant wasp plucked a train off the tracks in downtown Tokyo. Then, in her dream, she saw Bradley. He dangled by one hand from the train's undercarriage and held on to something with the other. He screamed and screamed as the wasp buzzed out to sea.

She awoke with a start, and realized what was missing from the Rover's interior. Bradley's jacket had been in the car, and a pair of Vuarnet sunglasses. But not the champagne.

5

Hannah drove downtown early Monday morning, negotiating the traffic around the Plaza and sliding onto Grove Street without having to brake.

Here, along this narrow street, lay the antithesis of the Orange County ideal. Most people gravitated to the county because it was big and still partly undeveloped, free of burdensome layers of history. The county was known for its sprawling, town-sized malls, stuccoed three-bedroom houses, planned cities with misspelled Spanish names, and miles of freshly topped toll roads that had required the uprooting of centuries-old oak trees.

But the mania for tearing down history had never infected Las Almas, and in the wake of Bradley's death, Hannah found its order comforting.

The city's past, slightly out of order, lay along Grove Street. Hannah passed a filling station from the 1930s, which sat next to an adobe ranch house from 1844. She paused, as usual, to covet the Craftsman house that had belonged to Douglas's founder, Virgil Rattigan. The lawyer arrived just after 1900, and used his knowledge of water to turn the county orange with groves and green with cash. Las Almas couldn't have taken root without him.

At the campus entrance, she privately saluted the marble-and-gilt marker that bore the school's name. The outrage over that little drama lingered still in Orange County, and that delighted her.

For years, the institution was the Orange County College of Business and Law. But in the late seventies, the civil-libertarian great-grandson of the school's founder proposed renaming the school after the Supreme Court justice. That set off a vicious battle with the trustees, mostly Republicans who thought Douglas helped bring down the presidency of Orange County's most illustrious son: Richard M. Nixon. The trustees had their ideology, but the heir had the money. The name was changed.

Conservatism had its revenge, however. Douglas was remembered in a well-established California law school, but it still was a rung down the prestige ladder from Boalt Hall or Stanford. Nixon, meanwhile, had a multimedia museum and presidential library in Yorba Linda, the town where he was born. Tourists could see it and Disneyland in a day, if they pushed it. Few, on the other hand, bothered to stop by Douglas to pay their respects.

Monday's first class was criminal-law theory, and Hannah was thankful for its distraction. She loved it passionately, even though she wasn't sure she was going to pass.

The readings covered everything from Dostoyevsky to Abbie Hoffman and the students argued with their hearts as well as their minds. Every Monday, before class began, the room buzzed with pent-up intellectual energy. People yelled. Arguments boiled over. At times, Hannah felt she was watching a troupe of histrionic Mensans rehearsing *Twelve Angry Men*. It was a wonderful jolt of adrenaline to start the week.

But, as on every Monday morning, the students fell immediately silent as Emilia Dove entered and began to pace in front of the room.

Dove ruled with a glacial glance. Queen of the Night, indeed. She was imperious, darkly frightening when a student didn't have an answer at the ready. Tall, nearly anorexic looking, she strode behind her desk, finishing her transits with predatory, swooping turns. She tapped her red-lacquered fingernails together, a tiny sound, like the last thing a rabbit heard as a raptor's claws snapped its spine.

Dove had been Hannah's instructor for first-year criminal law, and despite the terror she struck in Hannah's heart, Hannah came back for more. During the summer, she'd read one of Dove's books, an examination of the felony-murder rule, and found she was an exquisite writer as well as an extraordinary teacher.

"We were talking last week about the law of murder in England," Dove said.

Her voice was unusually soft today, perhaps to induce calm in the room. Hannah had heard Bradley's name whispered all around her that morning.

Bobby Terry nudged Hannah's hand off her notebook. He barreled in just as class began and they hadn't had a chance to talk.

He's dead? I can't believe it, he scrawled in the margin of her notebook.

"I can't either," she whispered. "The paper this morning said his blood-alcohol was high—zero-point-fifteen. He was blast—"

"Ms. Barlow," Dove said, smiling without any warmth, "will you give us the commission's view on how murder can be shown when the perpetrator did not intend to kill?"

Hannah straightened in her chair and gave thanks for the reading she had done that morning. Her cram memory was good enough for parroting, but to really sow the concepts deep, she would have to go over the material again and again.

"There has to be an intentional act, which the killer knows will be likely to kill," Hannah said, "even if he didn't intend it to happen."

"An example?"

"A woman who leaves an infant in a place where she couldn't reasonably expect someone to find and save it."

"Fine," she said. "Care to continue, Mr. Terry?"

Bobby tugged off his glasses. "I didn't get that far in the reading, Professor," he said. "I just kept thinking about Bradley Cogburn."

Dove's smile disappeared. Hannah shivered. Dove didn't fall for dodges like that. She was going to rip Bobby some new orifices.

"It was a horrible thing," Dove said. She walked to the window and adjusted one of the blinds. The room dimmed, as though the sunlight had been sucked out of it. She paced again, slowly, with her arms tight across her chest.

"Bradley Cogburn had a genius for the law," she said. "He took first in my criminal-law class last year. I have never seen a better exam essay."

Bobby and Hannah looked at each other. Bobby raised his eyebrows. Dove never praised anyone. Poor Bradley, Hannah thought. It would have delighted him to hear the Queen sing paeans to his intellect. Maybe the praise resonated to wherever his essence now resided.

"He had a future," Dove said. "But that has been cut short. It isn't clear what happened, but we can't ignore the possibility that it was the toll taken by the pressures here. You all face them. So I just counsel you not to let things get out of proportion."

Bobby nodded sagely, then leaned toward Hannah as Dove paced to the other end of the room.

"What is she talking about?" he whispered.

Hannah shook her head. Dove waxing mystical and mushy. It was strange to hear.

Dove stopped walking in front of Catherine Spinetti's seat.

"I've asked Ms. Spinetti to collect any money the second-years might want to contribute. We'll donate it in Bradley's memory to the scholarship fund."

Dove went on with the lecture. But Hannah heard none of it.

When class ended, she signed herself up for a twenty-dollar donation. Then she scratched out Bobby's ten-dollar pledge and doubled it. He whined, but she told him to stop it.

"You are not a very convincing starving student," she said. Bobby looked down at his belly and shrugged.

Evidence class was starting in less than five minutes, up two floors. She asked Bobby to save her a seat in the front row. Any farther back and she'd fall asleep once the Ruminator got started.

She waited in the hall until Dove came out of the classroom.

"Did you have a question, Miss Barlow?" she asked. "I thought I made it all very clear, but go ahead."

Hannah thought she'd glimpsed actual humanity in the classroom. But Dove had slipped back behind her icy persona. Maybe she had *Paper Chase* on video at home and practiced the John Houseman role on the weekends, Hannah thought.

"You said something about the pressures taking their toll," Hannah said. "I thought the police considered Bradley's death a robbery homicide. His wallet was gone."

Dove considered the question for a minute, putting the key into the classroom door.

"You were a friend of Bradley's?" she asked.

"I thought I'd gotten to know him pretty well. We were moot-court partners."

"I heard. Your brief has gotten quite a bit of attention, I understand."

"I hope I can untangle all of that," Hannah said. "Was that the pressure you were talking about?"

The professor turned away from her, fitting the key in the lock.

"The dean sent a memo around, summing up what he's been told by the police. They haven't ruled out suicide, apparently," she said. "It will hit some people hard, when they hear that's one of the possibilities. If someone like Bradley cracked, others will wonder if they're next. He wanted us to remind all of you not to let things get out of balance, as Bradley might have."

"That's just it," Hannah said. "I saw Bradley at M'Naghten's Friday night, and he seemed too balanced—not as worried about the hearing as he should have been. I can't believe he'd then go out and kill himself."

"You never met Bradley's father-in-law, I take it?"

"No," Hannah said.

"Alexander German had excruciatingly high standards when it came to his son-in-law." She paused. "If Bradley's future was at all in jeopardy, Alexander would have taken a keen interest. That's the kind of pressure I was talking about. Excuse me now. I'm late for office hours."

Hannah stared after her, wondering how Dove knew about Bradley's relationship with his father-in-law, and why she was so willing to share it with her. Then she tried to imagine a drunken Bradley lying down on the tracks, arms outstretched, waiting to sacrifice his great weight of despair to the steel wheels. But the scene wouldn't take shape. Not featuring the Bradley she had seen at M'Naghten's. He was already celebrating their victory. As she trudged upstairs to evidence she chided him for tempting fate—she had warned him that the champagne was bad luck.

6

Hannah couldn't believe the size of the place: two stories, overlooking the Back Bay, a shallow inlet linked to the Pacific. But here it was a pool of still water, ringed by waving grasses. Expensive homes terraced down the hill, nudging their way toward the reedy shores.

Hannah sat in her car at the end of the driveway for a moment, looking at the house. She could see now that it was attached to another unit—there were two entries, two door-bells. But it was like no duplex in her neighborhood. It looked like something from the cover of an architecture magazine: muted gray stucco, glass brick around the front door, and a gallery of small and large windows, all shaded in Japanese mulberry-paper blinds. Hannah guessed that the condominiums sold for triple what detached houses of twice this size went for in Las Almas.

She had never been to Bradley's house before. It was too far from school. She assumed that the house was some sort of gift from the families. Bradley had told her a little about Alicia's father, Alexander German, who was a founding partner in a prosperous Newport Beach firm, and he'd said his own father had made "a few million" in real estate.

Hannah had tried calling Alicia all Monday afternoon, but no one answered. Maybe she unplugged the phone, Hannah thought. The local papers had made a one-day wonder out of Bradley's death, complete with sidebars on how not to get car-jacked, or, in case it was a suicide, how to cope with the psychological pressure of school, work, whatever.

Hannah rehearsed what she was going to say one last time and rang the doorbell. She heard footsteps inside. Then Alicia Cogburn opened the door.

She was short, about five-two, Hannah guessed. She was snapping an elastic band around her fine brown hair, drawing it into a ponytail.

Hannah realized she had expected a female version of Bradley: tall, sculpted, and patrician. But Alicia had the body of an odalisque: wide hips strained at the seams of the khaki shorts. She wore an oversized Laguna Canyon College T-shirt. It must have been Bradley's, Hannah thought. She smelled a man's cologne wafting from it as Alicia leaned out the door.

Alicia Cogburn scanned Hannah's face warily, as though she expected even more bad news. Her eyes were pale green, almost the celadon of Chinese porcelain. The makeup she had daubed under her eyes had at some point smeared with an onslaught of tears. Hannah introduced herself and held out her hand.

"I'm so sorry," she said.

Alicia's face sank, but she put her hand in Hannah's. It was cold, shaky. She looked up and the tears shimmered in her eyes. She motioned Hannah inside.

"I'm sorry," she said. "Sometimes I just can't do anything but cry."

"I didn't mean to intrude," Hannah said, chiding herself for self-centeredness. This woman needed support, not someone pawing through her husband's things. "I'll come back later."

"No," Alicia said. "I'm glad to have someone to talk to. Let's go out back. I like to watch the sun set."

Hannah followed her through the living room, which was open to the second floor and surrounded by a gallery upstairs. The carpet under her feet was thick white Berber. Impossible to keep clean, yet it was immaculate. The art on the walls was abstract, muted. Everything else in the room glowed eggshell, white, or beige. Hannah felt as if she'd been dropped onto an ice floe.

Outside, she stood with Alicia on the wooden deck that jutted into the marsh. Alicia was watching tight formations of shorebirds skim the water, their shadows blurring on the surface as they flew. The setting sun glazed the sky with flat, metallic light. Hannah held her breath as an egret came close, picking its way along the edges of the reeds, its knees bending like soda straws. It was cold outside, but Alicia didn't seem to notice.

"Bradley never understood why I like this place so much," she said. "He wanted a place overlooking the ocean. Like my father's house. Actually, it was my father's house he wanted. But all that empty water used to scare me. You knew it just went on and on, for thousands of miles. Here, you can see the other side. It's nicer, I think."

"It's beautiful," Hannah said.

Alicia shook herself out of the reverie. "You were out there, Friday night. You told the police who he was, didn't you?"

Hannah nodded.

"And you told them Bradley said he was coming back here?"

"That's what he told me," Hannah said.

"He never made it. I could have seen him one more time, if—"

She stopped herself. Alicia faced a lifetime of that, Hannah thought. Ifs. If onlys.

"So you saw what happened to him?" Alicia said.

This was no safer ground for her, Hannah thought. She knew Alicia didn't really want to have it described to her in detail. She might actually want someone to tell her it was nothing but a bad dream. Hannah was sorry she couldn't do that.

"Yes," she said. "It was . . . well, it was bad, Alicia."

"My father told me so." She drew a deep breath. "He identified the body. I just couldn't do it. Was it suicide? Did Bradley kill himself? The reporters kept asking me that."

"I don't know," Hannah said. "It's just one of the things the police are looking at. Robbery's a possibility, too."

"His wallet was gone, I know that," Alicia said. "I think that must have been it. Robbery. He struggled with someone for it, and fell and hit his head and the robber panicked. I know he didn't kill himself."

"He didn't seem depressed to me, despite everything that happened last week," Hannah said.

Alicia nodded vehemently. "That's right. I told my father that." She stopped suddenly. "Oh, God. I didn't realize. You need your rough drafts, don't you? Your hearing is coming up."

Hannah nodded. "But I should have waited. I'm sorry."

"No, no," Alicia said. "He told me he'd found some of them. Come on."

They climbed the stairs, passing a wall devoted to pictures of Bradley. As a toddler. In his high-school cap and gown. On a camping trip, with a day's growth of golden stubble on his chin. His wedding day, resplendent in a morning coat. Bradley, from baby to groom. Half the wall was empty, and would stay that way. Alicia picked up a stack of papers from a glass-and-metal desk in the gallery and handed them to Hannah.

"Bradley was looking through these Friday morning," she said.

Hannah flicked through the stack: articles and opinions on Indian sovereignty, California gambling statutes, and the structure of tribal governments. What class was that stuff for? She didn't see her draft, Bradley's sections, or the final draft that knitted their work together.

Alicia was watching her anxiously.

"There's nothing here," Hannah said. "Maybe it's in the car."

"The police thought they'd be done with it soon. I'll know by the funeral Thursday. Will you be able to come?" Alicia said.

Hannah said she would be there.

Alicia was silent, lost in thought. Then she looked up at Hannah. "Can I show you something?"

She didn't wait for Hannah to agree. She went into the bedroom and returned with a gray plastic box. She unlocked it and pulled out two guns: a blue steel nine-millimeter semiautomatic pistol and a .38-caliber revolver. Hannah felt herself tense at the sight of them in Alicia's shaking hands.

"His father's guns. Bradley knew how to use them. He kept them in good condition," she said.

Hannah hoped Bradley knew to keep them unloaded, too.

"If he killed himself, he would have done it with one of these. Isn't that the logical thing? He wasn't depressed, and he didn't use the very weapon he knew would work. It doesn't make any sense."

Hannah agreed. But not every suicide took the expected form. She'd known a crack-shot cop who'd hung himself in his backyard.

Alicia put the guns away, locked the box, and sank into the chair at Bradley's desk, cradling the box in her lap.

"I should get rid of these. They scare me," she said. "But they were his." She began to cry again.

Hannah reached for her hand. Alicia grasped it tight and shook her head.

"Sorry, sorry," she whispered.

"It's okay," Hannah said. "It will be okay."

She wondered if that was anything like the truth for Alicia. Hannah knew what sudden, violent death left behind. She had seen fathers smolder in angry, consuming fury. It burned out their very souls. Some children swallowed guilt, gulped it in, choked on it. She knew that feeling herself.

The husbands and wives had it the worst, she thought. She had seen women and men slip into grief's cocoon at the moment of a spouse's death. They receded deeper, year after year, into opaque layers of loss. She thought she could see that thin film beginning to wind itself around Alicia.

Hannah was walking down the driveway when a black BMW 850ci pulled up. The driver talked on a car phone as he set the parking brake, turned off the headlights, and opened the door. Hannah stepped around the door and looked at him.

In the car's dome light, she could see his white-gray hair, straight nose, and cleft chin. He wore a dark business suit. Three buttons, dramatic lapels. Hugo Boss, perhaps. Or something custom-made. He glanced up at her as she passed.

The man snapped the phone shut and got out of the car. Hannah heard the door slam. She turned around. His eyes flicked down to the Douglas sweatshirt she wore.

"You went to school with Bradley?" The voice was sharp.

"Yes," Hannah said.

"I'm Alexander German, Alicia's father," he said as he strode back toward her. He was tall, and he looked down at Hannah, his eyes narrowing. Her hand disappeared into his. It was huge, the palm soft but the grip firm. Almost painful.

"Hannah Barlow," she said. "I was your son-in-law's moot-court partner."

"Oh, yes," German said. "Alicia told me there was a problem. . . . An allegation."

"I'll be able to work it out," Hannah said.

"I hope so. It's too bad he got you mixed up in it."

Hannah looked up at him.

"In what?"

"In his problems," German said. "I'd hoped it wouldn't come to this. Not everyone is cut out for law school. It's not just a question of intelligence. It takes a kind of sustained pacing. Like running a marathon."

For a man who'd just lost a son-in-law, German seemed rather cool, Hannah thought. Here he was, chatting about Bradley's death as though it was an unfortunate end to a small-claims case.

"I thought Bradley handled school pretty well," Hannah said.

German sighed. "He was running himself ragged, but keeping up the facade, as usual. I told the police, of course."

"They think it might be robbery. His wallet was gone," Hannah said.

"Maybe, maybe," German said. "But who knows? Bradley could have ditched it, trying to muddy things so that the life insurance would pay off." German's face softened slightly. "It would have been a thoughtful thing, for Alicia's sake. And I've had clients do it before—trying to make some amends to the loved ones, I suppose. But insurance companies don't usually fall for it."

"You seem so sure," Hannah said. "How can you be?" The question bubbled up out of her amazement at his chilly demeanor. "Sorry. I don't mean to pry."

He shrugged, the sangfroid unmelted. Apparently he didn't mind a stranger's analytical probing.

"It's partly a hunch, and it's history. Bradley's father killed himself, too."

Hannah thought of the guns. If his father had used one of them, it might be why Bradley hadn't.

German held out his hand again and smiled. It was a glimmer of cold, uncomforting moonlight. "Nice to meet you, Hannah," he said. "Perhaps we'll see each other again."

Hannah smiled back. But she was fairly sure she never wanted to see him again.

7

The idea formed slowly on the drive home, almost against her will. She tried to beat it back with logic: Bradley had no reason to cheat. Good grades, law review, it made no sense.

But some parts of Bradley's story—Fernando picking up the brief in the library, Bradley telling the Ruminator he'd noticed the plagiarism—rang false. Perhaps he'd given Fernando permission to copy it, with the promise that Fernando would make enough changes so that no one would notice the similarities. She could almost imagine Bradley doing that. It would have pleased him to show Fernando how brilliant he was. The whole thing could have been Bradley's ego backfiring.

On Tuesday morning, after her classes, Hannah tried to ask the Ruminator about how the plagiarism turned up. But in a long string of polysyllabic dithers, the professor told her to schedule a deposition or send him an interrogatory. In an honor-code matter, he had to be punctilious. Certainly she understood.

She did, Hannah thought. Whatever Bradley had done, and however he'd died, he'd left her to face the disciplinary case alone.

As she parked in front of the yellow stucco house, she told herself again that she had nothing to lose by talking to Fernando Ruiz. Maybe he'd level with her. They could work something out.

Ruiz lived on Las Almas's east side, an old barrio of

bungalows washed to pastel colors by time and weather. Ruiz's house crouched behind a tall wrought-iron fence. Looping letters had been spray-painted on the curbs and cinder-block walls flanking it: MONOS 187 PENGUIN CITY. One eighty-seven was police radio code for a homicide—that's what the Monos had in store for the rival gang in Anaheim.

A knot of boys in baggy chinos and white T-shirts huddled at the corner, eyeing Hannah as she parked her car. Probably some of the selfsame Monos. It was early afternoon, and Hannah decided she would be gone well before dark.

From the curb, she could hear the shouting inside the house. In Spanish, a woman and a man. She rang the bell anyway.

The wooden door swung in. Then the black grillwork security door slammed out and Ruiz stood there, glaring at her. He crossed his arms over his chest, tilted his chin up, and looked down his nose at her, his head cocked to one side. Then he flicked her a smile.

"La Rogue Cop come calling," he said. "What an honor."

Hannah smiled coolly back at him.

"Your committee needs to do better homework," she said. "I didn't get fired. I quit the department, and I never had any kind of beef filed against me for beating up anybody. Not even Monos. Ask around."

Ruiz leaned against the doorjamb.

"Okay, so maybe Celestina employed a little dramatic license. But the core issue remains: equal justice. I won't get it."

"Maybe we can do something about that," Hannah said. "Can I come in?"

Ruiz shrugged and led the way. "Not for long. I've got to get to work."

"Nights?" Hannah said.

He nodded.

"Hard to do that and study," Hannah said.

"Yeah, well, what am I going to do?" he said. "We can't all be rich like Bradley, now can we?"

Hannah followed him into a living room awash in yellow shag. A stack of law books sat next to a burned-orange sofa.

A woman, no more than four-eleven, walked out of the kitchen, drying her hands. In Spanish, Ruiz introduced Hannah to her. The mother nodded to her. Then her reddened eyes strayed to the wall above the sofa.

There was a plain black shelf mounted there, holding a vase of roses and a flickering red votive candle. The smoke from the flame left a black smudge on the glass of the photograph hanging above the shelf. It showed a middle-aged man, suntanned and wrinkled by a life outdoors. Fernando had his eyes.

He motioned for her to sit down. "So, what have you got to say to me?"

Hannah told him Bradley's version of the plagiarism story. Ruiz listened, his eyes never leaving her face, his expression flat and unchanging.

"That's not what happened, is it?" Hannah said.

Ruiz said nothing.

"I'm trying to make this thing go away," Hannah said. "I could use some help. Knowing the truth would be a start."

"I have absolutely no reason to trust you," he said.

"Look," Hannah said. "I wish I could show you my research, the parts of the brief I wrote. I can't. Bradley had my copy, and I don't know what he did with it. I didn't rip you off. I swear to you. Why not be honest with me?"

"I don't know," he said. "I'll have to talk to Celestina. There's a lot at stake here. It's not just my problem." He glanced up at her and then away.

"It's the cause?" Hannah said. "White versus brown? At my expense?"

"I've been humiliated," he said. "I'm sorry you were hurt, too, okay? But it's different for me. You don't know me, but take my word for it—this is about what they can pin on me, not who I am or what I did. I know how this is going to go down if I don't fight back hard. So I don't think I want to do a deal. I'm sorry."

Hannah threw her backpack over her shoulder and was ready to leave when Ruiz's mother brought a tray out of the kitchen. She looked sideways at Hannah as she set two cups and a carafe on the coffee table.

"That man, he ruined us," she rasped at Hannah. "We give up everything so Fernando goes to school. And now? We have nothing, but *vergüenza*."

Shame.

"But the man is punished," the woman said with a grateful sigh. *"Gracias a Dios."*

"Mama," Ruiz snapped.

She glared at him, muttered something in Spanish, and trudged back to the kitchen.

"The hand of God shoved Bradley in front of a train?" Hannah said. "Is that what you think, too?"

He stared at her, silent and defiant. Gang-bangers called it mad-dogging. She thought about the tattoo on his hand.

"Maybe," he said. "I heard the cops think it might be suicide. I could see him doing that, offing himself so he wouldn't lose face when it all came out. But the thing is, like I said before, Weiss was going to let him off. I know it. Cogburn knew it. He was rich, he was white. He was one of them."

"So there really was no reason to kill himself," Hannah said.

He looked at her and his eyes narrowed. He sugared his coffee and impatiently tossed the spoon into the saucer.

"So what happened?" he said.

"Robbery, and a fight. Or just a fight," Hannah said.

"Could have been a car-jacking gone bad. He had a nice car," he said. He had stopped looking at her.

"Maybe," Hannah said. "Why wasn't the car taken? I don't think that washes."

"Oh really?" Ruiz said. His head snapped up, and the sarcasm of the question twisted his mouth into an ugly curve. "And what does wash?"

Hannah shrugged. "I've got no answers. What about you?"

Ruiz suddenly slammed his fist on the table and stood up.

"Shit. Get out of my house."

The shift from annoyance to sudden fury caught her off guard. "What's wrong?"

"I get it, okay?" he said. "I won't play along with you, so you present your real tactic. You'll tell your former colleagues at Las Almas PD how pissed I am at Bradley. You'll tell what happened last week, in Weiss's office and M'Naghten's. Suddenly, I'm not just a plagiarist, I'm a killer. Get the fuck out." He started picking up books next to the sofa.

"The cops will love it—gang-banger shoves frat boy under train in payback. We never really change, you know."

"I'm not saying any of that," Hannah said. But now she began to wonder. Why was he so jumpy, so quick to make those connections? Perhaps he'd expected the police to show up.

"I told you to get the hell out," he said. He snatched another textbook and cocked his arm. *Criminal Law and Its Processes* looked like it weighed about five pounds. The hard cover had sharp edges. She picked up her pack and left.

As she drove home she thought about how he'd acted. He had followed Bradley out of the bar Friday, and disappeared. My God, Hannah thought, what happened out there?

The Las Almas station was only five years old, but it had been designed to look like a depot from rail's golden age— hacienda architecture, a cavernous lobby, a shoeshine stand, and spaces for restaurants and shops. County officials hoped commuter trains would make a comeback. Soon.

Hannah's footsteps echoed on the waiting room's terra-cotta tiles. A few travelers sat on what looked like pews from a Mexican church, facing a television mounted high on the wall. The sound was turned off. They stared reverently at the screen anyway.

Hannah walked onto the patio and up the stairs to a balcony that overlooked the tracks. She imagined she could see where Bradley had died: silver rails, brown ties, and ballast—chunks of rust-red rock. They were the color of dried blood. She felt queasy.

Bells clanged, and a block away, the crossing gates at the street jolted downward, just missing the bed of a cruddy gray pickup whose driver decided to race the train. He was lucky, and real stupid, she thought. Cars were no match for trains.

She felt a low, throbbing hum in her collarbones. An air horn blasted two tones in a piercing major second chord. Then she saw the Amtrak commuter train as it slid around a curve and into the station. People spilled out of the cars. Passengers on the platform clambered on. The train pushed its bulk north, sun glinting on the silver metal.

Hannah walked downstairs and south, to the end of the platform. She pushed her sunglasses up on her nose and picked her way across the ballast beside the tracks.

Her old partner, Devlin Eddy, used to do this. He came back to a crime scene and walked around, kicking the dirt, chatting with the passersby. The first few times it drove Hannah crazy. It's a waste of time, she told him.

People have habits, he told her. Sometimes a witness you missed the first time will turn up later. Crime-scene teams don't get every little bit of evidence all the time. You never know.

In time, it became her habit, too. And it came back easily.

A few people stood on the platform, waiting for the train to take them south to the mission at San Juan Capistrano, the beach at Del Mar, or the last stop, San Diego. Hannah saw heads turning to watch her as she stopped and stared at the trash on the ground. She did it over and over, and eventually she was blocks away from the station.

Muddy paper cups. Taco wrappers. A work boot. Nothing more, she thought. Maybe it is a waste of time.

Something glinting in a clump of weeds around a eucalyptus tree caught her eye. Hannah crouched, picked up a twig, and poked out a chunk of glass.

At one jagged edge, an elongated green-and-white leaf trimmed in gold had been painted on the glass. The glass curved into a well. Something was stamped into the surface. Hannah peered at it: *750 ml.* She took the green bandanna out of her hair, folded the glass into it, and walked back to the station.

The loudspeaker spewed feedback. Then, with a nasal bray, a voice announced the arrival of the San Diegan.

On the platform, a boy in an engineer's hat and sagging overalls seemed to be giving the rails a Third Reich salute. Then Hannah saw the microphone in his hand. The cord led to the tape recorder slung over his shoulder.

A sunburned tourist—what other grown man would wear a Mickey Mouse hat?—was trying to talk to him.

The boy twiddled a dial and interrupted him.

"I need to get the sound level," he said. "Be quiet for a second."

And Hannah remembered him then, standing in the shadows Friday night, headphones clamped over his ears and eyes riveted on the tarp that covered Bradley's body.

She walked up behind him. He seemed to be holding his breath as the locomotive approached. When it stopped, he held the microphone near the air brakes, catching the harsh gasp as they blew off pressure. Then he snapped off the recorder.

"Good," the boy said. His voice was squeaky with joy.

"Hey," Hannah said. "Can I talk to you for a minute?"

His eyes widened as he looked up at her. Before Hannah could even move, he jumped off the platform and ducked under the first car in the train.

Hannah shoved the sunburned tourist out of her way as she crossed in front of the locomotive. No way was she going under a train.

Please God, don't let there be a freight on the other line, she thought. The image of Bradley's mangled face floated up behind her eyes and her throat tightened.

The boy darted down the siding, holding his hat with one hand and the tape recorder with the other. He didn't look back. He swerved left and ran down one of the side streets.

Hannah sprinted after him, grateful to be off the right-of-way. She gained on him as he wavered at a corner.

The boy glanced back.

"Wait!" Hannah panted. Out of breath, goddamn it, out of shape. "I only want to talk to you!"

But the boy sprinted away, cutting diagonally through a vacant lot. Hannah groaned to herself and took off after him.

The boy skittered up a grape-stake fence and disappeared into the yard behind it. Hannah ran at the fence to get some momentum, grabbed the saw-toothed edge, and threw one leg across the top. Splinters bit into her hand. She looked into the yard. He was nowhere in sight.

At that moment a snarling, brindled pit bull launched itself from the back porch. She dropped back into the lot, not waiting to see the top of the canine's trajectory.

Hannah raced around the corner and rang the doorbell at the pit-bull house. A chubby Hispanic teenager answered. She smiled at Hannah.

"Avon?" she said.

"No," Hannah replied. Avon ladies must be a dusty, sweaty bunch these days. "Is there a little redheaded kid here?"

"*Quien?* Uh. Who?"

Hannah exhaled hard. She hadn't spoken Spanish in a while. *"Un niño con pelo rojo."* She ruffled her hair to demonstrate.

"No," the girl said, laughing. She tugged on a strand of her black hair. *"No hay."*

Hannah muttered thanks in both languages and headed back down the street. Her knees ached. Her hand throbbed.

She circled the neighboring blocks, but saw nothing of the boy. She walked back to the station, hoping the tourist she'd assaulted was gone.

At home, she plucked the slivers from her palm with tweezers. Then she unfolded the bandanna and looked at the shard of glass. Had Bradley guzzled the champagne to numb the fear of the train? Or had he thought to slash his wrists, but lost the nerve and opted for the five-thousand-ton train instead? Maybe he had fought with someone. Where had Fernando been? Hannah rewrapped the shard and put it in the library table's drawer.

She rubbed her legs and winced as she rotated her shoulder. A pulled muscle. Nothing more, she hoped.

I don't run like I used to, Hannah thought. Not much left of the investigator's people skills, either.

But maybe it could come back. Everything she had learned couldn't have been erased so quickly. She'd spent five years as a detective. Off the force now for nearly three years. It seemed so long ago. And it had all ended with Janie Meister.

8

Hannah was in her second year working sex crimes when her life began to crumble. For the first year, she had liked the job. She was assigned to rape cases. The work was never easy or enjoyable, but she was good with victims and good with suspects, too. She eschewed bullying and kept her anger in check. And as a result, they talked to her. More than they should have, sometimes.

But in the second year, it seemed to Hannah that more and more of the cases involved children. And the sexual assaults were within the family. The victims were so young—mostly under five. One was just a baby. It sent razors through her stomach to think of how tiny they were.

It took a while before she realized how much the work was taking out of her. Sleep eluded her two or three nights a week. She tended to snap at people, like Eddy, who would wander over from robbery homicide for a chat. She'd been working on a sensitive case, and as it was assigned for trial she realized it was going to be a disaster. Later, she decided, that was really the beginning of the end.

The victim was a four-year-old. Her mother met a guy in a bar and moved him into her motel room. She worked days and "Daddy" stayed home with the girl. He insisted on giving her baths, morning and night. During these, he raped her. The girl had described the assaults to her mother after the man had moved out and another boyfriend moved in.

Within a four-year-old's abilities, her accounts didn't vary much. There was even physical evidence—hymenal tearing. It wasn't going to be easy, but Hannah thought the right deputy DA could win it.

The prosecutor was new to her. The pale young man seemed profoundly uneasy with the job of asking a little girl to talk about the "yucky stuff" that had come out of the man's penis. He told Hannah that he really considered these cases family matters. He never called the child by her name. On the day before trial, he sat behind his desk and in the worst lawyer gobbledygook explained the process to the child and her mother. Voir dire to reasonable doubt, with no translation. The girl's eyes glazed and she hung on to Hannah's hand tighter and tighter.

Hannah tried to hustle another DA to take the case, somebody who could handle it. But she was told that the office was swamped, and hey, the guy had to start somewhere.

On the second day of trial, the defense produced its expert witness, an earnest white-haired doctor, who explained that hymenal tearing wasn't always a sign of molestation. A playground injury could account for it.

The prosecutor's tough cross-examination bordered on parody. His voice broke every time he said the word *hymen,* and attempts at bullying the old doctor only managed to make him seem more credible. Hannah passed up a note: *Ask him what he got paid for the testimony.* He crumpled it in his hand.

In a break, she dragged him into the stairwell.

"What's the problem?" she said.

"I feel lousy," he said. "It's the flu or something."

"Then ask the judge to adjourn for the afternoon," Hannah said. "You can't let her take the stand when you're not a hundred percent."

The prosecutor shook his head. "I'll be okay," he said.

He made a series of convoluted objections during the defense lawyer's cross-examination of the girl. The judge waved him off, and all the while the defense lawyer softly trapped the child in a net of inconsistencies and memory lapses.

Mommy had brought guys home before, hadn't she? She told you to call all of them daddy, didn't she? Don't you mix up the daddies, sometimes? Which one had the red truck?

Which one took you to Disneyland? Did any other daddy ever give you baths?

Hannah groaned to herself in the back of the courtroom. The lawyer was using the SODDI defense: it usually meant "some other dude did it." In this case, some other daddy.

The prosecutor shuffled through his notes, made up some ground on the redirect. But not enough. The lawyer had sketched the child as confused, perhaps coached by a bitter mother.

The child craned her neck, looking for Hannah. Even sitting on a restaurant booster seat, she barely cleared the witness stand. Her lip was trembling. Hannah nodded and mouthed the words. *Good. You did fine.* But, she thought, the big idiot at the counsel table has failed you miserably.

The jury took five hours to acquit Daddy.

After that, the assistant DA in charge of sexual assault met with some of the county's sex-crime investigators and let it be known he didn't want any more cases he was going to lose. They had to be solid. He wanted a kid who could testify and withstand a cross-examination. Physical evidence was a big plus.

"Competent prosecutors wouldn't hurt, either," Hannah said.

He told her to sit down and shut up.

Hannah was close to asking for a transfer then. Homicide was looking better all the time. No murder could have been more chilling than what that child went through.

A week later, before she could file her request, Janie Meister came into her life.

The girl had compressed herself into a child-sized chair in the interview room at the Child Abuse Investigation Team's office. Her hands were clamped between her knees, her chin was buried in her chest, and thin brown hair veiled her face.

A tattered stuffed lion peered out at Hannah from between the girl's thin arms. She glanced up and down again when Hannah smiled at her.

"If I talk to you, can I go home?" she said.

Hannah hiked up her skirt and sat down on the floor at the child's feet.

"You don't have to talk to me if you don't want to," she said.

"When we're done here, a doctor is going to take a look at you and then you can watch *Cinderella*."

Janie looked at Hannah.

"Then I can go home, right?"

"No," she said. "I don't think you're going to go home right away, Janie."

"I'm in trouble. I shouldn't have told Gretchen," she whispered, her voice shaking. "He told me not to tell. He said I could never go home if I told."

Hannah gave Janie a Kleenex and looked at the incident report while the girl sobbed.

Janie had told her friend what her father did to her on Saturday mornings, during cartoons. Later he would buy her a dress for her Barbie doll. Janie's mother apparently didn't know. Saturday was her morning to sleep in, after she and her husband enjoyed a few drinks on Friday night.

But one day Janie went to Gretchen's with a full case of Barbie clothes. She dumped them all on the floor, and as her friend admired them the girl collapsed on the heap, crying and rocking inconsolably. She refused to go home. Finally, she told Gretchen the price of the wardrobe.

Gretchen told her parents. They called Janie's mother, who came and listened silently to their story. She told them to mind their own business, wrenched Janie to her feet, and stormed from the house. Gretchen's parents called the police.

Two officers picked Janie up from school the next morning and brought her to the abuse team's scaled-down interview room.

"Janie," Hannah said. "Our job is to help make you safe. We need to find out what's happening in your life to do that. Okay?"

"It was supposed to be a secret. He made me promise," Janie said.

"Sometimes grown-ups make kids promise things they shouldn't," Hannah said. "Some secrets are fun, and they make you feel good. Some are bad, and they make you feel bad."

Janie nodded her understanding.

"How do you feel, Janie?"

The girl's whisper could barely be heard. "Bad."

Behind the one-way window, Hannah's boss and a social worker were watching the interview and videotaping it. If Janie was lucky, this was the last time she would have to tell anyone the details until trial. If it got that far.

They sat in silence for a time. Then Hannah talked to Janie about school, her friends, and her toys, like the lion she held so tightly.

"He's my friend," Janie said.

"Lions are strong and very brave," Hannah said. "He's a good choice for a friend."

Janie was muttering into his ear, where the tawny plush had matted with her tears. She beckoned Hannah to lean close. Her voice was soft, but loud enough to be picked up on the tape.

It all spilled out. Porno-movie scenes, delivered in a kindergartner's words. The girl's voice was high and breathy. The story was full of pauses. In just those few minutes, Hannah came to dread the stops. On the other side of the chasm lay the next horror. She made herself keep the neutral face, the encouraging, comforting voice. But inside, she felt something breaking.

She waited a day before interviewing the father.

Hannah could still remember his eyes. They were the only remarkable thing about him. Milky, pale blue, but with a frightening glare in them, like the moment when lightning struck. He wore a starchy blue dress shirt and a neat navy tie with a pattern of red chevrons. The navy chalk-stripe suit was subtly expensive. She watched him cross and uncross his legs. The shiny black Italian loafers were thin-soled, free of wear.

His voice was smooth, and he found the right tone: civil, but aggrieved. He told Hannah he was new to Las Almas. He had just gotten a job in Newport Beach. He marketed investment opportunities, he said. Hannah heard the slippery sound of scam in the words.

He denied everything, and Hannah played along. She steered the interview to his youth, his family. He covered pretty well, Hannah thought, but there were a few slips, a few times when his own pain sliced through the glib lies. She wondered how long his own molestation had gone on.

The girl's mother was fierce, combative, tearful. A stranger did it, she insisted, if anything was done. The persecution of her family was unconscionable. Her husband would sue. They'd do what they had to do, but they wouldn't let anyone take their child away. Hannah thought of giving her the reality check: who do you love more—your child or your husband? But she doubted it would do any good. The woman would hear nothing but her own outrage and denial.

Given the lecture the DA had delivered, Hannah doubted that there would be a criminal prosecution. She looked over the medical report. A colposcopy confirmed Janie's account. She had not been penetrated. There wasn't any physical evidence. Only the child's story of how her father taught her to give him blow jobs in exchange for doll clothes.

So it would probably be a child-protection case. The county social workers would keep Janie safely out of the home until Daddy owned up to his problem or Mom got over her denial.

Probably, Hannah thought. The number of incest cases seemed to be exploding. Foster parents were scarce these days, and as a result, the children's shelter was stuffed. Kids slept on mats in the gym, sometimes. A backlash group of accused parents—SOFT, or Save Our Families Today—had filed a lawsuit alleging substandard conditions at the shelter. So the social workers were under a lot of pressure to return children to their homes unless there was a solid reason to keep them out. Hannah was afraid that Janie's case was one of those. She was right.

"Janie hates the shelter," the social worker said. It was a new one, a man Hannah didn't know.

"Mom visited and Janie hung on to her like a limpet," he said.

"So she's going to a foster home?" Hannah said.

"Well, I was thinking real home," he said.

"Think again," Hannah said.

"Provided that Meister moves out and has no contact with her—I think it'll be okay."

"He's a manipulator. He's got his wife bamboozled. She's picked her side. With him," Hannah said. "It's not safe."

"I'm sending Janie home," he said. "The family's profile is good."

"They've got money, you mean," Hannah said. "They look nice and white and middle class to you."

"It's an informal agreement," the social worker said, ignoring her. "No court order."

"There's no court order?" Hannah yelled.

"The court's jammed. They want as much diversion as possible, and the Meisters qualify," the worker said. "I'll keep an eye on it."

"I think you should at least get an order," Hannah said mildly.

"Don't tell me how to do my job," the social worker said, and slammed down the phone.

That night after work, she drove to the Meisters' house. She looked at it: white clapboard and green lawn. A plastic swing turned slowly in the evening breeze. The mother's car was there. The father's wasn't. The porch light shone into the night. It all looks so normal, Hannah thought.

Three hours later, at eleven o'clock, she was thinking about leaving. Then the move-yourself truck pulled up outside and Meister got out. Hannah watched him trot up and down the path, loading box after box into the back. She bit on a nail and squinted. Maybe she was wrong. It looked like he was moving out.

Then Meister came out of the house with the stuffed lion in one hand and Barbie's fold-up Model Mansion in the other. He put them on the lawn and undid the swing. His wife followed him, threw her arms around his neck, and kissed him. Hannah felt a dizzying rage surge into her head.

She dialed the social worker's after-hours number on the car's cellular. It was clear he didn't appreciate being bothered after midnight on a Friday. Sleepy and annoyed, he told Hannah he'd check on it midweek. Hannah reminded him that Janie was supposed to go home Monday.

"They're going to take off with her," Hannah said. "What are you going to do about it?"

"Goddamn it, I know what I'm doing," he said. "I'll check it out. It's not your job, detective. It's mine. I'll look into it."

Hannah called her lieutenant. He had been asleep, too.

"Back off," he said. "It's not our problem anymore."

"It's a little girl, not a problem," Hannah said. "I don't mind following it up."

"No," the lieutenant said. "And that's an order."

She called the social worker's boss right away. He hung up on her after making her spell her name. By the time she got to the boss's boss, her lieutenant was on call waiting.

"So help me God, Barlow, if you don't back off of this, I'll bust you back to traffic duty. I mean it. This is not our problem."

Hannah was about to tell him off when she stopped herself. She'd worked eleven years to get where she was. It was her career. Her life, really. What else did she have? She muttered an apology to the lieutenant and hung up. And all that night she prayed, as she never had before, that Janie would be all right.

On Tuesday, she called the social worker to see how the return home had gone.

But he wasn't there. She got his supervisor.

"They're gone," she said. "We dropped Janie off Monday, and everything seemed fine. But this morning we sent a worker by. The whole family is gone."

The supervisor seemed suddenly tongue-tied as she tried to apologize without sounding responsible. Hannah hung up on her.

That afternoon the lieutenant sighed and handed her the newest stack of cases.

"It's tough," he said. "But you did your job. Don't sweat it."

Hannah felt no comfort. She forgot about asking for a transfer, and for the next month she spent every free moment trying to track them down. Where had the rental truck been returned? Any new hires at the telemarketing boiler rooms in San Diego County?

She forgot to eat for hours at a stretch. She felt achy and exhausted, but her sleep was light, fitful. When she did dream, it was of Janie.

Eddy convinced her to take a week and go to his cabin at Big Bear. She went, walking distractedly along the hiking trails, half reading books, and avoiding Eddy's collection of single-malt scotches. She called in daily from a pay phone downtown.

"Give it some time, Hannah," he said. "Something will turn up on the girl. You'll see."

He was right.

The decomposing body surfaced about a month after Janie disappeared. It had been in the water nearly that long. It was a girl, four or five. Brown hair. No distinguishing marks. No match to any children reported missing in the area.

Hannah talked to the detective in Gaviota Bay. He said they might be able to pull enough DNA for testing. But the testing was expensive. They were a small department, and other distraught parents had called, thinking it might be their missing kid. He'd let her know how things progressed, he said.

For a month Hannah felt she had died, too. One morning she woke up and realized what she had to do. The resignation letter was two sentences long.

"I can't do this anymore," she told the captain when he summoned her. "I can't start caring, stop caring, leave behind a problem because it isn't supposed to be 'mine.' "

"Well, Jesus, Hannah that's part of what this job is about," he said.

"I know," Hannah said. "That's my problem with it."

He told her to take more vacation time. Try a leave for a few months. Take a new assignment.

"It's ridiculous to quit because somebody else fucked up," he said.

But that wasn't it, Hannah thought. Someone else didn't fuck up. I did. I knew what had to be done—anything, everything—to make sure that child was safe. Instead, I worried about being demoted. Losing my career. That was more important. But it was my responsibility, because I knew what was happening. And so, it was my fault.

After a couple weeks she got a job working for Roy Carruthers, a cop-turned-lawyer friend of Eddy's. She served summonses and filed court papers like an automaton. The demands of Carruthers's busy office were a relief for her. The job made her get up in the morning, get dressed, get in her car. She used part of her pay to hire a PI, a jumpy, fast-talking New Yorker who ran up a four-figure bill with little to show for it. Finally, he came up with a good lead. A secretive family—investment broker, submissive wife, and a new baby—had just moved into a small town near Omaha. Hannah ran up her Visa bill with a flight there. But it wasn't them. She'd spent everything she could, and the search was going nowhere. She had to put it aside.

Carruthers seemed to know something was wrong. He left her alone for a while, and then became something of a cross between the bighearted buddy and a Dutch uncle. He dragged her into his office for a cup of coffee every other day or so. She talked to him, because he refused to shut up otherwise. She ate, because Carruthers told her she looked like a wraith. She got on the scale, and realized she'd lost ten pounds.

He talked up his cases and the law business to her. He told her she'd be good at it. He brought her a practice book for the Law School Admissions Test. It was something to do at night, something to crowd out the thoughts that ran through her head. She started working the sample tests and enjoyed them. Almost in spite of herself, she signed up for the exam.

When the score came in, it surprised her. She showed it to Carruthers, who gave her a hug and the recommendation letter he'd already written.

"Law school is rigorous stuff. Brain boot camp," he said.

Good, she thought. Rules, procedures, adjudication. A refuge of the intellect. After school, she could specialize in bankruptcies. Corporate law. Tax, even. Anything that dealt with big companies and money and nothing like human lives. But no family law. No criminal work. From now on, she told herself, work is work and my life is my life. She would build a cinder-block wall between the two.

That was two years ago. Most of the time Hannah could avoid thinking about Janie, except in the aftermath of the dreams. They brought everything back, and managed to twine Janie and her own mother together. Two instances in which she hadn't done everything she should have done, she thought.

She woke up some mornings, her throat tight and her stomach churning. It was all those feelings, the guilt and the pain, she thought. They had to come out somehow.

At times she wished she could go back to the church. She saw, perhaps for the first time, the merits of confession. Tell all to the priest, get your penance, do it, and feel the hand around your neck unclench. But what could you do if people told you it wasn't your fault, not your sin?

If only God, or someone, could give her a penance for avoidance. She'd committed sins of omission. Failed to act. And what was the penance for that? She'd gladly do it, whatever it was. Anything to feel whole again.

9

Armed with a take-out double latte from M'Naghten's, Hannah faced Wednesday's classes. By midafternoon, she was weakening. And after a hour of hearing Professor Borden extol the genius of the three forms of Babylonian land-lease systems, her head was pounding.

She popped three aspirin at the drinking fountain outside the dean's office. The dissolving tablets left a powdery bitterness in her mouth. She took another gulp of water.

Behind her, she heard high heels clicking on the tiled floor. They came close, stopped. Then the heels stamped, the sound an impatient child would make.

She turned and found Lois Popich waiting, arms folded. Today, like every day, Popich's blond hair was wound in a chignon. Glasses perched primly on her nose. Her oversized gray suit fell in a straight, boxy line from her shoulders to below her knees. A stand-up collar and a pink lace jabot peeped out between the lapels.

"The dean asked me to give you something. Wait here."

Hannah scanned the confetti of posters on the bulletin board next to Weiss's door. Writing competitions, financial aid announcements, scholarships. A notice, left over from the spring, was partly hidden, but for the name—Catherine Spinetti. Hannah flicked the other papers away. Spinetti had won the Lungren Fellowship. Full tuition and a hefty stipend for a top student preparing for a career in prosecution. Some people have all the luck, Hannah thought.

Lois leaned around the corner and grandly held out an envelope. Hannah tore it open and read the paragraph in one glance. She read it again. Popich seemed to be waiting.

"I made *Law Review*," Hannah told her.

"You should have been selected in the fall," Lois said. "The dean told Harrison Onizaki that you would be an asset to *Law Review*. But—" She stopped herself. "Congratulations." She turned on her heel and closed the dean's office door behind her.

Hannah let out a little sigh, then laughed. It echoed in the empty hall. *Law Review* was a lot of work, but if she did well and got selected as an editor for third year, it would mean full tuition. Of course, the letter noted, the acceptance was provisional. If the plagiarism charge was sustained, she'd be removed.

She stopped at the doorway of the *Law Review* office and breathed in the scent of burned coffee and old paper. It was glorious.

Harrison Onizaki, the law-review editor, stood by a table of cubbyholes, punching out a plastic label. He wore a vest made from a kimono. He pushed his shoulder-length hair out of his face and peered at Hannah over his trendy maroon-tinted half glasses. Every day the same look: retro-hippie Kabuki.

"Welcome aboard. This one will be yours," he said, pointing to a fat stack of cite-checking assignments crammed into one of the boxes. A sick wave rose in Hannah's stomach as she watched him peel the old name sticker from the cubbyhole.

"Bradley left a lot of stuff undone," Onizaki said. "If you could start ASAP, it would be great. And we can talk about ideas you have for your article. You're going to have to work fast."

"I'll come back tomorrow, after class," she said, and backed into the hall.

One of the fluorescent tubes over her head flickered white and blinked out. Runner-up to the dead man, she thought. She felt stupid for not realizing it the instant she read the dean's letter.

She looked up at the sound of the mincing footsteps. Lois was marching down the hall, lugging a black attaché case. She snapped her eyes right and wished Hannah a good night as she passed.

"Wait," Hannah said, running to catch up with her.

"I'm in a hurry," Lois said.

"Just tell me this much," Hannah said. "I'm on *Law Review* because Bradley died. Isn't that right?"

Lois turned into the stairwell and trotted down the middle of the steps, forcing Hannah to walk behind her.

"That's not it," Lois said over her shoulder. "Not exactly."

"You said the dean thought I should have been put on the review in the fall, but Harrison chose Bradley," Hannah said.

"I didn't say that," she said.

"That's what you started to say," Hannah said. "Did the dean think there was some reason Bradley shouldn't be on the review?"

"No," she snapped. "Look, if you're upset because you think you got the job because Bradley's dead, you shouldn't be."

"Why not?" Hannah said.

"He wasn't long for *Law Review,*" Lois said, pushing open the lobby doors and taking the small steps to the sidewalk two at a time.

"Why?" Hannah called. Then she realized what Lois meant. He was going to be expelled. So suicide wasn't that farfetched.

"Did Dean Weiss have the evidence to make an expulsion stick?"

"I don't really know," Lois said. They had reached the parking lot, and she was fidgeting with her keys under the Popsicle-orange glow of the sodium lamps.

Lois loved the power that streamed out of the dean's office, Hannah thought. She was no older, no smarter than most of the students. She'd probably never earn as much as Bradley, or Catherine or Bobby. But she knows all about us: grades, scholarships, who gets disciplined, who flunks out. More than a few secrets, Hannah thought. And she likes people to know she knows.

"Lois, come on," Hannah said. "He's gone. You can't slander the dead. Tell me what was going to happen."

Lois unlocked a white Geo Metro and got in.

"Suspension, and removal from the review while he was on academic probation."

"That's it?" Hannah said.

She nodded. "Dean Weiss thought suspension would be sufficient punishment."

Hannah held the car door open. "But I thought expulsion was standard for plagiarism. Why not for Bradley?"

"That was the dean's call. Or it would have been, if . . ." She tugged the door towards her. "I'm late. Good night."

Hannah held on to the handle.

"You know a lot about this, so let me ask you. Do you think Bradley killed himself?" she said. "Why would he, if he wasn't going to be pitched out of school on his ear?"

Lois didn't answer right away. She plucked a pink valet ticket from the dashboard and tossed it onto the passenger seat. Hannah saw a heraldry shield and its lion passant. The logo of the Creston Hotel. It was only four blocks from school.

"You've been talking to Alicia," Lois said. "She doesn't believe it either."

"Have you talked to her?" Hannah said.

"No. She talked to the dean. They've known each other for years. Her father and Dean Weiss were classmates here."

"Maybe she's right," Hannah said. "Suicide doesn't seem like something Bradley would do, does it?"

Lois shrugged.

"People are unpredictable," she said. "You never really know how someone will react when they're humiliated." She tugged the door out of Hannah's grip.

As Hannah watched her drive away she saw a dark blue Sentra at the edge of the lot. Two people stood beside it, looking at her.

In the deepening darkness, Hannah wasn't sure who it was at first. But as she got closer she recognized Celestina Pacheco and Fernando Ruiz.

She said hello to them both. It wasn't too late to straighten this all out, she thought.

"I'm back," Ruiz said. "The dean couldn't keep me out of class."

"No, you're no threat to Bradley now. Not anymore," Hannah said.

"That's as good as saying he used to threaten him," Pacheco snapped. "We've had it with your slander. There are state defamation laws, and there is a hate-speech code on this campus. We won't hesitate to employ them."

"Celestina, save the speeches for the masses, okay?" Hannah said. "I haven't defamed anybody."

"Fernando told me you all but accused him of murder," she said. "If the police, or anyone else, begin harassing Fernando because of what you've said about him and Bradley's death, we'll bury you with paper."

"Don't we have enough to do without threatening lawsuits?" Hannah asked. "We have until tomorrow to file an answer with the dean's office. The hearing will probably be scheduled before the end of January. Let's put all this crap aside and lay out for the dean what really happened."

Celestina shook her head. "No way. You just stay out of his face."

They got into the car. Hannah tried to catch Ruiz's eye. But he looked away.

Hannah felt adrenaline drumming at her temples. Every time they showed up, it was guerrilla theater. She told herself to calm down. Celestina was apparently bent on some larger political goal. She was using the situation for that. But Ruiz? Maybe he really was a victim. Maybe he had the right to be blindly furious with everyone, including Hannah. More and more, she believed he had written the draft, and Bradley copied it. But his defiance and defensiveness were all out of proportion.

10

That winter had been capricious. Days of gloom and rain alternated with brilliant mornings, like this one. The cemetery's hills sported a buzz cut of vivid green rye grass. Sparrows twittered in the Brazilian pepper trees next to the imitation English chapel.

Hannah slipped off her black wool jacket, put on a pair of sunglasses, and waited outside the chapel. She was coated in sunscreen, so she could afford to soak in the summery weather.

Most of the second-year class, minus a substantial number of Latino students, seemed to be here. Professor Dove nodded a hello. Dean Weiss followed her, smoothing dry straws of hair across his head. Hannah had filed her answer to the plagiarism charge that morning. It had been easy enough. She denied all the allegations and asked for the earliest possible date to review the brief Bradley had submitted.

A black Lincoln Town Car stopped on the gravel road. Alexander German got out first and offered his hand to Alicia. She was wearing a billowy black dress that made her look like a plump abbess. She opened her arms to Hannah.

"Thank you for coming," she said as she hugged her. "Bradley would be glad to know you cared."

Over Alicia's shoulder, Hannah saw a blonde in her thirties walk toward the chapel with a towheaded boy of about eight. There was a picture of Bradley at that age in Alicia's gallery. This boy looked just like that.

"Bradley's brother and sister?" she asked.

Alicia glanced back and then away. "Stepbrother. And stepmother."

As the woman approached, Alicia talked faster and softer, and an edge crept into her voice.

"Bradley's father married Susan after his first wife died. Bradley was a junior in high school then. His father had made a lot of money in Palm Springs. Millions in real estate. That's where he met her." She flicked her eyes to the woman, who passed with barely an acknowledgment of her.

German took his daughter's arm gently and walked her into the chapel. Hannah followed them.

Inside, candles flickered around an ebony casket. Hannah pulled on her jacket. The sun's warmth hadn't penetrated the chapel's granite and slate.

The minister's eulogy was short. He praised Bradley's scholarship and dedication to the highest principles of the legal profession. German read from Ecclesiastes. God's fine balance—a time to be born, a time to die—sounded less than fair at a young man's funeral.

At the end, the organist played a transcription of the "Pie Jesu" from Fauré's *Requiem*. Hannah knew the piece. A soprano from the church choir had sung it at her mother's funeral.

She looked over at Bradley's stepmother. When she wasn't staring straight ahead, she was checking her watch.

Afterward, Alicia told her the police had released the Range Rover. There hadn't been much to glean, they said. Alicia invited her to go through it anytime and then stay for dinner. They agreed on Friday.

German, Weiss, and Alicia piled into the car and drove to the grave site. Dove had disappeared, probably to hatch some new brain-twisting hypothetical for Monday's class.

Susan Cogburn and her son lagged behind. As the boy knelt on the flagstones to pick up some of the pepper tree's fallen pods, Hannah introduced herself as one of Bradley's class-mates and offered her condolences.

Susan Cogburn seemed to be suppressing a smile.

"Bradley talked about me?" she said, raising her eyebrows. They had been artfully sketched and shadowed to frame her golden-brown eyes.

"No," Hannah said. "We didn't talk about family much."

"I wouldn't have thought so," she said. "Well, thank you for coming. Geoffrey!"

Geoffrey held up the pods for his mother to admire, oblivious to the twigs and dust on his knees. Susan Cogburn tugged the pods out of his hand and shoved them into her purse. She flicked the dirt off his pants with a linen handkerchief and took his hand.

Hannah watched as they crossed the road to a Mercedes sedan. The boy's giggle drifted back to her. He swung his mother's arm. She laughed, and skipped the last few steps to her car.

On Friday evening, Hannah put on a black wool turtleneck, a pair of jeans, and her indulgence for the year; tooled-leather cowboy boots. Red ones. She brushed her hair over her shoulders and tamed her bangs with a spritz of spray gel. At Trader Joe's, she bought a five-dollar bottle of French chardonnay.

Alicia walked her to the garage and pressed the door opener. Hannah saw the Rover inside, shrouded in something like parachute silk. It fluttered as a wind swept into the garage.

Alicia shivered. The cold, Hannah thought. Or the memories.

"Dinner should be ready in about twenty minutes. I'll call you," Alicia said.

Hannah pulled off the cover and unlocked the passenger door.

The car smelled of leather and lemon polish. Across the backseat sat the half-dozen manila file folders Hannah remembered seeing that night. She opened the first one: commercial outlines and a notebook full of semicomprehensible jottings from what looked like criminal-law class.

In the next folder she found a handful of newspaper clippings. The first was a one-inch story on an unidentified man found dead in his Stanton motel room. Then an obituary. Hannah compared the dates of death, the age of the man. It seemed to be the same person. The rest of the stories dealt with Tim Gallagher.

Hannah vaguely remembered Gallagher. He was either a victim of a family plot to steal his inheritance or an intelligent, sociopathic murderer with the face of a Romantic poet.

Hannah skimmed the first story. Gallagher had gone to dinner at the home of his brother, Jack, an electronics genius whose computer hardware company was just beginning to flourish. Neighbors heard glass breaking, heard a car roar off. Twenty minutes later the house went up in flames, taking the brother with it. When the will was read, the kin were amazed to find he'd left everything—an estate of more than five millions dollars—to Tim, the ne'er-do-well brother.

But then arson investigators decided accelerant had been used to hurry the fire along. The pathologist noted the lethal mix of barbiturates and alcohol in the victim's system. Murder charges were filed, much to the joy of the brother's ex-wife, whose children were next in line for the money.

Gallagher fired a string of court-appointed lawyers and announced he could do the job better himself. He'd studied history at Pomona College before proclaiming the professors dolts and dropping out, so the press snickered at first. Then, after his first pretrial motions proved to be more than the usual pro-per gibberish, a columnist dubbed him "counselor." He comported himself well at trial, and in the end, the lack of a real lawyer wasn't much of a disadvantage. The best criminal defense attorney in the county probably couldn't have gotten him off. The jury convicted and voted for the death penalty.

Hannah skipped the rest of the articles—there had to be a dozen of them. Even though he'd aced Dove's class, she didn't realize Bradley had that much interest in criminal law, let alone one particular case.

In the last file, Hannah found a padded envelope. The cops had unsealed and opened it, and shut it closed with the metal clasp. Inside was a computer disk labeled SCHOOL STUFF. It wasn't the disk Hannah had given him, but maybe he'd transferred her draft to this one. She decided to go through it at home.

Hannah heard Alicia's voice outside. She slipped the print-outs, clips, and disk back into their envelopes, tucked them under her arm, and locked the car.

Alexander German's BMW was parked in the driveway. He greeted her at the door and announced that he was staying for dinner. Hannah found herself suddenly less hungry.

Alicia refused Hannah's help in the kitchen, leaving her to keep German company in the living room.

"You're starting a second career, I assume," he said.

"You could tell I'm not fresh from UC Irvine?" Hannah said. "Time for a face-lift, I guess."

"Let me guess. You did something artistic. The way you dress—an actress?"

"I played a few ladies of the evening early in my career. Not my favorite roles," she said.

"So I'm right?"

Hannah laughed. "No. I was a police officer. I worked vice, against my will, but the guys couldn't fit into the skirts. I liked other assignments more."

"You worked homicide?"

"I was thinking about a transfer there. But I decided to get out."

"Too much violence, I would think."

"That's everywhere," she said. "It went deeper than that."

"Dean Weiss and I were talking about pervasive violence at a fund-raiser," German said. "And not two hours later Bradley was dead. Suicide is different, but still, you never know when something like that is going to erupt in your life."

Alicia called them to dinner. She had set the table with her best china, rimmed in gold. A stuffed Cornish game hen sat on each plate. The scent of raisins, cinnamon, and cloves filled the room.

Alicia put her father at the head of the table. She ran her hand lightly across the back of the empty chair at the other end and sat down across from Hannah. Hannah noticed that she only ate when German looked up at her. But she drank almost greedily. And German kept his daughter's glass filled.

He tipped the bottle toward Hannah's goblet when it was still half-full. She put her hand over it.

"Rationing?" he asked, raising his eyebrows.

"Tonight I am," she said. "I have to study later."

Alicia swigged the wine and sighed.

"Bradley studied night and day sometimes," she said. "In first semester, he was so scared of flunking out that he was always at the books. Mostly in the library—he said he couldn't concentrate here. I kept interrupting." Her face flushed and she fumbled with her fork for a minute.

"Alicia," German said. "You loved him. You wanted his attention. There was nothing wrong with that."

"I loved him, and he loved me," she said. "He wouldn't have done this to me. Hannah thinks I'm right."

German raised an eyebrow at Hannah.

"Really," he said.

Hannah said nothing at first. She hadn't meant to say anything to bolster Alicia's position. German still stared at her, waiting for an explanation.

"I told Alicia that Bradley didn't seem depressed—to me," Hannah said.

"And you're, of course, an expert, having been a police officer," German said. He spat out the last two words. Wine sharpened his tongue.

"No, I'm not an expert." What a jerk, Hannah thought. Why is it so important to prove Alicia wrong?

Alicia was staring down at her plate, her cheeks blotched, shoulders hunched, and her lower lip quivering.

They were heading for an argument. Hannah tried to shift the course before it was too late.

"I looked through the papers and notes in the car, Alicia," she said. "They're Bradley's study materials, mostly, some other things I haven't looked at yet. May I take them home with me? I'll return them when I've sorted through everything."

Alicia nodded.

German poured himself more wine.

"Still wrestling with your plagiarism hearing? Alicia could be a witness. You have insight into Bradley's character that Hannah might find helpful, don't you, sweetheart?"

Alicia didn't answer him. She got up and went into the kitchen, returning with three miniature trifles in stemmed dishes. The glass edges rattled against each other, a crystalline jangle set off by her shaking hands.

"I know neither Bradley nor Hannah would cheat," she said. "It's all a mistake."

Hannah glanced at German. He was staring at the custard and poking through it with little jabs of his spoon.

"Perhaps the other student . . . the Mexican guy," Alicia said, searching for the name.

"Ruiz," Hannah said.

"He might have needed Bradley's help. Maybe Bradley just felt sorry for him."

"Please, Alicia," German said. "Bradley giving his paper up

like alms for the needy? Don't be absurd. He didn't give a damn about anyone else."

Now it was Hannah's turn to stare at the dessert. It sounded like Alicia and her father had argued about this before.

"He cared about you, Daddy. He respected you. I know he turned to you for help and you gave it," Alicia said, her voice thin and high as she struggled to control it. "He was grateful, and so am I."

German's face turned white, as though his blood had drained out through the soles of his feet. He slammed the palm of his hand on the table. The plates and cutlery jumped. Hannah's glass swayed and she caught it before it fell.

"I don't want to hear about Bradley's gratitude," he said to her, his voice a growl. "Ever."

Alicia pushed herself away from the table and stumbled up the stairs, sobs spilling behind her. Hannah followed her to the bedroom.

Alicia was nestled in the sheets, her face buried in her hands. Hannah knelt next to her and touched her shoulder tentatively. Alicia reached for Hannah's hand and clutched it.

"I'm so sorry," she stammered. "I had too much wine. And I upset my father. He's not usually like this. It's my fault. He might be right about Bradley, and suicide, you know? He's trying to make things easier for me."

"But he can't talk you into something you don't believe," Hannah whispered. "You need facts. Evidence."

Alicia nodded. "There's not much of that now."

"I know," Hannah said. "But the police will come up with something. Try to get some rest now. We'll let ourselves out."

Alicia nodded and closed her eyes. Hannah sat beside her, and in a few moments she was breathing evenly in sleep.

As Hannah came downstairs German was draining wine from his glass. His face was red and his silver hair seemed to have slumped out of its perfect coif. He looked more than a little drunk as he turned to stare at Hannah. The sight of him infuriated her. What kind of father acted that way toward a child he professed to love?

Her outrage must have shown. German looked away from her and fumbled with the bottle of wine Hannah had brought.

"She'll be all right," he said. "I just can't stand seeing her tear herself up like this, torturing herself with how he died. She's obsessed with it." He hoisted the bottle. "Is this stuff drinkable?"

"How about some coffee instead?" Hannah said.

He shrugged. "Beans are in the fridge. Grinder's behind you."

As the coffee brewed German dropped himself into a kitchen chair. He was falling asleep. Hannah watched his head sink toward his chest, then jerk up as he awoke. She put the cup in front of him and sat down. He seemed less combative now. Maybe she could try to talk to him, for Alicia's sake.

She thought about her own father. At the end of a whiskey-soaked evening—in the days when he still drank—he sometimes slipped into a softer mood, a place where Hannah could talk to him. Sometimes he even remembered what she'd said the next morning. What was there to lose? All German could do was scream and yell. She'd heard that already and it didn't scare her.

"Look, Mr. German. I'm sure you love Alicia, but you're awfully hard on her. You seem more interested in forcing her to accept Bradley's death as a suicide than helping her cope with her loss. She could use your understanding now."

He frowned and stood up, swaying slightly. Hannah tried to steady him, but he batted her hand away.

"Let me tell you something. First, you've got no business lecturing me on how to talk to my own daughter. Second, she's making a martyr out of him and it's crap, and that's the understanding she needs from me. Not a bucket of crocodile tears." He patted his coat pockets and glanced around the kitchen.

"Perhaps it would be better if you stayed here tonight," Hannah said.

German sneered at her. "Oh? And would you like me to close my eyes and touch my nose? Pee in a cup?"

"I don't think Alicia could handle it if you wound up dead on MacArthur Boulevard," Hannah said softly. "That's all I'm thinking about."

German wiped his nose with the back of his hand. Jesus, Hannah thought, he's going to cry. He stumbled into the dining room and Hannah followed him. The keys lay on the coffee table, and he picked them up.

He flapped his hand toward the darkened hall. "There's a guest room down there. I'll take a nap, okay, Ms. Officer?"

"Promise?" Hannah asked.

"For Christ's sake!"

"For Alicia's," Hannah said.

He sighed, dropped the black leather case into her hand, and zigzagged toward the bedroom.

Hannah took the keys upstairs and put them on Alicia's nightstand. The light still was on. It gleamed on Alicia's damp eyelids as they ticked with the motion of dreams. She whimpered once, like an anxious child.

When Hannah got home, she found Bobby Terry sitting at the top of the stairs. The mouth of the biggest man on campus was slathered in mascarpone cheese.

"Tiramisu," he said, wiping his lips. "I learned to make it last weekend. I did bring some for you, but . . ." He shrugged at the empty plate.

"Oh God, Bobby, sorry. I forgot you were coming."

"I thought you'd deserted me," he said. "It's cold out here."

Between his bulk, his aura of curly brown hair, and the fuzzy beard that ringed his face, Hannah had come to think of him as some kind of shy, huge animal. Bigfoot, perhaps. She had a hard time thinking of him as Robert Terry, Jr., Esquire, but then he would start jabbering to her about his latest expedition into some obscure treatise on future interests. He didn't brag, but she thought he probably was sneaking up on Spinetti for the number-one spot in the class. He was, of course, on the review.

"I'm sorry," she said. "I was at Alicia's."

"I didn't know you two were friends," he said. He got to his feet and the boards creaked a little under his weight.

"I went to find the rough drafts for the brief and stayed for the dinner from hell," Hannah said. "She's in shock, and her father treats her like an imbecile. What a jerk."

"I saw him in court once," Bobby said. "He's pretty good. Very smooth. Charming."

"Then he saves it all for the juries," Hannah said. "He was vicious tonight."

As he did every time they studied, Bobby began with a foray to the kitchen. Hannah gathered up the mail that had been dropped through the slot in the door and scanned it. She heard the clatter of plates and cups in the sink.

"I don't understand why you can't just wash these dishes up after you use them," Bobby called over his shoulder. "It takes no time."

"It takes even less time if I leave them around till you do them," Hannah said. "And thanks."

"Didn't Catherine look terrific today?" he said.

Hannah smiled to herself. Bobby loved women. Actually, he loved Woman, and every few months, he found a new creature who perfectly embodied the feminine for him. He favored bright women, but their packaging didn't seem to matter. Since first year, he had worshiped a tiny, chain-smoking librarian, born in Vietnam and graduated from Stanford; a lanky, intimidating Afrocentrist-feminist first-year; and a shy, plump, pale-eyed blonde in admissions.

None of these, as it turned out, had been able to see past Bobby's corpulence to his considerable charm. Women could complain all they wanted about how they hated being judged on their looks, but Hannah thought they judged men just as brutally. Fat guys really had it tough. Still, I'm just as guilty as the rest, she thought. As much as she loved Bobby, she didn't think she could be in love with him.

Bobby seemed emotionally indestructible. His romanticism undimmed by rejection, he loved on, often from afar. The Cyrano of the second-years. Now, for weeks on end, Catherine had been the only woman for him. Bobby always set himself a challenge, but as far as Hannah could tell, Catherine was Mount Everest.

"Catherine always looks the same to me," Hannah said. "A vestal virgin at the temple of law. Does she ever not have a book under her nose? Can she smile? She's going to have to get a charm transplant if . . ."

"If what?" Bobby said.

"I was going to say if she's going to be *Law Review* editor. But now that Bradley's dead, who else?"

"I'd say she's it," Bobby said. "You're hard on her, Hannah. She's no icier than you. She reminds me of you, a little."

"I'm not icy at all," Hannah said, without much annoyance. Usually, a comment like that would have gotten a rise. But she was thinking of something else.

"Really? Then why haven't you had a date in six months?"

"Too busy," Hannah said. "What were you telling me about the early positioning for *Law Review* editor?"

Bobby shook his head and clucked his tongue at her. Since his pass had failed, he'd advanced himself from suitor to romance coach.

"Changing the subject. Still hiding out emotionally, aren't you? When are you going to let someone into your life?"

"I don't have the energy for a relationship right now," Hannah said. "After graduation, I'll see if Agustin is still available. But listen—you told me Bradley was really pissed off about Catherine pushing to be editor?"

"Yeah. He said she'd sewn up a job with the DA's office. Didn't need editor on her résumé. He said he did," Bobby said.

"He did, because why?" Hannah said.

"He said he wanted to prove something to his father-in-law—that he didn't need nepotism to get job offers," Bobby said. "He thought Catherine wanted the job just to tweak him."

"When was the vote going to be?" Hannah said.

"March," Bobby said. "Early bets were on Bradley. More outgoing, more of a motivator. I was lobbying for Catherine, though. Steadier, more reliable."

That was Catherine—cool, steady, levelheaded. But at M'Naghten's, not an hour before Bradley died, she'd seen Catherine about to boil over in a rage. She remembered Catherine jabbing her pen in the margin of the book. Still, the meeting had ended with Catherine smiling. And then she left, just a little before Bradley did.

Bobby was back in the kitchen.

"If Catherine gets the job, I'll never see her," he said as he rustled around in the cupboards. "As it is, she's too busy to talk to me at school. And she's never home on the weekends. I've checked. Called her a dozen times. She never answers."

"Bobby, maybe she doesn't want to talk to you. Maybe you should back off," Hannah said.

He shrugged. "Maybe just a little."

Hannah dumped Bradley's files on her desk, turned on the mica lamp and then the computer. Bradley wrote at a computer, as she did. He might have merged her draft onto a disk—the one from his car, if she was lucky. She slipped it into the drive and punched at the keys; she hoped she was doing something right.

If he was working on stuff for *Law Review*, maybe he'd used Microword. That was the program the staff used and Hannah had it, too. She hit the directory command. Several file names came up. She thought two might be related to school: TORTURE and SERMONS. She called up the first one. Notes from tort class. SERMONS was a sketchy outline from contracts, the class taught by the Parson. Very clever, she thought.

She read over his outlines. How had he managed even to pass those classes with crappy notes like this? They were sloppy, confused, sketchy excerpts from lectures. He had even written a note to himself: *Huh? Get her outline for this.*

Three other files caught Hannah's eye: PAWN. ROOKED. QUEEN. Hannah wouldn't have taken Bradley for a chess player. He seemed more the poker type. ROOKED was short: the address in Palm Springs of someone named Raymond O'Reilly. PAWN was just letters and numbers:

ABA 135000458 OCBA 0678987503

The letters were familiar enough—probably American Bar Association and Orange County Bar Association. But the numbers didn't mean anything. Were they membership numbers? And why keep the stuff in a computer file?

Hannah stored it and retrieved the file called QUEEN.

A convoluted fact pattern, something about a rural murder committed by a trio of addled suspects: one drunk, one blasted on cocaine, one mentally retarded. It was followed by an outlined answer, with points given for each issue spotted. It all had to do with defining criminal conduct. Culpability—*actus reus, mens rea.* This was criminal law, Dove's field. A study outline? No, Hannah thought. She had a dim memory of the fact pattern. Where had she seen it before?

Then she knew: in an examination room, with a blank blue book in front of her. But then, she had only seen the bizarre hypothetical. She had been expected to supply the answers, all on her own.

"Jesus," she said. She pushed her chair back and stared at the screen from the dimness outside the light. She felt the skin on her arms contract, as though someone had rubbed ice over them.

Bobby ambled into the room, gnawing on a water cracker

topped with mashed Roquefort cheese and a twist of black pepper. He looked over her shoulder.

"What's that?"

"It's law-school lite," she said. "Fifty percent less studying."

11

"Hannah?" Bobby, lying on the floor, his shoes off, nudged her thigh with his foot.

Bobby had been dissecting exceptions to the hearsay rule for two hours. Hannah couldn't concentrate on any of it.

"So, could the insurance company use the wife's dying declaration or not?" Bobby said.

Hannah realized it probably was the second time he'd asked the question.

"Sorry. I wasn't listening," she said. "That outline Bradley had. I'm just stunned."

Bobby sighed. "I guess I'm not. He always seemed too perfect to me."

"It would have been nice if you'd shared those suspicions when I started working with him," Hannah said, only half joking.

"Sorry," Bobby said, taken aback. "It was just a feeling, and I racked it up to jealousy. He had everything."

"He had a stolen test," Hannah said.

"Well, that's definitely a bad sign."

"I'm beginning to think there aren't any notes. He didn't have a first draft," Hannah said. She'd printed out the stuff on the disk and she tapped the paper. "I don't think Bradley wrote his half of the brief. The outline makes me very suspicious."

"It's evidence of his proclivities, all right," Bobby said. "If he got hold of that outline and used it, then he probably wouldn't have flinched at ripping off Ruiz's brief. You got stuck with a cheat for a moot-court partner. You should argue that."

Hannah nodded. "If Bradley plagiarized him, why won't Ruiz just tell me how he did it?"

Bobby shrugged. "Blame Evita, his sidekick."

"Cut it out," Hannah said.

"I'm un-PC," he said. "So sue me."

"Stop," Hannah said. "No more litigation."

"It's what we do, Hannah," he said. "We're born disputing, we die demurring."

"Bradley died while he was cheating his way through school," Hannah said. "Suicide, or a fistfight with Ruiz or something happened. I don't think it's a coincidence that he got himself killed while all this was going on."

"What do the cops think happened?"

"I don't know."

"Well, ask them. You've got contacts." He looked at his watch. "It's after one. I'm going home."

Hannah nodded, still distracted. She walked Bobby to the door.

A few leaves skittered across the threshold and she brushed them out with her foot. She watched Bobby lumber across the yard and slam the gate behind him.

At first she didn't see the car. It was parked under the camphor trees. Then the wind blew the branches back, and the streetlight's glow showed a compact car parked the wrong way, in front of the Victorian house next door. She was sure that the car was Fernando Ruiz's Sentra. There was someone behind the wheel.

12

Hannah sat in the darkness, making herself wait fifteen-minute intervals before checking to see if the car was gone. When it still was there at two, she punched in 911 and reported a possible prowler.

But by the time the patrol car pulled up, the Sentra was gone. She knew one of the officers, a widow who was raising two kids. Hannah apologized for the bother. No problem, she said. You can't be too careful.

Hannah saw them out and sat down on the sofa with the cases she had to read for evidence class. He's trying to scare me, she thought. I came to his house, now he's coming to mine. She thought about him taunting her: no threat to Bradley, not now. And he's no threat to me, she thought. She told herself that several times as she studied, jumpy and sleepless, until dawn.

As soon as it was light, she knew, Eddy would be up, slurping coffee and schmoozing with other cops on the Internet. She called him and told him what she wanted to know. He told her to meet him at the Plaza at nine.

Many things in Hannah's life had changed. Her former partner was not one of them. He loped toward her, the pockets of his tan corduroy jacket bulging with God knew what. He sucked black coffee from a foam plastic cup.

He kissed her cheek, collapsed on a bench, and stretched out his feet. Hannah looked at his shoes, loafers in a vile liverish shade.

"Plastic?" she said.

"It's chic now," he said. "Saving our companion animals and all."

"But you do it because you're cheap," Hannah said. "You haven't quit eating meat, have you?" she said.

"Do I look nuts to you?" His fuzzy black mustache twitched like a nervous caterpillar when he talked. His hair was too long, slopping over his collar and falling into his eyes. He smelled like an ashtray.

"So," he said. "Here's the lowdown. It's Ivan Churnin's case, and you owe me because I had to wake him and make up some cockamamie story about why I needed to know."

"Churnin," Hannah said, trying to place him. "Do I know him?"

"No, lucky you. Came to us from LAPD. About forty-two, smart, but pretty fucking cocky. He's clearing cases left and right. Anyway, the suicide theory has dropped to the number-two slot in the hit parade."

"Why?"

"Santa Ana PD arrested a guy Monday. One of the 'urban settlers' your classmates are so touchy about."

This was a sore point between the city and the law school. The homeless drifted into Las Almas when the neighboring city, Santa Ana, expelled them from their shantytown around the county hall of administration. A few had taken to spending the night on the lawn around Rattigan Library. The security guards were forever shooing them off.

But the bulk of the homeless had taken up permanent residence on the outskirts of town, along the banks of a trickle known as Pico Creek. The city's mayor had been elected on her promise to clear them out. The police chief, always on the lookout for a budget-expanding problem to solve, proclaimed the campsite a breeding ground of crime and backed the mayor's pledge with a series of sweeps.

But three determined students at Douglas's community legal clinic had outmaneuvered the city, picking out constitutional flaws in the roundups and a subsequent anticamping ordinance. The students' brief had called the homeless "urban settlers." There was another, less euphonious name for them at city hall.

"What's the deal? I haven't heard anything about an arrest," Hannah said.

"They got him at Mountain Man. He was trying to buy a two-man tent and a sleeping bag he could have used in a Himalayan snowstorm—with Cogburn's American Express gold card. It had been canceled, of course, but the guy was too addled to have thought about that."

"He robbed Bradley?"

Eddy shook his head. "He says not. Says he thinks he found the card in some bushes on the right-of-way, a mile or so from the crash site, Saturday afternoon. The guy's not too coherent. His brain is fried from vodka and speed. But he swears up and down he didn't rob anybody. Churnin thinks he's lying."

"Bradley's wife hasn't said anything to me about it," Hannah said.

"She doesn't know," Eddy said. "Churnin isn't sure what he's got, so he's being low-key about it. But he thinks he can get the guy to cop to the murder, with enough time. Anyway, he had an outstanding warrant for probation violation, so they're holding him at county jail. He's a Pico Creek regular."

"So Churnin has a chance to make some points for himself," Hannah said.

"The mayor and the chief are reported to be very pleased with his work thus far," Eddy said with a sigh. "Churnin is going places."

Hannah didn't say anything. Ambition had been draining out of Eddy even before she left the department. He and Hannah had gone a few rounds before she could convince him she wasn't trying to make him look bad. He just wasn't working hard enough.

His first marriage had foundered on late nights and gonzo-cop life, so he was reforming to win the love of someone called Gudrun, a bookkeeper in the city's finance department. That meant keeping regular hours and, sometimes, pretending the batteries in his beeper had died.

"You could retire, go PI," she said. "Gudrun would like that."

"Naw," Eddy said. "Things are okay as long as I keep my head down." He took a slug of the coffee and belched. "So why do you care about Churnin's case?"

Hannah told him about the plagiarism and Ruiz's threats.

"You think there's a connection between Cogburn getting smashed by the Midnight Special and this term paper of yours?"

Hannah shrugged. "When I say it out loud, it sounds farfetched. I wanted to run it by somebody."

Eddy lit another cigarette. "I wouldn't recommend running it by Churnin. He's hot on his bum theory. He hates distractions."

"What if he's wrong about the bum?"

"That's not possible, to hear him talk," Eddy said. "And he's got a one-track mind. It's a body, Hannah. A body with a record who's sitting in jail without an alibi, and the whole enterprise has the chief and the blessed civic mother beaming down on it. What have you got that will make Churnin harder than that?"

Nothing but my lovely smile, Hannah thought later, after she'd bought Eddy breakfast. If Churnin was any good, he was probably right about the bum. But something nagged at her. Was it all coincidence? The bad brief, the fight in the dean's office, Bradley's death, and Ruiz's weird behavior?

And the kid. Hannah felt sure he'd seen something. Maybe just the accident itself. But she didn't think anyone had talked to the kid.

Forget it, she told herself. It's not your problem. Not your responsibility. The words rang in her ears, echoes of Janie.

At least I'll tell Churnin about the kid, she thought. That's just a potential witness, no threat to his theory. He can't balk at that. And I'll tell him about Ruiz. If he knows there are other possibilities, he'll have to at least ask some questions. By not telling him, the bum might be railroaded—a fine term under the circumstances—for something he didn't do. If Ruiz wanted to sue her ass for telling the cops he'd assaulted Bradley in the dean's office, let him. It was the truth, and that was an absolute defense.

She called the homicide division and got Churnin's voice mail. She left her name, number, and told him she wanted to talk about Cogburn's death. She told Churnin she'd been Eddy's partner. That should count for something, she thought.

She went back to the outline. It had been filed under QUEEN, Bradley's nickname for Dove. Now, suddenly, a memory pinged at the back of her brain. She closed her eyes to bring it into focus.

The memorial grove, late one afternoon in the spring. The air smelled of orange blossoms, rich and so sweet you could almost taste the fruit. Hannah was studying, sort of, by an open window in the Rattigan Library. She looked down and saw them there, under a tree. Bradley was wearing an ivory Stetson hat. He doffed it to hide a folded sheet of paper that Dove handed him. He said something, and Dove laughed. Really laughed, her mouth open and her white teeth gleaming. Then she ran her hand through her cropped hair, languorously, as though she were Rapunzel.

Dove had talked to the class about the pressures of law school. But what kind of pressure was being applied that day, under the trees? Hannah wondered. And what had been the result?

13

From Las Almas, it was a half-hour drive to Silverado Canyon. The road wound past rows of creamy-white houses with red tile roofs that packed the hillsides like legions of match heads. It curved around Irvine Lake, where a few cattle stood drinking, and plunged into the sage hills. Lean, masochistic bicyclists wobbled up one rise and plunged down the next. A hawk floated above them, circled back, tipped its wings, and slid down into a thicket of glossy-green live oaks.

Hannah rolled down the window of the Hyundai and trailed her arm outside for a moment. A hot day for January, and she reveled in it.

She turned off on Silverado Canyon Road. The road narrowed, running between a rocky cliff on the right and a drop into a grassy ravine cut by a stream on the left. She passed the fire station and turned right on Thisa Way, then a left on Thata Way. Professor Dove must love giving directions.

Thata Way abruptly became a gravelly rut, about as wide as the Hyundai, and started to climb. The branches of sycamore trees steepled overhead. Hannah could almost touch the shiny leaves as the shuddering car crept up the sharp incline.

"Come on, Tin Man," she urged.

At the crest of the hill, Hannah saw another wooden sign: HIDEA WAY. She turned left and followed it to the end.

Dove's house was a blue stucco box ringed by red geraniums and white impatiens. Hannah knocked, but there was no answer. She heard a horse whinny and followed a trail that led behind the house.

Dove was in a corral, brushing a roan mare. The horse had a brand in the shape of a heart on her hindquarter. Dove squinted at Hannah, then took off the straw hat she was wearing and wiped the sweat off her face with her forearm. She wore leather gloves, to protect the nails, no doubt.

"Beautiful horse," Hannah said. "At school, I never would have taken you for the western type."

"I like to keep school and home separate." She was tapping the metal-toothed brush against her wrist.

Hannah nodded.

"I'm sorry to intrude on your weekend. I didn't think this was really something we should talk about at school."

"What do we have to talk about?" Dove said.

Hannah pulled the printout from her jacket pocket.

"This came from a computer disk I found in Bradley Cogburn's car."

Dove scanned it, blinked, and started again from the top. She looked back at Hannah and walked to a redwood table in the shade. She peeled off her gloves and read it again.

"It's the exam outline from last year's criminal-law final," Dove said. "You're saying he had this? Then?"

"You said it was the best exam you'd ever seen. I guess it was too good."

Dove shook her head. "This is unbelievable."

Hannah nodded. "How do you think he got it? Could he have taken it from your office?"

"I don't keep exam materials there," she said.

"You keep them here?" Hannah said.

She nodded.

"Maybe he stole it during one of his visits," Hannah said. "When he came out here to go riding."

Dove stared at her, saying nothing for a long time. It worked well for her in class. She would stare until an unprepared student started to babble an answer, any answer. Hannah fought the impulse to fill up the silence.

"I don't think that is any of your business," Dove said finally.

"The honor code says the problem of cheating is everyone's business," Hannah said.

"It's supposed to be handled through the proper channels," Dove said.

"I'm telling a professor that her test security has been compromised. Perhaps that's something she doesn't want to hear."

Dove didn't answer. She turned the paper over in her hands.

She was fifty, maybe older, Hannah thought. It was hard to tell. Her hair was subtly dyed, soft black with a hint of aubergine. But in the sunlight, Hannah could see the web of lines around her eyes. Now, without one of her trademark scarves as camouflage, the skin of Dove's throat was exposed. It sagged slightly, like a piece of fine, crimped silk.

"He came here just once, on a Saturday, during spring break," Dove said. "We rode out into the canyon a bit and he stayed for a drink. On the deck. He never was inside the house." She handed the outline back to Hannah. "And I didn't give it to him."

"He got it from somewhere," Hannah said.

Dove snatched the currycomb and strode back to the corral. She brushed the mare's shoulder with long strokes. The horse shied as she stroked harder, harder.

Hannah folded up the paper and walked back to her car. She was starting the engine when Dove ran up the path and leaned in the window at her.

"You want to know how Bradley got my exam? Think about this," she said, her eyes narrowing. "What would Weiss do to make sure Alexander German's money kept rolling in?"

The Rattigan Library closed at six. As of five-thirty, Hannah had filled a carrel with binders full of endowment updates, alumni newsletters, and American Bar Association accreditation reports. Now she knew how much money Dove had been talking about. In the previous five years, German's firm, German, Friedenthal, and Block, and German himself, had given Douglas more than $100,000. In an alumni newsletter, Hannah read, the firm had pledged a half million for library renovations during the next ten years.

The numbers supported what Dove suggested. Douglas needed German. But German had given money before his daughter's marriage. He was an alumnus and a trustee. Maybe it had nothing to do with Bradley. He didn't seem to like him much. Yet Alicia said he'd helped Bradley. It had made German furious.

She dug a quarter out of her backpack and dialed Alicia's number. She answered on the eighth ring, her voice groggy and raw. When she heard Hannah's voice, the string of apologies began. She was humiliated, she said, she'd had too much to drink. The stress, she thought she could handle it, but she had been wrong.

Not a word about German's behavior. Hannah wondered if she remembered the evening at all. Or had German simply put his own spin on it before he collected his keys and left?

Hannah told her no apologies were needed.

"But you said something last night to your father. About him helping Bradley," Hannah said.

"I did?" Alicia said. The voice was intentionally childish. Her defense mechanism, Hannah thought. It probably worked very well with her father.

"It made him angry. Furious. You remember that part, I'm sure," Hannah said.

"Yes," Alicia muttered.

"How did he help Bradley?"

"I don't know, exactly," Alicia said. "I just heard him and Bradley talking about it."

It had been that Thursday, the night before Bradley died, she said. Bradley came home in a fury, upset about Ruiz's attack and the plagiarism allegation. He said he was going to be a scapegoat, strung up by the "Mexican mob."

"Those words," Alicia said. "He's not a racist, but he was distraught. I've never seen him like that."

He stormed upstairs, asking Alicia to leave him alone for an hour or so. She picked up the phone to call her father when she realized he was already on the line—with Bradley. Before she hung up, she heard her father's voice.

"Daddy said he would take care of it, and Bradley said he'd be 'eternally grateful.' Those words," she said.

"How can you be so sure school was what they were talking about?" Hannah said.

"When Bradley came downstairs, he was much calmer. He hugged me and said everything was going to be fine," she said, her voice strained and finally breaking into a sob. "And I never said anything to him, or my father. Not until last night. I just wanted him to know I knew what he'd done. I shouldn't have ever mentioned it. He compromised himself—for me, and Bradley. But something went wrong. What?" Alicia was sobbing, verging on hysteria, blaming herself for everything, including Bradley's death.

"What if he did kill himself?" she said. "I didn't see anything wrong? My father did. Why didn't I?"

"It's not your fault." Hannah hesitated telling Alicia about the bum's arrest. It would make her feel better, but Hannah wasn't convinced it was what had really happened. Still, she thought, she deserves to know. "Alicia, the police have a suspect in custody."

"Oh my God," Alicia gasped. She sounded more fearful than relieved. "Who?"

"A homeless man, who tried to use Bradley's credit card. It's not a solid case yet, or so I'm told. But Bradley didn't kill himself. I'm almost certain of that."

"I knew it," she said, her sobs subsiding. "I just knew it."

Hannah spent ten more minutes soothing Alicia. She was hanging up when an exasperated librarian appeared at her side, rattling her keys and pointing at the clock. The library had been closed for a half hour.

At home, she found a message from Churnin, the homicide detective. He had a voice as smooth as oil. It coated every word, but Hannah felt the edge beneath it.

Her interest was, of course, appreciated. But it seemed the plagiarism theory, as Eddy described it to him, was tangential at best, given other information gathered in the investigation. Any other leads that were of merit were, naturally, welcome. She could call him anytime.

Faultlessly polite. And unquestionably dismissive. She had been told to go away. She wasn't about to do that. She dialed his number, and this time he answered. In his unctuous voice, he agreed to meet her Sunday morning. Breakfast at eight. At Cluckin', he said. He'd buy.

Cluckin' was, in essence, breakfast with the Dead. The group's CDs played nonstop, an ostinato to the clatter of iron skillets on the grill. The restaurant seats were covered in tie-dye and the menu was adorned with dancing bears and fiddling skeletons. Every omelette was a Grateful Dead song title: "Friend of the Devil" (habañero chiles and cheese), "Ship of Fools" (shrimp and sherry cream sauce), and "Uncle John's Band" (sausage and avocado).

She picked out Churnin easily among the jean-clad crowd. He wore shiny gray polyester pants and a white short-sleeved shirt. He was bald as the eggs behind the counter, and the only person over forty in the place. With his jacket off, Hannah could see the nine-millimeter in a shoulder holster. He was tucking into a "China Doll," a concoction of stir-fried vegetables and egg whites.

Hannah introduced herself and he motioned her to sit down. In her pack, she had a sketch she'd made of the kid and the shard of Perrier-Jouet bottle, still wrapped in her scarf.

"You a Dead fan?" she said.

"A vegetarian," he said. "I like some of their country stuff. But not the long jams that sound like Ravi Shankar in a blender. What are you having?"

Hannah ordered coffee.

"So you think there's some connection to this plagiarism thing, I take it," Churnin said. He was smiling at her, one eyebrow cocked.

"Possibly," she said. She told him about the fight in the dean's office, Ruiz's behavior at M'Naghten's, and the conclusions Ruiz jumped to when she went to talk to him.

"Sounds like you're angling for my job," he said. "Thought you were tired of police work."

Now his coolness made sense. He had done some checking on her.

"I was just trying to get him to talk to me about the brief," Hannah said. "He went ballistic on me."

"You pushed him a little, right?"

"What do you mean?" Hannah said.

"I heard you were like that. Didn't know when to leave it alone. But that was three years ago. Maybe you changed."

She could guess which version of three years ago he'd heard and chosen to believe: Barlow the stress case. Flipped out over a kid. Told everyone else they'd fucked up. Too bad she cracked. Women aren't tough enough for this stuff. You can't let it get to you.

"I don't see what bearing that has on anything," she said.

"You should leave this stuff to the people who can handle it."

"I'm asking you to handle it," Hannah said. "You might be overlooking some things." She reached into her pack for the sketch and the packet of glass.

"You know, I usually don't take too kindly to people telling me how to do my job," he said, spearing a pea pod. "But since you were so good at being a detective, I'll be happy to listen."

He folded his hands and smiled at her. If the table had been narrower, Hannah was sure he would have reached across it and patted her on the head.

Hannah sat back and stared at him. He was determined to discount anything she told him. If she told him about the kid and gave him the shard of glass, God knows what he'd do with them. He could easily bully a kid into an identification. He could smear the bum's fingerprints all over the glass, for all she knew. She left the picture and shard where they were.

"I'm just telling you that there might be more to this than a bum and a credit card," she said. "Bradley had a stolen exam on one of the disks in his car. Why doesn't that interest you? Did you even check it out?"

"Ms. Barlow," he said, "in the best of all possible investigative worlds, I would sit at my desk and ponder all the interesting hypotheticals, from CIA involvement to an invasion by Sasquatch. A stolen exam, for instance, is a problem for your institute of higher learning, not me. I know I've got the guy, and soon enough the DA will file on him."

"Whatever it takes, you'll make the case," Hannah said.

He put the glass down and wiped his thin upper lip. He smiled again.

"No. I've got what it takes to make the case," he said. "Now, why don't you go back to learning how to defend scumballs like our urban settler and let me do my job." He grabbed the check and smiled at her once more.

"My treat," he said.

14

Three hours later Hannah was at Bobby's, hoping the churning rage in her stomach wouldn't ruin her appetite. Once a month, Bobby made Sunday brunch for her, and it always bordered on being a religious experience.

Hannah wasn't a bad cook, only a hasty one. Anything that required more than two ingredients took too much time. She stuck to broiled fish, steamed vegetables, and five-minute rice. An occasional splurge consisted of a steak, or berries puréed and poured on chocolate ice cream for dessert. Since starting school, she had been known to descend to burritos from a drive-through, but only in times of desperation.

Bobby speculated that Hannah's tastes were the remnants of a prior, abstemious life: as a discalced Carmelite in Avila or Zen Buddhist nun in Kyoto.

More than once she had offered to reciprocate for the sumptuous meals. He wouldn't hear of it. After all, he said, he had the recipes, the practice, and the copper saucepans. The most she could hope was that he'd dictate a shopping list and let her buy the raw materials.

Bobby lived in a chipped Spanish duplex on the fringes of a dangerously louche Las Almas neighborhood. Prostitutes decorated the corners on Saturday nights. Drive-bys were commonplace. On any evening, Hannah left well before midnight, the hour at which neighborhood etiquette dictated that domestic shootings could commence.

Hannah smelled smoke and sweet, burning sauce as she

came up the walk. Bobby was in the backyard, tending something in the smoker he'd had shipped from St. Louis. He sent her into the kitchen to slice the French bread.

"I baked it yesterday," he said.

Hannah shook her head. "Bobby, come on. You made it?"

"I had nothing else to do," he said, cradling a duck in two oven mitts. "I was stuck here, studying hearsay. I'd stop every now and then, punch the loaves down, cite an exception—think of an excited utterance, for instance, let the dough rise some more. Punch, recite, bake. No trouble."

He sliced the duck and layered it over a salad of black beans and white corn. He sprinkled the concoction with a dressing.

"Cayenne vinaigrette," he said as she sniffed at it. "Even you could make it."

By the time they'd gotten to the white-chocolate mousse and espresso, she'd told him about the kid, Ruiz's surveillance, Dove's blame shifting on the criminal-law exam, German's largesse to the law school, and Alicia's eavesdropping.

"Have you heard from the cops yet? Told them any of this?"

Hannah was looking jealously at Bobby's half-eaten mousse. He passed it to her without a word.

"The investigator has a one-track mind and a bum in jail. He had Bradley's credit card," she said. "But for some reason, I don't think the bum did it. And I don't think Bradley killed himself."

She half hoped that saying it aloud would dilute her certainty, the way a bad dream faded in the glare of morning. But she felt a chill pass through her body and knew it as real fear, not the frisson of a dark fairy tale.

"You think somebody killed him?" Bobby said. "Not for his credit card?"

She nodded.

"Who would do that?"

"I think Bradley stole Fernando's brief, but he was going to get away with it," she said. "Meanwhile, Fernando was facing expulsion."

"Okay," Bobby said. "He's the one? Tell the cops."

"I don't know that he's the one," Hannah said. "I think Dove was having an affair with Bradley."

Bobby nearly dropped his demitasse. "Dove? You're kidding me. I didn't think she had—"

"Bobby," Hannah said warningly.

"—an ounce of romance in her."

"She might have given him the final," Hannah said.

"Because they were sleeping together? And then she killed him?"

"She might have had good reason. Maybe Weiss's plagiarism investigation turned up the perfect final, too," she said. "Maybe Bradley knew that, and was trying to shift the focus from what he did to what she did for him. That could be the reason he was only going to be suspended, not expelled. He was going to rat her out to save himself."

"Hannah, this is crazy stuff," he said.

She pointed her spoon at him.

"There's another possibility. Maybe Dove didn't give him the test. It could have been Weiss, doing a favor for German's son-in-law, to keep in German's good graces."

Bobby didn't say anything. She realized she was talking fast. She felt excited, alive. She realized she had always liked puzzles, liked testing her theories and working them out. It was one of the things detective work and law had in common.

"And no one found out," she said, spacing the words for emphasis. "So things were fine. But then Bradley plagiarizes and gets caught. German intercedes for him again with Weiss. Weiss is stuck. He has to do some kind of investigation. But his solution is to go easy on Bradley, to keep German's money coming."

"So Weiss killed Bradley?" Bobby said. He was chuckling now. "How? Did he bore him to death?"

"I'm serious, Bobby," she said.

"What other suspects have you got? Isn't the devoted wife usually the killer, in lieu of a butler, I mean? And have you considered my motives?"

Hannah felt an embarrassed flush rising to her face. She put down the dessert.

"I've been thinking about everyone who was wound up with Bradley. Everyone he'd crossed and taunted."

"Who else?" Bobby said.

"How about Catherine?" Hannah said.

Bobby gaped at her. Then his face twisted in disgust.

"Jesus, Hannah," he said. "That's the most ludicrous thing

yet—you think she killed him over who was going to be *Law Review* editor?"

"He had a lot of weird games in motion," she said. "I don't think he realized how close to the edge he was playing. Something caught up with him."

"Hannah, lighten up already." Bobby suddenly looked earnest and worried. "You're obsessing on this. You don't want to have it happen again."

"Have what happen again?"

"You know, like with that little girl. You kind of lost it, you said."

"I didn't lose it." Hannah was sorry she'd ever told him about it. "I cared about what was happening to her. She was being molested and I tried to stop it. I didn't do everything I could, and now she's gone. Dead."

"So you went crazy, blaming yourself. It was out of your hands. So is this," he said, reclaiming the mousse. "You knew Bradley pretty well. You saw him dead, and I'm sure that it was awful. You found out some nasty secrets about him, and suddenly you think you see connections everywhere. But you're too wound up in it to know. Just let the cop sort it out. If he doesn't, you can't blame yourself. Forget about it."

Hannah shoved herself away from the table and plucked her backpack and coat off the sofa. She was on the brink of an anger so explosive she was afraid to speak.

"I tried to tell him," she said. In her ears, her voice was choked, tight. "He's got his bum, his easy answer, so he's not listening. So now I'm supposed to brush my hands and say, 'Oh well, Bradley's gone and, goody, I'm on *Law Review*?' I don't think so. I'll see you in class."

Hannah left the door open behind her. She unlocked the car and sat for a moment behind the wheel before she started the engine. Bobby watched her from the threshold, then stepped inside and shut the door.

Forget about it. She started the engine and pulled out into the street. It's not something you did. It's not your fault.

With her mother, with Janie, she'd tried to coat herself in those phrases, as though they were a balm, something to ease the pain, to banish the bad dreams. It hadn't ever worked, not for long.

She hadn't walked away and let Bradley die. That was the

difference, this time. But if she doubted Churnin's pat story and ignored her doubts? If she had pieces that made a different picture, and despite that, she walked away, she was no less culpable.

Whether he meant to or not, Bradley had pulled her into his death. His secrets had trickled out, stained her. Just the way his life bled out, smearing the stones and steel that night. There was no turning away from that.

Halfway home, she glanced out the passenger window. Here, in the old town, the train tracks paralleled the street. She thought of the boy. He had run away that night, his face cold with fear. He's as stained as I am, she thought. It seemed right to her that she should find him.

She tried to think of what he would be like. He loved trains. That was clear. He dressed like a brakeman, he taped the sound of the brakes and engine. How had that started? Maybe a house near the tracks, clacking rails a lullaby. A shortcut that took him past a crossing every day, and pennies on the rails. Maybe it started with toys. Miniatures. Models.

She stopped for a light. There was a phone booth at the Mobil station on the corner. She pulled over, grabbed the phone book and the notebook from her pack. One hobby store was nearby, a mile or so from the tracks where Bradley died. A second one was closer still, less than a few blocks from the station where she chased the kid that day. Both were open from ten to five on Sundays.

There was a For Lease sign in the window of Train Town, and a clearance sale in progress. A preternaturally clean-cut teenager was chasing a kid away from a display of HO-scale boxcars and lecturing the kid's mother about sticky little fingers. He finished his tirade and shrugged at Hannah's description of the redheaded boy. He didn't remember him. There are bunches of stupid kids in and out of here all day long, he said. I don't look at them any longer than I have to.

Good approach, Hannah thought, no longer wondering why the store was going out of business.

Hobby Junction was next. A bell pinged as Hannah opened the door, and somewhere from the back, she heard a sad, undulating hoot, like a bassoon wailing for its lost mate.

She followed the sound to a man blowing on a fat wooden

whistle, drawing out the hollow tones. In front of him, a model train sped around a landscape built on a table, taking the curves at precarious speed.

The man had hair the color of cinnamon mixed with sugar. He could have been the redheaded boy grown up—and spread out. Two ham-sized rolls of fat spilled from the open sides of his overalls. An engineer's hat sat pushed back on his forehead. His horn-rim glasses were held together with a twist of thin wire.

"Nice sound," Hannah said as he hooted again.

"Yes, it is," he answered. "Carved this one myself. 'Course, the real thing, up close, is pretty near earsplitting."

Hannah told him she was looking for a boy, a train-loving kid who looked like a nearsighted rabbit.

"That would be Teddy," he drawled, with a trace of Oklahoma in his voice. "Sure. They don't make rail fans much like him anymore. Some of the kids won't even admit they like trains. I guess their friends tease 'em. Tell 'em it's a geek thing."

He pointed at the landscaped layout.

"Teddy did some of this—painting the foothills, laying the track," he said. "But he'd really rather be out around the real thing."

"Isn't that dangerous?" Hannah asked him. She thought of the way Teddy dived under the Amtrak train and ran across the rails.

"Sure. You've got to know your way around trains. Teddy does."

"I saw him the other day, with a tape recorder and a microphone," Hannah said.

"Rail fans do that," he said. "Teddy can tell you when an engine was put into service, how old it is, pretty much everything, just by the sound of it. He's stayed up all hours, even got a friend of mine to take him out to the Cajon Pass once, just to catch him some train or other. He's got a heck of a collection by now."

Hannah nodded. "Has he been in here lately?"

"Been a couple weeks," he said, taking out a penknife and shaving the whistle a bit.

"Do you know where Teddy lives?"

He waved the knife. "Nope. Just around here, somewhere. I know he gets here on his bike."

"How about his last name?"

"Never asked. Why you looking for him?"

"I saw him at the station. I thought it was an interesting hobby. My son might like it," she said.

"Model trains are a lot safer," he said.

"He likes being outside," Hannah said.

He shrugged. "Can't tell kids what to like," he said, and busied himself with the whittling.

Hannah wandered the aisles and paused for a moment at a display near the front of the store. There was a rack of cellophane packets, full of trees and bushes. Next to it was a rolled-up poster of distant hills and mountains. Landscape in a bag. Horizon in a tube. How nice to be able to set up your own world.

Right above the ballast in a box, she noticed a sign plastered on the inside of the front window.

The Coast Daylight would be in Las Almas at noon Saturday. The poster called it the most beautiful train in the world, and Hannah could see why. A photograph showed a sleek Art Deco engine pulling cars painted red, orange, and black. The locomotive had an emblem on its side—an orange sun trailing streamlined wings.

"The sun's for California, and the wings stand for speed," said the whittling man, who had walked up behind her. He peeled the poster off the glass and rolled it up for her.

"Your little boy would love this train. It's a gem. Bring him out to see it. Every rail fan from here to San Berdoo will turn out for it Saturday. Teddy's bound to be there."

Hannah took the poster. She felt bad about the make-believe son, particularly since the man seemed to have taken quite a liking to him. She forced a smile.

"He's got soccer practice," she said. "But I'll be there."

15

Bobby tried to catch Hannah's eye in the hall outside Dove's classroom on Monday morning. Hannah ignored him and went inside just as the clock ticked over to ten.

She decided she'd sounded crazy Sunday. And she should admit that to him. But she didn't want to hear his solicitous questions about her mood, her mind. She didn't want her psyche's pulse taken. She knew it was running fast, and Bobby was right to warn her. She was spending too much time theorizing, web spinning, probably over nothing. But she felt she should find the boy, Teddy. No one else knew enough about him to do it. She would talk to him, tell Churnin about him if necessary.

There was one last thing she wanted to do to snuff out her lingering suspicion. She would take the criminal-law exam to Weiss that day, explain how she got it, and press him to open a full investigation into test security. If he agreed, she would forget the notion that he gave the exam to Bradley. Silly idea, really. Weiss toadied to money and power, but he wouldn't stoop to that.

Would he? What if he treated her approach as an opening to make a deal and drop the charges against her. That would mean something else. And she would tell Churnin about that, too.

In the meanwhile, she had real work to do. In the real world, not Bradley's shadow land. She found a chair away from Bobby and sat in the back of the room—the dormitory. Big

Bubba Dave was there, resting his head against the windowsill and snoring.

The door opened again and Catherine Spinetti calmly surveyed the room for a place to sit. Bobby cleared a spot for her and offered the roll sheet as though it was spun from gold. As she leaned down to sign her name she looked at Bobby and tilted her lips into a polite smile. Bobby grinned back. Lord, Hannah thought, if he had a tail, he'd be wagging it.

Hannah flicked through her notes for the day's topic: issues in capital punishment. She'd fretted over Bobby and Teddy and whether to call Churnin again for most of Sunday afternoon, so she had stayed up late to read the essays.

Dove walked in, and the buzz in the room died. She put down her briefcase and scanned the faces of the students. Her eyes met Hannah's for a moment. Hannah tried to read her expression. Impossible. She wore the Queen of the Night's dark cloak again.

"Let's look at this question as Barzun did," Dove began. "There's so much attention put on the sanctity of life that abolitionists ignore the reality of prison. The hours and years of boredom, the cell's claustrophobia, the monotony, and the omnipresent threat of rape and violence and sudden death. The loss of whatever humanity is left. Isn't that cruel and unusual?"

Hannah raised her hand. Dove nodded to her.

"No. It's justice. We're keeping them from killing again," she said.

"Wouldn't we be more certain they'd never kill again if we executed them?" Dove said.

"To execute, society has to be absolutely sure of guilt. We aren't. Not always," Hannah said. "Even some Supreme Court judges have said they can't be sure innocent people haven't been executed."

"With your background, I would think you'd find such a possibility rather remote," Dove said.

Hannah waited for a moment before answering. Was Dove baiting her?

"The police make mistakes. So do juries and judges and appellate courts," she said. "I do think the number of pure saints and angels on death row is pretty small, however."

"They could dance on the head of a pin, no doubt," Dove said.

"That's a credit to our justice system," Hannah said. "But the trend to limit appellate hearings when there's new evidence has to make you think twice. What if the system does err at some point? There's no correction for it. I wouldn't want to be on the court of last appeal and find out later I let an innocent person be executed because he missed some bureaucratic alibi deadline."

"Nevertheless, the odds are in our favor, you say," Dove said. "Some would say there's no perfection in any system. We do our best, and go on carrying out executions, because society demands justice. Is that right?"

Spinetti's hand rose and unfurled.

"What people really want is revenge, not justice," she said. "We simply have to accept that."

"I take it you're opposed to the death penalty," Dove said. "Another surprise, coming as it does from a would-be prosecutor."

Spinetti shrugged.

"I believe guilty people should be executed for capital crimes," she said. "I just think we shouldn't fool ourselves about what execution represents."

"Okay," Dove said. "But this is rather monotonous. Let's say you're opposed to the death penalty. Tell me what's wrong with it."

Spinetti paused for a moment and then nodded.

"It is cruel and unusual. The argument that says it's not ignores science and eyewitness accounts. Twenty minutes gasping away in a cloud of cyanide gas isn't painless. People suffer. They choke and they writhe. That's what a bloodthirsty society wants. And it would really like it if it were on television."

"Lethal injection is available. California will be using it soon," Dove said.

"There will be less suffering, that's true," she said. "But no less waste of life, no less vengeance. Prison is harsh, but lives have been transformed there. You can't say that about execution. It's murder, even when we tell ourselves it's righteous punishment."

Hannah looked up from her notes. Spinetti was staring down at her notebook, her hands folded over each other.

"Fine. Good argument," Dove said. "Hang on to it, Ms.

Spinetti. You can use it with the Ninth Circuit when you get fed up and leave the DA for a lucrative criminal-defense practice."

There was a smattering of applause and Bubba Dave shouted "Brava," much to Hannah's astonishment. Catherine ignored him, still gazing down at her notes. But finally, she fluttered her right hand in a diva's acknowledgment of him. The sunlight glinted on a ring as she waved. Maybe, Hannah thought, Spinetti is human after all.

Hannah left the room before Bobby finished collecting his books. Later, she thought, I'll talk to him later.

Someone tapped her on the shoulder in the hallway. Hannah turned and found herself looking up into Spinetti's face.

Her eyes were brown, almost as dark as the black pupil. Her skin was olive, nearly sallow. Law-school pallor. Hannah knew a few students who foolishly moved from Michigan or Illinois, thinking they'd get a California tan along with the juris doctor degree. As far as she knew, all of them were still bleached white as midwest snow and saw the ocean only on TV weather forecasts.

"Nice job in there," Hannah said. "You turned the argument on a dime."

"Actually, it's part of something I'm working on for the law review," Catherine said. "Dove thought she had me, but she's not the only fast thinker in the room."

Hannah nodded. "I think she knows that."

"Anyway, Harrison wanted me to see if you wanted to do something for the review's capital-punishment issue. Do you have a minute? We could stop by Bork for some breakfast and talk about it."

"Sure," Hannah said.

The student services—lounge, bookstore, and what passed for a cafeteria—were in the basement of Bork Hall, an intentional rebuke to the school's liberal namesake. The trustees didn't give up easily.

Weiss arranged the coup. Two coups, really. By naming the building after Reagan's defeated nominee to the Supreme Court, he thrilled the trustees and managed to woo an endowed chair from a Newport Beach Mercedes dealer. The dealer idolized Bork, copied his beard, and in television ads proclaimed that like his hero, he, too, believed in original intent.

In his interpretation, that meant the Founding Fathers intended everyone in Orange County to have a Mercedes.

The cafeteria was mostly myth. Despite the students' clamor for their right to frozen yogurt and fresh doughnuts, it was only a collection of vending machines. It looked like a prison for wayward junk food, Hannah thought, surveying the stacked cell blocks of Ho Hos, Ding Dongs, Fritos, Cheetos, and Doritos.

Spinetti got a coffee and liberated a pallid apple. She talked about the special issue, and the topics that hadn't been covered yet—lethal injection, access to appellate counsel, costs of incarceration versus those of execution. Hannah realized she couldn't think about plunging into research like that. Not right now. Apparently her distraction showed.

"You don't seem very excited about *Law Review,*" Spinetti said.

Hannah shrugged and stirred the watery coffee. "I feel sort of strange, coming on because someone is dead. It seems so ghoulish."

"You didn't kill him to get his spot on *Law Review*, did you?" Spinetti said.

"No, of course not." Hannah sipped at the coffee to give herself time to think. It was essentially the same accusation she'd made against Catherine. "That would be ludicrous, wouldn't it?"

Catherine nodded. "People get so wound up about stuff like that—law review, moot court, AmJur awards, class ranking. It's not important, in the long run. We only need to graduate, pass the bar and do our work."

"Easy for you to say," Hannah said. "You're going to be the *Law Review* editor."

Catherine smiled. "No, I'm not," she said. "I told Harrison I didn't even want to be nominated."

"Why not? It's yours for the taking," she said. "Now."

"It's too much responsibility. I told him I'd take articles editor, or something else that doesn't require me to baby-sit a bunch of legal prima donnas."

Hannah took another sip of coffee. So if she never intended to be editor, why would she dispatch Bradley?

"It's not because of the gossip," she said. It was as though she read Hannah's mind.

"The gossip that says what?"

"You know," Catherine said. "You implied it, with one word—*now.* But you should know this. People are saying the same thing about you."

"That I killed Bradley because of *Law Review*?" Hannah was dumbfounded at the thought.

"As you say, it's ludicrous. Just juicy speculation to relieve the tedium of school," Catherine said. "Besides, if anybody wants to know where I was that night, all they'd have to do is check at the library. I was logged onto WESTLAW until eleven. They kicked me out."

I will check, Hannah thought. Or at least tell Churnin to do it.

"I didn't mean to throw accusations around," Hannah said. "I know how serious things like that can be."

"You mean the disciplinary hearing," Catherine said. "I heard about it. Do you think Bradley plagiarized his sections?"

"I don't know anymore. I think it's possible. But Bradley said Ruiz was about to flunk out, so copying his work wouldn't make a lot of sense."

Spinetti munched the apple and gazed at a spot somewhere over Hannah's shoulder.

"I think Fernando is an underrated student," Spinetti said at last. "He's not flunking out. He looks rough around the edges, and so people presume he's not bright. But some of the sharpest lawyers don't fit the pinstripe image. Tony Serra, Gerry Spence."

"You think Bradley plagiarized the brief?" Hannah said. "Not the other way around?"

"I don't know," Spinetti said. "Bradley had the opposite problem from Fernando. He seemed too perfect, so people envied him. School seemed effortless for him, so it was natural that people would suspect he cheated, schemed, or manipulated his success. I don't happen to think that's what he was about."

"Now you seem to be saying Fernando did it," Hannah said.

Catherine smiled. "Lawyer mind. I was examining all the arguments. I suppose it's more likely that Fernando did it. I know things didn't come as easily to him. He's making up for some lost years."

"Lost how?" Hannah said.

"He was in a gang. Did you know that?"

"He mentioned it, but only because he seemed to think I already knew."

"I'm surprised you didn't," Catherine said. "We're all grist for the gossip mill—as we've discussed. Bradley was the worst of the rumormongers. He dug and pried until something came loose. So it only seems right that he's the subject of the gossip now."

"Well, we can't be the only suspects," Hannah said.

"We're not. Nor is murder the only explanation," Catherine said. "Suicide still is popular with the psych-major crowd. At least, with the would-be Jungians. They favor the Icarus archetype—brilliant guy flies too high with a flawed psyche and so plummets."

"You hang around with a brainier crowd than I do," Hannah said.

"It's all a cover for morbid fascination—people just enjoy watching the wax melt and hearing the big splash. Still, if he killed himself, he certainly chose a brilliantly metaphorical weapon—mowed down by the engine of law."

"Do you think he killed himself?" Hannah said.

"He'd been distracted for weeks. That wasn't like him. He let his work pile up in *Law Review*. Harrison cut him some slack, but it was reaching the point where someone was going to have to address the issue and figure out what was wrong."

"He didn't talk about it?"

"Not to me," Catherine said. "He didn't like me."

"Why?" Hannah said.

"You know why. He was instinctively competitive. He harried me about who was the better student. Rather, who was ranked higher," she said. "He heard I was number one in the class and he wanted me to confirm it. I don't know where he got that. I told him it was none of his business."

Bobby, Hannah thought. If Catherine finds out, he'll never get anywhere with her.

"But anyway, Bradley assumed it was true. And he assumed I was going for editor of the review. He just assumed that, and to tweak him, I never contradicted him."

"I heard it infuriated him," Hannah said.

Catherine laughed. It was an odd sound, brittle and squeaky, like a gate about to crumble from rust.

"He said I was imperiling his future—that unless he made

editor, he would never be able to prove that he could compete in the job market on his merits, not his connections," she said. "He told me over and over I didn't need to be editor. I told him, just to twist the screws a bit more, that needing it wasn't the point. What if I just wanted the intellectual challenge before I plunge into the pit?"

"Criminal practice."

Catherine nodded. "I love it. But Bradley, damn him, got the highest score in Dove's class. Beat me out of an AmJur award. That irked me."

"I gather he had a gift for criminal law," Hannah said.

"Well, he and I were in a DA's internship last spring, and you wouldn't have known he was good at it. He seemed bored most of the time."

"Really?"

"It annoyed some of the deputy DAs, who expected us to be gung-ho and soak up the law-and-order mentality. You know, hang out with them, go on police ride-alongs, learn to shoot, all that stuff. We all did it, but Bradley rolled his eyes and muttered. Only one thing got him excited."

"What was that?" Hannah said.

"The access he had to criminal records: Department of Corrections reports, probation records, rap sheets, the Cal-ID fingerprint system. All that fascinated him. Volunteered for any task that involved it. He knew all the computer stuff inside out."

Hannah thought about the clippings she'd found. What had he been looking for? Did it have anything to do with Gallagher? She glanced up at Spinetti, who seemed to be reading her mind.

"I don't know what he was doing," she said. She looked at her watch. "I've yammered on without getting to the point. Sorry. Stop by the office, though. I think Harrison has some stuff to show you."

16

"I've boxed up his personal papers and sent them to his wife," Harrison said. "I know it's kind of weird, putting you here. But there was nothing we could do."

Bradley's former desk was in the middle of the *Law Review* office, facing the door. Hannah opened the middle drawer. Empty.

"It's okay," Hannah opened the side drawer. There was a sheaf of paper in the hanging file. Blank typing paper, but behind it, something typed. She pulled it out—Bradley's write-on.

"Here's the stuff he was working on," Harrison said, coming back with a stack of pages. "Later we can talk about the production schedules and your article. Catherine had some ideas, right?"

Hannah nodded. "I'll pick a topic by next week."

"Good. I'll let you get organized here."

Hannah picked up Bradley's article and skimmed its ink-noted pages. It was as irritatingly smooth as she had remembered.

In the light of its perfection, she saw the foundation for her suspicions: envy. She didn't want to accept the fact that she'd been bested by a lazy genius. She was willing to believe that he'd cheated his way through law school and been killed for it. That was better than facing the facts: he could sleepwalk through Douglas and learn more than she ever would, cramming and reading and torturing herself.

When she thought rationally about it, she didn't know with certainty that Bradley had used Dove's criminal-law-exam outline to ace the test. He could have gotten it later. The plagiarism wasn't proven yet, either. And from the minute they were summoned to Weiss's office, it was Ruiz who behaved like the cheat, not Bradley.

He probably never cheated at anything, she thought, Yes, he was brash, competitive, flaunted his intellect, and belittled people like Fernando. But were those motives for murder?

Venturing into the wrong part of town at night in your expensive car—that was a mistake. Looking like a rich, easy target—that's making yourself a victim. And that's how he got himself mowed down by a train. Churnin's right, she thought.

She put the essay back in its folder and resolved to forget it, forget Bradley. Forget everything but school.

She took up the first piece Bradley had been cite-checking: an article about the legality of asset forfeiture. The yellow stick-on notes with his questions stopped after page thirty. Hannah opened the citation handbook and went to work.

Most of the staff lit out after lunch. She stayed, enjoying the quiet. The office's institutional blandness offered nothing to distract her. But after three hours, the edges of the tiny letters in the footnotes looked like they were sprouting fuzzy molds. Hannah blinked and rubbed her eyes.

She took two aspirin from the gallon-sized office bottle. She could easily finish a few more pages at home later. She yelled good-bye to Onizaki, who was cocooned with his computer in the editor's cubbyhole.

Halfway down the stairs, she heard someone calling her name. Lois Popich stood above her, a square of yellow paper clinging to her fingertip.

"I think you dropped this," she said.

Hannah walked back and peeled off the note. She was about to thank Popich when, suddenly, the woman snatched back the paper.

"I did drop this, right?" Hannah said.

"Yes," Lois said, again thrusting the slip into her hand. "Here."

Hannah thanked her and trudged back down the stairs. Her head was pounding. She blinked to make her eyes focus on the note.

It was a phone number. Nothing more. No name. Bradley

must have jotted it down for a reason. The asset-forfeiture article was written by a criminal-defense attorney Hannah didn't know. Maybe it was his home number and Bradley had it because it would be handy if there were questions. Better find out, she thought.

She stopped at a pay phone on Founder's Walk and punched in the digits he'd scribbled. Three rings, and then the click of connection. A few notes of cool tenor sax. Hannah recognized it: Coltrane's "Blue Train."

And then Bradley spoke to her.

She knew it was an answering machine. But the voice shot past reason and hit her at nerve and bone. Her knees went rubbery.

Bradley didn't identify himself. He just gave the number and asked callers to leave him a message.

Hannah hung up, fished out her address book, and looked up the number in Newport Beach for Bradley and Alicia. It wasn't the same as the one she'd just dialed. That number had a 497 prefix. She flipped to the front of the booth's phone book—it was a Laguna Beach exchange. She called information, but the operator said there was no address listed. The number was new—not even a year old.

Hannah looked at the note again. The seven was slashed with a crossbar, European style. It took a moment for the memory to bubble up—something about the footnote she'd seen in the write-on, a last-minute edit. She went back to the office and took out the article again.

She could see how she wouldn't have noticed it that first time, six weeks ago. She didn't know Bradley's handwriting then. But now, after the moot-court brief and going over his *Law Review* work, she did. And the black scribbles on the write-on weren't his. Someone else had edited it for him— even written in a footnote. He'd taken the credit for it, bragging that writing was rewriting. But someone else had revised it. Maybe even written it in the first place? It could have been Dove, she thought, remembering the book she'd read that summer. More and more, she saw Dove in it: the exam, the editing. It would be like her to show her love with an exam and a write-on.

Hannah looked at the phone number again. The innocent explanation was that it was an office he kept. But Alicia never mentioned such a thing. In her gut, Hannah knew that was not where the number would lead. She knew what she should do: give the note to Churnin. But just as certainly, she knew she wasn't going to. Not without seeing what Bradley's other life looked like first. He was a cheat, after all.

In the Rattigan Library reference room, Hannah skimmed the shelves and found the volume she needed. The gray directory cross-indexed every address and phone number in the county. She flipped to the section that listed phone numbers in sequence and started to write down the address across from it. Then she stopped, checked the front of the book. It was more than a year old, so this address probably was stale by now.

But when libraries subscribed for the crisscross service, they usually got updates. Hannah scouted the room for a librarian she knew.

She spotted one she'd seen before: a fortyish woman who had aged so fast since the summer that Hannah wondered what part of her life had collapsed under her. She was stacking books on a cart next to her desk. She shook her head when Hannah asked if she could call for the address.

"We're cutting back. Don't have the money to do general-library services. One call a day, and only for internal library business, that's all we've got this year. Try the Las Almas Public Library, downtown branch."

Hannah mulled this over for a minute as she scanned the librarian's framed pictures. One showed a chubby girl, a boy in a Little League uniform, and the librarian herself. The edge of the picture was jagged, showing the brown cardboard behind it. She'd cut someone out.

"How long have you been divorced?" Hannah said.

The woman blinked at her in surprise.

"About six months," she said.

"Let me ask you something," Hannah said. "What would you think of a man who was married, but who kept another place for himself, without telling his wife."

"I'd say he was screwing around, and that's about par for the course," the librarian said. "Your husband?"

"No. But a friend's, and she won't believe me unless I have some proof. This is the number. I need the address. Please."

The woman looked at Hannah for a long moment, then held out her hand for the number.

"One more favor?" Hannah said.

The librarian nodded. She jotted notes as Hannah talked and then frowned at her.

"That's not information I'm supposed to give out," she said.

"I know," Hannah replied.

"Was this woman, you know, with this guy?"

"That's what I'd like to find out," Hannah said. She was telling the truth, after a fashion.

The librarian nodded. Twenty minutes later she was back with an answer: Catherine Spinetti had indeed been logged onto WESTLAW from nine forty-five until eleven, when the library closed. And the librarian gave Hannah an address—an apartment on Jasmine Drive in Laguna Beach.

Just north of downtown Laguna, the Pacific Coast Highway crested a hill, opening a view of turquoise and malachite sea, a strip of white sand, and two basketball courts filled with lean men, untroubled by paying jobs, playing pickup games in the sun.

Hannah got out of the car and felt the swirl of cold January wind cut the warmth. The sky was washed in pale, pure blue and streaked with clouds.

In summer, Laguna Beach choked on art-fair crowds and reeked of coconut oil and car exhaust. In winter, the city could breathe again. The air smelled of sea salt and west wind. Hannah took a deep breath of it.

Before her sat the apartment house, a case study of sixties charmlessness. Hannah thought it showed a bit of humor, at least, that someone painted the complex in that decade's hideous avocado color scheme. Not just one variety, but two: neon Fuerte, with black-green Haas trim. She went upstairs. Bradley's apartment was on the corner. It looked as though a slice of ocean and sky might be glimpsed from the bedroom.

She knocked, not expecting anyone to answer. A picture of Bradley began to take shape for her as she thought more about Catherine's description of his internship with the district attorney. He was intelligent, no question about that. But law school was not his main occupation. She wasn't sure what purpose school served, but there had to be one. Or more than one. It got him into the DA's office, for example, and gave him access to criminal records the public would never see. Bradley's enterprise, whatever it was, was more important than cite-checking assignments, final exams, and moot-court briefs. Yet he was determined to be thought the best at Douglas. Why?

Alicia said she seldom saw Bradley—that he was at the library almost constantly. Hannah had tried, but she couldn't remember seeing him there, not during all the hours she spent in the stacks. He was here, she thought. What was he doing? She knocked again.

"He's not there," a man's voice piped from below her. "I haven't seen him in three weeks."

Hannah looked down at a short middle-aged guy in a tan Roy Rogers T-shirt and cutoff Levi's. His ears flared from his head like handles on a sugar bowl and his dyed brown mop-top haircut gave him a startling resemblance to Moe Howard. Gardening stained his knees green and he grasped a plug of crabgrass in one hand, like a proud hunter with his prey.

"The rent is way past due," he said. "I was just about to send Bradley a three-day notice. If you're a friend of his, you'd better let him know he's about to find his stuff on the sidewalk."

Think fast, she told herself. He clearly didn't know Bradley was dead. If she told him, questions would arise that she didn't want to answer. The cops would arrive. The apartment would be searched and sealed. For all she knew, he'd left her research and brief drafts inside. At the very least, she was determined to get them out.

"He's so sorry," she said. "He was called out of town. Family illness, and he was so distraught, he just let everything slide. He asked me to come by to pay the rent."

"Oh," he said. "Well. Come on down, sweetie. Let's take care of this."

The manager, who introduced himself as Vernell, led her to his apartment. This turned out to be three rooms of purest cowboy kitsch. Barbed wire framed a picture of the open range. On the back of a leather chair, an embossed horseshoe haloed a sensitive portrait of Trigger. An ottoman, covered in brindled, hairy cowhide, stood on buffed cow hooves and sported a scrawny tail. Hannah sat down on it and got out her checkbook.

"That's eleven hundred and ninety, with the late fee," the manager said.

Hannah smiled to keep her jaw from dropping and scribbled out the amount. She might have to sell the Limbert plant stand sooner than she'd planned.

"I do have a favor to ask," she said as she slid the check to him. "Bradley is going to be in Ohio for another couple weeks, anyway. He wanted me to send him a few things he needs. Do you think you could . . ."

He scrunched his face in agony, as though someone was branding his sofa.

"I can't go in there without the tenant's permission." He brightened at a thought. "I could call him, though."

"He's at the hospital so much," Hannah said. "I hate to bother him. It's, well, it's touch-and-go with his mom."

Vernell tapped on his lip with his finger.

"I *am* paying the rent," Hannah said.

"I couldn't let you go up there by yourself," he said.

"Of course not," Hannah said, trying to look horrified at the very notion.

"Let me get my keys," he said.

The spare Danish furniture, the bare hardwood floors, and the white paper window shades made the apartment seem large, but it set a mood for monks, not lovers. A large faux oak desk filled one corner, its top stacked with binders and neat piles of paper. If her notes were there, it would take a while to find them.

"What is it he needs?" Vernell said.

"I've got a list here," Hannah said. "A shirt he likes. Some stuff for school."

"School? He never told me he was in school. I didn't think you needed a degree to be a tennis pro," he said, narrowing his eyes at her.

"Right," Hannah said. "But I think he was looking for a new career. He had tendonitis, or something."

She couldn't keep this up for long. Bradley told a big pack of lies to the guy, but Hannah was amassing a bundle herself.

"Too bad. It sounded like a great life. He was out in Palm Springs a lot, he told me. Private lessons, right?"

Hannah half nodded. What if this guy was trying to trick her. He opened his mouth for the next query, but from below, they heard a phone trill.

"That's mine," he said. "Could you hurry up?"

"It's going to take me a minute to find this stuff. Go ahead," Hannah said. "I won't be long. It's okay, really."

He padded out and Hannah headed for the desk. There were

piles of surveyor's maps, and binders filled with photocopied cases—every one about a tribe suing or being sued by a state. She recognized the names of three California attorney generals on the lawsuits. All centered on Indian gambling. There was a copy of what looked like a partnership agreement. Signed, but she couldn't make out the names. At the bottom of the stack was an eight-by-ten picture of three men in black tie.

She knew two of them: German and Weiss. The third man must have been Bradley's father. The lines that lent character to Bradley's expression were deep cracks on the older Cogburn's face. The smile that carved them was sharp, rapacious. Hannah shivered at the sight of it and replaced it in the stack of papers.

Bradley had taped a newspaper clipping to the lamp. Tim Gallagher again. This time there was a picture of him. He was being dragged out of a courtroom, finally bound for San Quentin after managing months of delay, according to the cutline. She folded the paper and stuck it in the pocket of her denim jacket. Why the fascination with Gallagher?

She gave the desk one more review, but couldn't find her notes or her half of the brief. She went to the bedroom. The closet was empty. She went through the dresser drawers. Underwear, socks, T-shirts. She saw a knit polo shirt and reached for it. It would cover her lies to Vernell. Her hand touched something silky stuffed behind it.

She drew out a pale pink scarf, a long rectangle of silk with a paisley pattern woven into the fabric. The kind of scarf Dove wore. A hint of perfume wafted to Hannah's nose as she picked it up.

Outside, she heard Vernell's feet on the landing. She jammed the scarf into her backpack and strolled back into the living room, hoping she looked more innocent than she felt.

"Got it," she said, waving the shirt at Vernell, who seemed markedly less friendly than he had been when she gave him the check.

She thanked him all the way down the stairs and even from the window of the car, but he said nothing. If he sensed something was wrong and called the police, she would have a lot of explaining to do.

She looked back. Vernell was on his knees in the middle of the lawn, digging fiercely at the weeds with a screwdriver. He seemed to have forgotten about her already.

17

Hannah thought about the picture of Weiss, German, and Bradley's father. Maybe Weiss wasn't indebted to German for the school's financial support. It could have been a link to Bradley's father. She decided it was an omen that Weiss was involved in this mess.

She decided not to talk to him at school. In his office, with his big desk, pictures of presidents and officious Lois outside the door, he'd be too much the dean and she the supplicant student. She went to his house, that night. At dinnertime.

Weiss lived in Las Almas Heights, where the two-story houses dated from the twenties. Lights glowed in front windows. The sloping lawns glistened with dampness and the tang of hearth fires drifted in the night.

The Weiss home was in the Tudor style. Perfect for a dean, Hannah thought. There was a Cadillac in the driveway and music, a string quartet, came through a half-open lead-glass window. Perfect as a stage set. The trustees probably issued it all to him when he got the job.

The woman who answered the doorbell was tall, square-jawed, dressed neatly in a burgundy corduroy jumper and teal wool sweater. All very Lands' End and timeless good taste. Hannah recognized her from the grip-and-grin pictures in Weiss's office. Maybe a preppy wife was also part of the dean's perk package, she thought.

Something, though, was amiss. The dean's wife's eyes were glassy and ringed with dark circles. She blinked softly as

Hannah introduced herself and explained she needed to talk to Weiss.

"It's important," Hannah said. "I'm sorry for disrupting your evening."

"Nothing here to disrupt," she said. She wobbled as she swung the door wide open. Hannah could look down the long hallway, through an open kitchen door to a table where a water glass sat, filled to the top with a golden liquid. A faint whiff of scotch floated out on Mrs. Weiss's breath.

"The dean," she said, with a false grandeur, "is not at home. Not last night, not tonight. Another school affair. It always is."

Hannah felt a sting of embarrassment. In her drunkenness, Mrs. Weiss seemed more than willing to take Hannah on a guided tour of a troubled marriage.

"I've seen the pictures in his office," Hannah said mildly. "The fund-raising events seem to come with the job." She knew she should leave Mrs. Weiss to dissolve into her scotch. But she didn't. Not just yet, she thought.

"I'm not going anymore," Mrs. Weiss said defiantly, through her clenched jaw. "There's only so much polite chitchat I can tolerate. I nearly died of boredom at the last one. An hour into dinner the dean left me with a table of car dealers."

She glared at Hannah, waiting to have her indignation matched. She wanted to be pushed to higher levels of outrage, Hannah thought. So she would oblige.

"A few minutes with car dealers? How bad could that have been, Mrs. Weiss?"

"Three hours!" she bellowed. "Three. I told him no more, I didn't care how much paperwork he had in his office. If he wanted their money, *he* had to suck up to them."

Hannah felt a chill down her back.

"When was that?"

"Three? No—two weeks ago. A Friday," she said.

"The night Bradley Cogburn died?"

Mrs. Weiss's nodded, a doll's head bobbing on a spring. She'd known Bradley since he was a baby, she said. He was a beautiful young man. Booful, she said. The word melted, like the ice in her drink, into two syllables.

Hannah nodded. Gone for three hours. She looked up and realized Mrs. Weiss was still talking to her.

"You want to see the dean outside school, try around the pier.

Huntington Beach," she said, stepping toward Hannah and stumbling out of one of her oxblood pumps. Hannah broke her fall.

"Sorry," Mrs. Weiss said. "The pier, any Sunday morning. That's something he still takes seriously."

Mrs. Weiss shut the door. Suddenly the string quartet was playing at full volume, the windows rattling with every pizzicato.

18

Hannah went to two classes Tuesday and then retreated to the *Law Review* office. Onizaki had decided he couldn't abide Bork coffee, so he brought his own machine. For a quarter, which Harrison donated to the campus chapter of Amnesty International, he was willing to share.

She dumped two packets of sugar in the coffee and sipped it, staring out at the empty hallway through the glass panel in the office door.

Then the clock jumped to three, and the passage was jammed. She realized how small a community Douglas really was. She could sit in one place, and eventually, everyone who had some connection with Bradley would appear.

Dove strode by, flicking a jade-green scarf over her shoulder. Hannah wondered if she had discovered yet that a piece of her neckwear collection was missing. Perhaps she wasn't worried that sooner or later someone would find out about Bradley's apartment. Or maybe she would drop by, to tell Vernell a lie or two and get her belongings back. Hannah wondered where Dove had been that Friday night.

Fernando Ruiz was across the hall, talking to Agustin, the professor Hannah liked so much that she felt compelled to avoid him. Ruiz was catching up on the classes he missed, Hannah thought. He was rubbing his mouth in tense, repetitious circles.

Weiss passed him, his hands deep in the pockets of his suit pants. Ruiz glanced away from the dean, only to find himself staring at Lois Popich. She was trailing her boss by a half step, making notes as he talked to her over his shoulder.

The whole crew, Hannah thought. Which of them knows what really happened to Bradley that night?

The door opened, and Catherine leaned in. She nodded a hello to Hannah and pulled papers out of her box. Bobby, Hannah realized, was hovering behind her. Maybe he's making some progress with her at last, Hannah thought. That was good. She'd talk to him later, apologize, and explain that she was going to hand over all the possibilities to Churnin. They were indeed not her responsibility.

The possibilities were growing. There was the brief, the stolen exam, and the boy, who'd seen something. And now there was Weiss's disappearance just before Bradley died.

Mrs. Weiss had been incredibly drunk, but her memory about that evening was faultless, Hannah found after some checking around. The fund-raiser had begun at seven. The Bork-loving Mercedes dealer had indeed been the guest of honor. He and two sales managers sat with the Weisses. Dinner began at seven-thirty. Mrs. Weiss said the dean left at eight-thirty and came back at eleven-thirty.

Bradley died around ten. If Weiss hadn't gone to his office—if he had gone somewhere else—no one would have known. No one was around school on a Friday night. Except, she thought, the security patrol. Whoever worked that night would know if Weiss had been on campus.

Hannah had a nodding relationship with some of the guards. Their primary job was keeping students out of the faculty parking lot and escorting the more drunken of the urban settlers off the Rattigan Library lawn.

She found one of the guards in the security office at the campus gate. He was a balding crossword-puzzle addict. Bitten, his last name, was embroidered on his uniform pocket. The president of Women in Law complained about him after he pointed to this emblem and told her leeringly, "Once Bitten, twice shy." Bitten apologized, but turned sullen after that, muttering about how some women just couldn't take a joke.

Bitten nibbled on a cuticle while he thought about Hannah's question.

"Friday. Friday two weeks ago. I think I was working that night. Think I saw him. But the dean's here a lot at night, late."

"There's a logbook, right?" Hannah said.

Bitten nodded. "A meticulous recording of after-hours visitors. The dean demanded it after a VCR was stolen from the faculty lounge." He licked his finger and turned back the pages of a black ledger. "What time?"

"Eight-thirty. Thereabouts," Hannah said.

He ran his finger along a column. It left a damp, smeary trail. Hannah could see why he gave women the creeps.

"Why'd you say you want to know?" he said archly.

"I didn't say," Hannah replied. He was disgusting. She didn't want to owe him any favors. Maybe she'd try another of the guards, later. "It's not a big deal," she said casually. "Never mind."

"Wait a minute, wait a minute." He reached for her hand. Hannah slid it just out of reach. Bitten smiled. He loved a challenge, Hannah thought.

"Don't go getting all huffy," he said. "I'm just curious, you know? Curious, and detail-oriented. It's what makes me good at my job."

Right, Hannah thought. She'd sneaked the Hyundai past him into the faculty lot at least three times. With his nose buried in the *New York Times* crossword puzzle, he wouldn't have noticed if a tank convoy rumbled by.

"Here you go," he said. He slid the book around so Hannah could read it. Weiss had printed his name and the time: eight forty-five. She looked at the time-out column. It was blank. He could have stayed five minutes, or three hours.

Bitten still was nibbling, seemingly devouring his finger a millimeter at a time. He didn't realize the meticulous recording of campus access had been violated by the dean himself.

"Thanks, Bitten," she said. "You're doing a hell of a job."

He grinned and threw her a smart salute.

There was a message waiting for her Wednesday at the *Law Review* office. It didn't make sense at first. She didn't know anyone named Susan. The phone number was in Newport Beach.

"What's this about?" Hannah held up the slip to Harrison, who was counting the day's coffee receipts.

"Ten bucks. Now I know why everyone is so jittery," he said to her. "Oh. That. She said Alicia Cogburn gave her your number. She wants you to call her."

*   *   *

As she drove across the coastal hills Hannah faced up to her prejudice. She disliked Orange County's upper crust, even with minimal exposure to it. As a cop, she'd met the wealthy at the times they least wanted to be seen: domestic-violence calls in Las Almas's nicest neighborhoods. Busting a guy in a Rolls-Royce as he cruised the hooker corner west of downtown. And that was just the rich of Las Almas. They were paupers, pikers, compared with the breed's Newport Beach variety.

She imagined that Bradley's stepmother lived in one of the cold, cavernous, and tastelessly nouveau riche mansions that had sprung up along the Emerald Coast, just south of Newport.

Some of the most ostentatious new houses hadn't survived the fires that swept down the canyon the previous fall. A clan of radical environmentalists who lived in the canyons and put out a photocopied newsletter each month had praised the fires as nature's retribution against the rich who relentlessly despoiled the coastal hills. Hannah thought the theory was anthropomorphic eco-manure and it conveniently overlooked the role of the arsonist who'd started the fires in the first place. She doubted if he'd acted out of environmental rage. Arsonists' motives were usually more primal than that.

The fire hadn't worked its way down to Susan Cogburn's house. It was one of the homes that predated the conspicuous consumption of the eighties. The thick plaits of ivy that wove through the fence and around the front door were at least twenty years old. A For Sale sign stuck out of the grass on the front lawn.

Susan Cogburn led her into the living room. The carpet was strewn with Geoffrey's toys and a huge kilim-covered sofa sat in front of the fireplace. On the hearth lay a slobbering, tubby golden retriever, introduced as Duke. A honeyed scent drifted into the room from a bouquet of gold, lavender, and russet roses on a sideboard. Hannah had never seen such colors in roses before.

Susan Cogburn, in a cashmere sweater and jeans, was buttoning her son's jacket. Geoffrey stood close to her, watching Hannah. The Cogburn eyes were his—violet blue and seemingly guileless. Susan kissed the boy on the head and sent him to play outside. Hannah watched through a window as he wriggled up a rope ladder that hung from a wooden fort about the size of Hannah's apartment.

Susan pulled her bare feet onto the sofa and seemed in no hurry to tell Hannah why she had wanted her to visit. She pointed out a lithograph, an ocean scene she'd bought in Laguna. She loved it there, she said.

They talked about Laguna, and how the city had changed. The rise in T-shirt shops and the decline in galleries. The protests over plans for a tollway that would mar the canyon and disgorge even more people into the city every day. How AIDS hovered over the city like a dark whirlwind, plucking man after man out of bright life. They each knew at least one victim. The talk stopped for a moment. Hannah didn't mention Bradley's apartment in the town.

"I wanted to see you again, and thank you for being so good for Alicia," Susan said.

Hannah shook her head.

"I don't know that I've done very much."

"You took her side against her father. No one ever does that," Susan said.

"He's adamant about the fact that Bradley killed himself," Hannah said. "He was bludgeoning her with it over dinner. Not a pretty sight."

"Alexander can be that way. He thinks he can bully people into sharing his opinions. But I don't believe Bradley would have killed himself."

"Why not?" Hannah said.

"He was the only thing he loved in this world. The only person he wouldn't hurt."

"It sounds like you didn't care much for him," Hannah said.

"I tried to build bridges to him. But it's hard for a second wife," Susan Cogburn said. "Particularly when she's marrying a rich man with an only child. Bradley was very attached to his father. Bradley wanted to be his father."

Hannah thought of how much Bradley resembled him.

"What did that entail?" she asked.

"Being smart, charming, one step ahead of the other guy," Susan said. "Henry could sweet-talk money out of a bank. Actually did it, once or twice. And he could make you think you knew him when you didn't."

He'd come down to Orange County, still powdered with the

dust of his mother's failed farm near Bakersfield, she said. It had fallen to drought, just as his grandfather's farm in Oklahoma had done in the Depression. So Henry Cogburn had learned never to trust his fortunes to what grew in the earth. He just bought and sold the land itself.

His real-estate business flourished, first in Orange County and then in the desert around Palm Springs. He wanted a family, but his wife miscarried with frightening consistency until Bradley took hold inside of her and hung on through the ninth month. They decided he was a miracle child who would want for nothing. She died when Bradley was in high school.

"They spoiled Bradley," Susan Cogburn said. "He might have grown up to be a nice man. But they let him have whatever he wanted, do whatever he wanted to do. Henry disciplined him occasionally, usually too much and too late."

Susan Cogburn said that she had been working at a Palm Springs bank when she met Henry Cogburn, who came down to the desert for business and shuttled back to Orange County on weekends to be with his dying wife. Susan was twenty then, and Henry was fifty-five. They had something in common: she had been born in West Virginia and her family had known the hardscrabble life, too.

After Henry Cogburn's wife died, he took Susan out to dinner at Le Vallauris. The romance moved fast, and Bradley hadn't liked the outcome.

"Isn't that what you'd expect?" Hannah said. "You were just a few years older than Bradley."

"Six years. He was such a shit about it, though," Susan Cogburn said. "He made me miserable every chance he had. He accused me of screwing his father while his mother was dying in the hospital. It wasn't at all like that."

She picked a few browning leaves out of a pothos in a copper pot on the hearth and put a log on the fire. Hannah noticed that her fingernails were short and unpolished. Her hands were cross-hatched with tiny scratches. She saw Hannah looking at them.

"Roses. You've got to cut them back this time of year, but they do resent it," she said.

"You don't have a gardener?" Hannah said, looking out at the acreage behind the house. She saw row after row of rose stubble. Hundreds of bushes had been pruned.

"The gardener does the lawn. When Geoffrey is old enough

to push the mower around, he'll do it," she said. "Even if you get to be rich, you should work. Otherwise, you get out of practice and that's dangerous. You never know when you're going to be poor again. I tried to teach Bradley that."

She sat down again and patted the sofa for Duke to join her. The dog heaved himself onto the cushion with a grunt.

"A little late, wasn't it?" Hannah said.

"It sure was. Particularly since Henry was giving him other life lessons."

"Like what?"

"That he was too bright to bother with some petty things. It was easier to get someone else to do your work for you," she said. "Henry wanted his son to have the prestige of a college degree. But he didn't see the point in some of the requirements."

"So that's where Bradley learned shortcuts," Hannah said. She told Susan about the plagiarism charge and the stolen exam.

"I can't say I'm surprised," Susan said. "When Bradley was a sophomore in college, Henry paid one of his employees, a broker with an English degree, to write a paper for him. Then he had the gall to complain to the department head when it only got a C-plus."

"At least he didn't fire the broker," Hannah said.

"But he did," Susan said. "I was furious with Henry. I saw things differently after that. If he'd lived, I would have divorced him."

"He killed himself," Hannah said. "Why?"

"There's a saga here. Do you want to hear it?"

Hannah said she did.

East of Palm Springs, an Indian tribe lived on a reservation of sand that bore nothing but creosote bushes and a handful of fringe-toed lizards. But like the Morongo and Agua Caliente Indians, the Agua Dulce band had a hidden resource. Hannah already knew what it was.

"Gambling," Hannah said.

"The federal government had long ago said that Indian tribes were sovereign nations," Susan said. "The tribes argued that states' laws against gambling didn't apply to them."

Cases went to court a dozen times or more as the states tried to bar reservation gambling. But since the passage of the Indian Gaming Regulatory Act in 1988, federal law seemed to be on the tribes' side.

It was a green light, of sorts. But Henry Cogburn envisioned more than boring bingo games or even a Quonset-hut poker palace on the sands of the lower Colorado Desert. He wanted to bring a Las Vegas casino with roulette, blackjack, and baccarat to the Agua Dulce reservation.

"What the Indians in Palm Springs have planned to do," Hannah said.

Susan nodded. "Right. But this was years ago, remember. Henry was a visionary."

Hotels to feed the casinos could be built on leased tribal land, or developers could buy property bordering the reservation for their projects. This was land that Henry Cogburn happened to own.

Only one snag arose: the tribe wasn't sure it wanted gambling on its land. Some members did—they would get rich. Others, more altruistic, thought of the prosperity it would bring the tribe, which wasn't lucky enough to have a hot springs under their sand, like the Agua Caliente Indians in Palm Springs did.

Some saw the casinos as a darker river flowing into their world. They'd heard stories of the unusual money-management practices of some white executives who ran other tribes' ventures. As in many cash businesses, some dollars apparently did not make it from the gaming tables onto the books. Others opposed it because they thought tribal beliefs and traditions could never withstand the shift to a Vegas culture. A few believed gambling was just plain sinful.

The Agua Dulce tribal council voted four to three in favor of the project. Developers lined up to bid for the right to build the casino. Men with briefcases and bankrolls arrived to look at Henry Cogburn's sandy real estate.

Then it all fell apart. The state filed suit to block the venture. But Alexander German, Henry Cogburn's good friend and legal adviser, had warned him that this would happen. They were prepared to tough it out in court.

What no one expected was the suicide of Luz Gomez, the tribal councilwoman who had cast the pivotal vote.

Police found a note next to the vodka bottle and the vial that had held the Valium. She had taken money, a bribe to vote for the project, for the welfare of her grandchildren, not herself, she wrote. But she decided that what she had done was wrong.

She could not face the ugliness she already saw arising among her people. So she had chosen to confess, and die rather than face the shame.

With a new councilman and a second vote, the casino was dead, too. The tribe asked the state attorney general to investigate Gomez's allegations, but no bribery charges were ever filed.

"Who paid her off?" Hannah said.

Susan Cogburn shrugged. "Henry said he didn't know anything about a bribe. He said she was a cantankerous old drunk who was dying of liver cancer and decided to screw over her family by sinking the entire project. He said she'd found out the kids were going to tear down her house and lease the land to a hotel developer."

"Did bribe money ever surface?" Hannah said.

"No," she said.

Hannah said nothing for a moment. The desert. Indian tribes. Deals gone bad, and cheating. Rooked, she thought. That's what Bradley called one of his files.

"Did Henry ever know someone named Raymond O'Reilly?" Hannah said. "He lives in Palm Springs. Maybe he was involved in this deal."

Susan closed her eyes in thought for a moment.

"I don't think so," she said finally. "But this was four years ago, and Henry didn't tell me everything. After he fired Alexander, he stopped talking to everyone except Bradley."

Henry Cogburn had used every dollar he had or could borrow to buy land adjoining the Agua Dulce reservation. The acreage was cheap, and he bought a lot of it. But without a casino, it was worthless.

"He could have climbed back, I think," Susan said. "But he didn't think so."

Bradley was the one who found him on the floor of his study with the nine-millimeter pistol in his hand and the top of his head blown off.

"Bradley would never call it suicide, though," Susan said.

"Did he think it was an accident?"

"No. He said it was murder," she said. "And Alexander German might as well have pulled the trigger."

19

Before he died, Henry Cogburn convinced Bradley that German was responsible for ruining the deal. He'd even hinted that maybe Luz Gomez didn't kill herself. That maybe German was in cahoots with his competitors to ruin him.

"It was pretty crazy talk," Susan said. "Henry was drinking a lot. But he convinced Bradley that it was all German's fault."

And when he put a pistol in his mouth and pulled the trigger, Bradley blamed German for that, too, she said.

"Once, he'd loved German, because his father did. And when his father told him to, he loathed him, just as easily. Poor Alicia."

"They were already married?" Hannah said.

"Just a year. This just about tore them apart. From the day his father died, Bradley only wanted two things. First, to destroy Alexander. Alicia was heartsick. I don't know how she stayed in the marriage. Bradley was obsessed with revenge and didn't make any secret of it."

"What was the other thing?"

"He wanted to revive his father's business."

"But he went to law school instead? I don't understand," Hannah said.

"A long time ago Henry decided Bradley should be a lawyer, to help him run the business," Susan said. "He wanted Bradley to model himself on Alexander. Bradley wasn't sure law school was necessary. He just liked to make deals. That was his strong suit. They went round and round about it. When Agua Dulce blew up, he was determined that Bradley be a lawyer—and use everything he learned against German. Henry was out of his mind at the end, I think, but he knew the only way to get Bradley to put up with three more years of school was to give him a carrot. He made him a deal in his will."

"The business was Bradley's once he got a law degree," Hannah said.

"That's right," she said. "I was surprised when Bradley didn't try to fight it. But he didn't seem to mind, except for the time it would take. Bradley's impatient, like his father. Of course, after the Agua Dulce debacle, there wasn't much left of the business. But Bradley was sure he could build it up again."

Now Hannah understood why Bradley had been at Douglas. It was a means to a particular end. He didn't care about the law, outside of what he needed to ruin his father-in-law. Douglas was just another requirement, like his college English class. He was bright enough to work, when he wanted to, and unprincipled enough to cheat when he had the chance. Just like his father.

"But if he just needed to graduate, why was he so competitive?" Hannah said. "Why was it necessary to make law review, angle for editor, act so superior?"

"Well, I told you," Susan said. "He was just like his father."

Hannah gestured to the sign on the lawn as she was leaving.

"I'm going to find a place in Laguna," Susan said. "Real estate's depressed these days, but Henry bought this house a long time ago, so I might make a little money. I'm going back to work in any event, as soon as Geoffrey's in kindergarten."

"Back to banking?" Hannah said.

She nodded. "It's been a while, and the business has changed. But I had a knack for it. Served on a couple ABA committees, even."

American Banking Association, Hannah thought. The file on Bradley's disk, with those letters and a number. She had assumed it meant American Bar Association. But what if it didn't?

"Can I show you something?" Hannah said, reaching into her backpack for the printout of the file Bradley had called PAWN.

20

The moon hung from a length of gold cord that had been tied to one of the wooden ceiling beams. Made from papier-mâché and about the size of a beach ball, the satellite was coated in silver leaf. It glimmered as tiny white Christmas lights, posing as stars, blinked around it. The moon, at least here in La Luna, was a sad woman. Her mouth crumpled in anguish. Tears slid over her plump cheeks.

Hannah watched it turning in the center of the coffeehouse while she waited for Alicia. Sometimes it seemed to her that the moon had merged with a local legend: La Llorona, the weeping ghost of a woman who haunted the riverbeds around San Juan Capistrano, trying to recover the bodies of her children, whom she had drowned. The moon-woman radiated that kind of tragedy.

Alicia drifted in about ten minutes late. Hannah called to her, but she didn't seem to hear. The crush of people around the cash register—yelling orders, sprinkling cinnamon over cups, paying bills—enveloped Alicia for a moment. Hannah saw her face. Tentative, strained, and overwhelmed, it disappeared and then emerged as the press of the crowd popped her out. She stood swaying for a minute beneath the overhanging moon.

The scene gave Hannah a glimpse of how closed Alicia's world had been. It held her father. No one talked about the mother; Hannah assumed she was dead. There had been Bradley, and the icehouse in Newport, mostly paid for by German, Hannah guessed. Alicia didn't work, Bradley had told

Hannah that. She shopped. She worked for one of the genteel charities. There would have been a baby, sometime after graduation and Bradley's successful passing of the bar. Everything had been in place, kept there by the Cogburn-German alliance, a tissue of lies and illusions. Now it was all blown apart.

Hannah stood up, called to her again, and this time Alicia heard. She waved and worked her way to Hannah's table.

"It's so loud and crazy here," she said, her voice breathless. "I didn't think I was going to be able to find you."

Hannah ordered coffee and waited while Alicia peeled off her coat.

"I used to go to a place like this with Bradley, when we were in school," she said. "Laguna had coffeehouses, even when they weren't popular anyplace else in Orange County."

"Laguna is the wild hippie child of the nation's most conservative county," Hannah said. "It will never be like its parents, and its influence is spreading."

"Thank God," Alicia said.

The coffees came. Alicia was still staring around La Luna in a reverie. Hannah hated to break it. She seemed so happy.

"There's something I'd like to talk to you about," Hannah said. "It's not really any of my business, so you can tell me to go to hell if you want to."

"I don't think I'd do that," Alicia said.

"I've found out some things that are—disturbing. I wanted to talk to you about them before I talk to the police. I don't want to misunderstand anything."

Alicia said nothing. She was looking over Hannah's shoulder at the moon-woman. Hannah continued.

"I think Bradley did plagiarize the moot-court brief," Hannah said. "I think you have the proof of it. Did you bring the statements?"

Alicia nodded. She pulled three envelopes out of her purse and handed them to Hannah.

Hannah opened the bank statements and ran her finger down the list of electronic transactions. There it was, in December: $1,500 sent in a wire transfer to the account number she found in Bradley's PAWN file. She had made the wrong assumptions about what the letters and numbers meant. Susan told her that in this case, ABA was American Banking Association. The nine digits were a routing number for Orange County Bank-America—that was what OCBA stood for, not Orange County Bar Association.

Susan Cogburn had quietly prevailed on a friend to violate bank regulations and identify the second number. It was Fernando Ruiz's checking account.

"I think this is evidence that Bradley paid Fernando for the brief," Hannah said. "It wasn't the first time Bradley cheated. He got a criminal-law-exam outline and produced a perfect final last semester, too. He was used to cheating, wasn't he?"

Alicia nodded. Her eyes, once swollen from crying, now looked deflated and saggy. She sank back in her chair.

"I should have told you. You deserved to know, for your own defense in the plagiarism case," she said. "I hoped he had changed."

"I'm afraid he hadn't," Hannah said. "He hadn't changed when it came to his feelings about your father, either."

"What are you talking about?" Alicia said in a numbed voice.

"I've talked to Susan," Hannah said.

Alicia was fighting to hold back the tears.

"But she doesn't know everything," she said. "We had our difficulties, and they stemmed from our fathers' problems, but we were working things out. If you love enough, you can overcome anything."

It takes two people loving enough, Hannah thought. She looked at Alicia and wondered if she should tell her about the apartment.

Alicia was staring down at her wedding band, turning it around and around. The ring, dusted with a cluster of tiny diamonds, was loose on her finger. A few more pounds lost to grief and it could slip off, unnoticed. Maybe that wouldn't be a bad thing, Hannah thought, losing a symbol of a man who didn't love her enough to tell her the truth. About anything.

Hannah decided the apartment could wait.

"I know that Bradley would never have pleaded with your father for help with his problems at school," she said. "All Bradley wanted was to ruin him. That was still the case, wasn't it?"

"No. Well, I don't know," Alicia said. "Bradley's father convinced him of some crazy things. But we were working on that, on how he could honor his father's memory without hating my father. And I heard them talking. I told you."

"You heard part of a conversation and created a context for it," Hannah said. "I can understand that. You wanted to think that Bradley and your father had reconciled. But I think there might be another explanation."

Alicia picked up the coffee mug with both hands.

"Go on," she said.

"Bradley was turning up any information he could about the Agua Dulce land venture. He was building a case against your father," Hannah said. "He might have agreed to help Bradley, but it wasn't out of love for him. It was out of fear."

Alicia's coffee mug clattered to the table. She stood up and swept the envelopes into her purse. She was shaking with anger, her green eyes bright and fierce.

"There was nothing to use against my father," she said. "He didn't do anything wrong. It's not his fault, not about the deal, or the suicide or anything. Bradley's father was the crook, and Bradley just couldn't accept that. I don't know what lies Susan told you about my father, but he didn't do anything. Nothing."

"Where was your father the night Bradley died?" Hannah said quietly.

The sound in Alicia's throat grew from a growl to a shriek. She picked up a mug and flung it across the room. It clipped the hanging moon and set it spinning. The mug crashed against the far wall and the coffeehouse din froze into silence. Alicia screamed into it.

"You're crazy! And I'll tell the detective that!" she shouted. Before Hannah could reply, she shoved her way through the crowd around the table and through the double doors into the night.

21

Hannah got to campus early on Thursday and headed to Bork for a cup of yogurt. The scene with Alicia had unnerved her. She replayed it over and over during the night. She hadn't seen the fury about to boil over. After watching Alicia wordlessly accept lashings of humiliation from her father the night after Bradley's funeral, Hannah thought that nothing could enrage her. Nothing, apparently, except insinuations about her father. It struck her as the kind of furious protest you mount to convince yourself of something you know is false.

But if Alicia called Churnin, it would undercut anything Hannah brought to him. He didn't need much encouragement, as it was. Maybe Bobby was right, Hannah thought. I should leave this alone. Uncovering Bradley's secrets was doing her no good.

But it's not about me, she thought. There was a kid, Teddy, afraid of something he'd seen or heard. No one was looking out for him. And there was the bum, whom Churnin was determined to charge. He might be an ex-con with a brain as porous as a butterfly net, but that didn't make him Bradley's murderer.

It was just after eight, and the lunchroom was nearly empty. Except, amazingly, for Bobby. He had said more than once that he would rather starve than eat out of a Borkian vending machine. He had pronounced its coffee to be vile, undrinkable sludge.

He turned and spotted her. Unsmiling, he waved her over.

"Where have you been?" he said. "I looked all over for you yesterday afternoon."

"I took off early," Hannah said. "I had some business to take care of." She had hoped for time to work up a more graceful apology. But there was no way now. "Look, Bobby, about Sunday . . ."

He waved his hand.

"I know. I was wrong. I'm sorry."

"You were wrong?" Hannah said.

"Yes. Francisco, at least, is up to something. Look."

He shook open a copy of the school paper, the *Appeal*. A story on the editorial page was headlined BLAMING THE VICTIM. Fernando Ruiz wrote it.

Hannah skimmed the first paragraphs. It was addressed to her.

Her name was never mentioned. Nor was Bradley's. There were allusions to the railroading of the Sleepy Lagoon defendants, Ruben Salazar's death from a high-velocity police teargas shell, and the brutal end to the Las Almas pickers' strike of 1921. Those served to disguise the actual meaning of the piece, but Hannah knew a personal threat when she saw one.

Once again, Ruiz wrote, the wronged becomes the wrongdoer, simply because he is brown-skinned and speaks Spanish. The fears and prejudice of the Anglo make a perpetrator out of a victim. But the victims are not powerless, and the victims are not alone. *Those who twist the truth will find themselves tied up in the very knots they have made*, Ruiz wrote.

"Subtle," Hannah said.

"Well, I know what he really means," said Bobby. "I'm walking you to class."

But nothing happened that day. Hannah borrowed Bobby's notes at lunch and caught up on what she'd missed. It was as though their argument never happened. She didn't know whether Bobby believed her theories about Bradley's death, but he no longer looked at her like she was crazy. That was enough.

Bobby wanted to hang around while she was at a *Law Review* meeting. Hannah told him she'd be fine.

"It's going to take at least two hours," she said. "There's no point in waiting. I'll be fine. Fernando isn't going to jump me on Founder's Walk, for God's sake."

Bobby finally agreed to go if Hannah would call him when she got home. She promised she would.

The meeting lasted three hours and Hannah stayed to talk to Harrison about her article after it was over. When they were done and Harrison gone, she looked at her watch. Nearly seven. With a twinge of discomfort, she looked at the darkness outside. She leaned out into the hall and saw no one except Lois Popich, who was locking the door to the dean's office. She stamped down the stairs and Hannah heard the oak door clunk shut behind her.

Hannah stuffed papers into her pack, threw on her wool coat, and walked downstairs. The security lamps flickered orange along Founder's Walk, not yet bright enough to illuminate the grove or the shadows between the buildings. Night classes didn't begin until seven-thirty. The professors who stayed late to teach them usually took a dinner break now. Hannah heard nothing but her own footsteps.

This is ridiculous, she thought as she felt her heartbeat quicken. I've walked to my car hundreds of times at this hour. There's nothing to be afraid of. Twisted in their own knots, she thought. She saw hands holding a rope and looping it into a noose. She shivered, and told herself it was the cold.

Halfway to the lot, she turned and walked back to the security office. She peered in the glass window set in the door. Bitten sat with his back to her, his feet propped up on the desk. There was a newspaper crossword puzzle on his knees and he peered at it in fierce concentration. Most of the squares were empty, smudged gray. She pounded on the door, but Bitten didn't move. Hannah looked closer. He was wearing earphones. The music apparently was so loud that he couldn't hear her slamming her fist on the glass of the door.

Now you're scaring yourself, she thought. You're panicking for no reason. She picked up her backpack and walked up the path, fighting the urge to run.

She reached the edge of the Rattigan Library lawn. If she cut across it and sidled through the hedge, she'd get to the parking lot faster. If she followed Founder's Walk around, it would take her past the eucalyptus grove, close-planted, full of leaves, fallen bark, and furtive noises. The grove had a sharp, acidic smell, like the reek of cat piss.

Hannah started up the slope. It was darker here. Only the dim glow from the lamps in the library stacks shone through the windows, like a gentle night-light. No wonder the bums liked to camp here.

She was halfway across the lawn when something caught at the leg of her jeans. She tried to shake free of the branch, the bush, whatever bit of vegetation had clung to her. That was what it had to be.

But now she felt a hand close around her ankle and tug it, hard. All she could see in the darkness was a man crouched on the ground, one hand holding her, the other reaching for her. Hannah kicked, felt the toe of her boot connect with flesh. The man toppled onto his back.

"Uhnff! My node, goddamn it," said a voice, unaccented and flat as a Kansas plain. Not Ruiz.

Hannah knelt next to him. She saw now he was old and unshaven. He smelled of vodka.

"I didn't mean to hurt you," she said. "But Jesus, you grabbed me."

"I thought you was someone else," he said. "My friend comes out here to keep me warm sometimes. Thought you was her."

Hannah got to her feet, wondering if it was the bum's vodka vision or if she should consider some new clothes.

"You should take off," she said. "The guard'll be on rounds soon."

"Not tonight," the bum said confidently. "We chipped in and got Bitten a *New York Times*. He won't be done with that puzzle for hours."

She jogged down the rise and brushed through the hedge, the ignition key jammed between her fingers. The parking-lot lights were brighter than those on the walk. She could see her car, just two lanes away. Jump in, lock the doors, drive home, call Bobby, and tell him nothing happened. Because nothing had, not really.

She was nearly at the car when she saw it. The spidery lines in the glass extended into every corner from the crater at the center of the windshield. He must have used a hammer, she thought, something with a handle, so he could really swing. Another message, Hannah thought. More direct this time.

Hannah felt the adrenaline pumping into her legs and arms as she got into the car. She knew she should stop, take the keys out of the ignition, call the auto club, get a grip.

But she was sick of being an intimidated recipient of his missives. If Ruiz had something to say, she was going to make him do it in person. The windshield would hold for as long as this would take, she thought. She knew Ruiz worked nights. She didn't know where.

After a few minutes with M'Naghten's nightside bartender, Hannah had her answer. She wondered for a moment if the guy was joking.

"Marimba?" she said.

"It pays good," he said.

Marimba was the whitest, blandest, least authentic, and most expensive Mexican restaurant in Las Almas. It had also paid out several thousand dollars in a civil-rights lawsuit two years before.

The bar had a lucrative dance party every weekend. But the owners, two rich erstwhile football players from Dana Point, hadn't liked to see too many swarthy men in the room. It gave the club a cachet they didn't like. So the bouncers were instructed to keep the "Swedes" at a minimum. The code, not surprisingly, had been deciphered, suits filed, money paid. The dance scene moved on. The scent of discrimination lingered on at Marimba, but it didn't seem to hurt its dinner business. When Hannah arrived, the parking lot was full.

And here was the host, Fernando Ruiz, holding the menus and checking off names. He wore an orange shirt, open at the throat to show curly black chest hair. He wore tight black pants tucked into boots. A striped sash wound around his waist. Lime-green ball fringe bobbed on a black vest as he scribbled reservations.

He looked like Gaucho the Clown. Hannah had to struggle to keep her rage from releasing itself as derisive laughter.

Then she thought of how much he must hate this, and himself. He might have a scholarship for school, but it wasn't enough to support the mother and sisters. He was proud, but pride didn't pay rent or buy groceries. She imagined Bradley taunting him about the job, his high principles, and the gap between. She no longer felt like laughing.

Ruiz was staring down at the seating chart when he began the mechanical *bienvenido,* delivered with an artificially warm smile. Then he glanced up. Hannah could feel his misery and embarrassment.

"I want to talk to you," Hannah said.

"I'm busy," he said.

"I could mention to Celestina that you're the token Swede here. Or you could make a minute for me," she said.

He glared at her.

"Wait in the bar," he said.

He stalked in a half hour later as Hannah sipped at a cup of coffee.

"What the fuck do you want?" he said.

"I want you to pay for my windshield," she said. "I want you to stop making veiled threats and I want you to stop following me."

"Your windshield? I don't know what you're talking about," he said.

"I know you're not the persecuted innocent you make yourself out to be," she said. "You sold out to Bradley, just like you've sold out with this job. You're a hypocrite, and you're scared of what will happen when people find that out."

"You don't know a fucking thing about me, or my life. I don't have to answer to anyone except to my family and God. Period."

"You might have to answer to somebody in between, depending on what you've done," Hannah said.

"Now who's making threats?" he said.

"I'm just telling you that you don't fool me."

A doughy man in the restaurant's ludicrous uniform cleared his throat, pointed at his watch, and motioned for Fernando to get back to his post.

"I think that's the end of your break. Be a good little Swede and get back to work," Hannah said.

22

When Hannah was a first-grader, there was a cartoon-show host named Engineer Bill. He'd worn a puffy engineer's hat, mattress-ticking overalls, and played a milk-drinking game called red light, green light.

On this Saturday morning, it looked to Hannah like he was back. In a big way. There were a hundred or more Engineer Bills, and not a few Bill-ettes, lined up on the platform at Las Almas station. They were waiting for the Daylight, and Hannah waited with them.

She'd spent Friday morning having the windshield fixed. She didn't tell Bobby what had happened on Thursday night. He would only worry, or hover, or threaten Ruiz. She wanted Ruiz to think she had turned the tables on him. She had seen him on the stairs between classes Friday afternoon and smiled coolly at him. He just sneered back.

Hannah scanned the crowd on the station platform, but she didn't see Teddy. She did find the flabby trainmaster of Hobby Junction, who pointed to a red-and-black bike leaning against a pillar. Teddy was here, he said, that's his bike. But maybe he'd walked up the line some, to get away from the crowds. She should try the McFadden Street crossing in Santa Ana.

The Daylight was due in the station in eight minutes.

Hannah jogged to her car, jammed the key in the ignition, and headed west, paralleling the tracks.

At the crossing, a cluster of rail fans stood with their video cameras and tape recorders, consulting their watches, setting sound levels, and leaning into the tracks to scan for the Daylight.

No Teddy. Hannah parked a half block away and waded into the thicket of people.

The morning sun was melting away, leaving a leaden sky. Wind eddied scraps of paper in the gutters. A mother slipped a sweater around her toddler's shoulders just as the girl pulled away and ran pigeon-toed toward the rails. The woman scuttled after her.

Teddy stood in the gap that opened behind the running mother. The wind flapped his oversized jeans. He held a microphone aloft, his eyes fixed on the tracks. The Daylight, its orange-and-black paint cartoon bright against the gray sky, rumbled toward them.

The train's horn shattered the stillness, and Hannah felt its vibrations rattling her body. The fans applauded and cheered. Hannah stepped into the crowd behind Teddy and held him by one shoulder. The kid was bony and small.

He jumped at her touch and squirmed to look back at her. The glasses magnified his brown, watery eyes. He seemed to be looking at her from inside a fishbowl.

"I don't know what you saw. But I know it scared you," Hannah said. "I'm not going to hurt you, so don't run, okay?"

He nodded stiffly and stared down at his shoes, scruffy black high-tops with shredded laces that he had salvaged by knotting them in two places.

Then he fished around in the pocket of his jeans. He held a cassette in his hand. His hand was shaking.

"I didn't do anything." The boy's voice trembled. "I just listened."

Teddy shivered as they stood on the landing outside Hannah's apartment. His skinny arms, pebbled with gooseflesh, stuck out of the short sleeves of a baggy gray T-shirt. Hannah saw a fading brown scar in the skin, about the size and shape of an eraser. Or the tip of a cigarette. He hugged himself to stop the shaking. His teeth chattered.

"I can make some hot chocolate," Hannah said as she unlocked the door. "How does that sound?"

The boy nodded. He scanned the living room and his eyes lit on the computer. He plopped down at the library table and drew his knees up to his chest. He drummed his fingers on the keyboard as he watched Hannah dump cocoa mix into mugs and put the kettle on the stove.

She pulled up a footstool and sat at his feet. Their eyes were level now. Teddy's glance darted toward hers and then away, like a minnow confronting a cat.

"I should introduce myself," she said. "Hannah Barlow."

She put out her hand. He cautiously extended his. There was a bandage with green dinosaurs taped over his knuckles.

"Teddy Czerwinski," he said. The hand was small, the grip tentative, almost as though he feared some injury. "Are you a cop?"

Hannah shook her head. "You're perceptive. I used to be a cop. Not anymore."

"I saw you out there, that night. You act like a cop."

"You've talked to cops before?"

"Couple times." He pushed his glasses up on his nose and glanced around Hannah's apartment. He unwound himself in the chair and seemed to relax. "If you're not a cop, why were you looking for me?"

"The man who was hit that night was someone I knew."

He stiffened again. His eyes flicked to the door.

"It's okay. I don't think that you hurt him," Hannah said. She thought she was right about that.

"I didn't," he said. He looked at his feet and then up at her. "Sorry I ran away from you last week. Pendejo didn't get you, did he?"

Hannah laughed. It was a good name for the lunatic pit bull.

"My butt is unbitten," she said.

The kid smiled. For an instant there was some warmth in his eyes. But when he saw her looking at him, the glimmer went out. He hides his feelings, Hannah thought. What taught him to do that, so young?

In the kitchen, the kettle whistled through a breathy glissando to a shrill scream. Teddy tensed at the sound. Hannah could feel his eyes following her as she brought the steaming cups of cocoa to the table. He took a tentative sip and blew across the surface.

"I thought you were a cop. I wasn't supposed to be out there, at the tracks, at night. I didn't want to get in trouble," he said.

"What happened that night?" she said.

Teddy lowered the cup, pulled himself into the chair, and looked away from Hannah. The sudden stillness made it seem that he'd left the room. Camouflage, Hannah thought. If you're not attracting attention, perhaps you won't be the target.

"Teddy? It's okay. Go ahead and tell me."

He blinked and brought his eyes back to Hannah's.

"Monty doesn't know I was there. I'll be in trouble if she finds out," he said. "Is there some way she doesn't have to know?"

Monty? Why didn't he call her mom?

"I'm not sure," Hannah said. "I don't want to make you any promises I can't keep. You might have to talk to the police. It's up to them."

"I didn't do anything wrong," he said. "Not a big thing, anyway."

Hannah nodded.

He reached for the mug and took a sip of chocolate. Then he started.

There was a new diesel in service, he said. He didn't have it in his sound library yet, and he'd found out that it would be one of the locomotives hauling the ten-forty-seven freight, from Kansas City to San Diego.

"I hid under a boxcar that was sidetracked so the railroad detectives wouldn't see me," he said. "They don't care if I tape stuff in the daytime, but they don't like having kids out on the sidings at night. It's dangerous."

"I'll bet," Hannah said.

"But it's fun watching them move the containers with the straddle buggies and everything. It's just that it's pitch-black on the sidings. You can't see what's coming. And they freewheel the cars and containers out there. They're so quiet that you can't hear them, almost until they're right up on you. I heard some guys have been hit by them."

"Scary stuff," Hannah said.

"You've just got to watch what you're doing," Teddy said nonchalantly. "I got there at ten and sacked out under a boxcar with my microphone. Then I heard them."

"Who?" Hannah said.

"Security guards, I thought. But they have flashlights," Teddy said. "These guys were walking in the dark. They didn't talk. Then they stopped, and one of them laughed. I decided to tape it."

"Why?" Hannah said.

"I thought maybe they were going to break into one of the containers," he said. "Sometimes the thieves pull the pins—"

He saw Hannah's confusion.

"They take apart the cars and that sets the brakes and then they can break in," he said. "One of my friends saw that happen once and called the railroad cops on his dad's cellular. They caught them. The Santa Fe let my friend ride up in the cab with the engineer and gave him some cool pins—and some savings bond or something. I thought maybe these guys would say their names or talk about where they were going to fence stuff. You know."

Hannah asked him for the cassette. He pulled it out and offered it to her.

"Can I copy this?" she said.

"No!" Teddy howled, grabbing it back.

"Whoa. What's the matter?" Hannah said.

"You'll just take it to them, and tell them I was there, and then they'll say I should have called them, and—"

"You don't trust me," Hannah said.

He didn't answer.

He was eleven years old, with a cigarette burn on his arm, an acquaintanceship with cops, and eyes that rolled down on emotion like security shutters. She could guess why trust was no longer in his repertoire.

"Okay," Hannah said. "We'll do this your way. For now, I'll just play this. And we'll stop it every now and then, and you'll tell me what was going on."

He nodded, relieved. Hannah sat on the floor, put the tape in the deck, and pushed the play button.

A faint metallic crackle, like tinfoil. And then Bradley's laughter. Bright and easy, as it had been when he was insulting Ruiz at M'Naghten's a half hour before. A cold chill curled through Hannah's stomach.

"I haven't opened one of these since my wedding," he said. *"Should I shake it up first?"*

A faint voice answered, so softly that Hannah couldn't make out the reply.

"No? Well, I'm in the mood to make a real mess."

There was a second or two of silence. Hannah stopped the tape.

"Could you see them?"

"I crawled out a little bit, but they were standing right next to the car. All I could see was their pants and shoes. I was afraid they'd see me."

Hannah started the tape again.

"Anyway," Bradley said. *"I just brought this to say thanks. You're a lifesaver. As always. Sorry there are no glasses."*

A sharp pop.

"What shall we toast? How about the future?"

A silence.

"No? You might want to revise your future," Bradley said. *"If they find out what you did, you'll be looking for a new career—at least. Personally, I think it's a felony. But as long as we've got a deal, no problem. You keep up your end of things and I keep quiet."*

Hannah glanced at Teddy; he was shivering again, though the room was warm and he had finished the hot chocolate. She stopped the tape.

"What was happening then?"

Now the boy was shaking so hard that the chair squeaked. Hannah grabbed the afghan from the sofa and went to him. He pulled away at first, but then eased against her. She folded him into the blanket.

"It's okay, Teddy. Nobody's going to hurt you here. Tell me what happened next."

"One of them sat down. His back was right in front of me. He put the bottle on the ground," Teddy said. "The other one picked it up."

Hannah restarted the tape. They heard the crunch of feet on the ballast.

"You want more?" Bradley said. Then he gasped. *"No!"*

There was a dull thud, like meat being pounded. A scream of pain.

"The guy on the ground fell over. There was blood on his forehead. His eyes still were open." Tears spilled from Teddy's eyes. He dashed them away with the back of his hand.

"I got really scared and I grabbed the recorder and pulled way back under the car. The other one picked up the bottle and grabbed the man under his arms and dragged him away. I got out on the other side of the car and ran, as fast as I could."

"Did you see either of them after that?"

Teddy nodded.

"I was running home when I heard the train. They don't

usually sound the horn at night like that. The engineer just was wailing on it. I came back, and I saw the man, the one who'd fallen over. He was lying on the tracks and the train . . . I couldn't do anything."

He began to sob. Hannah held him closer and rocked him. They sat there for a long time, until the boy's shuddering stopped.

"I was really scared," he said, his voiced muffled in her shirt. "I knew I'd get in trouble. I wasn't supposed to be out and I wasn't supposed to be on the siding and I saw him get hit and I didn't tell."

He began weeping, each sob racking his shoulders. Hannah felt she was holding a terrified bird whose thin bones would snap if she grasped any tighter.

"What if he wasn't dead before?" the boy gasped. "I could have gotten help. What if I left, just let him die?"

Hannah felt tears stinging her own eyes. Don't, she thought, don't take that on.

"You couldn't help him," she said. "You didn't do anything wrong."

She reached over to the stereo and plugged in the earphones.

"I'm going to listen to the end of this, all right?"

He nodded, sniffling.

Very faint, through the jostle as Teddy moved the recorder, she heard a word. Hannah cranked up the volume and played it again.

The voice was raspy, pitched in a nether range that could be a woman's growl or a man's throat-tightened spit of rage.

"Bastard."

Teddy watched Hannah's face as she replayed the last bit of the tape. She took off the earphones and held him tight.

It was late afternoon by the time they retrieved Teddy's bike from the station and came to his house, a bungalow three blocks away from the street where he'd left Hannah clinging to a fence.

The bungalow made Hannah think of Candyland, the board game she played when she was no more than a toddler. The house was painted a sugary pink. The shutters' white and red slats alternated, like a candy cane. But as they got closer she saw the shutters were bare in places, and the pink paint was cracked and peeling.

Teddy insisted she park away from the house. Hannah hauled the bike out of the Hyundai's backseat. The boy got on it and fidgeted for a second. He again refused to let Hannah copy the tape. She knew she couldn't push him much more without him disappearing on her. And if he was sufficiently nervous, he could destroy the tape. She didn't want that.

"You're not going to call the police now, are you?" he said.

"Not yet," Hannah said. "But soon. We have to."

Teddy glanced toward the pink house.

"Monty isn't your mom, right?" Hannah asked. It seemed a logical guess.

The boy nodded. "Foster mother. Best one so far."

"How long have you lived with her?" Hannah said.

"About a year. Her husband used to work as a brakeman with Union Pacific. He's dead now."

"And you're going to tell her about all this, right? She'll understand."

He nodded. They sat in silence for a moment.

"When will I have to talk to them—the cops?" Teddy said.

"I could call you," she said mildly.

He shook his head. Hard.

Hannah thought for a minute. "Why don't you come by Friday afternoon, when school lets out? I'll know by then. I'll buy you a burger, okay?"

He nodded, turned the bike, and zigzagged across the street, momentarily terrifying a tawny cat. As he neared the house a heavy woman in a housecoat waddled out on the porch. Her hair was a fluffy pink-tinged cloud, floating around her head.

Teddy opened a chain-link gate across the driveway and stowed the bike before running up the stairs. Monty kissed him on the top of the head. He pushed himself under her arm and supported her slow, arthritic progress back into the house. He glanced back at Hannah and gave her a furtive wave.

Hannah dialed Churnin's number. The recording was different from the first time: he was out of town until Thursday. He'd check in for messages.

Hannah didn't leave one. This would take too long to explain. She wanted to do it in person. And it wouldn't hurt to have someone on her side. She thought about that for a moment and dialed Eddy's pager number.

23

Hannah pulled into the bluff-top parking lot and turned off the engine. Twenty minutes until sunrise on a Sunday morning. She found nothing romantic or inspirational in watching the dawn.

Her mother, hoping some sanctity would rub off, used to rouse her from sleep and send her with Michael to Mass and communion every day before school. In college, she'd pulled all-nighters before exams and partied until morning. Police work meant graveyard shifts that ended with daybreak. And insomnia had shown her more than one morning like this one.

The clouds thinned until only a gauzy sheet veiled the sky. Hannah saw the outlines of the offshore oil rigs and, across the channel, the masses of dark rain shadows that hung over Catalina Island.

She wanted a cup of coffee. She had read the next week's cases the night before, waiting for Eddy to answer his pager and call back. Finally, she called him at home and got his answering machine. She left a third message on his office voice mail before giving up and going to bed.

Lying there, she replayed Bradley's taunts in her mind: If they find out what you did, Bradley had told his killer, you'll be looking for a new career—at least. That was certainly true for Weiss, if he'd secured the exam for Bradley. The words could just as easily fit Ruiz or German. She didn't know where any of them had been at ten o'clock that night. Ruiz should have been at work, but wasn't for some reason. Odd, because Fridays were probably big at Marimba. German said he had gone to the fund-raiser.

Bradley had said it was more than just loss of a career. It might be a felony. That would apply to German, if he had indeed bribed and possibly done worse to Luz Gomez. But for the others? Stealing a test or cheating on an exam wasn't a crime, that she knew of.

Hannah got out of the car and scanned the water. A few surfers bobbed in the waves. She wondered why it was necessary to practice this sport so early in the morning. Maybe, like communion, surfing was a sacrament best taken before full consciousness. Middle-aged men like Weiss might not do it if they thought about it too much.

Surfer magazine had first revealed Weiss's passion to the world. The story mingled legalisms and surfer patois and proposed that Weiss represent the locals who wanted to sue outsiders for trespassing on their waves.

Weiss had laughed along at first when Douglas students razzed him about the article. But then someone posted a doctored photograph on his office door. The dean's scraggly neck, thinning hair, and pinched face had been plastered atop the body of a buff sixteen-year-old who cuddled a blond water nymph in a thong bikini. The picture disappeared along with Weiss's good-sport smile.

Hannah walked down a flight of splintering wooden stairs to the sand. The wind blew a steady, gritty spray at her, but the sun was rising, warming her face. She strolled along the water, straining to make out a figure riding out a frothy wave a dozen yards down the strand.

It was Weiss, wearing a neon wet suit. He kicked out, caught a second wave. His turns were mushier than some of the teenagers surfing around him, but he didn't seem bad for a fifty-year-old academic. Weiss rode in one last wave, slogged out of the water, and made for a flight of stairs. Hannah followed him.

He was walking out onto the bluff when she reached the top of the flight behind him. She was about to call his name when she saw the blonde running toward him. The transformation was so startling that she almost didn't recognize her as Lois.

Her hair was down and parted on the side so that it fell over one eye, a blond wave glowing with sunlight. She wore tight jeans and a lush, pale pink angora sweater that clung to her heavy breasts. Hannah backed down a step, but Lois didn't appear to see her.

She fell into Weiss's arms and sealed her lips to his, pulled her face back, and laughed, a throaty, feline sound of pleasure.

She and Weiss talked quietly, intimately. Hannah couldn't make out the words. But she could make a good guess at what they were saying to each other.

Did Bradley know about them? Maybe this was the hold Bradley had over Weiss. It made sense. If German threatened to pull out his endowments, Weiss could always woo another car dealer who'd survived the recession. Not all the buildings on campus had names yet. So maybe he didn't sell himself for Douglas's sake.

But what would he do to keep his job, his reputation? He might offer Bradley a criminal-law crib sheet or a slap on the wrist for plagiarism to ensure that the board of trustees never found out about Lois. Maybe he'd been willing to kill to keep it quiet. But since when was an affair felonious? She thought about that all the way home.

Hers was clearly a home no one had bothered about in several weeks. Since Bobby hadn't been over, the dishes were undone. Hannah had been tossing clothes on the closet floor, intending to get to them later. Later, she decided, could be now. Sometimes mindless tasks—dishes, laundry, showering—helped her thoughts click into place. With her hands engaged in sorting, washing, shampooing, her brain went into overdrive.

She picked up the denim jacket and went through the pockets. Sometimes she found money she'd forgotten about. More often she found a tissue with the potential of shredding and dispersing itself all over her black jeans.

This time she found the clipping from Bradley's apartment and looked at it again, more closely this time.

Tim Gallagher clutched the shoulder of his lawyer as he looked back at a burly sheriff's deputy, who was leaning against the paneled wall just outside the courtroom rail. Gallagher's face was red and twisted in a spitting rage. Hannah could almost hear him bellowing.

The deputy's lips puckered in an obscene rosebud. He was throwing Gallagher a dainty good-bye kiss.

Beside the deputy stood a man in a pinstripe suit. He was trying to suppress a smile. He was Bradley Cogburn.

She abandoned the laundry and got out the folder she'd

found in Bradley's car. The first story about Gallagher was dated June fifteenth, three months before the prison transfer.

GALLAGHER WINS RIGHT TO COUNTY-PAID CLERK

"Counselor" Tim Gallagher, who acted as his own defense attorney in his murder trial, has won the right to be assisted in legal research for his appeal by a county-paid law clerk, an appeals court has ruled.

Gallagher, who was convicted of murdering his brother in order to gain a family inheritance, has been sentenced to die in the gas chamber at San Quentin. He is currently appealing the verdict. Through a series of legal maneuvers that have even won the grudging admiration of the prosecutor, Gallagher has been able to prevent his immediate transfer to death row.

While working on his appeal, Gallagher is entitled to the assistance of an attorney and a law clerk, the court ruled. In a telephone interview from Orange County Jail, Gallagher said he will start interviewing prospective clerks this week.

"I've got a lot of work ahead of me," Gallagher said. "I think that with a little assistance, I'll be able to win my case on appeal, and avoid having to spend one day in the hellhole that is our state prison system."

Next to the story was a picture of Gallagher, apparently taken before his arrest. He was wearing a gray suit, oxford-cloth shirt, and red tie. His arms were crossed defiantly. A hexagonal gold signet ring caught the light of the camera's flash. He could have easily passed for the lawyer, not the client.

Hannah read the last story in the stack. Gallagher was transferred to prison in late August. Bradley had finished his internship in May. Bradley was bored with the DA's office, or so Catherine said. Yet, there he was, in a packed courtroom, watching Tim Gallagher lose a round with the system.

Catherine said that all he'd really wanted from the internship was access to criminal records. He might have found something about Tim Gallagher.

She looked through the stories. A sociopath, the cops said, over and over.

In the middle of the pile was a strange article: all the sources were unnamed. The writer employed plenty of *possibles, allegedlys,* and other journalistic hedging techniques against libel suits. The story posited that the brother's murder might not have been Gallagher's first—or last.

It alluded to an unnamed, potential witness in the brother's murder case. The story described the man as a barfly and a small-time fence. He surfaced after the conviction, but could have been handy to the prosecution if Gallagher had won a new trial. The witness claimed he'd struck up a conversation with Gallagher in a bar a few days before the brother's death. They introduced themselves by first names only. After a few beers, Tim had mentioned he would soon be leaving California. He was coming into some money.

After the murder, the witness saw Gallagher on the news, put the pieces together, but kept his mouth shut. Later, facing jail time for his unorthodox retailing methods, he decided to talk. Unfortunately, he died before making a sworn statement. He'd ingested the equivalent of thirty Darvon tablets—the exact lethal dosage recommended in the suicide manual found at his bedside. If he had been lying about Gallagher, and was on the verge of being discovered, he might have killed himself. But the story's source—Hannah guessed it was the DA investigator who busted hump to check out the guy's story in the first place—speculated that it might not have been suicide. The problem was, Gallagher didn't know where the witness was living. And he was in jail when the man died.

Hannah flipped back to the one-inch story and obituary she'd first read while sitting in Bradley's car. That man died in a Stanton motel room in July, a possible suicide. It sounded like the same guy. The obituary finally revealed the name: Bud Peavey. How had Bradley put it together? He wasn't working for the DA then.

It was another suspicious death by drugs, much like Jack Gallagher's and Luz Gomez's. Hannah wondered where Gallagher had been when Gomez died. Did Bradley's father know

Gallagher? Did German? There was no hint that he was a killer for hire, but he sounded capable of just about anything.

She drummed her fingers on the table, and then reached for the telephone. Where was Eddy, anyway?

She beeped him twice, and he was prickly with annoyance when he called back.

"You're annoying Gudrun, who was still asleep," he said. "What is it?"

"Will you help me get into San Quentin?" she said.

"Commit first-degree murder and you won't need my help."

"Just for a visit. I want to talk to Tim Gallagher for a few minutes. If you don't set it up, it will take forever to get cleared."

The line hummed with Eddy's uncertainty.

"You're not bigfooting in Churnin's case, are you?"

"Not really," Hannah said. "It's something he would think was a waste of time. Maybe it is. But there's something else that's solid, Eddy. I found a witness."

"If he can ID the bum, Churnin will cover you in kisses."

"Where is Churnin, anyway?"

"Michigan. The bum has a record there. Armed robbery. Beat a guy with a lead pipe and shoved him in front of a bus when he wouldn't give up his wallet. Sound familiar?"

"Yes, but he didn't kill Bradley," she said. "Bradley knew his attacker."

"Churnin would be disappointed to hear that. It conflicts with his theory," Eddy said.

"But he'll listen, right?"

"Depends. Can your witness ID the guy?"

"No," Hannah said.

"No ID? Then he'll be real skeptical. Might not go too easy on the witness."

"He's a kid," Hannah said. "What will Churnin do? Beat him with a blackjack in the interview room until he changes his story?"

"Naw. Look, I don't like the guy, so I expect the worst from him. But Churnin is a straight-up cop. He'll do what's right. Call him when he gets back."

"I will. About Gallagher . . ."

"I'll see what I can do," Eddy said. "Gallagher is probably pining for some company anyway, since he killed off the only family he had."

24

When Alexander German called that night, Hannah was wary, waiting for him to scream at her for the insinuations she'd made to Alicia. But German didn't sound angry. His voice was smooth, engaging. He asked if he could take her to dinner, to apologize for his behavior at Alicia's the night after the funeral.

Hannah said yes. She wanted to know what he was up to.

"Is this a fancy place?" Hannah said.

"Yes," German said. "Leave those cowboy boots of yours at home."

She twisted her hair into a chignon and put on a pair of sterling earrings. They were shaped like rain clouds and showered dangling, silvery droplets. She put on a black knit dress: long sleeves, high neck, a modest V in the back. The dress looked best with her suede pumps, the ones with three-inch heels. Exactly the kind of shoes she didn't wear when she was a detective. She couldn't stand in them for long, let alone run. That shouldn't be a problem, she thought. This is dinner, not the Olympics. She slipped them on.

He picked her up in a Porsche 356, a 1963, one of the bathtub models Hannah had always admired. It was just before dusk when they headed north, then west, toward the coast.

Hannah had expected the Ritz-Carlton, or Antonello's—someplace where the Newport Center lawyers tended to cluster. Outside such places, the lolling Rolls-Royces, rumbling Mercedes-Benzes, and tawny Jaguars made her think of big cats resting around the best watering hole on the savannah. But the real predators were inside, tearing into steak and osso bucco.

Tonight, though, they headed north along the coast, toward Seal Beach and the Los Angeles County line. German pulled a cellular phone out of his jacket and spent five minutes peppering someone named Janice with questions about a discovery motion.

"The case that won't die," he said, clicking the phone shut.

They pulled into a parking lot a half block from the beach, under a looming wooden water tower.

In the seventies, the tower had been converted into a showplace home, but now, in its second reincarnation, it was a small, expensive seafood restaurant. Hannah had read about it. The chef was apt to top the sea bass with a nasturtium or slide a salmon fillet studded with three shades of cracked pepper onto a bed of caramelized onions.

The access was a rattletrap elevator rigged in the middle of the structure. Hannah and German stood nearly nose to nose in the car, and when it slammed to a stop, Hannah had to catch German's wrist to keep from falling against him. He steadied her and smiled. Not the chilled smile of that first day, but one with actual charm. He had put her at ease, she realized. Perhaps she had misjudged him before.

They stood in the entryway for a moment as the host took their coats. The restaurant was only half-full, a sedate Sunday-dinner crowd. Hannah caught German's eyes sweeping her body. And to her slight surprise, she realized she didn't mind.

"I'm glad you agreed to come," he said. "I was afraid that you had written me off as an arrogant jerk."

"My pen is poised," she said.

German laughed.

She let him amuse her with small talk during the appetizer and the salad. He picked an expensive Sonoma chardonnay and kept her glass filled. Hannah sipped it slowly.

"I've bored you with a short history of civil litigation in Orange County," he said. "It's your turn."

"To bore you?"

"I don't think you could," he said.

Hannah shrugged and ran through the lines of the résumé:

Orange County native. Cal State Fullerton, and the sheriff's academy. Eleven years with the Las Almas PD.

She left out her other life, the one in the margins. My mother? Oh, she was crazy and drunk, and one day we fought, and I shoved her. And left her to die. Maybe I actually killed her. My family? Well, they blame me. Won't ever say it, of course. They shower me with prayer and baleful glances instead. Ever married? No. Who knows what I could do to a husband?

"I've already figured out what made you a good cop," German said.

"Really? What?"

"Getting people to talk to you," he said. "But evidently you decided you could make more money talking in court than grilling petty thieves."

Hannah toyed with the salad. She wasn't about to tell him that she blamed herself for letting a child die and had been inches from emotional death herself.

"I just decided I wanted something different for myself. So now I'm crunching casebooks as hard as I can."

"Where will you go after you graduate and take the bar? The DA's office?"

"That would be the logical place, I suppose," she said. "I haven't really decided. I have a clerkship with Dare and Dare this summer."

"Bankruptcy?" German snorted. "You'd be a good litigator. A no-nonsense attitude in a smart, beautiful woman makes a formidable package. You're not daunted by much, are you?"

She looked at him. The candlelight on the table illuminated his face, and his half smile sparked a cold shiver.

"Everyone is daunted by something," she said. "Aren't you?"

"We could find out," he said.

The female animal in Hannah was flattered. But after a lifetime with her, Hannah knew her weaknesses. She was hormonally driven, a wild thing with no sense whatsoever, and Hannah meant to keep her on a short leash. Particularly in the presence of someone like German.

It couldn't be a straightforward seduction, Hannah thought. He has something else in mind. She steered the conversation back to safe topics, much to the female animal's dismay.

"How is Alicia?" she said.

German shrugged. He poured himself more wine. Hannah covered her glass, as she had at the last dinner. He smiled at the gesture.

"Better, I hope," he said. "I persuaded her to stay with my sister in the desert for the weekend. Then I'll be able to spend some time with her. I still think it's best for her not to be alone."

"I met Susan Cogburn this week," Hannah said.

"Did you? How is Susan?"

"Fine. She told me Bradley hated you. And that the feeling was mutual. It explained a lot to me about our last dinner together."

German seemed unruffled.

"Susan is common as dirt," he said. "A gold digger. She mined Henry Cogburn down to the last penny, not that he minded as much as his wife would have, had she been conscious. Did she tell you about the affair?"

"Her affair with Henry Cogburn?"

"No. Bradley's affair. After he married my daughter."

With Dove, Hannah thought. She imagined Dove unwinding the silk scarf from her long, thin neck and looping it around Bradley's.

"I heard he was cheating on Alicia. Just a rumor," German said. "I had some people check it out. It was true."

"How awful for her."

"Alicia knew nothing. She trusted him utterly. He did it to torture me."

Hannah looked at him over the lip of the wineglass. What kind of thinking was this? Her incredulity must have showed.

"It's not egotism. He was out to get me. I could stand Bradley's enmity. His father panicked, lost everything, and killed himself. That's hard for a son to face, so he blamed me. Fine. Maybe he'd get over it, or not. But just hating me wasn't enough. He used Alicia to punish me."

"What did Alicia think of your investigation?"

"She didn't know about it. And I knew that if I told her what I'd found out, it would be playing into Bradley's hands. It wasn't enough to wound me by hurting her. He wanted to drive a wedge between us, too."

"Who was he sleeping with?" Hannah said.

"That's not the point. Any woman would have done. His aim was to make sure I knew about it."

"So what happened?" Hannah said.

"I saw to it, obliquely, that Alicia found out. A phone call from a hotel to verify a bill. A florist misdelivering flowers. It didn't take much. She was the one who told me, ultimately."

"And you were able to feign hurt and outrage," Hannah said.

"When I saw her face, I didn't have to feign anything," he said. "But she had to find out, and that was the only way. I hoped she would see him for what he'd become, and end the marriage."

"But she didn't."

"She was devastated, but not angry. That's her way, unfortunately. She confronted him and he made up some brilliant crap about the pressure of school, and if she had been loyal to him and not me, it would never have happened. Alicia forgave him. Another round to Bradley. You see how he is."

"Was," Hannah said.

"How he was. Of course," he said nonchalantly, as though Bradley was a dead houseplant. He motioned to the waiter for the check. "Sometimes I forget he's not with us."

German was nearly silent as they drove back to Las Almas. He insisted on seeing Hannah to her door and unlocked it for her. Before she could turn to thank him and end the weird date with as much grace as she could muster, he was inside.

He stepped close to her. Hannah judged him to be a foot taller than she was.

"Did I invite you in?" she asked. She looked at him quizzically. Did he think he was going to kiss her good night?

"There's something I have to ask of you," he said. "Don't bother Alicia anymore."

Instantly, Hannah knew that German had exhibited all that charm only in the service of this moment. Her first instincts about him had been right.

"Is this your idea? Another instance of you taking charge of Alicia's life for her?"

"No," he said.

"Then why isn't she telling me this?"

"She doesn't want to talk about it," he said. "All of this has upset her. Bradley is dead, whether by suicide or murder doesn't really matter. She won't realize it for a while, but this is the best thing that could have happened to her. You're not helping, digging around, looking to unearth mysteries and intrigues."

It could be true, Hannah thought. Alicia was furious at her at La Luna. But the outrage was because Hannah had implicated German. She was sure Alicia hadn't told him what had happened. If she had, German would have torn Hannah up one side and down the other, not bought her dinner. So Alicia hadn't asked him to call Hannah off. He was bluffing.

"I'm sorry I upset Alicia," Hannah said. "I'd like to clear things up." She opened the address book on the library table.

Suddenly German was behind her, reaching around her. She could feel his chest pressing against her back. He slammed the book shut and held his hand on it.

"Look, I know that you're honestly interested in helping here," German said in her ear. "There are pressures on you, I know that."

"No there aren't," Hannah said, "except you. Get off."

"You're trying to keep up with your classes while coping with this plagiarism thing. Maybe you're in over your head," he continued. "I could get you some help."

Hannah felt her throat tightening.

"The future is blurry for you right now, but I could help you. I told you, I think you'd be formidable in a courtroom."

Hannah picked up the phone and punched three numbers.

"For Newport Beach," she said. "The last name is Cogburn. C-O—"

German wrenched the phone from her hand and slammed it back on the receiver. He spun Hannah around to face him and held her by the shoulders. Hannah winced at his grip and he tightened it even more.

"Let me go. And get out before I call the police," she said.

"You thought you could get something out of Alicia, is that it?" His voice was low, but packed with venom. "You'd feed her choice bits of suspicion and then cry poor. You were going to bleed her, when she was most vulnerable. You were trying to make her think Bradley was some innocent victim, and only you cared enough to find the truth."

"And you would rather keep the truth to yourself," Hannah

said. Her heart was pounding. His strength, the bitter sneer on his face frightened her. But she couldn't show him that.

For a moment the grip faltered.

"I don't know what you're talking about."

Now it was her turn to bluff.

"Raymond O'Reilly," she said.

He pulled her up by her shoulders. Her feet were barely touching the ground. His cheek was next to hers. She could feel the stubble on his jaw and smell him—cedar, vanilla, and a hint of wine.

"Goddamn you," he whispered into her ear. "If you so much as suggest that to anyone, I'll have you out of Douglas and slapped with a defamation suit so fast you won't know what hit you."

He dropped her to the ground, but held on. Hannah recovered her balance and sank one of her three-inch heels into his foot. He screamed and lurched back. Hannah reached for the phone, but he hobbled out and was gone, the door wide-open behind him.

25

Her dreams that night were full of dark alleys, where she hid, or where others hid from her. She heard German whispering to her and felt his hands. In the morning, she could see the yellow tinge of a bruise forming on each arm.

Eddy called just after seven. The state Department of Corrections had cleared her visit, on his statement that it was a police matter.

"Don't screw me over on this, Hannah," Eddy said. "I'm going out on a limb for you."

"I won't," Hannah said. "Thank you, Devlin." She almost never used his first name.

"Don't get all gooey. It doesn't mean Gallagher will see you," he said. "It's just a license to hunt. You can go today, if you want."

It meant skipping classes. She could get notes from Bobby, if she begged. She made a reservation out of John Wayne Airport for a nine-thirty flight and reserved a rental car in San Francisco. She put on a cream silk blouse, an emerald-green wool suit, and a pair of matching suede pumps. She didn't want to look like a drab would-be lawyer. Let Gallagher think, at first glance, that she was a groupie, a rich one who had a thing for guys in prison. Gallagher looked like a man who would like to lay eyes on a woman.

The plane touched down just after ten forty-five. She drove north on 101 through San Francisco, where a gray cape of fog engulfed the skyline and streets. Hannah had never managed to see the city in the sunshine, and wouldn't this time, either.

But halfway across the Golden Gate Bridge, the whorls dissolved and she had a view of the Marin headlands, their hills glowing gold and green.

Hannah passed Sausalito and Corte Madera. She turned east, back toward the bay, and had her first glimpse of the prison. It sat on its own peninsula, Point Quentin, and had a fine view of the water. But she doubted if the residents admired the scenery much.

She parked in a visitors' lot and joined a line of people filing into the entrance building. A guard found her name in a black binder and slid a wooden tray toward her.

"You'll have to remove anything that could trip the machine," he said, nodding at the metal detector.

Hannah took off her earrings, watch, and belt.

"Take off your shoes, too, just in case," he said. "Metal shanks set it off. Then you can give it a try. See if you're going to have to part with your bra, too."

"Excuse me?" Hannah said.

The guard, who couldn't have been more than twenty-five, was blushing, ever so slightly.

"It can detect the underwire ones, sometimes," he said.

"I had a boyfriend in high school who claimed the same thing," Hannah said.

The guard laughed and Hannah walked though the arch, feeling the chill of the linoleum through her nylons.

"Okay," the guard said, sliding her the tray and a visitor's badge.

She waited for Gallagher in the visitors' area, a room of low tables, vending machines, and a thicket of signs: NO SMOKING. Four of those. VISITORS AND INMATES MAY EMBRACE AND KISS AT THE BEGINNING AND END OF EACH VISIT. NO OTHER CONTACT IS PERMITTED. One sheet near the door repeated acceptable visitor dress. No denim. The state didn't want an inmate in his prison blues to slip out, disguised as a jeans-wearing visitor.

The hall quickly filled with women and small children. Some of the women led their kids to a toy-filled corral or sat them in front of a TV to watch videotaped cartoons.

From the door opposite the public entrance, a trickle and then a stream of men filled the room. Hannah saw a lot of tattoos and bulging muscles. Two popular ways to pass the time when you're down for fifteen years to life, she thought. Weight lifting she understood: a way to press and lift and drive the demons out. But prison tattooing was a strange hobby: chess pieces were melted down and mixed with shampoo and water for ink. The needle, driven by a cannibalized Walkman motor, was concocted of guitar string run through a pen tube. A great way to contract AIDS, she suspected.

Nearly thirty minutes passed. Hannah hadn't realized how nervous she was. But the silk blouse felt clammy against her back, and her head was beginning to ache. She realized she'd skipped breakfast. And the thought of the dinner made her queasy.

She read the clippings again, but the words were dancing away from her eyes. The din in the room rose and ebbed with each new arrival. She kept her eyes trained on the metal door.

She glanced at her watch. She had waited forty-five minutes. A guard appeared at the door and scanned the room.

"Hannah Barlow?" he shouted.

She stood up, and the guard threaded his way through the tables.

"Death-row inmates just finished with showers," he said. "Gallagher will be down in about ten minutes."

Gallagher's eyes were dark blue, like a stain of bottled ink on white paper. His hair was light brown, cut short and parted on the side. His nose was thin and sharp and it gave his clean-shaven face a boyish innocence; Hannah realized she didn't know how old he was. He had the serious mien that won the newspapers' nickname, Counselor, even without the gray suit. He could have passed for a junior partner at German's firm.

Except for the tattoo. It must have been done after the picture had been taken, and by a professional. This was no crude prison piece.

The artist had rendered the boa in green and red. It wound around Gallagher's neck like a scarf and must have continued under his shirt, because it emerged from the rolled-up sleeve of his denim shirt and coiled down his right arm. The top of his hand bore the boa's head. Its eyes shifted as he flexed his fingers. The flicking tongue extended down his middle finger and forked around his nail.

He smiled at Hannah as he sat down, taking her in from red head to green high heels in one swoop of his eyes. He noticed her gazing at his arm.

"Prison culture," he said, flexing a forearm. The serpent wriggled. "You spend any time inside, you get a taste for tattoos. But I wanted something more than the usual big-breasted woman done in basic black. What do you think?"

"I've never seen one like it," Hannah said, honestly enough.

"But we've slid right past the introductions and into dreary prison rituals," he said. "Are you the police officer?"

"No," she said. "Hannah Barlow. I'm a law student."

"Oh," he said, frowning slightly. "Somebody said Las Almas PD was sending a homicide investigator up here to see me."

"Must have been a misunderstanding," she said. "Still, I wanted to ask you about someone. Someone who died recently. But I'm not a cop."

Gallagher laughed. "Sure, no problem. I prefer not to talk to cops. They like to blame me for things I didn't do."

Hannah opened the envelope of clippings and took out the picture of the court melee.

"Do you know this man?" She pointed to Bradley.

Gallagher looked at the clipping for a long time.

"I remember the day, certainly," he said. "He looks vaguely familiar. But the courthouse is full of slick lawyers in expensive suits. Is he the dead man?"

"That's right," Hannah said. "His name is Bradley Cogburn. He was a classmate of mine. He worked in a criminal-law internship last spring and I thought he might have clerked for you after that. You were interviewing in May, right?"

Gallagher looked at the picture more closely.

"You know, maybe that's why he looks familiar. I interviewed him, I think. Yes." He tapped Bradley's face with his finger. The cuticle was neat, the nail buffed to a low gleam. "He was very full of himself. He talked about his father-in-law being a big-shot lawyer, that kind of thing."

"His father-in-law is Alexander German."

"Newport Beach, right? He was president of the Orange County Bar Association last year, I think."

"Do you know him?" Hannah said.

"No. I know the name from the bar magazine. Someone put me on the mailing list. A compliment, I guess. Anyway, Bradley wasn't the guy for me. It was a game to him, something cool for the résumé. It was my life. I took a pass."

"Why would he have been in court that day?"

"Looks like he was gloating, doesn't it? There was plenty of that going on. Was he your boyfriend?"

Hannah shook her head. "Where were you living four years ago?"

"Let me see. I was busted for this ridiculous bullshit in Las Almas, November, four years ago. Before that? Stanton. I wasn't too flush at the time."

"Spend much time in the desert?" Hannah said.

"Where are we going with this?" he snapped.

He had slipped into defensiveness before he could stop himself. So, he doesn't have perfect control, she thought.

He shrugged and patted his pale cheek. "I burn easily, so I try to stay out of the sun."

"Do you know someone named Raymond O'Reilly?"

Gallagher didn't answer her. He scanned the ceiling, glanced around the room, lit a cigarette, and blew some smoke, thoughtfully aiming it away from Hannah.

"I don't think I do. What's he look like? Where's he from?"

"I don't know what he looks like. He lives in Palm Springs, or did."

"The desert, huh?"

Hannah nodded.

"What happened there?" Gallagher said.

"You tell me," Hannah said.

"Never laid eyes on the place." He stubbed out the cigarette. "I told you. Is that it?"

"No. I'm curious. How did you find out where Bud Peavey lived?"

Gallagher laughed. "I read that story, too. What a crock. It would have required mind reading and astral projection for me to kill him. I'm talented, but I'm not psychic."

Hannah nodded.

"Well. I've got to get some lunch before two or wait for dinner. Not that the food's great." He got up and held out his hand. Hannah shook it, hoping he didn't see her distaste at touching the red python's head.

"I wish I could get Domino's to deliver," he said. "But they won't take collect calls. I might have to wait for the warden to order for me—and we both know when that would be."

He smiled at her. The dark blue eyes were peaceful, gentle. The corners crinkled charmingly. A lovely facade, Hannah thought. He could probably make a woman believe the earth was flat.

She smiled back at him. "By the way, who did you hire for a clerk, back in Orange County?"

He tapped his lips.

"I'll remember it in a second. It was some wimpy guy from Western State. Ed something. Helped me write one hell of a motion to suppress—for all the good it did me. The judge couldn't have understood the legal arguments we presented in a million years."

The thought wiped the charm from his face. Hannah watched him as his eyes slid left and right, as though he saw the prosecutor and the judge conspiring against him. Then he realized she was watching him.

"So I lost that battle," he said, smiling. "But not the war. I'm not dead yet." He swung out of the chair and strolled out of the visiting room.

Hannah picked up her briefcase and handed her visitor's pass back to the guard at the door. This one was a woman, slight, with biceps round as pippin apples. She looked like she could sprint the length of the prison and still have energy enough to bust some heads.

"Are you working for that guy?" the guard said. "What happened to the other one?"

"What other one?"

"The lawyer that's here every week. The only person who visits our Timmy."

"I thought Gallagher was defending himself," Hannah said.

"It's his secret that he's getting help, I guess," the guard said. "He likes all that publicity bullshit about how brilliant he is. But it's his life, right? Why gamble?"

"So who's the lawyer?"

"Don't know. I've never actually seen him," the guard said. "Just heard that he's here, every week. I figure it's some bleeding heart. Working for free."

"It's not appointed appellate counsel?"

"Nope. He's pro bono. It's taking three years for the death-row boys to get a paid-for lawyer. Gallagher's only been here since August. This guy's a total pro boner. That's what we call it. Because someone's got to have a hard-on for lowlifes like Tim, taking no money to get them off."

German, Hannah thought. It's got to be. She scribbled her name and phone number on a piece of paper and handed it to the guard.

"If you can find out the lawyer's name, number, that stuff, give me a call, will you? I think your Timmy's up to something."

"I wouldn't be surprised," the guard said. Her smile was vulpine, the teeth pearly and sharp, as if they'd been honed. And she seemed delighted at the idea of sinking them into Tim Gallagher's condemned hide.

26

It wasn't a completely wasted trip, Hannah thought. She knew Gallagher was lying about something, maybe many things. The story in the newspaper didn't mention names. And Peavey supposedly never gave Gallagher his last name in the bar. But Gallagher knew instantly who Hannah was talking about. She was convinced he'd had him killed. But how did he find him?

Clearly, Gallagher knew who German was, but maybe not from the bar's mailing list. He knew Bradley, but not necessarily as a job applicant. If Gallagher was linked to the Agua Dulce fiasco, Alicia might have heard of him.

Hannah knew she had to see Alicia. She had pushed her too hard about her father, and she had to apologize for that. But she had been right about him. She had the bruises to prove it.

She called Alicia from the plane, and again when she got home. No one answered. Maybe she really did go to the desert, Hannah thought. She called information, and the operator gave her the numbers of the five Germans in Palm Springs.

Hannah tried them all, including a Bavarian delicatessen. No, no one there was related to Alexander German, the woman said. But had she tried the spa? Sylvia usually was there during the week. Hannah was nonplussed. What spa?

"Bad German, in Desert Hot Springs. Sylvia German runs it," the woman said, as though it was a city landmark that everyone knew.

A receptionist there answered with a cheerful *guten Tag*.

"Ja," the woman said when Hannah asked for Alicia.
"Moment, please."

Alicia answered in a faint, fragile voice. The line went dead
as soon as Hannah spoke her name.

Hannah sat back on the sofa and ran her hands through her
hair. Alicia might not have been alone. German might have
been there, listening. Maybe he was intentionally keeping
Alicia away from her.

She glanced at the clock. Five. She could get there in two
and a half hours.

Just before eight, Hannah pulled into Desert Hot Springs, a
poor man's Palm Springs that drew tourists with the lures of
pure air and healing waters. It got quite a few health nuts, but
the area's biker bars, wide-bodied mobile homes, and cheap,
isolated ranchos also attracted an odd mix of hell-raisers,
sun-addled desert coots, and methamphetamine kooks.

Bad German was a cut above the other spas in town. The
one-story motel, paneled in redwood, was surrounded with
sand verbena, creosote bushes, and palo verde trees. Flood-
lights illuminated the patio and the steaming pools. The spa
was busy, even in the cold desert night.

A man whose belly sagged onto his legs played cards with
his equally corpulent wife under an umbrella heater. Nearby, a
masseur with white-blond hair pummeled a nearly naked man
under the shifting shadows cast by a palm. From the pools
arrayed around the courtyard rose a vapor of East European
accents, Czech or Croat or Hungarian, Hannah guessed.

Alicia Cogburn lolled in the shallows of the largest pool. Her
pale face had turned pink in the steam. As Hannah came closer
she caught a whiff of the water: sulfur, tinged with the tang of
rosemary.

Alicia looked up at Hannah and glanced down again.

"I had to come, Alicia," Hannah said. "I wanted to make sure
you were all right."

Alicia splashed water on her shoulder.

"I'm fine. Go away and leave me alone."

"Alicia, I don't know what your father told you," Hannah
began.

"That he took you out for dinner and you turned on him, like
you did on me. That you're unstable, and you've had at least

one breakdown before. That's why you're not a police officer anymore."

Hannah sat down on the pavement. He worked fast, she thought. Maybe even talked to Churnin.

"I don't suppose your father mentioned that he tried to bribe me? That he threatened me?"

Alicia looked up at her suddenly. Something Hannah said had rung true. She recovered, though.

"If you don't leave, I'll have to call Roland over here to make you leave," she said petulantly.

Roland was the one pounding the flab of the man in the microscopic bathing suit. The man gestured and talked as he lay on his stomach on the massage table. Roland's biceps glistened in the lights and jumped with the effort of kneading the man's shoulders. His eyes made a circuit around the patio and came to rest on Alicia. They shifted to Hannah. He looked at her for a long time, and she could see his mouth forming monosyllabic responses to the man's windy speech.

"Did you send your father to see me, to tell me that I'd upset you?"

"No. Of course not," Alicia said. "I'm not six years old."

"Your father acts like you are," Hannah said.

Alicia's hauteur melted slightly.

"I wish he'd stop," she said.

"He's not going to stop with me, because he has something to hide. I know it, and you know it, too, Alicia."

Alicia wouldn't look up at her. She frowned down at the swirling water. Hannah took out the clipping of Gallagher's courtroom farewell and pointed to Gallagher.

"Who is this?"

Alicia peered at Gallagher's face and slowly shook her head.

"I don't know." She scanned the story. And then she spotted Bradley in the picture's background. Hannah could see her eyes redden. "Why was Bradley there?"

"I don't know," Hannah said. "He'd met Gallagher. I think he believed Gallagher was involved with your father."

"This man's a murderer," Alicia said. "My father doesn't know anyone like that."

"We don't know everything about our parents' lives," Hannah said. "I think your father hid things from you, to protect you. Or he was protecting himself, for fear you'd hate him. I don't know how far he went to make sure that would never happen."

Alicia wiped her eyes and swam to the far side of the large pool, disappearing in the thick billows of steam. She glided back and motioned to the white robe on a chair. Hannah handed it to her as she got out.

"When you asked me where my father was the night Bradley died, something happened inside me," she said. "I'd been so afraid someone would ask me that. I thought if no one did, it would mean everything was all right. That it was just my stupid imagination."

"When I asked, that told you everything was not all right?" Hannah said.

Alicia nodded. "I don't know where my father was," she said. "And he won't tell me."

She had called him at ten-thirty, just before the police showed up at her door. He wasn't home. He'd gone to the fund-raiser for Douglas, but told her he'd be leaving early, by ten.

She called him again, after the police came to tell her about Bradley. No answer. She finally got him on his cellular phone at ten forty-five. Later, when she asked him where he'd been, he told her he'd been having a drink with a friend.

"But he wouldn't tell me who it was," Alicia said. "I couldn't think what to say to that. Bradley and my father did hate each other. And God help me, it was the first thing I thought when they told me Bradley was dead—that he'd confronted my father, and something awful had happened."

"You didn't tell anyone?" Hannah said.

"The police? About my own father? No," she said. "I didn't want to believe it. I just . . . tried to pretend I'd never had the thought. I was getting pretty good at ignoring it. Until you came along."

"Alicia, it might be that your father wasn't involved. But you owe it to yourself to tell the police your suspicions. It's the only way this is going to be resolved. Things don't go away by ignoring them."

Alicia half nodded.

"Can I ask you about one more thing?" Hannah asked.

"Go ahead."

"Do you know someone named Raymond O'Reilly?"

Alicia's face registered surprise and, Hannah thought, fear.

"Of course I do," she said. "He used to manage this place for my aunt."

"Did he know your father?"

Alicia nodded. "He showed up here one day threatening to kill him. That's why he was fired."

27

Alicia had only heard about the confrontation. O'Reilly had shouted about German owing him money. Sylvia thought she saw a gun in O'Reilly's waistband and Roland chased him off. Alexander German told her he didn't know what O'Reilly was talking about and convinced her not to bother calling the police.

"When was this?" Hannah said.

"Two years ago, I think," Alicia said.

"After the Agua Dulce project cratered, and Bradley's father killed himself."

Alicia nodded. "I think O'Reilly lives in the north end of Palm Springs. Sylvia sees him downtown now and then. She's still afraid of him."

Someone called Alicia's name. The women realized they were nearly alone on the patio. It was after ten.

"I need to talk to this guy," Hannah said. She reached into the backpack for the printout of Bradley's files. He kept O'Reilly's name under ROOKED.

"Not tonight," Alicia said, suddenly maternal. "A guy who carries around a gun and threatens people? You're not going there alone in the middle of the night."

And so she didn't. Alicia went behind the desk and got the key for the room next to hers.

Just before eleven, Alicia showed up at her door with a pot of herb tea—and Roland. He looked less frightening up close. He had his massage table with him, but Hannah demurred.

"He has a big towel. You'll be more covered up than you are at the beach," Alicia said.

"It will be good for you," Roland said. The words bobbed with a Nordic cadence. "You are tense, yes?"

"Maybe another time," Hannah said.

Alicia shrugged and unlocked the door to her room. Roland followed her in. Hannah wondered for a moment if Alicia was as wounded and long-suffering as she had assumed. Perhaps Alicia had found her own way of dealing with Bradley's infidelities. Or maybe, Hannah thought, chiding herself for her dirty mind, a massage was just a massage.

In the morning she headed down to Palm Springs. O'Reilly's apartment house was on the windy, unglamorous edge of town. The white stucco was blasted off in places, and the building stood alone amid blocks of blowing sand, scrawny palms, and twisted yucca trees. The water in the apartment pool was thick with fluorescent green algae, and from the sound of it, there was about to be a murder in one of the downstairs apartments. Hannah was glad she'd waited for daylight.

A bloodshot eye was all she saw as the apartment door opened a crack.

"New PO?" croaked a voice. The eye squinted at her.

So he's on probation for something, Hannah thought. This was not surprising.

O'Reilly's mood improved a bit when she told him she wasn't the PO. She was pleased when he stepped outside instead of asking her in.

O'Reilly was a bandy-legged, potbellied runt, shorter than Hannah. His hair hung down his back in a stringy ponytail held by a pink elastic band. They stood on the cracked walkway while O'Reilly rolled a joint and blew its smoke out over the swamp below.

"I heard you were out to get Alexander German a couple years ago," she said.

"Totally righteous beef," O'Reilly said.

"What was the problem?" Hannah said.

"Money."

"For what?" Hannah said.

"Not a cop, right?"

"Right," Hannah said.

"So what are you?"

"A law student. German's son-in-law was killed a few weeks ago. I went to school with him."

"No shit? I knew him."

"I thought you might," Hannah said. "Your name was in his computer. What was going on?"

"Said he'd get my money."

"In return for what?"

"Telling him what I knew."

"Which was what?"

"About my auntie."

"Who's your auntie?" Hannah wondered if the guy ever said more than five words at a time.

"Luz Gomez."

She coaxed the story out of him.

He'd been at his aunt's house one day, before the council voted, and saw German handing her a fat envelope. The next time he saw her, she was buying vodka at a Circle K with a hundred-dollar bill. She gave him one, and told him the lawyer had plenty more.

When she died, O'Reilly had decided there was some good to be salvaged from the sad situation. He'd looked German up and demanded money to keep quiet about the bribe. German offered a grand, and O'Reilly, apparently a man of limited foresight, told him that was plenty.

But a couple years later he came to his senses. German had promised more, but then backed out. O'Reilly made the scene at Sylvia's spa, and then, when German contacted him, he threatened to talk to the police.

Two days later somebody grabbed him as he was coming out of the Elbow Room and beat him black and blue. O'Reilly decided that he was in over his head.

"So you didn't tell the cops about the bribe, or that you'd been beaten up?"

He looked at her as though she was crazy.

"Fuck the cops," Raymond O'Reilly said. All had been quiet until the previous summer. Then Bradley Cogburn called him. O'Reilly had just gotten out of jail for possession. "Didn't know the guy," he said.

Hannah thought of Bradley scrolling through arrest records and probation records at the DA's office. Where had he heard of O'Reilly in the first place? Probably from Alicia recounting the incident at Sylvia's spa.

With a bottle of Jack Daniel's and a sympathetic attitude, Bradley had wheedled the tale out of O'Reilly. At the end, he'd promised he'd get money from German.

"Never came back, though," he said.

"Now you know why," Hannah said.

O'Reilly flicked the roach into the pool and sighed.

"Bummer," he said.

28

Hannah poured a glass of wine and sat down at the library table. Her head was crammed with questions, theories, and snippets of fact. All of them a knotted mess, like bits of yarn and frayed threads carelessly heaped in a basket.

Her body was in no better shape. Her neck was stiff from driving. Her skin felt dry to the point of cracking, thanks to the hour she'd spent on O'Reilly's sandblasted terrace. And her head ached from a two-hour microfilm session at the Palm Springs library, where she had read about the Agua Dulce debacle.

She had had this feeling in investigations before. There was a bone-weariness, as though she'd hiked fifteen miles. But that was nothing compared with the mental ache. It was like having someone pull your brain out through one nostril.

The only consolation was that this stage didn't last forever. Eventually, with enough effort, things could be untangled, sorted, and woven together properly. Then a pattern would emerge. She would be able to see what fit, what didn't, what should be kept, and what could be discarded. She could tie it up with a ribbon and give it to Churnin.

Two hours later she was making notes for herself so her headache would go away, when someone hammered eight times—in the rhythm of Beethoven's Fifth—on her door.

Bobby stood on the landing, a ridiculous smile lighting up his face. He wasn't wearing his glasses, and Hannah would have sworn he was fifteen pounds thinner. That wasn't possible, of course. It had only been four days since she last saw him.

"It happened, Hannah," he said, amazing her further by kissing her smack on the mouth. She smelled beer and realized he was slightly drunk. "It finally happened."

"You've lost your mind?" Hannah said.

"My heart," he said with a flourish, and enveloped her in a hug.

She slid out, got him to sit down, and demanded he explain what the hell he was talking about.

"We went out, Hannah. We had a date—you could certainly call it that. And she asked me."

"Who?" Hannah said. "Catherine?"

He nodded. "I was studying at Rattigan and she was there, too. I just waved at her, but she came over and started talking. And then she asked me if I wanted to go to M'Naghten's. We were there for three hours."

"And a lot of beers," Hannah said.

"I'm fine. I really didn't drink that much. It was so great. She's fantastic. I'm having breakfast with her tomorrow."

Hannah nodded. She'd seen Bobby wax ecstatic about women before, but this was the first time it had been about an encounter that had actually taken place. She tried to keep from smiling. It wouldn't have been fair to deflate Bobby at this point.

He was well into a word-by-word account of the date when the phone rang. First there was silence. Then Hannah could hear the breathing. She hung up.

"Wrong number?" Bobby said.

"A breather," Hannah said.

The phone rang again. Hannah picked the receiver, ready to tell the guy to give it a rest. But the caller spoke first. The voice was low, rough, almost an angry buzz. It rasped her ear. Like the voice on the tape.

She held on to the phone, hearing its echoes. Bobby got up, took the receiver away from her, and listened to the dead line.

"Are you okay?" he said. "Did he say something this time?"

" 'Back off bitch,' " Hannah said.

"Jesus, Hannah, who was it?"

"I don't know. But if he's trying to spook me, it's working."

Before Hannah could say more, Bobby was at the linen

closet, hauling out a blanket and two old pillows. He made up a bed on the sofa.

"I'm staying here, just in case," he said. "If it was Ruiz on the phone, maybe he'll show up. We know he likes to do that."

It wasn't O'Reilly, she thought. She hadn't thought it wise to leave her number with him. But it could have been German. Hannah told Bobby about the dinner and German's threat.

"He knows where I live," she said. "I was stupid to let him pick me up here."

"Hannah, you really should call the cops," he said. "At least call your friend."

She dialed Eddy's beeper number and waited. Bobby sacked out on the sofa and was soon dozing. Every few minutes he'd jerk awake, get up, and do a circuit of the apartment, peering down into the night from every window. Then he'd lie down and go back to sleep.

When Eddy called, she told him what had happened— German, the windshield, Ruiz's veiled threat in the *Appeal,* and the phone call.

"I've got to get Churnin to talk to the witness," she said. "This shouldn't wait. Someone knows I know something. They might find out I know there's a witness."

"The one you told me about?"

"Teddy Czerwinski. He saw everything. He lives on Daley Street, not far from where it happened. He's a kid, like I told you," she said. "Someone's got to hear this tape of his."

"What tape?"

She told him Teddy's story. Eddy took a deep breath.

"Christ," he said. "I'll get hold of Churnin, tell him to come back. If he kicks, I'll interview the kid myself, okay?"

Hannah started to thank him, but found herself crying instead.

"I'm tired," she said. "And I guess the call got to me."

"It's okay. You get yourself some sleep," Eddy said. He sounded tired himself.

She did sleep, but only fitfully. She woke up to every noise—the sofa's squeaks as Bobby turned, a dog yipping in the next yard, a bougainvillea scraping the screen of Mrs. Snow's parlor downstairs.

She got up after seven to find the living room vacant. Bobby had written a note, saying he was off to meet Catherine. He left

Hannah a pot of espresso. She drank it, showered, and dressed. She was locking the door behind her when the phone rang.

It was Eddy. Churnin had grudgingly agreed to come back. The kid could come in on Tuesday morning, early.

"Great," Hannah said.

"After I talked to him, I asked a patrol unit to swing by the kid's house, to make sure nothing was amiss," he said.

"Thank you, Eddy," she said.

"They know this kid," Eddy said.

"From when his dad beat him up?"

"They didn't mention that," Eddy said. "They know Teddy because Teddy likes to run away. He's done it at least a half-dozen times."

"I didn't know that," Hannah said. The news made her uneasy.

"They understood when it was his dad, who was a really nasty drunk, apparently. But he still does it, whenever he and the foster mom disagree. He's apparently kind of a hellion. His old man screwed him up pretty good. Are you sure he's not yanking your chain about this?"

"No. I've heard the tape."

"Okay, Hannah. Just make sure the kid and the tape are here on Tuesday for Churnin," Eddy said. "He's not happy about cutting his trip short."

He hung up abruptly. And that wasn't like him.

29

On Friday morning, Hannah woke up relieved, almost happy. The feeling of lightness, bordering on joy, was unfamiliar. She savored it, and realized why she felt that way.

Yes, someone was stalking her, trying to scare her. But she could deal with that. Bobby was protective, and bulky enough to be intimidating. Besides, she knew how to handle herself. The important thing was that Eddy had convinced Churnin to take her information seriously. When he met Teddy and heard the tape, that would cinch it.

Eddy told her Churnin was upright, so he'd have to admit, despite the wishes of the mayor and chief, that his case against the bum wasn't ironclad. She might have derailed a bogus prosecution. Penance, she thought, and smiled to herself.

With the information Hannah had garnered, Churnin would have a choice of suspects. She ran the list through her mind. Everybody but Bobby, she concluded. And herself, of course, rumors notwithstanding. Soon enough, all that would be Churnin's problem. She had a disciplinary hearing to think about.

The committee set the hearing date for the end of the month. The Parson had called to say she could review the administration's evidence on Thursday.

Hannah knew what she'd find—the brief Bradley had purchased, the way he'd have bought a tie. She wondered if he'd bought his own death along with it. Again, a problem for Churnin.

Hannah decided her defense before the disciplinary committee would be simple. She was going to tell them the truth. She had the evidence ready. Alicia had sent her a copy of Bradley's bank statement, showing the wire transfer of $1,500 to the account number in Bradley's PAWN file. She would give all of that to the committee. Let Ruiz try to explain it away, if he could.

But she still didn't have a paper trail to prove that sections of the brief were really hers. The committee would wonder why she couldn't show them her earlier drafts and research. Goddamn Bradley, she thought. He had said he'd found her disk. Had he lied about that, too?

She was certain she hadn't missed it, or any printout he made of it, in her searches of his car, his desk at the *Law Review*, or the Laguna apartment. Alicia had gone through the Newport house a second time at Hannah's request, but turned up nothing. Bradley was a keeper, Alicia told her. He didn't throw things away.

Keeping, Hannah thought. She suddenly saw Bradley, old as Emma Snow, awash in a sea of briefs he hadn't written, tests he'd purloined.

The picture jolted her memory. She suddenly knew where her lost notes were. They weren't the best ones, but anything would be better than the nothing she had.

On the day the moot-court topic was assigned, she had gone to the library, planted herself at a WESTLAW terminal, logged on, and stayed logged on even as she scoured the stacks. She emerged hours later with twelve or thirteen pages of notes outlining the law that she'd have to cover in her research. They were in a spiral notebook. Not a new one, but just one she'd had floating around in her backpack.

And when she got home, she'd used the same notebook to scribble estimates for an air conditioner. She brought it downstairs to Mrs. Snow and was about to tear out the pages, but Mrs. Snow said she'd only lose them. So Hannah gave her the whole notebook, telling herself that it would be impossible to mislay a book with a neon-orange cover.

Hannah ran down the stairs and pressed the doorbell. Inside, she could hear the tubular chimes' hollow ring and Emma Snow's shambling walk.

She shook her head at first.

"Oh dear, that was months ago, wasn't it? I wouldn't have any idea where that book was now."

"Can I look, Mrs. Snow? It's important."

"It's probably there somewhere," She pointed Hannah toward the kitchen.

Every square inch of floor space was stacked to shoulder height with newspapers and magazines. Mrs. Snow had left narrow aisles leading to the sink, stove, and kitchen table. There, one of the four chairs was clear of debris. Mrs. Snow's packrat problem had clearly grown worse in the last six weeks.

Hannah began the search at the sprouting heaps on the kitchen table. She promised any listening deity that she'd help Mrs. Snow clean up, if only she could find the damn notebook.

The prayer was answered. An orange cover peeped out from a stack of ancient *Arizona Highways* magazines on the floor.

She thanked Mrs. Snow and kissed her on the forehead.

"It's a good thing I don't throw anything out," Mrs. Snow said defiantly.

Hannah smiled at her. "Today, Mrs. Snow, I have to agree with you," she said.

Hannah caught herself smiling again as she parked the Hyundai at school. So far it had been a good day. Almost magically blessed. Maybe that was the grace that came after penance. She remembered a drawing from the Baltimore Catechism—grace pouring down like rain from the billowing cloud that surrounded a dove—the guise of the Holy Spirit.

But within an hour Hannah's joy ended. All it took was Lois Popich leaning in the door of the *Law Review* office and crooking her finger at Hannah. Her skin was tinged pink and her blond hair was noticeably lighter. They must have spent hours at the beach Sunday, Hannah thought.

"If you have a few minutes, Miss Barlow, the dean would like to see you," Lois said.

Her first thought was that Lois and Weiss had seen her. But Lois seemed marble cold, as always. If she knew they'd been found out, would she be so calm? Hannah wondered how much of an actress Lois really was. She followed her to the administration building.

Lois tapped Weiss's door and swung it open. Weiss motioned

Hannah to sit down. He walked behind the desk, folded his arms, and frowned down at her.

"Miss Barlow, I have to say that I am dismayed at having to call you here again."

"I have the feeling I'm not going to be happy about it either, Dean Weiss."

"You have a stolen criminal-law-examination outline in your possession," he said.

Hannah felt like she'd been hit by lightning. How did Weiss know? Dove could have told him, but why would she? Could Alicia have told German, and he told Weiss? Jesus, Hannah thought, I've been so stupid.

"I found it in Bradley Cogburn's car, after he died," she said. "He used it to cheat on the final."

"And what did you intend to do about it? When were you going to bring it to the school's attention?" Weiss asked.

He had her. What was she going to say? That she was going to use it to smoke Weiss out?

"I think it was part of Bradley's pattern of cheating," she said. "I intended to use it at the plagiarism hearing."

"It will indeed be discussed at your hearing," Weiss said. "As another possible honor-code violation."

"This is outrageous."

"Is it? I have no way of knowing who used this outline. You say you found it in Bradley Cogburn's car. You say he used it. You say that he was a habitual cheat. All of that is certainly possible, but there is perhaps another explanation."

Hannah clasped her hands in her lap. Her fingers were numb with cold. She knew where he was going, but she had to hear him say it.

"And what is that explanation?" she said.

"We will subpoena your final examination, and if it reflects possession of this outline, the matter will also be referred to the discipline committee."

"That's crazy," Hannah began.

"Is it? If you found the exam, as you say, why didn't you report it? Reporting it wouldn't preclude you from using it as evidence."

Hannah couldn't answer him. Maybe he knew that she suspected him of giving Bradley the exam. He might even know that she'd found out about Lois. But he had the upper hand at the moment. She couldn't prove he'd given Bradley the test. He could, however, make her look like the thief. Why else hadn't she reported a stolen test to the administration?

But she had told Dove. She wondered if Dove would vouch for her. No, Hannah realized with disgust. If Dove had given Bradley the test, she would do anything to steer the investigation away from her. Aiming the disciplinary apparatus at Hannah would be the easiest way to accomplish that.

"You can go now," Weiss was saying. "The formal complaint will be mailed today." He sat down and began squaring up papers on his already immaculate desk.

Hannah grasped the arms of the visitor's chair and got up. Her palms were damp, as though all the ice of a moment ago had melted.

In the outer office, Lois typed briskly. Hannah caught a glance of the text on the screen. It was the complaint.

"Twice in one month," Lois said under her breath. "I'm shocked."

Hannah was at the door, her hand on the knob. She knew she should let the remark pass. But she couldn't help herself.

"Oh, I understand. You're so shocked you're blushing," she said mockingly, looking at Lois over her shoulder.

Lois looked up, surprised.

"I thought it was sunburn," Hannah said. "Fair-skinned people like us should avoid the beach. It can get us into trouble."

Lois's face turned a shade redder. She looked quickly away and began typing again. Hannah had never heard a student talk to her that way. No one except Bradley, teasing her about a hall pass. He'd put her in her place.

Hannah slammed the door so hard that the glass rattled. She was sure the noise had made Lois jump. And somehow, that made her feel better.

30

Hannah met Teddy on the deserted patio of Serrano's in Santa Ana that afternoon. The lunch crowd had cleared out hours before. As Hannah talked about meeting Churnin, Teddy nibbled at a chili burger and seemed more brooding than usual. He watched the cars on Grand Avenue and the steady traffic of women and children into the *lavandería* behind the taco stand.

"Teddy, what's wrong?" Hannah said.

"Nothing," he said.

"He's okay, Teddy. Just a detective who wants to make sure he solves his case. Up until now, he's been on the wrong track."

Teddy looked up at her.

"What wrong track?"

"A homeless guy found one of Bradley's credit cards. The detective thinks he robbed Bradley and then killed him."

Teddy ran his fingers over his lips.

"What is it?" Hannah said.

"Nothing," he said, too quickly.

Hannah bit into the *carne asada* burrito, wiped a trickle of sauce from her chin, and waited. Nudging Teddy did no good. She watched him as he bit his lip and twisted his hands in his lap.

"I'm not doing it," he said finally. "Forget it."

"Teddy, come on. What's wrong?" Hannah said.

"I don't want to do this," Teddy said. "You tell them what happened."

"It's not the same, Teddy," she said. "They want to talk to you, and hear the tape. Please, Teddy. This is important."

"Okay," he said. "All right."

She didn't know why Teddy was suddenly so touchy. But now that she knew he ran away—and not just from her—she had to be careful with him.

"You told Monty, didn't you?" Hannah said.

"Stop bugging me," he said. He got up suddenly. "I'm not a baby, okay? I said I'll be there, I'll be there."

"Okay," Hannah said. "You know that this is something important. Give me your number, just in case, all right?"

He impatiently reeled it off, got on his bike, and pedaled away, glancing back at her once.

She'd seen that vacant expression at her apartment. It was as though the real Teddy was already gone, leaving behind only his skinny body to pump the bike and his empty eyes to stare back at her. A frightening premonition swept her: she would never see him again.

When she got home, she dialed the number he'd given her. The Oklahoma drawl of the man who answered told her all she needed to know. Teddy had given her the number for Hobby Junction.

On Saturday, she drove to the Candyland house early, and waited. Teddy's bike wasn't behind the gate. Lights burned in a room toward the back of the house. Through the window, Hannah saw a glimpse of kitchen shelves crowded with bric-a-brac.

She was getting out of the car when Monty eased her way out the front door and down three concrete steps to the yard. She paused for a moment on each one, catching her breath. Then she stooped slowly, picked up a hose and began watering the lawn.

"Monty?" Hannah said.

She turned and glared up at Hannah. Up close, she was older than Hannah had thought. Seventy, not sixty. The pink tint in her hair had faded. Now it was the color of dirty ice and so thin that Hannah could see her scalp below it. A few lashes were left around her rheumy blue eyes. She was wearing a flowered housecoat and pink slippers. Her ankles were swollen, traced with blue veins.

"You selling something?" She said. "Take it on out of here, missy. I'm not buying."

Hannah shook her head.

"I came to introduce myself. And to talk about Teddy."

"What about Teddy?" Monty said. "Now, right off I know you're not his teacher, or the principal. We're real well acquainted. New social worker? You should have called me first."

"No, no," Hannah said. Damn it, Teddy hadn't told her anything. "I'm a friend of Teddy's."

Her eyes bored into Hannah. She put down the hose.

"Oh. And you're Russell's latest 'friend,' too, I reckon. You don't dress trashy like the other ones, I'll give you that."

Hannah's exasperation eased slightly. The old gal was feisty.

"Look. I assume Russell is Teddy's dad. I don't know him."

Monty shrugged.

"But thanks for the fashion assessment," Hannah said. The corners of the old woman's mouth turned up.

"Is Teddy around?" Hannah said.

"Off to the yards," Monty said. "Like usual."

"We have to talk about something important," Hannah said.

Monty looked at her for a long moment, and finally beckoned her inside.

The shelves of knickknacks were not confined to the kitchen. Every wall of the living room was taken up with them, packed as tight as steerage berths. Indeed, Hannah felt like she was standing on the lower deck of Noah's ark. The shelves were crammed with hundreds of animal-shaped salt-and-pepper shakers. Pottery pairs of cats. Porcelain pairs of dogs. Glass penguins, salt in their bellies and pepper in their wings. Stoneware seals and clay raccoons. Even a pair of crystal unicorns.

Hannah sat down on the sofa, uninvited. Monty planted herself in the middle of the room, her hands on her hips.

"You had better tell me what's going on," she said. Her voice was thin as the glassware around her. Hannah could hear the crack and the imminent shatter.

It took a half hour. At first, Hannah thought Monty was hard of hearing, or in early-stage Alzheimer's. She insisted Hannah go over things again and again. Who she was. How she met Teddy. What he saw that night.

Finally Hannah realized Monty wasn't senile or deaf. She was trying to catch her in a lie. Canny old thing, Hannah thought.

"I know this sounds bizarre," Hannah said. "I'm telling you exactly what happened. I don't know why Teddy didn't tell you."

Monty sat back in an upholstered chair, its fabric shiny from the rub of the woman's back. She lit a thin brown cigarette.

"I only do this when he's not here," she said conspiratorially. "He gets after me." She blew out the smoke with pleasure.

"No surprise that Teddy didn't tell me. The child has seen a lot: his father, drunk and high, beating on his mother, on him. He don't talk about it. Thinks all that's his fault." She pulled a tin ashtray out from the seat cushion and tapped the cigarette on its edge. "When bad things happen, Teddy hangs on to 'em. Blames himself. So, seeing someone die, well, I'm flat-out stunned he told you anything. He runs, 'stead of talking."

"He did run, at first," Hannah said. "And I'm afraid he'll do it again. I think I pushed him too hard."

"It doesn't take much," Monty said. "He thinks they'll take him back."

"Back where?"

"The children's home. It's not a bad place. It's just the neighborhood."

"I don't understand," Hannah said.

"The social worker told me. It came out at the hearing, when they decided the county should keep him. Nobody has been able to convince Teddy it's not the God's truth," Monty said.

"Teddy lived with his dad for a while, after his mom run out on them both. When he did something bad, Russell would beat him and then tell him that someday just thrashing him wouldn't be enough. Someday he'd have to tell the police what a purely evil boy he was, and they'd put him in one of the places on the riverbank." Monty raised her eyebrows at her. "You get it?"

Hannah frowned. "No," she said. "Go on."

"If he was bad at the first place, the children's home, he'd be moved down the line, through some secret tunnel. And if you were bad, bad, bad, way down the line, then there was the last place and the special chamber that sucked out all your air so's you'd die. He told Teddy he would wind up there, and no one would ever know what became of him."

She dragged on the cigarette. "The bastard. Now do you know what Russell was talking about?"

Hannah nodded. The county had lined a stretch of the Santa Ana River with its places of confinement: the children's shelter, juvenile hall, a men's jail, and finally, the animal shelter with its euthanizing chamber. It was cruelly ingenious. Russell could drive Teddy there, point out the buildings to him, giving his story enough truth to make the terror stick.

"Then he won't come to the cops," Hannah said. "There's no way he'll come."

"Don't you worry. We'll be there Tuesday," Monty said. "I know how to get Teddy places he don't want to go."

The second disciplinary complaint from Douglas was waiting when Hannah got home. She read it almost mechanically, without the feeling of sick panic that the first complaint evoked. She couldn't believe she found a cheating accusation routine. But now it was.

On Monday, everyone at school seemed to know about the second allegation. The gossip was not just that there was another charge. Now the subtext was that if there were two instances of alleged cheating, Hannah must really have done something wrong.

It was as though everyone assumed she'd be expelled— Douglas's version of the death penalty. Harrison Onizaki told her he'd scheduled another article for the capital-punishment issue. Her piece could go into the next volume.

"If things work out," he said.

Hannah nodded curtly at him and left the office.

Bobby caught up with her just after that exchange, looked dolefully into her eyes, and asked in a hushed voice if there was anything she needed.

"What, a last meal? A call from the governor?" she snapped. "Jesus, Bobby, you know I didn't do anything. Don't treat me like that!"

Bobby wisely retreated to the nearest classroom and left Hannah alone to fume.

By noon, the solicitous looks and the whispered conversations were too much. She headed for the parking lot.

Halfway across the Rattigan lawn, she heard someone calling

her name. Guillermo Agustin was waving at her, motioning her back.

"Rough day," he said.

Hannah nodded. "Awful."

"Look, there's a lot of stuff buzzing on the rumor network, but I'm sure you had nothing to do with Kennedy, Watergate, or IranContra."

Hannah had to smile. He was terrific.

"I just wanted you to know that if you need a character witness, someone to talk about your hard work and unassailable honesty, I'd be happy to do it," he said.

"Thank you, Professor," Hannah said.

"And if you need to bail out of here for a few days, I can give you my outline for the stuff we're going to cover Wednesday and Friday."

He handed her a note. "Take this to the gals in word processing. They have my stuff on disk. They can spit it out for you in no time."

Hannah looked at the note in her hand. The ground under her feet seemed to be giving away. *The gals in word processing.* She looked up, saw Agustin staring at her.

"Thanks again," she said.

Agustin smiled. "I've got to get back for office hours. You're okay?"

She nodded and looked at the note again. *The gals in word processing can spit it out in no time.*

She thought about the scarf she'd found at Bradley's apartment and nearly groaned at her own stupidity. It was pink—not red, not emerald green.

If she hadn't jumped to a conclusion about the damn scarf and if she'd realized that Dove was like every other professor, using word processing for her outlines and tests, she would have seen it so much sooner. Now she knew how Bradley got the criminal-law final. And she was furious at herself for not realizing it before.

31

The white Metro lurched through the late-afternoon traffic on the Pacific Coast Highway. Every now and then Hannah lost sight of it. But it didn't matter. She knew where Lois was going.

The compact swung into a parking place just north of the pier. Lois got out. Her hair was loose and it blew in the wind that rose off the water. She shrugged on a white wool coat and walked down the pier. Hannah followed her.

The sun was low on the horizon, pressed down by coils of low clouds. A half-dozen surfers plied the water around the pier, seal sleek in their black wet suits. The thought of the icy water made Hannah shiver.

Lois was pacing the width of the pier. She hugged herself against the cold and occasionally glanced at the street as she walked. She didn't see Hannah. She pushed back her sleeve and looked at her watch.

"He's late, isn't he?" Hannah said.

Lois turned on her heel. A spasm of panic passed over her face.

"What do you want?" she said.

"To talk to you. About some secrets you've been keeping."

Lois shrugged unconvincingly. "The marriage is over. He's moved out. We've got nothing to hide."

"Maybe not—not the two of you. People understand that marriages fail," Hannah said. "But you have secrets from the dean, don't you?"

Lois crossed her arms and glared. "Get to the point."

Hannah reached into her backpack and pulled out the pink silk scarf. It fluttered prettily in the breeze, like the tail of an elegant kite.

At the sight of it, Lois put her hand over her mouth. Then she grabbed for the scarf.

"Give it back," she snarled.

"When I found it, I thought it belonged to someone else," Hannah said. "But she's dark-haired. She wears red and green—primary colors. She would never wear something this pale. But for a blonde, like you, it's just right."

"You want me to get Frederick to stop the hearing, isn't that it?" Lois said.

Hannah shook her head.

"I'm not Bradley. I'm not going to play games like that. I just want to know what happened. You and Bradley had an affair, right?"

The wind was whipping Lois's hair across her face. It covered her eyes and mouth in a latticework of golden strands. Lois glared through the web for a moment before she gave Hannah a tight nod.

"You worked in word processing then. How long after you started sleeping with him did he ask for Dove's criminal-law final?"

She didn't answer.

"Lois, there's no point in lying about this," Hannah said. "It's obvious."

Lois sighed and hugged the white coat closer to her body.

"He never really asked for it," she said. "He didn't have to."

"Why was that?" Hannah said.

"He told me about his father, and German, and all the work he was doing to make sure German didn't get away with what he had done. It was serious work for Bradley—every weekend, when he told Alicia he was studying, he was in that apartment, poring over his father's files and journals, trying to find people who knew what really happened."

"Amazing he had time for you," Hannah said.

"He told me he could talk to me about things he couldn't tell Alicia. She wouldn't hear anything bad about her father."

"And you saw that he would fall behind at school. So you stole him a test?"

She shook her head.

"It wasn't like that, exactly. I saw he wasn't studying. I knew he'd be in trouble. So I got him Dove's outline. There was no harm in that. It wasn't a secret document. I thought it would help him. But when I gave it to him, he just kind of fell apart."

"How do you mean?"

"He acted really upset. It was acting, I see that now," she said. "Anyway, he told he'd need more than an outline to pass the class. He'd need a miracle, or he'd have to quit school. And that meant he'd never inherit the business. German would get away with his father's death. It meant the end of everything, he said."

"He let you fill in what that really meant," Hannah said.

She nodded again. "So I got the test for him."

"And then everything was wonderful."

Lois shook her head and clenched her eyes shut.

"And then everything was shit," she said. "When the semester ended, he told me it was over."

"Just like that?"

"Like he'd paid me by the hour," she said. "It was awful. But I managed to make it worse. I went back to him a month later. Pleaded with him to take me back. I asked him how he was going to get through second year without my help. Without my love is what I meant." She wiped her eyes. Mascara and pearly shadow came off on her hand.

"But that's not how Bradley took it. He thought I was talking about getting outlines and tests for him. He told me I was too much trouble. He'd found a better way to get what he needed."

"What was that?" Hannah said.

"Fear."

32

"Who was afraid? Was it German?" Hannah said.

Lois shook her head. "I don't know." She looked anxiously at her watch and then at Hannah. "He'll be here any second," she said. "Please just leave."

"Bradley could have meant you—that he didn't need to sweet-talk you anymore. He had information that could cost you your job."

"It wasn't me. He'd moved on. But he did let me know that if I tried to expose him, he'd turn it all around on me. I knew I was vulnerable, particularly after I began to see Frederick."

"When was that?"

"September. I'd worked with him for a month or so."

"Does he know about you and Bradley?" Hannah said.

"Yes," she said. "I told him."

"But not about the exam."

"No, of course not," Lois said.

"How did he find out I had the exam?"

"I don't know. I think someone called him, Wednesday or Thursday."

"He doesn't even suspect that you stole it for Bradley?"

"He did. He asked me, last night," Lois said. "I swore to him that it wasn't me."

"So you lied to him."

"I had to lie," she said. "He would never have forgiven me. He's a scrupulously honest man."

She didn't realize the web she was weaving for herself. Hannah didn't say anything for a moment.

"What else happened with Bradley?" she asked.

Lois looked at her strangely.

"Nothing else happened," she said. "He used me, he threw me away. He was ruthless about it."

"Bradley's dead, Lois," Hannah said.

Lois stared at her for a moment. She seemed genuinely amazed.

"I had nothing to do with that," she said.

"What if Bradley told Weiss that you'd stolen the exam and threatened to expose you? Wouldn't Weiss have protected you? Maybe that was why Bradley didn't get expelled for plagiarism."

"I don't think Frederick would do that," she said.

"Then why else would he go easy on Bradley?" Hannah said.

"I don't know," she said.

"What else did Bradley try to wring out of Weiss, before Weiss struck back?"

"Frederick couldn't hurt anyone," Lois said. "And I'm telling you, if he knew I'd stolen that test, it would be over between us."

"You might be underestimating his feelings," Hannah said.

Lois shook her head. "I can't think about this. It's frightening me."

"Where was Weiss, that Friday?" Hannah said.

"With me," Lois said. "At a hotel."

Hannah remembered the valet parking tag in her car, from the Creston. "Not all night," she said. "He was at a fund-raiser."

"For a few hours. He got away for a while, to see me," she said. "It was our four-month anniversary."

"There should be witnesses, then, someone at the hotel who saw him, who saw you."

Lois pressed her fingers to her lips. Her hands were white, shaking.

"I registered. But Frederick tries to be discreet. So many people know him. The hotel is so close to school."

"You should think hard about who might have seen him,"

Hannah said. "It's information you're both going to need. Soon."

"But we didn't do anything." Lois looked over Hannah's shoulder to the highway. "Oh, God."

A Volvo station wagon squealed to a stop, its tire bouncing off the curb. Weiss bounded out of the car and then jerked himself back into a casual stride. He waved to Lois.

She moaned. It was a harsh, painful sound.

"For God's sake," she said to Hannah. "You're not going to tell him all this, are you?"

Hannah wanted to say something to her. Lois had been badly used by Bradley. But she could be lying. She could be protecting Weiss. So Hannah forced herself to stay silent. She walked to the pier's railing, turned to the water, and pulled up the hood of her sweatshirt to hide her face and hair.

She glanced back and saw Weiss gather Lois in his arms.

He kissed her, his eyes closed and his face taut with desire, as though this was all he wanted from life. He opened his eyes, saw the smeared makeup and the dampness on Lois's cheeks. There was a question on his lips, as intense as the kiss had been.

Lois shook her head and smiled. She pulled his face to hers, kissed him deeply, and turned his back on Hannah.

Hannah slipped away. She looked back once as she got to the highway.

Weiss was gazing up at the sky, almost reverently. Maybe he thinks he sees grace pouring down, Hannah thought. He smiled out at the sea, and back at Lois, the woman he loved, who held him to her with a thread of deceit.

33

Hannah wove her way through the maze of mini-offices in the Las Almas Police Department's robbery-homicide division on Tuesday morning. Memories rushed at her from every corner. She could almost see the parade of cops, victims, and suspects that had made up her life then. The room was the same, but the faces she saw around her were utterly different. She recognized only a secretary and one detective. Churnin hadn't been the only change in the past three years.

She found Eddy's cubicle, the one farthest from the door. The cubbyhole next to it still contained a battered steel desk about the size of a Volkswagen. It had been her office, if you could call the four metal-and-fabric dividers an office. When she worked there, the top of the desk had resembled a Mayan ruin: the listing, stepped pyramids of reports towered over ceremonial avenues lined with pencils and pens. A hapless fly occasionally sacrificed itself in the cenote of day-old coffee. In short, it had been a mess. But she had known where everything was, and she'd done good work there.

She could guess at the character of the desk's new user from the immaculate blotter and rectilinear tower of letter trays: orderly but rigid. More concerned with appearance than substance. Prone to trimming out messy facts to avoid upsetting certain tidy theories.

The report on the bum's arrest sat squarely in the center of the blotter.

"Churnin around?" she said over her shoulder to the secretary.

She shook her head. "He's coming in from John Wayne. And Eddy will be right back. He said to make yourself at home."

Hannah sat down and skimmed the report. The bum had a name: Ballard Goodacre. A record, too: armed robbery, assault, and manufacture of methamphetamine, more than ten years ago. More recently he'd done some time at Metropolitan State Hospital. A judge deemed him incompetent to face trial for assault on another urban settler.

The summary of his interview was there. Goodacre told Churnin he found the American Express gold card on Saturday afternoon in some bushes, about a mile from the place where Bradley had died the night before. He'd been collecting cans, and there it was, he said. He claimed to have been in his plastic-tarp tent at Pico Creek when Bradley died, but none of his neighbors remembered seeing him.

Hannah heard someone kick open the squad-room door and stood up to see Eddy's entrance. He balanced a tray on three fingers and swept down the row of desks like a snooty headwaiter.

Hannah squared up Churnin's report and tried not to look guilty. Eddy seemed unconcerned about her snooping and ushered her into his cubicle.

He put down the tray, which held a dented gray thermos and two SWAT-team mugs, and poured out the coffee with a flourish. Hannah sipped it. Irish cream.

"And it's Tuesday, too," she said, laughing. "Perfect."

"For old time's sake," he said. "For my favorite FNG."

When she first made detective, it was onto an all-male squad. They taped a list of rules for the FNG—Fucking New Guy—onto her desk. Rule number one: Come in every day for the first month at seven A.M. and make coffee. Rule number two: It couldn't be just any coffee. There was a set menu: Columbian on Monday, Irish Cream on Tuesday, Sumatra on Wednesday, and so on. Rule number three: She was responsible for buying good coffee. Fresh ground from Diedrich was preferred, but Starbucks was okay, too. Demerits were handed out if she dared bring some supermarket vacuum can.

Hannah had fumed silently. Make coffee for a month? Eddy,

then her new partner, took her aside and told her not to take it personally.

"They had me shine shoes for a month," he said. "It's a test, and I'm telling you that if you pull any feminist shit with these guys, they'll make your life hell."

"Okay. I'll be a good little Betty Crocker," Hannah said.

Like hell, she thought.

She arrived at seven the next day, armed with fresh-ground Irish Cream. She measured out ten ounces of water and dumped in fifteen scoops of coffee. Strong enough to blast them out of their chairs, she thought. Café à l'IRA.

At the end of a week she found a gold-sealed certificate on her desk.

"You're off probation, and don't make coffee again," Eddy told her that day. "The EPA says sludge like that has to be stored in a low-level nuclear waste dump. We don't have one in Las Almas."

Hannah smiled to herself, remembering that day. It had bonded her with the guys, and particularly with Eddy.

"You know, some people still think you made that lousy coffee on purpose," Eddy said as he poured her second cup. He wiggled his ridiculous mustache at her.

"Really? Me?" Hannah said.

The doors at the end of the squad room banged open again and Churnin strode in, a bulging garment bag hitched over his shoulder. He dropped it next to the immaculate desk and leaned over the divider to smile coldly at Hannah.

"See what a dedicated public servant I am, Miss Barlow?" he said. "You insult me, tell me I don't know how to do my job, imply that I'm cooking up evidence, and yet I come from across the country when you call."

He'd said nothing about Alicia, Hannah noticed. She was sure that if Alicia had called him, he would have flatly refused to come back, no matter what Eddy told him. Alicia had apparently decided she didn't want to open a discussion with the police about her father or his whereabouts the night Bradley was killed.

"If your bum robbed Bradley, where are the other credit cards?" Hannah said.

"He could have sold them," Churnin said.

"But no one has tried to use them," Hannah said.

"No," Churnin said.

"Where's the wallet? You didn't find it at your guy's camp, did you?"

Churnin looked down at his desk and didn't answer.

"You didn't come back because of me," Hannah said. "You came back because these things began to bug you, and you're enough of a cop to know something's not right. You know Teddy is a lead that needs following."

"Oh, Ms. Barlow, I'm all squishy and warm now," Churnin said.

"Hey, Ivan. Go easy, huh?" Eddy said, holding out a cup of coffee to him. Churnin shot him a disgusted glance and disappeared below the divider.

Eddy put the cup down and shrugged to Hannah. It embarrassed her to see him fawning and scraping to Churnin.

"Look, I've got an appointment," Eddy said. "Can I leave you two alone without fear of mayhem?"

From his cubicle, Churnin mumbled assent. Hannah nodded. Eddy picked up his mug and left.

Hannah looked at her watch. Eight-fifteen.

"Where's this witness?" Churnin said, standing up. He rested his elbow on the divider and looked down at her.

"He'll be here."

"Sure he will," Churnin said.

By eight-thirty, Hannah was sure he wouldn't be. She stood up and glanced over at Churnin, who was hunched over a trash can, idly trimming his nails with the scissors of a Swiss Army knife.

"I'll call and see what's going on," Hannah said.

"Good idea," Churnin said coolly.

Hannah punched in the real phone number, which Monty had supplied Saturday. No one answered.

"I should have picked them up myself," Hannah said.

"Right," Churnin said. "And you could have brought along Santa Claus and the tooth fairy."

"I'm going over there. Perhaps you'd better come, too."

"Oh, no. I'll let you handle this," he said. "But tell me. This purported tape. Why didn't the kid give it to you? Why didn't you just make a copy of it?"

"He wouldn't let me."

Churnin's eyes widened. "Big, threatening kid, is he?"

"He's a child who doesn't trust adults. I was trying not to scare him off."

"And you've done a great job. But there is a tape, right?"

"Yes," Hannah said. "I've heard it."

"And this kid—it's Teddy, right?"

"Right."

"Not Janie?"

Hannah felt her cheeks burning.

"That's not funny."

"But you are." He stood up and crossed his arms. He was smiling a wide, ugly grin at her. "I can't believe Eddy went out on a limb for a nutcase like you. Particularly since he doesn't have much limb left. But I got it figured now. This is more than old-partner loyalty. You must be fucking him on a regular basis."

Hannah wanted nothing more than to dump her coffee on Churnin's head. But that would be the irrationality Churnin wanted to see. Instead, she put the mug down and left without a word. She could hear Churnin snickering behind her, but she wouldn't look back at him.

When Hannah pulled up, Monty was pacing her yard. Rather, Monty took a step, winced at the pain in her arthritic knees, pivoted, and winced again. Hannah could see she had been crying.

"Monty, where is he?" Hannah said.

"He ran," she said. "I was going to call you, but I hoped he'd come back. I'm so damn mad at myself."

"It's okay," Hannah said. "But he ran, right? Nobody grabbed him?"

"Run off on his own," she said. "I was trying to tell him there was nothing to worry about and I usually can do that, like I told you. But this time he wouldn't listen. He wouldn't talk to me. He just took off on his bike."

"I think we should call the police," Hannah said.

Monty nodded. "They're not going to be much help. We've been through this before."

"This time is different," Hannah said.

In the kitchen, Hannah could hear Monty talking to the emergency operator.

"It's not like the last time," she said. "Or the time before that."

Apparently, Eddy hadn't exaggerated when he said the whole department knew about Teddy's disappearing acts.

Monty put her hand over the phone. "Honey," she said to Hannah, "what's that detective's name?"

Churnin wouldn't be any help, Hannah thought. She bit her lip for a second.

"Have them page Detective Eddy." Hannah would have to call and tell him what had happened. But she didn't know what had happened. Teddy had been fine with the idea of talking to the police at first. It all changed after she told him the cops had a suspect in custody. Why had that frightened him?

"No," Monty was saying to the operator. "Teddy didn't make this up." She paused, listened, and then rolled her eyes. "I know he did, that time. This is different."

Great, Hannah thought. Now I find that Teddy not only runs away, but makes up stories, too. He couldn't have made up the tape. The tape, she thought.

Monty dropped into one of the easy chairs with a disgusted wheeze and reached for her cigarettes. The match bobbed and shook as she tried to put it to the tip.

"They'll put out the call, but they're 'noting that he's a habitual runaway,'" she said scornfully. "Some help that will be. I can tell you some places you should go looking for him."

"Do you mind if I look around Teddy's room first?" Hannah said.

Monty opened the door to a place so neat that Hannah doubted a real child could inhabit it. Books were arranged from tallest to smallest on the shelves. The pictures of locomotives, cabooses, and boxcars had been cut from magazines, matted, and then framed in plastic shadow boxes. A trainman's lantern, surrounded by timetables and rail-company stock certificates, hung over a table railroad layout.

It took a moment, but Hannah recognized old Las Almas. Teddy had re-created it on a slab of particle board. A white-gloved policeman stood at an intersection to direct traffic.

Hannah reached down to touch him and saw that he was standing in front of a tiny version of the Douglas campus. She imagined minuscule law professors inside, ranting at invasion of the Hand, not allowed in a C-2 zone.

To the right, what would have been west, was a model of the Coast Daylight, the size of her little finger. It sat on a minuscule siding, surrounded by a crowd of tiny plastic people. A red plastic woman and a white boy stood somewhat apart. Hannah realized he'd not only created a place, but a moment: the morning when she found him and he hadn't run from her. Tears unexpectedly stung her eyes. She wiped them and turned to Monty.

"Do you keep the room clean like this?" Hannah said.

Monty shook her head. "He does. Hates to see a thing out of place."

He controls this, Hannah thought. Everything else outside might be going to hell, but Teddy creates his worlds and keeps them well ordered.

Hannah picked up three cassettes from one of three plastic boxes on his desk.

"U28 B, Paris, Kentucky; EMD F7A, West Detroit, Michigan," Hannah read from the labels. "What does all this mean?"

"Those are locomotives, and the places where the sounds were recorded," Monty said. "Teddy gets them by swapping with other rail fans."

The tape could be among them, mislabeled on purpose. But there were dozens of cassettes. It would take too long to listen to them all.

"If he was going to hide something this size, where do you think he'd put it?" Hannah said, showing Monty the cassette.

"I don't know his hiding places," she said. "He's secretive as a little squirrel. But I saw him stick his Christmas money in one of those." She nodded to the shelf of train videos. There were fifteen or twenty of them, with titles like "Western Pacific," "Steam on Saluda" and "Challenger #3895." Hannah opened them all, but found only videotapes.

Monty watched Hannah rifle through the closet and desk drawers. Hannah flipped through a couple of the thicker books, thinking he might have hollowed one out for the tape. But she found nothing.

Hannah looked at the bed. Perfect hospital corners. Sheet and blanket tucked tight under the mattress.

"Do you make the bed?"

"Heck no," Monty said. "I can't bend like I used to. He does it."

Hannah knelt next to the bed. Monty told her Teddy hung on to his secrets. Held fast his faults. All tucked away inside.

Hannah lifted the mattress and ran her hand between it and the box spring, feeling nothing at first but the muslin covers. And then she touched something soft and pliant. Something folded in half. She slid out a black ostrich wallet and opened it.

Bradley smiled in his driver's-license picture. His Douglas library card was in one of the plastic sleeves, backed by a video-rental card. But the wallet was otherwise empty. No credit cards or cash.

She tried to imagine what had happened: the killer emptied the wallet and Teddy found it and kept it. Or Teddy found the wallet, threw out the money and plastic, and Ballard Goodacre found them. Or Teddy gave it to Goodacre. But if it was any of those things, why hadn't he just told her about it? If it was something innocent, why had he run?

She slid out the library card. There was something behind it—a rectangle of light green paper, folded into fourths.

Hannah opened it. She saw the name, the date, the amount, and the signature in one glance.

She blinked and forced herself to read each line again. *Pay to the order of Bradley Cogburn. Two hundred and fifty thousand dollars.* Signed by Alexander German. Dated January 12. The day before Bradley died.

34

It was late afternoon before Hannah came to the last of Teddy's known hideouts. She had already been to a half dozen of them, including a hollowed-out bush behind the stables in Las Almas Regional Park and a culvert at the end of Shelton Street. She showed his school picture to stable hands, picnickers, and assorted winos, but no one had seen him.

She parked on the side of the dirt road bordering Pico Creek and clambered down the embankment in two steps. It was steep and the crumbling dirt slid out from under her. Hannah grabbed a branch of a gray-green saltbush and used it to regain her footing. Her heart was beating fast and she coughed in a cloud of the dust she'd kicked up.

Something rustled and hissed in a stand of buckwheat at her feet. A whip of thin, tan, and sinuous skin flicked aside a branch. Hannah froze, expecting a rattler to slither out over her feet. Instead, an annoyed opossum poked out its head and skittered across the baked channel, dragging its hairless, snaking tail behind it.

Hannah exhaled hard and sat down to catch her breath. The earth was dry and cracked, peeling back in a pattern of jagged diamonds. The creek bed smelled of dust, horse dung, and smoke, funneled from the Pico Camp's early dinner fires. The urban settlers' campground was up a quarter mile, on the opposite bank. Ballard Goodacre lived there. Teddy hid here. Hannah wondered if they knew each other.

She got up and continued north. She found Teddy's cave,

such as it was. He hadn't done much to disguise it, except stack tumbleweeds at the entrance. Hannah pulled them out and ducked inside.

Teddy had scraped back a sidewall to make a bench. He covered this with a green army-surplus blanket. It was damp and smelled of mildew. Hannah pulled it back and saw a lidded plastic cooler sunk into a well Teddy had carved in the bench. Hannah lifted the lid: a box of granola bars, two cans of Coke, a *Playboy,* and a flashlight. No tape. And no sign of Teddy.

Hannah looked back to the entrance. It would be dark in a couple hours. He might be hiding in the creek bed somewhere, having heard her noisy approach. She took out a piece of paper and flicked on the flashlight. She needed to write something to reassure him, to bring him home.

But she couldn't stop thinking about the camp, and Goodacre, who had lived so close to the cave. Teddy could have wandered up there and met him. He could have brought Goodacre along that night. Or Goodacre guided him. He probably knew his way around a train yard.

Teddy had taped a conversation between Bradley and someone Bradley knew, that was certain. But perhaps Bradley's companion left, and it was Goodacre who picked up the bottle and clubbed him. Teddy might not have been able to tell the difference. He hadn't seen any faces. Or he could have known it was Goodacre who did it, and lied about it. He might have unwittingly brought a robber in contact with a rich victim. That would be harder to live with than merely witnessing a crime. Maybe that's why he was hiding. She hated to think that Churnin might be right about Goodacre. He would be insufferable.

She jotted a note to Teddy, as bland and devoid of cop-threat as she could make it: *Call Monty. She's worried about you.*

Maybe that will work, she thought. She put the flashlight back in Teddy's cache, covered up the cave, and made her way to the camp on the other side of the creek.

The urban settlers at Pico Camp were civil and helpful, once Hannah convinced them she wasn't a cop and dropped the names of the third-years who'd represented some of them in court.

None of the campers recognized Teddy's picture. Most of them had nothing good to say about Ballard Goodacre.

"Kinda nuts," one woman said as the crowd around Hannah thinned.

She was in her fifties, Hannah guessed. Her hair was gray, going white, and she wore something like a sari over her jeans and T-shirt. Heavy pewter earrings had opened portholes in her earlobes.

"Ballard's synapses are fried crisp, like bacon, you know? Meth will do that to you."

Hannah asked if he'd flashed credit cards or cash. The woman shook her head and wandered off.

But as Hannah climbed the path out of camp, the woman caught up to her. She looked over her shoulder to be sure no one was watching and opened her hand to show Bradley's Visa card.

"Ballard gave it to me," she said.

"When?" Hannah said.

"That Friday night. Saturday morning, really, about three. But he made me promise not to tell, and said I had to use it quick. I knew it was wrong, so I didn't do it. Scared me too much."

Hannah nodded and thanked her.

"You wanna take it?" the woman said.

Hannah thought for a moment. Goodacre had lied to the police about when he found the card. There would be prints on it: Goodacre's. Possibly Teddy's, or someone else's. Hannah took out a tissue and the woman dropped the card into it. Hannah stowed it in her pack, along with the sketch, the shard, and the check. By the time she looked up, the woman was gone. The hem of her sari left a smooth track in the dust.

Hannah went back to her old habits. Twice she'd found Teddy by hanging around the tracks, so she tried there again while there still was some light left. She drove from one end of industrial Las Almas to the other, hoping to catch a glimpse of him crouching under a container car. That would be just like him. But in the fading light, peering through the triangles of chain-link, she could make out only dim silhouettes.

It was dark when she finally parked the Hyundai on a side street in the industrial strip along the tracks. The neighborhood was sad and sagging, the houses barely more than shacks. She was less than a mile from the spot where Bradley had died. And right around where Goodacre had told Churnin he'd found Bradley's gold card.

She took the flashlight out of the trunk and walked across the street. A chain-link fence separated the railroad's right-of-way from the road. Someone, in an inexplicable fit of civic pride, had planted a row of carizzos in front of the fence to block the view of the tracks. The ten-foot reeds waved and clicked in the evening breeze.

Hannah walked along the fence and shoved aside the canes, peering through the fence. Nothing seemed to move out there, behind the parked container cars on the side tracks. But at this distance, in the growing dark, she couldn't be sure. As she sidled along, something caught at the leg of her pants. She aimed the beam and saw a flap of fence that had been pulled away from its pole. The gap was big enough for a skinny kid to crawl through. Hannah wasn't sure she'd fit.

She dropped to her hands and knees. The reeds had been planted about a foot from the fence, but the branches had grown out and through the links. Hannah pushed the long thin leaves, shoved back the fence flap, and started through. The wire caught at the leg of her gray wool pants. Hannah heard fabric rip.

She got to her feet on the other side, inspected the small tear with disgust, and walked out to the tracks. She pointed the flashlight's beam under a row of sidetracked boxcars. Every few steps she bent low and said Teddy's name.

She listened for any reply, any sound. Out on the streets a dog gave a dispirited yip. She heard the hiss of air brakes and stiffened. Someone pulling a pin, she thought. I'm not alone here. It was time to go. When she reached the end of the boxcar line, she walked back toward the fence, flashing the light to find the flap.

As the reeds rippled sideways in a gust of wind, something reflected the flashlight's beam back at her. A glint of light off glass, metal, she didn't know what. Then she heard the slide of a semiautomatic pistol.

Hannah dropped on her belly, burying the flashlight under her. She clicked the light off and looked up. She saw nothing but the night, and through the gaps in the reeds, lights from the hovels across the street. She heard nothing but silence.

Then the carizzos rattled. The night was still, but the canes shook, a sound like the opossum made in the buckwheat. The noise stopped, started again.

Someone is out there, gun in hand, shaking the leaves, she thought. Looking for a way in. For a way to get to me.

She lay on the ground, motionless, trying to still her heart. It boomed like a kettledrum in her ears. The rustling moved systematically down the row of reeds.

Hannah had dropped in the open. She could run to the gap in the fence. But if she did, the shaker would see her, hear her. And yet she couldn't lie there, exposed. She crawled closer to the fence. The rocks clicked underneath her body. She stopped, held her breath. But the shaker apparently heard nothing. The canes shook on, thirty or forty feet away from her now.

Hannah wiggled through the flap and hid herself in the thickest part of the reeds, balanced on the balls of her feet, her fingertips on the ground. She nudged aside a branch and saw a shape, a deeper black shadow against the darkness, walk across the street and down an alley. An engine started. A white sedan pulled out and drove away. Hannah couldn't make out who sat behind the wheel.

She got back to her car and looked around. There wasn't anyone else to be seen in the darkness. In the dirt yard of the house nearest Hannah's car, a scrawny dog lay on its side, unmoving. The animal was tied to the trunk of a ravaged, stick-thin magnolia tree. A breeze slid through the scant, dry leaves. Maybe that was all she'd heard—the wind slicing through the carizzos. Oh sure, Hannah said to herself. An everyday, gun-toting downdraft.

No. Someone was searching for something, shaking the carizzos, as though there was fruit hidden in the reeds, ripe and ready to fall.

Not Goodacre. He was in jail. Not Teddy. Not driving a car. But someone looking in the spot where Goodacre said he found the credit card. If Goodacre was telling the truth about finding the cards, Hannah thought, maybe that someone was German.

If he killed Bradley, he could have been the one who scattered the credit cards and ditched the wallet. When she first met him at Alicia's house, he'd talked about suicide victims trying to make their deaths look like robbery, to get the insurance for their families. A murderer could just as easily dump a wallet to disguise the motive for a killing.

But German bungled it. He'd missed the check, the very thing that spelled out his reason for murder. He might have thought his son-in-law had already cashed it. Bradley could have told him so. But after the killing, he must have seen that the money hadn't moved from his account, and that worried him. He had to find the check; $250,000 paid to a son-in-law would make any cop ask questions.

It certainly made Hannah want to talk to him.

35

Hannah stood in front of the closet where she kept the .38-caliber revolver. More than two years since she last shot it. She pulled out the locked gun box, retrieved the key from its hiding place in the desk, and opened the container.

Hannah checked the cylinder to make sure it was empty, then dry-fired the gun. She took out the box of bullets and loaded it.

In eleven years as a cop, she'd never had to fire her gun at anyone. She'd done well on the range, though. She had a strong, steady grip. She liked the recoil of the gun against the heel of her hand, and the satisfaction of placing the shot just so. But those were paper targets, sunny days, the camaraderie of other cops. The gun felt altogether different at work, at night, running down an alley or crouching below a window. No sense of pleasure came with the gun then. There was only the reassurance of its weight, a counterbalance to fear.

Hannah put the gun in her backpack. She didn't have a concealed-weapon permit. But now that she knew German was armed, she was willing to risk the consequences. At least with the gun along, she had a better chance of being alive to face them.

She dialed Monty, and the phone rang just once before the old woman picked it up. Her voice was shaky, tired, tearful.

"Thank God," she said. "He's home."

Hannah breathed out, realized she was close to tears herself. "Is he okay?" she said. "Where was he?"

"He's fine, just fine," Monty said.

"Can I talk to him?" Hannah said.

"Well . . ." Monty hesitated. "He's . . . he's kinda tired."

"I understand. I'll come by in the morning."

"Oh," Monty said suddenly. "No. Come by tonight." Her voice shook. And something in that quaver worried Hannah.

"Monty? Are you sure everything is okay?"

"Oh, honey, it will be when you get here," she said.

Hannah paused. Monty was an old woman. She loved Teddy more than anything. All of this—the shock of his disappearance, Hannah's story—must be overwhelming. Of course she wanted someone there with her.

"I'll be there in a little while," Hannah said. "I have to talk to someone first."

Monty choked out a little sob and hung up.

36

Corona del Mar was still part of Newport Beach, but it preferred to think of itself as an autonomous village, more subtly wealthy than its glitzy parent city.

German's house was there, just as Alicia had described it—a hulking two-story hacienda overlooking the sea. There was a light on downstairs, but the upper story was dark. German had parked his Porsche on the street.

Hannah walked up the stairway, past the obligatory security-company sign and onto the bricked front patio. She peered through the slats of the plantation shutters into the living room.

She could see a black leather sofa, burled wood coffee table, and a marble-fronted fireplace. Louvers over a dining-room sideboard gave a view of the kitchen.

She rang the doorbell twice, but no one answered. She heard no sounds from inside. She checked the iron gates on either side of the house. They were locked. Probably wired to the alarm, too, she thought.

Hannah walked halfway down the stairs and looked up at the second floor. Now she saw a faint light. And one of the shutters moved, almost imperceptibly. She took another step back.

She was peering up when she heard someone turning the lock on the door. The door opened to show her . . . no one. Not at first. Then a tiny face, framed by a pair of black braids, peeked around the door at her. The girl stepped out. She was wearing a maid's starchy white blouse and black skirt and she couldn't have been more than eighteen. Hannah didn't blame her for not opening the door until she'd gotten a look from upstairs at whoever it was.

"Mr. German?" Hannah said.

"Is not at home," the girl said softly.

"Only you?" Hannah said.

Foolishly enough, the girl nodded.

"Do you know where I can find him?" Hannah said.

"His office," she said.

Hannah thanked her. At the bottom of the stairs, she looked back. The young maid was closing the front door. But someone else turned out the light upstairs.

She stopped at a stationer's on the way to Newport Center and bought two cardboard storage boxes, just in case. She parked a block away from the Bren Tower, assembled the boxes, and carried them out with her.

As she had expected, the doors to the building were locked. It was after eight o'clock. The guard station was far back in the lobby, and a man in a green uniform was reading a newspaper. He didn't see her. Hannah sat down on the steps to wait.

Hannah was about to give up the plan when she saw the light on an elevator blink. A young man in a dark gray suit got out. His tie was loose and his hair fell over his forehead. Even at this distance, she could see the pale skin, the rings under his eyes. A beleaguered first-year associate, she was willing to bet.

Hannah picked up the boxes. She'd put her backpack, and the gun inside it, in the top one.

The lawyer opened the door and saw her. Hannah smiled at him.

"Thank goodness," she said. "I was about to give up."

He looked at her, the boxes.

"You want to go in?" he said.

Hannah nodded and awkwardly extended her hand.

"Beverly Olswang. I'm a paralegal with CourTemps. I've got this stuff for Mr. German at German, Friedenthal, and Block. He was screaming for it. I couldn't get the guard's attention, and Mr. German's not answering his phone. Must be in the library."

She gestured at the door.

"Could you? Security is great and all, what with the crazies around, but it'll be my job if I don't get up there."

"Sure," the lawyer said. "I work at GFB myself. I know how tough he is. What case are you working on?"

Hannah froze. Then she remembered German, barking into his car phone as they drove to dinner.

"The case that will not die. With Janice," she said.

"Jesus, that one's a bitch," the lawyer said. He froze, embarrassed. "The case, I mean."

He pushed the door wide for her. He waved at the guard and gave him an okay sign. He rode up on the elevator with her and used his plastic card key to let her into the law offices of German, Friedenthal, and Block.

"Thanks," Hannah said. She smiled charmingly.

"Good luck with him," the lawyer said. "He's been up there since before seven this morning, and he's in a foul temper. Grovel, if necessary. It works sometimes."

The elevator doors closed as he waved to her. Hannah felt sorry for the guy. Too nice for this business, she decided.

From the dimmed reception area on the ninth floor, Hannah could look down on Fashion Island, a shopping center that so catered to the Republican *riche* that its local nickname was Fascist Island. Beyond its lights lay the darkness of the Pacific.

Then she scanned the room itself. A sleek arrangement of Japanese irises, daylilies, and spider chrysanthemums rose from a low table in the center of the room. The walls were covered with a small collection of modern art and photography: a watercolor of an impossibly dexterous, half-draped geisha using her toes to maneuver a piece of sushi to her lips. A photograph of a long-suffering weimaraner caught in a shower of flour. Huge photographs of the Yosemite Valley, draped in snow or dark with its forests in the summer.

Hannah got out her pack, stowed the boxes behind a sofa, took deep breaths to calm herself, and went to the receptionist's desk. In a folder next to the phone was a floor plan, listing names, office numbers, and extensions. A security consultant would be horrified, she thought. She was delighted. She got a fix on which corridor would lead her to German's office and crept down the darkened hallway.

The doors to most of the offices were closed. A few stood open to show her half-lit rooms, desktops neat or littered with paper. The plates next to each door gave the occupant's name.

At the first turn, she saw German's office. It was at the end of the hall, two doors wide, instead of one. The left door was ajar, giving her a glimpse of desk, burgundy drapes and, behind them, a slice of the darkness outside.

She walked down the far side of the hallway, trying to stay out of sight. German sat behind a walnut desk, reading a document in the pool of white light from a green-shaded desk lamp. With his head bent over the paper, Hannah could see the thinning hair at the crown. He rested his cheek on his long hand and murmured something under his breath. The hand looked bony, almost like a talon. She stopped and held her breath, hoping to hear whether he was talking to someone.

He must have heard her move, or at least felt a presence in the empty corridor.

"Janice?" he said, raising his head.

Hannah stepped into the doorway. German was alone.

German's mouth twitched almost imperceptibly when he saw her. He picked up the phone and punched in three numbers. Hannah was at his desk in two steps. She already had the check in her hand. She shook it open and held it in front of his eyes.

For a moment she thought he was going to faint. The color slid from his face and his eyes closed.

"Nothing, Jordan, sorry to bother you," German muttered into the phone, his eyes still closed. "Where did you find it?" he asked as he replaced the receiver.

"In the wallet, which you were looking for. But you wouldn't have found it. It wasn't where you left it," Hannah said.

German wiped his mouth with his fingertips once more and cleared his throat softly.

"I don't know what you mean," he said.

Hannah looked at him. The young lawyer said German had been in the office since early that morning. If that was so, it couldn't have been him out there in the reeds.

"All right," he said. "Tell me. Where was it?"

"Bradley had the check with him, the night you killed him," Hannah said. "Did he try to hold you up for more?"

"I didn't kill him. I was at home that night."

"No, you weren't," Hannah said. "You were at a fund-raiser,

and you left early, but you didn't go home. You weren't there when Alicia called you. Try again."

"This is absurd."

"Where were you?" she said.

"I had dinner with a friend," German said. "My friend prefers we keep our relationship private."

"Who is it?"

"I don't think that's any of your business."

"Fine," Hannah said. "Tell the police, then. I'm taking this check to them."

German sighed. "I'd rather you didn't."

"I'm sure," she said. "He was blackmailing you. Over the Agua Dulce bribe. Just tell me this. What did Tim Gallagher have to do with it? Did he kill Luz Gomez?"

"Tim Gallagher?" he said, shaking his head and almost smiling. "Counselor Gallagher?"

"You've been to San Quentin to see him. You know who I mean."

German shook his head. "Tim Gallagher has nothing to do with anything. And the money has nothing to do with Agua Dulce."

"Then what was it for?"

German shrugged. "Incentive."

"To leave you alone."

"To leave Alicia," he said.

Hannah stared at him for a moment.

"I don't believe it," she said.

"It's the truth. I convinced him that Alicia's patience was wearing thin," German said. "If she filed for divorce, he'd get virtually nothing. Alicia has very little money in her own right, not until I die. But if he left, I told him I'd make it worth his while."

"And what went wrong?"

"Nothing," German said. "He died without cashing the check. So I got what I wanted without having to pay for it."

"What about Luz Gomez and the bribe?"

"There was no bribe," he said.

"Raymond O'Reilly says there was," she said.

"Raymond O'Reilly is a burned-out drug addict. He told Bradley what Bradley wanted to hear, to get money from him."

"Then why did you pay O'Reilly off? Why did he threaten to kill you?"

"Look. I told you. I didn't kill my son-in-law," German said. "He wasn't worth killing."

"But he was worth paying off," Hannah said.

"For Alicia's sake, yes."

"But not for the sake of keeping Agua Dulce quiet."

"I told Bradley if he thought I'd bribed Luz, he should take the information to the tribe and the state. Nothing happened."

"Maybe you saw to that."

"If you take that check to the police, and I have to tell them what it really was for, it's going to humiliate my daughter. She doesn't need that."

"I think she would risk that, in order to know who killed her husband," Hannah said. "It wasn't a suicide and it wasn't a robbery. I know that."

"How do you know that?"

"There's a witness."

"Not a witness who saw me," German said.

"Prove it," Hannah said. "Tell me where you were."

German looked out the window for a moment, biting on the side of his thumb.

"With Emilia Dove. You know her, I think?"

Hannah nodded. Was she the one upstairs at German's house? What if she'd called German, told him Hannah was coming. Maybe it had been too easy to get in, Hannah thought.

"I can call her. She'll tell you I was there that night," German said.

His hand was edging toward the phone. Or to the drawer just below it. He was intent on holding Hannah's gaze.

Hannah kept his hand in her peripheral vision. If there was a gun in the drawer, she was in trouble. She couldn't get to hers fast enough. It was at the bottom of the pack. Stupid, she thought, to bring the gun and not have it in hand.

"I'll call her," German said. His long fingers hovered in the space between the phone and the drawer pull.

Hannah sprang across the desk and slammed German's chest with her palm. His chair rolled backward. He flailed and tried to stop himself. Hannah grabbed the phone and jabbed the redial key before he could get to her.

"Jordan, a guest needs an escort to her car," Hannah said.

"She'll be down in the lobby in a minute. Will you see to it?"

German glanced at her as she turned toward him, keeping herself between him and the desk drawer.

"Stupid bitch," he growled, massaging his chest. "What did you think I was going to do?"

She carefully refolded the check and put it in her inside jacket pocket.

"Maybe nothing. Maybe whatever you thought was necessary to shut me up," Hannah said. "Good night."

37

Hannah unlocked the apartment door, gathered up the mail on the floor, and dumped it on the desk. She looked at her watch—nearly nine-thirty. The answering machine was blinking insistently. One message. Hannah rewound the tape.

"This is Lena Montano," the woman said.

Hannah didn't recognize the voice or the name.

"I'm a correctional officer," the woman continued. "We met at the visitors' center at San Quentin."

Now Hannah remembered her: wiry, sardonic, not at all taken in by the likes of Tim Gallagher.

"I got the name of Gallagher's lawyer, like you asked," Montano said. "I guess I kind of made some assumptions. It's a clerk, not a lawyer. And she's not a man."

Montano laughed at herself.

"It's a woman, I mean, and she must not be a blonde, is all I can guess. Because if she was, the guys would have been talking about her all the time. The guys on my shift like 'em blond."

"I couldn't get her number. I'm sorry," Lena Montano was saying. "But her name—"

Hannah stopped the machine. She didn't need to hear Montano say it. She knew who it was, and she knew who had killed Bradley. Bradley had practically given her the reason on Founder's Walk that day. Hannah knew now the alibi was a fake. And Hannah knew how it had been arranged.

Her hands were shaking as she dialed Eddy at home. No

answer. The machine was off, too. She tried the office and got his voice mail, but left no message. She beeped him and waited, but she knew she couldn't wait long. She called the office again and left a message this time, telling him where she was going.

Teddy and Monty were safe, but maybe not for long, she said. She pleaded with Eddy to believe her, to meet her there and bring backup. She hung up and waited for a moment, hoping he'd call back. She had an eerie feeling that he was at his desk, maybe even listening to her message, and purposely not calling her back. In desperation, she called Churnin and left him the same message. She checked to be sure the gun was loaded and left for Teddy's house.

38

Hannah rang the pink house's doorbell twice and waited. Nothing. Lights were on in the kitchen, but the living room was dark. She could see in through the front window. The television flickered light patterns across the shelves of salt-and-pepper-shaker animals. Their shadows loomed small and misshapen, forming ranks of miniature gargoyles.

Monty must have fallen asleep, Hannah told herself. It was nine-forty. She knocked and called her name.

She heard a thump, and shuffling behind the door. The click of the dead bolt. The knob turned, and there stood Teddy.

She had never seen him without his glasses. His unmagnified eyes were still huge. And now they were red, from crying. He took one look at Hannah and began to sniffle.

Hannah dropped to her knees and hugged him. He didn't resist. He held her tight and she could feel the tears dripping onto her neck.

"It's okay, Teddy," she said.

"No," he whispered, "it's not."

Hannah looked up then, and saw Catherine. And her gun, aimed at the base of Teddy's skull.

She looked no different than on any day in any class at Douglas. Black pants, manly boots, black jacket, cream silk blouse. But instead of holding a black pen, she had a nine-milli-meter Glock semiautomatic. She held it confidently. She went to the range with the macho deputy DAs, Hannah thought with dismay. She remembered the figure in black running from the tracks the night Bradley died. It had been Catherine.

"Give me that pack," she told Hannah.

Hannah hesitated. Teddy was clinging to her, trembling. The door was still open and it was only a couple feet away. She could kick Catherine's feet out from under her, shove Teddy out the door. Maybe.

But suddenly the hallway echoed with a flurry of thumps, kicks, and throaty groans. It came from the closet behind Catherine.

"Monty!" Teddy wailed.

The moment was lost. Catherine picked up the boy by one arm and held him.

"She won't stop rolling around in there," Catherine said. "I told her I'll let her out when she quiets down."

The kicking and thumping stopped for a minute, then resumed.

"She's an old woman," Hannah said. "She could have a heart attack. Let her out."

"Later." Catherine held out her hand and Hannah saw the signet ring. She'd only had glimpses of it before. But now, seeing its shape, it all made sense.

"Give it to me," Catherine said again.

Hannah held the pack up to her. If she stalled long enough, Eddy would be there.

"I understand now," she said. "It didn't make sense that you'd do what you did for a client. But if you'd fallen in love with him, that would be different."

"I don't know what you're talking about." Catherine grabbed the bag and took out the revolver.

"I recognize the ring. It's Tim's."

Catherine's left hand slid over her right, covering the gold signet on her hand.

"I saw it in a newspaper picture," Hannah said. "Bradley had it. He had lots of clippings about Gallagher. But you know all about his research. He figured it all out—how Gallagher found the witness, about your relationship. But how did you find out about Peavey? You didn't work for the DA then. Bradley didn't, either."

"I don't have time for this now," Catherine said. "You are

going to sit over there and be still. But get this straight. I don't *think* I fell in love. I did. Tim is my husband."

She slammed the door, locked it, dragged the phone close, and sat down, the gun trained on them.

Teddy sniffled and Hannah gave him a hug.

"I'm so sorry," Hannah said. "I was trying to keep you safe, but I've done a miserable job."

He shrugged and smiled, shakily.

"I should have gone to the police with Monty. But I took off on my bike," he said. "I guess she was following me." He glanced at Catherine. "She ran me off the road," he said softly. He showed Hannah his arm, the skin scraped raw by asphalt. "And then she grabbed me and put me in the trunk of her car. She's strong."

"He was going to the police," Catherine said. "I needed time to think." She tried a smile at Teddy, but it was so false that it made Hannah cringe. "I'm sorry if I hurt you."

"Great," Hannah said. "Very sincere."

"Stop it," Catherine said, raising the gun. "I don't think you understand your position very well. You don't know how upset I am. I need to think."

Hannah said nothing.

"Can I just talk to him a little more?"

"Loud enough so I can hear," Catherine said.

"I know why you didn't go to the police," Hannah said. "It was because of the wallet and the check."

He stared at her, wide-eyed, and nodded.

"How did you get it?"

"She took it out of his pocket, threw it in the mud, before she dragged him away. It was her, wasn't it?"

Hannah nodded. "She took out the cash and the credit cards to make it look like a robbery. Why did you take the wallet?"

"Don't know," he said. "I guess I thought I'd give it to the police. But then I found the check."

"What were you going to do with it?" Hannah asked.

He dropped his head and whispered something.

"What?"

"Cash it," he said.

"You were going to try to cash it?" Hannah tried to imagine a teller doling out a stack of bills to an eleven-year-old.

"Russell—my dad—has a friend who knows how to do

stuff like that. I just wanted to help Monty. She's old. The Impala's transmission is about to give out. And she never gets to go anywhere. She plays the lottery every week, but she's never going to win. I wanted to help, but I didn't have it all worked out."

He was starting to cry again.

"It's okay now," Hannah said. She looked at her watch. Nine forty-five.

The phone rang fifteen minutes later. Teddy jumped and grabbed Hannah's hand. Catherine called to Hannah.

"Answer it in a normal tone of voice," she said, holding her hand over the mouthpiece. "Don't say anything strange, or so help me God I'll kill this little boy. Don't think I won't." She held the receiver to Hannah's mouth and ear and listened.

"Hello there," Hannah chirped falsely. At least, if it was Eddy, he'd know something was wrong.

But it wasn't Eddy. An operator asked if she would accept long-distance charges.

"Say you'll accept," Catherine said. It was clearly a call she'd expected. Hannah did as she was told.

"You should have stuck to your law books, Hannah," Tim Gallagher said. "I don't think this is your game."

"How did you know I'd be here?" Hannah said.

"Catherine called me. Attorney-client privilege is very useful that way. And normally, I'd have to book a call a day in advance. But not to my legal researcher. We agreed that if I called back, and you were there, then I'd know this was going right. I told you, this isn't your game."

"I don't think it's a game," Hannah said. "I think it's murder."

Catherine wrenched the phone away.

"You're doing that on purpose. You know they monitor calls sometimes," she said. "I'm warning you. Don't do that again." She put the phone to Hannah's ear.

"It is a game, you know," Gallagher said to Hannah. "I've won a few times. For a while I thought I was losing. But then I met Cathy. I'm not going to lose her. Not to that fuck, and not to you. Put her on."

Hannah nodded and Catherine took the phone.

"Okay," she whispered solemnly. "It will be fine. I love you.

Bye." She hung up and looked at Hannah. "This is all going to work out," she said. "You just have to cooperate with me. Listen to what happened, and you'll understand. You'll want to help."

"No, I won't," Hannah said. "I don't want to hear any of it. I know Bradley found out about you and Gallagher and what you did for him. He blackmailed you, and you killed him because he pushed you too far. I know how you covered yourself. You logged onto WESTLAW at the library and ran a huge search while you went out to meet Bradley. Then you came back and signed off. That's all I need to know. The rest is nothing but rationalizations."

"You think what I did was wrong. But I'm not a bad person. Bradley Cogburn was. And he did terrible things to me, and to Tim. I tried to stop it, but I couldn't. If you don't listen to me, things are only going to get worse."

She pointed the gun at Teddy and then opened the closet door. Monty toppled out onto her side. Her mouth was taped shut. Her eyes were open wide, staring frantically. Her arms were wrenched behind her back and tied there.

"For God's sake, Catherine, let her sit on the sofa or a chair. She's frail. You've probably already broken her hip."

"Are you going to listen to me?"

Maybe Gallagher was right, Hannah thought. She had been out of the game too long to do it right. She'd alienated her only ally, Eddy. He feared Churnin, feared for his job, that's why he'd abandoned her. She couldn't blame him. She'd pushed him beyond his limits. So there would be no rescue party. She'd have to figure a way out on her own.

"All right," Hannah said. "If you let Monty sit comfortably, let her talk to me, then you can tell the whole sorry story, if you want to."

Catherine and Hannah hoisted Monty to her feet and eased her into the battered lounger. With as much care as she could, Hannah peeled the tape from the old woman's mouth. She gasped in a breath of air.

"Thought I was dying in there," she wheezed. Her eyes were red, tearstained.

"Are you okay? Are you hurt anywhere?" Hannah said.

She shook her head. "I'm a tough old thing. Who is that girl? She's awful."

"Sit quiet now. Do you want some water?"

"No," Catherine said. "She'll need to use the bathroom then. I don't want anyone leaving this room."

"I'm not thirsty, you little bitch," Monty said.

Catherine stared at her, and then laughed.

"You've recovered," she said. "Good."

She picked up a roll of tape from the coffee table, tore off a piece, slapped it against Monty's mouth and dragged her back to the closet. The door slammed, and the old woman's kicks battered it, faster, then slower. Finally, the kicking stopped.

Teddy stared at the closet. Hannah put her hands on his shoulders.

"She'll be okay," she said.

"Teddy," Catherine said. "You're sure it's there?"

He nodded.

"Let's go," Catherine said.

"Where are we going?" Hannah said.

"I'll tell you when we get there."

Outside, Hannah paused on the porch, straining to hear a crunch of leaf or a rustle in the trees. No Eddy. No SWAT team. The street was quietly normal. No skulking shadows. No telltale stillness. A car passed the house. A neighbor picked up the newspaper on her porch. No one evacuated, nothing barricaded. That was that.

They got in the Hyundai, Hannah driving and Catherine in the passenger seat with Teddy on her lap. Teddy gave the directions, with Catherine's gun stuck in his belly. Right, he said. Left here.

Every few seconds Catherine checked her watch.

"I can go faster, if you're in a hurry," Hannah said.

"No. Stay at the limit." Catherine shifted in her seat. Then she began to talk, almost as if to herself. "He knew I was the one. He knew I was the only one who could save him. He knew, but I didn't."

Hannah glanced over at her. Her eyes were fixed on some far point, as though watching a movie of the day she met Tim Gallagher.

"He already had interviewed a half-dozen law students— even Bradley had gone down there," Catherine said. "Tim told me later he hated him from the minute he saw him.

"I went because I'd always seen everything from the other side—the prosecutor's view. I needed to know how criminal-defense attorneys thought, how they did things. It was going to be reconnaissance."

Hannah watched the street, looking for opportunities. She could swerve into traffic, cause an accident. But there was no way to be sure Teddy wouldn't be shot first. She looked over at him. He sat on Catherine's lap, his arms rigid, hands clamped on his knees. He was stiff with fear.

"I got to the attorney-client visiting room first," Catherine was saying. "It's a depressing place, even for a jail. One table, two chairs, a door with a window in it, and it's painted this sickly yellow orange.

"I was fidgeting with the briefcase I'd just bought when he came in. He surprised me so much that I dropped it. He wasn't what I expected. I'd seen his picture, but it didn't do him justice."

Oh Lord, Hannah thought. It's a romance novel.

"He was very genteel with me. I expected someone throwing around a lot of fuckin' this and goddamned that," Catherine said. "But he didn't talk that way. He was very soft-spoken, and asked me a lot of good questions about my qualifications.

"And he looked at me. Not leeringly. Not at my hair or breasts. There wasn't any of that."

Hannah had promised herself that she would say nothing. She wanted to concentrate on ways to get out, and attend silently to what Catherine was saying, alert to a panic or a change of heart. But the tale-telling scared her. The more Catherine told, the less likely she would be to let them live. At the same time, though, Hannah wanted to know what Catherine was thinking, not let her scheme their death in silence.

"He's not your average prisoner, granted," Hannah said evenly. "But truly, Catherine, he's not a priest. I met him. It's clear that he appreciates women. He's not blind to hair or breasts."

Catherine smiled. Good, Hannah thought.

"He's different from other men I knew, though. He doesn't belittle my intelligence. He doesn't try to prove that he's smarter than I am. Even though he is."

"He's certainly smart enough to know he would need someone brilliant to get him off death row," Hannah said.

Catherine shrugged, then nodded. She was vain about her intelligence.

"Did you think he was guilty?" Hannah said.

"What?"

"You'd read the trial transcript. What did you think?"

"I assumed he was guilty. That was the prosecutor in me. He never tried to convince me that he wasn't," she said. "And I never asked him outright."

Most defense attorneys didn't, Hannah thought. It's not their job to prove innocence. It's the prosecutor's burden to prove guilt. If the client actually did it, the lawyer doesn't want to know. It makes the whole process more difficult.

"Guilt or innocence really wasn't the issue. We had to go after the procedural errors to get a new trial," Catherine said. "But the more we talked, the more I thought he was telling the truth. It was an accident."

Hannah didn't say anything. She kept her eyes on the road. But she could see Catherine looking at her, all her attention focused on Hannah's reaction. She wanted someone else to believe it.

"They'd been fighting about money, no question. But Jack Gallagher drank heavily and had prescription tranquilizers in the house," Catherine said. "He had smoked in bed before. His ex-wife testified to that. The accelerant could have been spilled brandy. The experts said so."

"Defense experts said so," Hannah said. "That's what they were paid for."

"It was the truth," Catherine said.

"What about Peavey?"

"He was a liar. He would have sold out his mother to stay out of jail."

"So why is he dead?" Hannah asked.

"I don't know anything about that."

"What did Tim say?"

"That he was in Orange County Jail. He couldn't do—"

"Astral projection. I know," Hannah said.

Catherine looked out the window.

"He didn't do anything, or have anything done," she said. It was as though she had to repeat this to convince herself.

Hannah decided to change the subject.

"I wonder why Gallagher hired you in the first place," she

said. "Didn't he find it a little suspicious when you applied? Your scholarship, your history with the DA's office?"

"He knew my background. He thought it was an advantage."

I would think he did, Hannah said to herself. And he turned out to be right.

"I told him I'd do the best job I could," Catherine said. "I take my ethics seriously."

"Did you tell him about Peavey out of ethics?"

Catherine stared down at the gun in her hand.

"He heard a rumor about a witness. Sooner or later the DA would have had to tell us about him. Tim wanted to know who he was, have me go talk to him."

"So you just asked your friends at the DA? And they told you?"

Catherine shook her head. "I don't want to talk about this."

"Okay," Hannah said.

"Tim didn't do it. He didn't need to. He wouldn't have compromised me."

Hannah said nothing.

"He cared about me. Even before, when we were just working. He wanted to know what I liked to do when I wasn't working, where I grew up. All that."

Hannah nodded. Tim Gallagher would have listened closely, remembering it all for use later. Hannah thought she knew what he really wanted from Catherine, assuming for a moment that true love had not overtaken him.

A lawyer wife would be useful. He could write what he liked to her, and their mail would pass unopened in and out of prison: attorney-client privilege. If he ever got off death row, he could have conjugal visits with her. And even if she ceased to be his attorney, she still couldn't be compelled to testify to anything he told her. Spousal immunity. Very neat little package, Hannah decided.

"Tim was wonderful," Catherine said. "He listened. He understood me." She paused, momentarily lost in her thoughts. "Finally, someone who understood." And then it moved beyond empathy, she said.

"It was June. We were working on a motion. The hearing date was about two months away. We didn't have a lot of time, and I had come in on a Sunday. Let's wait here for a second."

Hannah pulled the car over as Catherine looked at her watch again. What was she timing? Hannah thought.

"I was prattling on about some issue I thought was useful and Tim was pacing in front of the door," Catherine said. "He glanced out from time to time, then he asked me for my sweater. I thought for a second he was cold—the jail is chilly sometimes in the morning, even in summer.

"He draped the sweater across the window and reached for my hand," Catherine said. "He pulled me close to him and kissed me. Once, very lightly. Then the sweater was down and he was pacing again, and I stood there like a statue. He smiled at me and told me to sit down before the deputies noticed something was wrong."

Catherine smiled at the memory. Her strained face relaxed. For a moment Hannah saw what Tim Gallagher had opened in her.

"After that, it was like a game. Could we touch? For how long? Kisses were chancy, and we couldn't manage it every time. We had to keep our hands on top of the table, that was a rule. But as we moved the books and papers around on the table, our hands grazed. I lived for those times."

Hannah could almost feel it. Catherine always seemed so cautious, so girded in her intellect. She'd banked her sexuality down to a dull ember. There was nothing like a dark, dangerous man, something from an unacknowledged fantasy, to bring it roaring to life. She could imagine Catherine trembling on the brink of an inferno in that jail interview room.

"When did he ask you to find out about Peavey?"

Catherine shook her head, as if she could jar the memory and expel it.

"Early in July," she said.

"How did Bradley find out?"

Catherine laughed.

"He was the one who made it all happen. If anyone was responsible for what happened to Peavey, it was him. Okay. We can go now."

Hannah pulled out and mulled that over for a moment. The only thing Bradley had excelled at during his internship was playing the keyboards, pulling information out of the computer networks. He must have learned the DA's internal systems, too.

But why would he do such a thing for Gallagher, who'd refused to hire him? And why help Catherine, his rival?

"He told you about Peavey?"

She shook her head.

"He gave you access to the system," Hannah said.

She nodded and pointed to a side road.

"Turn here."

Hannah knew where they were going, though she didn't know why. They were heading north, past downtown and the seedier outskirts, toward the foothills. These roads were still semirural, containing a few orange groves and strawberry fields, but yielding every year to another crop of identical three-bedroom houses.

"I'd surrendered my password when I left the office in May," Catherine said.

"Hadn't Bradley done the same thing?"

"They thought he had. He hacked a little, got one that still worked. He was good at that stuff, and he wasn't done tracking down whatever it was he was after. I told him I needed access to retrieve some of my personal files. He gave me the code."

Hannah tried to reason it out. Bradley might have guessed she was lying about that. Maybe he knew then that she'd fallen in love with Gallagher. Perhaps he gave her what she wanted so he'd have leverage with her later.

"I already had a senior deputy's log-in," Catherine said. "I used it."

"And found the witness's name and address," Hannah said.

Catherine nodded. "And the next thing I knew, he had killed himself."

"Do you honestly think that was what happened?" Hannah said.

She stared out the window again, saying nothing. If she hadn't convinced herself by now, then she had consciously thrown her lot in with a killer.

"Yes." Her mouth trembled and her eyes were downcast. She knew the truth, and that wasn't it, Hannah decided. But at the same time she didn't know because she wanted to believe Gallagher. She wouldn't let herself know because that would shatter everything. He was the only thing she had left.

"But the DA must have thought of you," Hannah said. "It was no secret that you worked for Gallagher."

"They talked to me," Catherine said. "I told them I didn't know anything. They believed me. They were even a little ashamed to ask me about it. They told me that what they really wanted was for me to find out, if I could, how Gallagher had done it. They were so sure I couldn't have been the one."

"They trusted you," Hannah said.

"I did what was best for my client," she said. "He had a right to know who was going to accuse him. He could have blown Peavey's story out of the water."

"If Peavey had lived long enough to tell it," Hannah said.

Catherine didn't respond to that. There wasn't much she could say, Hannah thought. She'd been responsible for identifying a witness to a killer. Hannah doubted if she had realized that when she did it.

"Bradley figured it out," Hannah said. "That's why he came to the hearing, wasn't it?"

"I didn't know why he was there. He showed up with a bunch of the prosecutors—guys he'd never much liked. He sidled over and told me he was sick of Tim sucking up the taxpayers' money. He said he couldn't wait to see the bastard get his. I told him Mr. Gallagher was only exercising his rights under the law."

"What did he say to that?" Hannah said.

"He laughed. And then he told me that I must really love my work. 'You're so passionate about it,' he said. I thought then that he knew something. I avoided him for the rest of the morning.

"The hearing was a circus, a complete debacle. I felt sick. I'd let Tim down. But Tim was keeping it together, until that bailiff started up. It was disgusting." She shook her head and grimaced.

"I went home and cried myself to sleep. But then Tim called. He said we should get married. I was stunned. But suddenly I was excited. I told him we could do it at prison, by proxy, whatever. I needed time to call my sister."

"But he didn't want you to do that," Hannah said.

"He didn't want anyone to know. Tim was worried about what it would mean to me in school, for the scholarship," Catherine said. "He told me we should keep it our secret—that it could be a confidential marriage. No blood tests, no license on public file with the county clerk, but still a legal marriage.

It was just that no one would know. I could keep working for him, and the scholarship wouldn't be jeopardized."

And no one need know that the jailhouse lawyer wasn't doing all the work himself, Hannah thought. He liked that image—the brilliant legal autodidact. Catherine was stupid not to realize how he was using her.

"We were married at the jail, that night," Catherine said. "We thought we could keep it quiet. The minister asked the watch commander if he could pray with Tim before he was transported. I was supposed to be there to have Tim sign some papers.

"I got Tim's ring from a friend who was keeping his things for him. I wore a white suit, and put a little bunch of violets in my briefcase. The minister talked very softly. Tim put the ring on my hand and said he'd always be with me. I started to cry, but I managed to keep myself together. A deputy came and told us it was time to leave.

"It was after eleven. There were only a few people in the lobby, some sleeping in chairs, waiting for someone to get processed out. The deputies were dozing off at the reception station. And there I was, the bride going home alone."

"When did Bradley begin blackmailing you?" Hannah said.

She didn't answer at first.

"Catherine, I've seen the write-on article," Hannah said. "It's corrected in black ink. From your fountain pen. I know you wrote it."

"He showed up at my house, on a Saturday, about a week after the hearing," she said. "He had his hands behind his back and he pulled out a little package, wrapped in white-and-silver paper, with little paper bells on top. He told me he was sorry he missed the ceremony, but a friend had told him about it."

"Someone at the jail?" Hannah said.

She nodded. "I think the deputy saw us. Then an inmate found out. Bradley said a snitch called the DA's office, wanted to make a deal for himself, bartering information about Gallagher, the great jailhouse lawyer, screwing his clerk while the taxpayers footed the bill. It was just icing on the cake, really. The real problem was Peavey."

"What did Bradley want?"

"To hear him describe it, it wasn't anything as grim as blackmail. He said it was a business transaction. I would work for him and he would pay me with his silence. He brought along a draft of the letter he said he would send to the DA, the state bar, and school. I would never get to take the bar, let alone be disbarred, he said. He said I'd committed witness tampering, at least. Maybe even accessory to murder."

"What did he want from you?" Hannah said.

"The write-on, he said."

"Was that the end of it?"

"It was supposed to be. When I gave Bradley the article, I asked whether he was going to keep his promise. He looked at me, as though I'd wounded him. 'I'm as good as my word,' he said."

Hannah couldn't help herself. "That's some guarantee."

"I didn't understand him thoroughly then. Not like now."

"Did you tell Tim?"

She nodded. "The next time I saw him. He was furious. He was angry that I had gone along. He told me that he knew people who would take care of Bradley in a heartbeat. No remorse. It would be like killing a mosquito."

Hannah said nothing. It was an unfortunate time for Gallagher to lose his veneer.

"That was very telling," she said.

"It scared me," Catherine said. "For a second I thought I didn't really know him. Then he stopped himself. He said he was sorry, that he hadn't meant it. He swore again that he had nothing to do with Peavey. He said he felt like he'd ruined my life. But he said we'd just go on now, and forget about Bradley."

"But that wasn't the end of it?" Hannah said.

"From the beginning, on *Law Review,* I saw that Bradley had no intention of doing any work. He blew cite-checking deadlines, over and over again. Harrison and he were always bickering.

"He called me one night, a couple nights before he died, and said I should meet him near the Las Almas train station. He was very revved up about something to do with his father-in-law. He told me he was too busy right now for school, and I'd have to do some extras—his cite-checking work and a paper he had to do for wills and trusts. I went out there, but I told him that I couldn't do his work anymore. I was swamped. I had my appellate work for Tim, my own classes, and *Law Review.* I was sleeping only three or four hours a night. I couldn't do it anymore."

"He told you that you didn't have a choice," Hannah said.

She nodded. "But I told him I did. If he was going to tell, so be it."

"What happened then?"

Catherine stared out the windshield.

"Nothing. I called his bluff," she said finally. "He gave up. It stopped."

"I don't think it stopped," Hannah said. "Bradley wouldn't just stop."

Catherine looked blankly at Hannah. Her face was gaunt, the skin pulled so tight that it was almost translucent. She looked like she hadn't slept at all in several nights.

But the gun in her hand was steady, and she was not so distraught that she would forget her training: it was up to prosecutors to prove guilt. She wasn't going to make it any easier by confessing to Hannah.

Good, Hannah thought. That means she hasn't decided to kill us. Not yet.

39

The road narrowed as it wound north, finally turning into a two-lane road with only occasional stop signs. Teddy peered out into the darkness.

"Here," he said as Hannah slowed for a stop. "Turn right."

Hannah made the turn and before them was Pico Creek.

"Park here," Catherine said.

The creek bank was even more perilous in the dark. Teddy scuttled down it without difficulty. Hannah went next, feeling her way down cautiously.

The silence of the countryside had been peaceful in the afternoon. Now it was oppressive, ominous. It was nearly pitch-black, moonless. But that could be a benefit. She wondered if Teddy could bolt, get himself lost in the night. It was a chance worth taking, if he thought of it.

But he seemed listless. Maybe the residue of his father's abuse clung to him still. Fearful of violence to himself or Monty, he became a dutiful boy. Maybe he even believed everything would be all right, if only he were good.

They came to the cave and Teddy pulled back the tumbleweed door. He squatted at the back wall and dug at it with his hands, like a terrier after a rat. He pried out a mud-smeared package and handed it to Catherine.

"Back to the car," she said.

She flicked on the dome light, undid two layers of brown paper, and slid a cassette into the player in the dashboard.

"Let's go," she said.

Hannah started the car, and a moment later Bradley's taunting voice filled it.

Catherine's face was emotionless. She said nothing, but her lips moved in reply to Bradley's questions. All but his last one.

"You want more?"

Catherine jabbed the stop button before his cry and the thud. She flipped the cassette out, put it in her pocket, and sighed. Then she began to talk again. Her voice was flat, icy. It chilled Hannah. Catherine was confessing.

"He called me that Friday, and told me he had one last thing for me to do. He swore, the last one. He'd meet me at the station, like before. I went to M'Naghten's to think about what I was going to do. I decided I wasn't going to put up with it.

"I had started thinking about it the night we met near the train station. You know, a lot of deaths that look like accidents are really suicides? I thought about that," she said. "And I thought about the bums, and the crime around there. So I guess I was thinking, but not planning, really.

"It was all up to him," she said. "And he made the decision himself. When he showed up at M'Naghten's, I told him I was through. I gave him his last chance and he threw it in my face. He taunted me. He told me he had the letter for the DA with him. He told me he'd mail it that night if I didn't do what he wanted." She laughed and shook her head.

"It was such an insult. He wanted me to create the moot-court research for him. He brought some of his messy notes and your disk. It wasn't just cheating, which was bad enough, it was covering up his inept plagiarism. I pretended to be afraid, told him I was sorry, and said that I'd see him out by the trains.

"So it was suicide. He had his life in his hands. He could have done the right thing, treated me like a human being. But he didn't. He made the decision to kill himself. He chose the place, he brought the weapon, he set everything in motion. Suicide."

Hannah said nothing. Victim as his own killer. It sounded like Catherine actually believed what she was saying. Maybe she learned it from Tim Gallagher. In their dark world, they were both blameless.

Catherine suddenly gave Teddy a hug. The boy went rigid.

"You were a good kid, to tell me the truth about the tape," she said. "Now let's take you home. You're going to forget all about this. You never heard anything. Never saw anything. You can forget all this, right?"

He nodded quickly, but then said, "I don't know about Monty."

"She'll forget all about it if you tell her to, won't she?"

"Don't know," he said.

"She will," Catherine said. "Now let's all go home. Take a left here."

"I know the way," Hannah said. "It's a right."

Catherine glared coldly at her. "Take a left."

"How much do you remember from criminal law?" Catherine asked Hannah suddenly.

Hannah didn't answer.

"There is such a thing as justifiable homicide," Catherine said.

"Self-defense."

"Exactly. Bradley was trying to kill me. Me, and everything I cared about. I did what I had to do to save myself. It was imperfect self-defense—the honest but unreasonable apprehension of the need to kill. It would be voluntary manslaughter, at the most."

As she listened to Catherine, Hannah suddenly thought of a game she'd played once at a school carnival. A piece of paper sat in the bottom of a cylinder. You paid a quarter and dribbled paint down on the paper, and the carny hit a switch. The cylinder turned furiously and the paint splattered. The patterns that the paint made were wild, insane. You could never guess what would emerge. Just like Catherine's words. Impressive sounding at first, until they spun off into a madwoman's babble.

"I thought you said Bradley committed suicide," Hannah said mildly.

"Morally, karmically, it was suicide. But I'm talking about legal issues now," she said. "It's an interesting defense."

"You're kidding yourself," Hannah said.

"Anyway, that's how I put it to myself, sometimes. But I don't have to worry about it, really. It won't come to that."

"Why not?" Hannah said.

"As far as everyone else is concerned, Bradley either killed himself or was robbed and bludgeoned and run over by the train. There's a lot of crime in the train yards, mainly because of the bums. The mayor's right. You never know who's going to die next.

"Teddy," she said brightly. "You know all this train stuff. What time does the eastbound freight go through Las Almas tonight?"

Teddy shuddered, shook his head.

Catherine slapped his face, hard.

"What time?" she rasped.

"Eleven-fifteen," he whispered.

Twenty minutes from now, Hannah thought.

They paralleled the tracks for three blocks. Then Catherine ordered a left turn. It was the fringe of the neighborhood Hannah had visited earlier that night. They passed warehouses, a foundry, a scrap-metal yard, and worn clapboard houses with iron grates over the windows.

Hannah slowed as she came to the tracks. They intersected Las Almas Boulevard at an ungated crossing.

"Take a right here and stop," Catherine said.

Hannah drove the car onto the right-of-way. The Hyundai squeaked and shuddered as it chugged over the rocky ground.

"Change places with me," Catherine said. "Don't think about running. I will kill him."

Hannah took Teddy out of Catherine's arms and got back in the car. He felt light, almost as though he could drift up and out of her arms.

Catherine started the engine, suddenly swerved wide right, and then back, driving the car onto the rails. She turned off the engine. The Hyundai sat squarely on the tracks.

"I'm not staying in this car," Hannah said. "You're going to have to shoot me. I won't sit here and get mowed down by a train."

"You're staying," Catherine said. "You don't have a choice."

"Catherine, you can't do this," Hannah said. "You're a good person. You don't want two more deaths on your conscience. Tim Gallagher isn't worth it."

"He is," she whispered. She looked at Hannah. "Why did you start all this? Everything would have been perfect."

*   *   *

They stood beside Catherine as she unlocked the trunk and surveyed the interior.

"It will be cramped," she said. "But I think you'll fit."

Teddy began trembling. Hannah felt her knees weaken with fear.

"Jesus, Catherine," she said. "You're out of your mind. No one is going to mistake this for suicide."

"No. But criminals are so violent these days. The woman in the closet, probably dead by now, her cash gone, your car stolen, your wallet gone, and the car smashed. It will be a story on the news, all right, and more crime for the mayor to campaign on. Get in."

Hannah bent and began to get inside. Catherine looked down for a moment. She was trying to see her watch in the dark.

It was the moment of inattention Hannah needed. She kicked hard, catching Catherine's wrist with the toe of her boot. Catherine cried in pain, and the gun fell from her hand. Hannah dove for it. But Catherine was faster. She swooped down, grabbed the pistol, and rolled to her feet.

Hannah lunged for her knees, trying to take her down. She looked up in time to see the butt end of the gun coming down on her.

Hannah heard the crack at the back of her head, before she felt the surge of pain. A thick buzzing noise filled her head and seemed to stop up her ears. She had thought the night was as dark as it could be, but the cloud that passed in front of her eyes was even blacker.

40

She was so hot. Choking. Couldn't breathe. She thought her eyes were open, but it was so dark that she had to blink to make sure. There was a small whimpering noise in the hot space, and for a moment Hannah was afraid it was her own voice.

Then she felt the child against her and realized it was Teddy. His back pressed against her belly and his legs curled in front of hers. Hannah put up her hands and touched metal. She tried to stretch her legs, but her feet clunked against the side of the trunk. Suddenly she felt a sick wave in her stomach. She had never felt so confined.

"It comes in about five minutes," Teddy whispered when he realized she was awake. "We've only got five minutes."

Hannah tried to fight down the panic. But it was a voice screaming inside, telling her it was useless, there was nothing to do. Her head pounded from the blow. She wondered if she had a concussion.

A thought was forming, but it came together slowly, like a bank of drifting clouds. She couldn't force it to move any faster. The thought might be something important, something to save them. But it broke apart when she tried to push it. They were going to die because she couldn't make a simple thought hold together. Something about the backpack.

"Where's my pack?" she said.

Teddy didn't answer. But he was whispering something. She realized he was counting aloud, keeping track of how long until the train bore down on them.

"Teddy?"

"Forty-five. It's here, but it's no good," Teddy said. "Forty-two. She threw away your car keys."

Something was poking Hannah in the back. She felt for it, and realized it was her flashlight. She drew it out and flicked it on.

It shone up on Teddy's face, the angle of the beam throwing dark pits over where his eyes should have been. The skin of his cheeks was sweaty, waxy, and he was breathing in little pants, like a frightened animal. She could feel his heart pounding.

"Okay. But where is my backpack?" It hurt to talk. Her tongue felt thick in her mouth.

"I'm on it," he said. "Thirty." He hitched his hip slightly, and she saw her backpack.

Hannah fumbled for the zippered inside pocket. She pulled it open and reached inside. Her fingers felt fat, slow, and swollen, but she knew she touched a lipstick, a coin, a pen. Then something sharp and cold. Good, she thought. Then she realized it was a pocketknife.

From what seemed to be a long way off, Hannah heard a horn, wailing high and then low.

Teddy stiffened. "That's it—" he said, his voice breaking off in a sob. "Three minutes to go."

Her slow brain was determined to wander away, like a senile woman. She tried to stop it, to get it to concentrate on now. Instead, it dredged up the image: she was six, the family was on its way to Chicago on a train, in a sleeper compartment. The horn sounded and Hannah laughed at the rumble it made in her bones. It was an adventure in the rocking car, where her parents played gin and talked and she and Michael watched the countryside of fields, then desert, then mountains and plains as they sped by the window.

The wail came again. Blood and death, she thought. We are going to die here, just like Bradley did. And that thought felt cold, sharp, pointed. It cut through the muck in her head.

Now the thoughts came too fast: what the crash would feel like, what it would leave behind. She saw Bradley, the caved-in skull, the sickening pink and red and his arm gone and his broken legs twisted tight around each other.

"Stop it," she told herself, and realized she'd said it out loud. The image obediently blinked out, and her head felt clearer.

She dug her hand deep in the pocket, and out came the extra car key, made the night Bradley died.

She held it out so Teddy could see.

"Hold this," she said.

"But the lock is out there," he said.

Hannah shone the light across the taillights. They sat in metal wells, but there was nothing over the back, no sheet metal or carpet, only a plastic housing. She flipped the flashlight and grasped it with both hands. She drove it hard against the plastic shell. She flipped the flashlight again and shone the beam. The plastic had cracked.

Hannah sighed with relief and got ready to slam again. But the flashlight was vibrating in her hands. The little car was buzzing, shaking. It was the train, she realized, telegraphing its weight and speed down the rails.

The air horn sounded again, longer and more urgently. The engineer must have seen them.

"It can take a mile to stop," Teddy said. "He won't be able to do it."

"I know," Hannah whispered.

She slammed the butt of the flashlight into the plastic again, and this time it went all the way through. Hannah felt a shard of plastic cut her arm.

She pulled out the flashlight, snatched the key from Teddy's shaking hand, and stuck her arm through the opening. She dove for where she hoped the lock would be. But the key tapped against the metal of the lid.

"Too far," she said. "I can't reach it."

The car was rocking now. Teddy's little cries were louder, coming faster. And then he started to scream. For a moment that was the only sound in the car. But when the train's horn wailed again, it blotted out even that.

She pulled her arm back and grabbed again for the flashlight. She battered out the plastic in the second well, the one closest to the middle of the trunk. Stupid, idiot, she told herself. Why didn't she do that one first? It might be too late.

She jammed her arm through and reached as far as she could. She angled the key, jabbing it against the trunk.

The car was rocking from side to side, and the horn was so loud that Hannah thought her eardrums were going to burst. She stabbed the key and felt it weak and shaky in her hand. She gasped, unable to get her breath. She felt she was about to drown.

The key plunged into place. Hannah screamed when she felt it drive home. She turned her hand. The trunk lid popped open. White light nearly blinded her.

She could barely see the train behind it. The light swept the tracks, right and left. Hannah grabbed Teddy at the waist and hoisted him out of the trunk. Together, they fell to the ground and rolled down the grade.

From the bottom of the incline, she saw how she might have died.

The blast of the horn was lost in the wrenching shriek of metal as the engine slammed into the car at the driver's door. Glass pellets rained down on ballast, glittering in the hard light. The engine thundered on, its force ripping the Hyundai in two. The front half of the car slid onto the siding. But the engine ground on, shoving the back of the mangled car ahead of it. The trunk gaped open, an empty casket sliding into the night.

Hannah held Teddy in her arms as the train, silvery and implacable, sped by them. It still was moving at forty or fifty miles an hour.

"How long until it can stop?" Hannah said.

"A half mile, maybe more," Teddy said. Now his body felt heavy and limp in her arms.

A yellow light glowed inside the train's cars. Hannah saw blurred outlines of passengers as they clustered at the windows, staring down at the eviscerated Hyundai on the far side of the track. Hannah longed to be inside with them, moving away, a watcher like the rest.

She stood up, and felt a stabbing pain in her left ankle. She must have twisted it when she fell. Her knees shook. She put her hand on Teddy's shoulder and they walked to a long line of boxcars on a side track before Hannah had to ease herself to the ground.

"I don't think I can walk," she said. "I'll have to wait till someone from the train crew comes back."

Teddy sat down and nestled against her side.

"I'll wait, too."

"Are you okay?"

"Yeah," he said. "I'm fine." But his voice was thin and stretched as he tried to make the words sound true.

"I just want to go home," he murmured. "I hope Monty is okay."

She kissed his forehead. It was cool and beaded with sweat. "I'm sure she is," she said.

Hannah touched the back of her head, where the gun's butt had struck her. The throbbing had subsided somewhat. She looked at the long thin scratches on her arms, extending from wrist to shoulder, as though she'd been pulled through a row of needles. Beneath those sharp spears of pain, her whole body pulsed with dull aches. She let herself imagine how it would feel to fall asleep in a hot bath.

Hannah flexed her foot and swayed with a wave of nausea that swept through her. With the sickness came a flickering strip of lights, like a failing neon sign.

It was then that she heard the footsteps. Someone walking toward them from the street.

Teddy started to shout something. Wait, Hannah thought. No flashlight. No one called out to them. She clamped her hand over his mouth and put her lips to his ear.

"It's not safe yet," she whispered. "Get away from here. Be very quiet, but get to the locomotive. Bring help."

She felt Teddy nod and she let him go. The loose rocks rattled under his feet.

The other footsteps slowed. Stopped.

Hannah held herself motionless. She saw that the night was not impenetrably black, now that her eyes had adjusted to it. She peered under the boxcar. She could make out a shape, moving up the row. Glimpse of white below the pale oval of a face. All else black.

Catherine had waited to see them die. Instead, she saw them escape. Hannah heard the metallic swipe of the Glock's slide. Then an exasperated sigh. Catherine might have been a mother whose child refuses to lie down for a nap.

"Don't make me do it, Hannah," Catherine called out.

Hannah dragged herself under the boxcar and watched as Catherine turned and began to walk down the other side of the row, the one closest to the open tracks.

Hannah wriggled out on the opposite side and eased herself

to her feet. Instantly, pain exploded in an agonizing spurt. Fountains of sparks flew behind her eyes. She bit her lip to keep from crying out. She tried a few hobbling steps. No good. She was too slow. Too noisy.

Hannah dropped to her hands and knees again. She crawled beside the track, peering under the cars for a glimpse of Catherine. But she saw nothing, heard nothing. Kick a rock, Hannah thought. Say something. Make a noise, damn it.

Ahead, she could see that the row went on for three or four boxcars. Then came an open stretch of siding. She would be an easy target for quite a distance, limping along out there. But there was a thicket of container cars on the other side. She could find a better hiding place. She wouldn't have to stay there long. Someone would show up, soon.

Hannah looked over her shoulder, saw nothing. She crawled on. She would rest under the last car, then sprint.

She never knew what made her look back again. A sound, perhaps. Maybe nothing more than a disturbance in the air. But Catherine stood twenty yards behind her, feet planted wide, arms outstretched, hands clasped. They dipped, rose.

She brought the Glock up and fired it. Hannah scrabbled under a boxcar and heard the bullet ricochet off the side. She had aimed too high.

Hannah heard Catherine running toward her. She knew that this time Catherine wasn't going to take any chances. She'd wait until she could shoot at point-blank range.

Hannah dragged herself to the edge of the car, put her hands on the rails, and crouched. The ankle throbbed, an engine of pain set at idle. It would hurt like hell in a minute, but she didn't have a choice.

Catherine was huffing now, no attempt at stealth. Hannah listened as she came closer, closer.

Hannah sprang out and tackled her at the ankles. Catherine toppled to the ground with a gasp and Hannah fell on top of her. She grabbed the gun and closed her hands around the barrel. She could hear Catherine panting in her ear, grunting with the effort of the fight. Hannah twisted Catherine's wrist, felt a satisfying snap, and rejoiced in her shriek of pain. Hannah felt the gun begin to slip from Catherine's hands.

Then, as though Catherine knew it would cripple her, she kicked Hannah's ankle. Hannah gasped and felt the gun slip away.

Catherine grabbed her under her arm and hauled her to her feet. They were in the open, easy to spot by the crew and police. Catherine dragged her back down the row of boxcars, saying nothing.

They were sheltered from view, but the cars were sparser here. Catherine dropped Hannah to the ground.

She lay there, dizzy with pain. The floating half thoughts were back. It's over. Only one question now: would she hear the shot?

After a moment she looked up. Catherine was standing in the middle of the track, staring down at her. Hannah looked around. There was a boxcar behind her. More on the side tracks on her left and right. The span of rail behind Catherine was empty, trailing away into the still night. Hannah heard no voices, saw no lights. No one was coming to find her, wherever that was. She had no idea how far she was from where Teddy left her.

She tried to sit up. She put her hand on the rails to support herself. In contact with the metal, she thought she felt a tingle traveling up her bones. Some nerve rubbed raw, she thought. But maybe not. Teddy had said it was dangerous here. They kicked containers loose and they slid along welded rails on roller bearings in near silence. Play for time, she thought.

"Catherine, it's not too late," Hannah said. "Put the gun down, and let's think of a way for you to save yourself."

Catherine laughed, a sound as sharp and jagged as a saw blade.

"I don't care about that," she said. "Tim is all that matters."

Now, not far away, Hannah thought she could see it over Catherine's shoulder. A boxcar rolled toward them. Not fast. Maybe five miles an hour. But it was nearly silent.

"Teddy got away. He's with the police now. They'll be here any second."

"Well then," Catherine said, "we'd better hurry."

She trained the gun down on Hannah. She almost seemed to savor the moment. Then Hannah lunged. Catherine fired wide, startled by her speed. Hannah shoved Catherine backward and stumbled off the tracks.

It happened in seconds.

Catherine staggered and fell against the coupler of the oncoming boxcar. She gasped, the wind knocked out of her, and lurched forward, grabbing for anything to break her fall and stop her from tumbling under the steel wheels. What she found was the fat, rounded coupler of the waiting boxcar. It stood open in a half-moon, ready to link with its oncoming partner. The cars were only yards apart.

Shaken, Catherine pushed herself straight and tried to step off the tracks. Her body twisted, but she seemed rooted to the spot. Hannah heard her scrabbling in the ballast. And then Catherine began to scream and tug at her left leg.

Her foot was wedged under one of the ties.

"Jesus Christ, help me," she shrieked.

The sound shuddered in Hannah's ears. She wrenched herself to her feet, but her ankle gave away and she fell. On the ground, she closed her eyes, but not in time to keep from seeing.

The boxcar's tons of metal, focused in the foot-square coupler, punched through Catherine's twisting body at the abdomen. Her screams ended sharply, knife clean amid the carnage.

Hannah managed to get to her feet. She was shaking and nearly sick at the sight before her.

Catherine's feet barely touched the ground. Her head and shoulders lolled to the right. The joined half-moon couplers, slick with viscera, held her upright. Catherine's eyes, dull as sand-blasted glass, drifted left, then right. But finally she focused on Hannah. She seemed to smile. A bitter expression, half sneer and half grimace. She mouthed words, but no sound came with them.

Hannah felt shrunken and empty, as though all feeling and strength had been wrung from her. She dragged herself to the boxcar. Catherine lifted her arms and dropped them on the bloodied link. Her hands slid over it as though she could open it and shove herself free.

Hannah touched Catherine's face. Her skin was chalky and her head drooped against Hannah's hand. The flesh felt clammy.

Catherine's eyes closed. Her lips moved silently, one word, one syllable, over and over. Him. Him. Him. Or perhaps Tim. Tim. Tim. She turned her head, pressed her lips against Hannah's palm, and opened her eyes.

Hannah saw the last flickers of consciousness there, fading pinpoints of light. Catherine smiled at her, but she was seeing someone else. Catherine recited her silent litany, fast and then slower, as though her mouth was forgetting how to form the prayer. Then the lips stilled. The eyes went dead, but they stayed open, fixed and staring at infinity.

41

She didn't remember exactly what happened next. She had vague impressions of hearing people running toward her. She heard their voices, hushed and frightened. Then someone picked her up. She thought it might be Eddy, and when she opened her eyes, she saw it was. He'd come, after all. She tried to thank him, but she found herself unable to speak.

She woke up in the hospital. Rather, she drifted awake and slipped into sleep again. The pain medication had made her woozy, and with sleep came frightening dreams. In one, she got out of the trunk, but couldn't save Teddy. She saw him grabbing for her, but something in the darkness of the trunk held him fast. She heard his screams through the howl of the diesel, just as the locomotive punched the car into scrap.

In another dream, she was still in the trunk, but could see as the train thundered toward her. Catherine and Tim Gallagher waved at her as they held Teddy above their heads, giving him a view of her death. In a third dream, someone stroked her forehead and whispered to her in words that were vaguely familiar, but didn't sound like English.

After two days, when the doctors were satisfied that the concussion was only a mild one, they sent her home.

The sight of the fading yellow house flooded her eyes with tears. She was alive. Achy and slightly dented, but breathing. But mingled with that relief was the stone weight of guilt. Catherine dead. Hannah had gone over it all, again and again. Was there any other way she could have saved herself? She didn't know. She hadn't planned any of it. She had just acted out of self-preservation. One lives, one dies. Hannah was glad she'd survived. But she would pay the price for it.

Bobby's hand tightened on her elbow, and she started up the stairs. Even with his help, each step hurt. The sprain was healing, but her ankle still throbbed when she put too much weight on it.

Over the next days Bobby cooked for her and, in deference to her condition, reined in his wilder culinary instincts. He made a pot of Chinese winter vegetable soup and smooth custards. Hannah suddenly saw what old age would be like: white food, stiff joints, pale sleep that didn't bring rest. She longed to be well again.

A visit from Ivan Churnin brightened her considerably. He came to take her statement the day after she got out of the hospital. Hannah hobbled to her bedroom and came back with the shard of bottle and Bradley's Visa card.

"I didn't know what you'd do with them before. I didn't trust you," she said.

Churnin, chastened and uncharacteristically quiet, put them in his briefcase and said nothing about withholding evidence. Then he cleared his throat.

"After you left that Tuesday, when Teddy was supposed to come in, I started thinking," he said. "The wallet began to bother me—why hadn't we found it? I went looking for it again, that night. The boxcars out there are creepy. Crawling with bums."

So it was Churnin she heard rustling around in the reeds. And he'd mistaken her for an urban settler. She chuckled to herself. First the bum on the lawn at Rattigan Library and then Churnin. She was definitely getting rid of the oversized navy coat.

"I went to see Gallagher," Churnin said.

"What did he have to say?"

"He said he didn't know anything about Bradley blackmailing anyone. He said Spinetti had been his law clerk, less than a paralegal, he said. I checked the courthouse. There's no marriage license."

Hannah nodded. "I know. But they're married."

She wondered if Gallagher had planned it that way from the

beginning. It would probably take a court order for the county clerk even to acknowledge the license's existence.

Catherine had risked her career for Tim Gallagher, killed for him and died loving him. But he had made sure she left no trace in his life. She thought of him smiling at Churnin, erasing Catherine with every word. It made Hannah feel sick.

The day after Churnin's visit, Ballard Goodacre was freed from jail. He immediately walked across the street to the courthouse with a hotshot Douglas third-year and sued the police for violating his civil rights. Shortly afterward Hannah read in the paper that the mayor had decided the conditional-use permit for Douglas's parking lot expansion was flawed. She threatened to veto the project and vehemently denied it had anything to do with Goodacre's lawsuit. Back to business as usual, Hannah thought.

42

But a bit of unreality remained: the disciplinary hearing. Bobby drafted a motion to postpone it, and Weiss promptly refused. So Bobby and Hannah got to work, although Hannah's head pounded and it hurt to stand for very long. She dug out her criminal-law final, as per the school's subpoena, and arranged for an appointment with Dove to discuss the grading.

Although Hannah had hit most of the points, Dove said she'd missed two key issues.

"No evidence of cheating here," she said.

"You'll testify to that," Hannah said.

"Of course," Dove said coolly.

They didn't talk about Bradley, or German. Hannah still didn't know if German was lying about being with her the night Bradley died. She wouldn't put it past him.

But would Dove have lied for him? Hannah shook her head. She didn't want to think about Dove and German together. What a bizarre pair.

While they prepared for the hearing Hannah reread the rules of Douglas's disciplinary process.

"This is interesting," she said to Bobby. "Weiss violated the procedure when he refused to continue the hearing."

Bobby's eyes lit up.

"You could sue over that," he told her.

Hannah sighed. "I just want this to be over. I don't want to spawn more lawsuits."

"It's just leverage," he said.

She shook her head. "I don't know."

He tapped the point of his pencil on his legal pad and cleared his throat.

"What are you scheming?" she said.

"There's something else you could do."

"What?"

"Meet with Weiss. Tell him you know who stole Dove's test, and why. Tell him you're prepared to argue that he brought the charge against you to protect Lois."

"I don't think that's what happened," Hannah said.

"Doesn't matter. You'd let the panel draw its own conclusion. That's all Weiss would need to hear."

It seemed like Bradley had left her an ugly bequest. All his machinations had created a filthy arsenal she could use with clean hands. She told Bobby she'd think about it. But it brought up an issue that troubled her: what to do about Lois Popich.

If Hannah called Lois as a witness, and Lois truthfully explained how Bradley had gotten the test, she would lose her job. And, probably, her lover.

Hannah mulled it over and decided Lois's secrets weren't hers to keep. Hannah had nearly died of secrets, of deals and blackmail and subterfuge. Bradley's games. Gallagher had been right, in a way. She was no good at them.

But she didn't want to sandbag Lois with a subpoena. That seemed unnecessarily cruel. She went to her apartment and told her what might happen.

"I don't know if it's going to be necessary, but if I have to, I will call you. I think you know that you'd be best off telling the truth. I'm sorry."

"I understand," Lois said quietly. Her tan had faded. And since that day on the pier, she had abandoned her haughty ways, at least with Hannah.

Hannah wasn't sure she did understand. Maybe she thought Hannah was just engaging in a more genteel version of Bradley's blackmail. Hannah didn't mean it that way.

But she knew she was giving Lois an opportunity to tell Weiss everything before he heard it in court. She wondered if Lois would gamble and say nothing, or confess to him. And what would Weiss do if she did? Forgive Lois? Leave her? Fire her? Maybe all three, Hannah thought.

*   *   *

The disciplinary hearings at Douglas were held in the school's walnut-paneled courtroom with its oak counsel tables, raised judge's bench, jury box, and witness stand. All the accoutrements of justice, Hannah thought. The last time she had been here, it had been for moot-court arguments. That had been acting. Mock justice. There was nothing mock about it this time.

Hannah sat in the chair designated for defendant's counsel. She rubbed the back of her head gently. The swelling had gone down, but it still ached.

She nervously swept a bit of lint from the navy wool suit jacket and checked her watch. This should have started ten minutes ago, she thought.

Bobby reached out and took her hand.

"I know it will be okay," he said.

"I think so, too." She wished she could sound more convincing. "Is Lois out there?"

"Yes," he said. He squeezed her hand tightly. "Hannah, I just wanted to tell you again, before this starts. I'm so sorry."

"Bobby, stop," she said. "Don't worry about it. You didn't know what you were doing. She engineered it."

Bobby nodded and pinched the bridge of his nose, unobtrusively wiping away a tear. It must be miserable. He had idolized Catherine.

Together, he and Hannah had figured out the scenario. Gallagher called Catherine after Hannah visited him. Catherine knew Hannah and Bobby were close. And she would have been blind if she hadn't realized how much Bobby ached for her. So it was easy for her to pick up Bobby in the library. And Catherine had some luck: that night, staying at Hannah's, he'd heard everything Hannah told Eddy about Teddy Czerwinski.

Bobby described how gently Catherine brought the conversation around to Hannah the next morning. Why was she so preoccupied? What was happening? And Bobby blithely told her the story of the boy and his tape, including his name and where he lived. He was so smitten, he didn't even realize he was being pumped dry.

"She would have been a good lawyer," Hannah told him. "She might even have gotten Gallagher his new trial."

Hannah looked at her watch again. Fifteen minutes late. Did

Weiss think he was a real judge, keeping them waiting like this?

Someone tapped her on the shoulder. Before she could turn around to see who it was, Bobby was on his feet, clenching his hand in a fist.

"Get lost," he was saying. "You have some fucking nerve, showing up here."

Ruiz was standing there, looking solemnly down at her.

"I need to talk to you," he said. "It will only take a minute."

"It's okay, Bobby," Hannah said.

Bobby shifted uneasily, uncurled his hand, and sat down.

"I wanted you to know, I went to the committee this morning and gave them this affidavit," Ruiz said.

He handed her two sheets of paper and she scanned them. Ruiz admitted giving his moot-court brief to Bradley, in return for $1,500. He attested that Bradley told him Hannah had completed her work independently and that it was only Bradley who was involved in the scheme.

Hannah looked up at him and nodded.

"This will probably get you expelled," she said.

He shrugged.

"It's the truth. I don't want to spend the rest of my life carrying around a load of guilt. I needed the money. Bradley was casual about it, said it was nothing. But it wasn't nothing. It was the very opposite of what we were supposed to be here for: honesty and ethics and law. I couldn't do it."

Hannah raised her eyebrows at him.

"And?" she said.

"And you could have proved I sold him the brief," he said, smiling ruefully. "Maybe they'll cut me some slack for admitting it."

"I'll tell them to go easy, if it will help," Hannah said. "There's one condition. Pay me for what it cost to fix my windshield. The car's totaled, but I'm still out the money."

"But I didn't do it," Ruiz said. "I told you I didn't."

"Then who?" Hannah said. And then she knew: Lois. Her windshield was smashed three days after Lois found the phone number Hannah had dropped. She must have recognized Bradley's number and feared that Hannah would discover the affair. She left the building before Hannah that night. There was enough time to do it.

Hannah nodded at Ruiz. "Okay. Forget it."

A door to the right of the judge's bench opened and the disciplinary committee filed in, followed by Weiss. He went to the plaintiff's table. Three professors sat in the jury box. The Parson took his place at the judge's bench.

Weiss glanced over at her once, but looked away before Hannah could engage his eyes. He fiddled with a pen and straightened a stack of papers in front of him.

"Ready?" Bobby whispered to Hannah. "Sic 'em."

Hannah was on her feet, starting to state her appearance for the record. The Parson waved her to sit down.

"After reading the student's answer and reviewing the evidence she has supplied, the administration has informed me the committee—"

A cough stopped him. He picked up a glass of water and sipped at it.

"For the love of God," Bobby groaned.

"The administration wishes to drop this action," he said. "And the committee concurs. Another student has confessed to selling his work to Mr. Cogburn, thus facilitating the plagiarism. That student will be dealt with."

Hannah sat back in the chair. Bobby took her hand and gave it a short squeeze.

"Congratulations," he whispered.

The Parson scowled at Bobby and continued.

"And the administration has decided the evidence against Ms. Barlow in the matter of the stolen exam is inadequate. We agree," he said. "The student is restored to full-time status. The administration and the committee apologize for any disruption in her studies."

He sounded genuinely sorry. Hannah nodded, might even have said thanks. She felt dizzy with disbelief. He tapped the gavel on the bench.

"The hearing is adjourned," he said.

Weiss stood up. His eyes swept the room, catching for just a split second on Hannah's. But she couldn't read the meaning in the narrowed slits, the slight darkness under the lower lids. He left the courtroom without a word.

Hannah stood up—too quickly. Her ankle buckled with a spasm of pain. Bobby caught her and enveloped her in a hug. Hannah laughed, and then felt the tears surge. She pressed her

face against Bobby's scratchy wool lapels and willed the
shaking and crying to stop. She didn't want to acknowledge
how terrified she had been. She eased back into her chair and
wiped her eyes as Bobby whooped and capered behind her.
Then, arm in arm, they went out in the hallway.

Lois stood against a wall, talking in a low voice to Weiss.
She was dressed for work, her hair was pulled up, schoolmarm
harsh, but she was wearing sunglasses. Weiss was listening,
saying nothing. He did not look at her. Finally, in a pause, he
turned away from her and walked out, back across campus
toward his office.

So she told him, Hannah thought. She felt a pang of guilt.
She'd forced Lois to tell him the truth. Had that really been
necessary?

"Hannah?"

She turned around at the sound of the voice.

Alicia stood there, holding a bouquet of baby's breath and
white roses. German stood behind her. Alicia smiled hesitantly.

"Did you win?" she said.

Hannah nodded.

Alicia shrieked with joy and grabbed up Hannah in a fierce
hug. The baby's breath tickled Hannah's nose. Over Alicia's
shoulder, she tried to gauge German's expression.

His face was haggard. He looked like he hadn't slept in
several nights. He cleared his throat. What came next sounded
rehearsed.

"We came to thank you for everything." His voice was flat,
almost numb. "You've eased my daughter's pain enormously
and restored her peace of mind." He stopped to cough, then
dabbed his lips with a handkerchief. "Now she can get on with
her future, and forget about the past. We all want to forget
what's happened."

Hannah nodded slightly. She read the meaning, clearly
enough. Forget that I bribed a woman, maybe had her killed.
Forget that I paid off my son-in-law to keep him quiet. Help me
cover up the crime that could ruin me.

"We can't ever really forget the past," Hannah said.

She had been thinking about that for more than a week and
had come to believe it. All anyone could do about the past was
undo its hold, work out the penances that its failures exacted,
and then look ahead.

"Alicia showed tremendous strength in dealing with Bradley's death," Hannah said. "I think she could handle anything."

He simply stared at her, face unmoving, but now a bit paler, more solemn. He knew what she meant. In a few weeks she knew she would have to call the bar's investigative committee and tell them about Raymond O'Reilly, and what he'd seen. She would tell Alicia first, and she hoped she would understand. Hannah thought she would.

Alicia pulled an envelope out of her jacket pocket.

"I want you to have this," she said. "You risked everything to find out what happened to Bradley. You nearly got yourself killed."

The check was nearly identical to the one German had given Bradley. But this one was made for $10,000. She saw her name as payee. A note in the left corner said: *for investigative services*.

She stared at it, closed her eyes, and opened them again. Counted the zeros. Yes, four of them.

"I just can't." She handed the check back to Alicia. What if, she thought. What if this is German's idea, his way of bribing me?

German seemed to be reading her mind.

"It's Alicia's money, and Alicia's decision," he said. "I thought it was excessive."

Alicia held the check out again. Hannah looked at it. The New York PI had told her that if she had some money, he might be able to reopen Janie's case, try to find out if she was the girl in Gaviota Bay.

But Hannah shook her head.

"Let me think about it."

She would wait until she'd told Alicia about her father and what he'd done. Then she'd see if Alicia still wanted her to have the money.

Hannah stopped at the *Law Review* office before going home. The room was dark and Onizaki's coffeepot was empty and cold—the first time in weeks. Then Hannah saw the note stuck to the staff bulletin board. Catherine's funeral was that morning, at a mortuary in Long Beach. That's where they were. Hannah was glad someone from school had gone. She didn't think she had any business being there.

She scanned the mailboxes. Onizaki had crammed hers with memos and a folder full of cite-checking assignments. She flicked through them and put them back. She might have to kiss off *Law Review*. She was behind in her classes.

Someone tapped on the window in the door. Professor Agustin.

"Nice going," he said.

Hannah smiled and held up the sheaf of paper.

"I've got a ton of work to do," she said. "Yours wasn't the only class I missed. And there's a draft of an article I've got to get to Harrison in about three weeks. I'm not sure I can pull it off."

"If you had some intensive tutorials?" he said.

"Evidence is the class that will kill me," she said.

"I'm terrific in evidence," he said. "Shall we meet in my office, say five tomorrow? We can get some dinner afterward."

Hannah thought for a moment. There had been that promise she made herself: no entanglements with professors. But this was schoolwork. At first, anyway. If things went slowly enough, she could keep her promise to herself. She only had two and a half semesters before graduation.

Bobby drove her home. The insurance company had told her to expect a check in a week, and she couldn't drive anyway, so she hadn't bothered renting a car.

She hauled herself up the stairs. The ankle throbbed with every step, and she felt little pinpricks of perspiration on her forehead. She sank onto the sofa and wiped her face.

"That's like running a marathon," she said. "Maybe I should move in with you for a few weeks."

"I'll cook feasts for you," he said.

"On second thought," Hannah said. "Between your meals and this foot, I'll blow up like a zeppelin."

Bobby shuffled the stack of mail into a pile and sorted it, bills going one way, junk into the trash, and the rest into Hannah's lap.

There was a card addressed in blue-black ink. Michael's handwriting. He had visited her in the hospital, he wrote, but she had been sound asleep. He prayed for her then, as he did every day, in the Mass. He prayed for all their family, living and dead. He hoped her healing would be speedy.

Hannah looked down at the card. She hadn't seen him more

than a half-dozen times in four years. But he had visited her in the hospital and left before she woke up? Maybe the words she heard intoned in her dream were Michael's Latin prayers. He always liked the old ways of the church. Maybe the touch on her forehead hadn't been a dream. She wondered if he had given her last rites as she lay there, fearful that she'd die in mortal sin. That would have been just like him.

"Get-well card?" Bobby said.

"Sort of a get-guilt card," she said. "But I'm not having it today. I hurt too much to feel any worse."

Bobby went to the refrigerator.

"You've had a major victory," he said from behind the door. "We need to celebrate."

"Not champagne, Bobby," Hannah said. The thought of it, an echo of Bradley's last toast, made her feel cold and shaky.

"Certainly not," he said. "Good micro-brewery beer from Mendocino. My parents sent down a case."

He flipped open the bottles and brought her one. Hannah took a sip and sighed at the cold taste on her tongue.

Bobby tossed a padded brown envelope to her. Hannah tore it open and shook it. A cassette dropped out, followed by a postcard. She read it.

"It's from Teddy," she said.

"How is he?" Bobby said.

"Good," Hannah said. "Better than I could have hoped."

She and Eddy had bought train passes for Teddy and Monty. They were working their way northeast now, and Teddy had sent postcards from Arizona and New Mexico. This one was from Colorado.

I recorded this for you, he wrote. The printing was neat and uncorrected. *There's a narrow-gauge line that runs through here, and I thought you might like to hear what a steam engine sounds like. It's kind of old-fashioned, but I like it. Monty says hello and thank you again. Her hip doesn't hurt too much now.*

"You're looking a little tired," Bobby said, shaking out the afghan and spreading it over her lap. "I think I'll let you rest a bit."

"Put this on first," Hannah said, handing him the cassette.

"You sure?" Bobby said.

Hannah nodded.

Bobby put the tape in and gave Hannah the remote.

"See you later," he said. He kissed her on the forehead and left.

Hannah hit the play button and settled back on the sofa.

The sound began in the distance, a soft chuffing, punctuated by blasts from a steam whistle. It drew closer and closer, rails clacking and engine pounding, a train from another time. Hannah closed her eyes and saw it: bare aspens and mountains cloaked in snow. All clean, white, with puffs of gray steam and bits of drifting cinder from the engine. The dream train wound through mountains and on high trestles, over deep, rushing rivers. She saw Teddy, microphone in hand, leaning out into the curves, capturing it all, blotting out the memory of other trains and dark, deadly landscapes.

Dreams salvaged from nightmares, Hannah thought. He's putting the past behind him, curving away from it, into the dreams ahead. I could go there, too, she thought. And with that, she found it easy to slip into sleep.